More critical praise for *Southland:*

"Fascinating and heartbreaking . . . an essential part of L.A. history."
—*L.A. WEEKLY*

"Compelling . . . never lacking in vivid detail and authentic atmosphere, the novel cements Revoyr's reputation as one of the freshest young chroniclers of life in L.A."

—*PUBLISHERS WEEKLY*

"The plot line of *Southland* is the stuff of a James Ellroy or a Walter Mosley novel . . . But the climax fairly glows with the good-heartedness that Revoyr displays from the very first page."

—*LOS ANGELES TIMES BOOK REVIEW*

"If Oprah still had her book club, this novel likely would be at the top of her list . . . With prose that is beautiful, precise, but never pretentious . . ."
—*BOOKLIST* (starred review)

"Subtle, effective . . . [with] a satisfyingly unpredictable climax."
—*WASHINGTON POST*

"An engaging, thoughtful book that even East Coasters can enjoy."
—*NEW YORK PRESS*

"*Southland* is a simmering stew of individual dreams, family struggles, cultural relations, social changes, and race relations. It is a compelling, challenging, and rewarding novel."

—*CHICAGO FREE PRESS*

"What makes a book like *Southland* resonate is that it merges elements of literature and social history with the propulsive drive of a mystery, while evoking Southern California as a character, a key player in the tale. Such aesthetics have motivated other Southland writers, most notably Walter Mosley."

—*LOS ANGELES TIMES*

SOUTHLAND

Nina Revoyr

AKASHIC BOOKS
New York

Published by Akashic Books
©2003 Nina Revoyr

Design and layout by Sohrab Habibion
Cover photo ©2003 John Dohrmann, all rights reserved
Author photo by Leslie Barton

ISBN: 1-888451-41-6
Library of Congress Control Number: 2002116775
All rights reserved
Sixth printing
Printed in Canada

Akashic Books
PO Box 1456
New York, NY 10009
Akashic7@aol.com
www.akashicbooks.com

ACKNOWLEDGMENTS

My heartfelt thanks to Dan McCall, Maureen McCoy, Lamar Herrin, and Kyoko Uchida for their insightful comments and suggestions about this book. Thanks also to Stephanie Vaughn for her unbending support; Alison Lurie for providing an office and refuge; Morna Pixton for her lucky table; Patsy Cox for always believing; Johnny Temple and Johanna Ingalls at Akashic for their enthusiasm and commitment; and Jennifer Gilmore for raising the bar.

I'm grateful to my agent, Tim Seldes, as well as to the Saltonstall Foundation and the Astraea Foundation. I am also indebted to several historical works and their authors: Keith E. Collins, *Black Los Angeles: The Maturing of the Ghetto, 1940-1950*; Carolyn Kozo Cole and Kathy Kobayashi (eds.), *Shades of L.A.: Pictures from Ethnic Family Albums*; Warren S. Rogers, *Mesa to Metropolis: The Crenshaw Area, Los Angeles*; John Tateishi (ed.), *And Justice For All: An Oral History of the Japanese-American Detention Camps*; and Arthur C. Verge, *Paradise Transformed: Los Angeles During the Second World War*.

Finally, I want to express my deep gratitude to Lauren Sanders. Had she not shown up on my doorstep in L.A., needing a place to crash, this novel might never have found a home.

*In memory of my grandparents
and Janine Werner*

PROLOGUE

NOW, THE old neighborhood is feared and avoided, even by the people who live there. Although stores wait for customers right down on the Boulevard, people drive to the South Bay, or even over to the Westside, to see a movie or to do their weekly shopping. The local places sell third-rate furniture and last year's clothes, and despite the promises of city leaders in the months after the riots, no bigger businesses, or schools, are on their way. A few traces of that other time remain—a time when people not only lived in the neighborhood, but never chose to leave it. And if some outsider looked closely, some driver who'd taken a wrong turn and ended up on the run-down streets, if that driver looked past the weather-worn lettering and cracked or broken windows, he'd have a sense of what the neighborhood once was. The grand old library's still there, and the first public school, with a fireplace in each of the classrooms. The Holiday Bowl's still open—although it closes now at dusk—where men came in from factory swing shifts and bowled until dawn. There are places where old train tracks still lie hidden beneath the weeds, and if the visitor knelt and pressed his ear against the dulled metal, he might hear the slow rumble of the train that used to run from downtown all the way to the ocean.

Now, the children feel trapped in that part of the city, and because they've learned, from watching their parents' lives, the limits of their futures, they smash whatever they can, which is usually each other. But then, in that different time—the neighborhood even had a different name—Angeles Mesa was a children's paradise. It was table land, flat and fertile, and the fields of wheat and barley made perfect places for young children to hide. The older children borrowed their fathers' guns and hunted rabbits and squirrels, because the Mesa was part of the growing city only in name; everybody knew it was country.

The children's parents loved the neighborhood, too. The ones who grew up in cities—either there in California, or in the dark, damp states of the Midwest and East—loved the space of the Mesa, and the fresh air that carried the scent of jasmine in spring and oleanders in the summer. The ones from the South couldn't believe they'd found a place with the ease and openness of home, but only a train ride away from their downtown jobs. It was a train that had brought them in the first place. The Chamber of Commerce sent an exhibit train to tour around the country, passing out oranges and pictures of palm trees to anyone who'd take them. Hopeful newlyweds, coughing factory workers, old sharecroppers with hands hardened by years of labor, all bit into the sweet juicy oranges and thought they tasted heaven. And the oranges were magical, because instead of quenching people's appetites, they fed them. That yearning and anticipation started out in their taste buds, and worked down into their hearts and stomachs until they grew teary-eyed with want. In Ohio, Mississippi, in Delaware and Georgia, you could see people trailing "California on Wheels," stumbling down the track after the slow-moving train as if they'd follow it all the way across the country. And they did. Maybe not that day, not that season, not that year, but they did. Packed up their things and arranged for someone else to send them on. Gathered the family and headed out to California.

Some of them went to Long Beach, seeking work in the bustling shipyards, or to Ventura, to draw their livings from the sea. Some went to San Fernando to be closer to the oranges that first seduced them, and some to the Central Valley to pick lettuce or grapes. And a few of them, after living someplace else for a year or several, after starting out in Little Tokyo or South Central or following the crops around the state, bought a plot of land in Angeles Mesa. The price was good, and what you got for it!—rich land nestled by wild hills. And if their neighbors spoke a different language, wore a different color skin, here—and only here—it didn't matter. Whatever feelings or apprehensions people had when they came, they learned to put them aside. Because their children played together, sat beside each other at the 52nd Street School. Because it was impossible to walk through the neighborhood without seeing someone different from you.

Now, even the All Are Welcome Church has steel bars over its windows, and half the storefronts stand empty and deserted. The strawberry fields and orchards are all buried under concrete, and lifelong residents won't leave their houses after dark. Those with the money but not the heart to leave the neighborhood completely cross the Boulevard and move into the hills. They never come down now, never stop at Mama's Chicken and Waffles or Otis's Barber Shop, which is closing, in its fortieth year, for lack of business. But then, in that other time, which wasn't really so long ago, the corner market could not keep its shelves stocked, or the Kyoto Grill cook enough food, or the Love Lifted Me Church on Crenshaw (which is actually on Stocker) make enough space to accommodate the faithful. And even as the area changed and grew—even as the Boulevard burst with commerce and people— the flavor of the Mesa didn't change. It was always country-in-the-city, but with a central place to gather. And since the Mesa had everything—food, bowling, church, and friends; not to mention trees, game, and a backdrop of hills—there was never any reason to leave. If a visitor had come through in 1958, he might have closed his eyes, and, listening to the voices around him, thought he'd taken a wrong turn and ended up in Texas. He might have walked into Harry's Noodle Shop and mistaken the town for Little Tokyo. He might see a group of men just released from the Goodyear plant, crowded around a radio and listening to a ball game. They'd be sitting on milk crates in front of a market owned by a young Japanese man, a veteran, who'd worked there since he was a teenager; who hired local boys himself; and who'd heard so many of his customers' stories he could almost forget his own.

The people who lived there, the people who laughed and drank and listened to the Dodgers, didn't know they were unusual.

They didn't know that their disregard for rules observed outside the Mesa made them exceptions, and their example did not stand.

Now, if that lost driver went through certain parts of the neighborhood, he would still see a few of the elderly residents—Japanese and black—in a place the rest of the city dismisses as ghetto. But their children and grandchildren, and their friends' children, too, have moved elsewhere to build their own lives. In the city where history is useless and the future reinvented every day, no one has any need for game you hunted and cooked yourself; for berries stolen off the vine; for neighbors in pairs and threesomes sitting on stoops with cups of coffee, faces lifted to accept the morning sun. No one thinks about the neighborhood, its little corner market. No one, including the children of the people who lived there.

CHAPTER ONE

1994

TEN DAYS after her grandfather died, Jackie Ishida pulled into the entrance of the Tara Estates, the apartment complex where he'd lived with her aunt and uncle. It was eleven a.m. on a Saturday, February, 1994. Normally at this time she'd be studying already—she was in her third year of law school at UCLA—but Lois had called the night before, voice rough with cigarettes and tears, and asked her to come over this morning. And since her aunt Lois was, hands down, her favorite person in the family, she'd decided that the library could wait. It was a beautiful day, she noticed, but Los Angeles always looked best in winter—free of smog, crisp and green, cradled by the mountains. She stared out the window at the snow-capped peaks and waited for the security guard to write her a guest pass, wondering, as always, why she had to complete this particular formality. The two shootings and numerous hold-ups that had scared the residents lately had all occurred *within* the Estates, not outside of them, so she didn't see why the guards were so concerned with visitors. Jackie, who'd grown up on the quiet, tree-lined streets of Torrance, could never get used to this haphazard clump of dingy, tan, threatening buildings. Some clever developer had named the complex after Scarlett O'Hara's plantation—which was, it turned out, not in Georgia at all, but instead had been built right there in Culver City, on the old RKO Studios lot just a mile away.

The security guard was a bulky young Latino man, and as he leaned down out of his parking hut, he stared at the pass he'd just filled out himself as if seeing for the first time what was written there.

"You're visiting Miss Sakai?" he asked, sitting back up in his chair. "Lois Sakai in 3B—Frank's daughter?"

"Yes," Jackie answered, holding her arm out the window. "I'm actually her niece. And his granddaughter."

"Aw, man," the guard said, clutching the pass. "Mr. Frank . . . It's just . . . See . . . Aw, man."

And as she watched him, her hand still extended to receive the blue pass, she saw that he was struggling not to cry. His name tag read "Tony," and he was about twenty-five—Jackie's age—but suddenly he looked like a child. "Hey," she said. "Hey, are you all right?"

He nodded, and then pulled himself together, finally giving Jackie her pass. "I'm sorry. I mean, you're family. And Miss Sakai, too. I guess I have no right. But it was just a surprise is all, and Frank . . ." He trailed off.

"It's OK," she reassured him again. "He had a good long life, you know? And we were all really lucky to have him."

Her words sounded empty and false to her, but they seemed to work for Tony. He nodded resolutely, gave his condolences, and then raised the gate so she could drive into the complex. And Jackie thought, not for the first time, that her ability to comfort people revealed a deficiency on her part, not a virtue. It is only those who aren't totally shattered by a loss who can comfort the others, who are. Lois, who'd stopped a mugging the previous fall by telling the three young would-be thieves that they were shaming their families; who'd once pulled a dying child out from under the wheel of a bus and held him while his mother fainted, had completely fallen apart at the death of her father. She'd collapsed in on herself—she wouldn't eat, would hardly talk, and she shivered no matter how warm it was. For the first time in her life, someone else—mostly Ted—had to watch after her and make sure she ate. All of this while Jackie made continual check-up phone calls, and while her mother Rose, Lois's sister, took care of all the funeral logistics.

Tony was right—her grandfather's death had been completely unexpected. At seventy-one, he'd still been in seemingly perfect health—he walked every day, ate lightly and well, and did repair jobs all over the neighborhood. With his tight, lean body, handsome grin, and just-graying hair, he'd looked twenty years younger than he was. The day he died, he walked a mile to an old widow's house to cut her overgrown front lawn. It was she who placed the call to 911 an hour later when she found him, laid flat out behind the idling mower.

Jackie parked her Accord in a visitor's spot, and then, sighing heavily, she walked up to her aunt's apartment, the last place she'd seen her grandfather alive. They had been close once, when she was much younger and had needed watching because her parents were so busy—her father practicing medicine and teaching at Cedars-Sinai; her mother going to medical school and then vanishing completely into her internship and residency. He'd lived in Gardena then, with her grandmother and sometimes Lois too, and Jackie had spent whole weeks with them when her parents were especially swamped. But then Jackie had gotten older, and her soft-spoken grandfather had been no competition for the excitements of the social world at school. He'd tried to stay involved in her life, right up until the end—he'd sent her clippings about women lawyers; he'd called her twice a month and pretended not to notice how she rushed him off the phone; he'd even sent her frequent e-mails on the computer her parents had bought him. But more often than not, Jackie hadn't answered, hadn't thanked him, hadn't noticed him much at all. By the time of his death she hardly knew him, and so her sense of loss now seemed shallow and unearned.

When Lois answered the door, she had the phone tucked between her shoulder and ear, and she was shaking out a section of the newspaper. She beckoned for Jackie to enter, which Jackie did, taking a seat on the couch. Lois held the paper in one hand now, and gestured as if whomever she was speaking to were standing right in front of her.

"You're being silly, Cal," she said. "If someone tells you she's prepared to spend a whole lot of money, it's not in your best interest to try and stop her." She paced silently for a moment, listening. Then, "Listen, don't mess with me. My dad just died, my cat has hyper-thyroid, and one of my students just got arrested for robbing a bank. If one more bad thing happens, I'm likely to snap. I'm a woman with nothing to lose."

Jackie was glad to hear her talk like this, even if her aunt's firm words were undercut by the fact that she was still in her blue plaid pajamas. Jackie had been worried about Lois these last ten days. Her aunt, a strong, brash, stout, stone lion of a woman, had been unusually subdued since Frank died. For the first time in years, she'd even taken time off from her job as head guidance counselor at Culver City High School. She'd lost weight, had to be forced to come to the phone, had been dazed and barely audible when she managed to speak at all. This return to her usual attitudinal self suggested that she was starting to recover.

"All right, then. Three o'clock." She hung up the phone. "Ted?" she called out in the direction of the kitchen. "We've got a date. Cal said three o'clock."

A vague sound of acknowledgment came from the kitchen. Ted was doing the dishes—Jackie heard the clinks of silver against stoneware, smelled the ghosts of burned eggs and onions—and she was sure he wasn't happy about it. "What's happening?" she asked, when her aunt turned toward her.

"We're getting out of here," Lois said. She pulled a cigarette out of a half-empty pack and lit it; she'd started smoking on the day of the funeral. "Ted and I are finally going to buy a house."

Watching her aunt cough a few times, lower the cigarette, and then take another pained drag, Jackie thought that maybe she wasn't improving after all. "A house?" she repeated, and then she noticed what her aunt had been holding—the real estate section, spotted with circles of red ink, question marks in blue, indecipherable notes in dark green. Lois had put the paper down on the coffee table and now her cat, Winston, jumped on top of it, circling and batting at the billowing corners.

"It's actually a great time to buy," Lois informed her, sitting in the armchair that was opposite the couch. "Prices have been plummeting because of the quake."

Jackie nodded. Not quite a month before, the Northridge earthquake had struck the city, destroying or damaging thousands of buildings, killing fifty-seven people, and terrifying everyone. Since then the aftershocks had been appearing like unwelcome guests, brazenly and when you least expected them. Frank, Lois told her later, had been oddly unperturbed by the quake, by the frequent aftershocks, as if he knew he wouldn't be taken by *that* catastrophe, but by one of a more personal variety. But Jackie wondered now if the heart attack hadn't been some delayed reaction to the trauma of the quake. The week before he died—just after the buildings on campus had been declared safe and classes had started up again—she'd come home to find her floor soaked, her carp wide-eyed and lifeless at the bottom of the empty aquarium. The tank's corner seam had been weakened by the quake; had finally given nine days after it. Maybe some seam in Frank's heart had been weakened as well, some internal fault line which waited two weeks, until the panic had lessened, to write its own smaller disaster.

"But isn't it kind of soon?" Jackie asked. She didn't press her on the rest of what she wondered, which was why they were doing this now. For six years, Lois, Ted, and her grandfather had lived in this small, cramped apartment, in this increasingly dangerous complex. It had never seemed strange that Frank had stayed here—when her grandmother died, it was a given that her grandfather would move in with Lois and not with Rose, even though the Ishidas had a huge place up in Ojai now, a four-bedroom house on a lovely five-acre lot. Lois was closer to Frank, always had been, and Rose had been closer to their mother. Now, with Frank gone, she and Ted would have more space—yet Jackie understood immediately why they had to leave. It was strange and awful to sit in this apartment, even for just a few minutes. She kept expecting her grandfather to enter the room, grinning when he saw her.

"I've just got to get out of here," Lois said, crushing out, to Jackie's relief, her half-smoked cigarette. Then suddenly Jackie was afraid that Lois, too, would leave her, move someplace where they couldn't see each other regularly. Her parents' departure she hadn't minded—they'd moved out of the house in Torrance and up to Ojai while she was going to school at Berkeley. And it was their absence, partly, that had made her spend more time with Lois when she moved back down to Los Angeles three years ago. That, and the fact that she *liked* her aunt—as opposed to how she felt about her parents, who were too much like herself. All of their

SOUTHLAND

major faults, all the things she'd spent her adolescence railing against—their tension, their rigidity, their inability to deal with strong emotion—she'd inherited right along with her mother's thin nose and hazel, light-for-a-Japanese-girl's eyes; and to avoid the reflection, she saw them as little as possible. Lois, on the other hand, was easier to be around—more generous, more interesting, both more intense and also somehow more relaxed. And if Lois was going to leave now, she didn't know what she'd do. There'd be no one in her corner, no relief.

Lois seemed to sense Jackie's fear, and she reached out and patted her niece on the arm. "We're sticking close by, don't worry. Culver City or West L.A. I just don't want to be *here* anymore— I'll never get used to Dad not being around, and I don't really want to. I mean, the day he died, all I could think was that I had to hurry home from the hospital so I could make him dinner in time for him and Ted to go out bowling. He told me that morning that he wanted black bean chili, and I took the cans down out of the cupboard before I went to school. They were still sitting there on the counter when we got home." She began to tear up at this, and Jackie looked away. "And I keep missing the stupidest things," Lois continued. "I mean, like the toilet flushing at two in the morning. Or the coffee grinder waking me up at five."

"At five?"

"Every day, including Sunday. Drove me fucking crazy, to tell you the truth. But I think it was something left over from when he used to have the store. Even after all these years, he always lived like he had to be at work by six-thirty."

The store. It was one of the many parts of her family's past that Jackie's mother had never discussed. Before Jackie, before marriage, before medical school, Rose and the rest of the family had lived in the Crenshaw district, where Frank owned and managed a little corner market. Jackie didn't know very much about that era—just that they left sometime in the sixties, after the riots down in Watts. As for Crenshaw itself, Frank's boyhood home, she'd only driven through it—by mistake mostly, and once or twice on purpose, when she was trying to avoid the traffic on the freeway. It was pretty much a black ghetto, as far as she could tell—

an image that had only been confirmed by the funeral.

The service was held in Culver City at her grandparents' church, which she hadn't entered in six years, since her grandmother died. *That* funeral had been uneventful, attended mostly by family and a few long-time neighbors from Gardena. But when Jackie walked into the church for her grandfather's service, she was surprised to see that half the people in attendance were black. She was even more startled, and then slightly embarrassed, when, during the service, the black mourners—who were mostly clumped together on the right side of the room—began to answer the pastor, to shout "Amen" after each of his supplications. Jackie had only been to this church once or twice, but she was sure this call-and-response wasn't a usual part of the proceedings. She learned later that the one thing Lois had managed to do in the days after her father's death was to put a notice in *The Sentinel*, the local black newspaper. Lois still seemed attached to the old neighborhood, unlike Jackie's mother, who always grimaced when she spoke of it. And it was Lois, mostly, to whom the mourners expressed their condolences—although some of them smiled at Jackie, too, or spoke to her warmly, gestures of reflected sympathy she knew she didn't deserve. One thing they made her realize, though, and she was seeing it more and more: Frank had had an existence outside of her, outside of the whole family. All the strangers at the church knew Frank Sakai not as an aging old grandfather, but as an individual with a story, as a man.

Jackie was about to ask her aunt why Frank had given up the store when Ted Kanda appeared, his booming voice filling the room. "Hey, gorgeous," he said to Jackie. "What's cooking?"

"Breakfast was, I guess," Jackie replied. "Not that you saved me any."

"I'm sorry," he said, and sounded it. Ted was a big man, shaped exactly like Lois although a good foot taller, and it was funny to see his strong, wide shoulders fall into an exaggerated slump of remorse.

"You didn't miss much, believe me," Lois said. "He burned the omelet so badly I had to throw half of mine out."

"I'm a *good* cook, usually," he insisted to Jackie, who knew differently. "I've cooked for some very important people."

Lois rolled her eyes. "He served some pasta to Jerry Brown once in the dining hall in college. To hear him tell it, he made a ten-course gourmet meal for heads of state."

He turned toward Lois, his ponytail swinging. "You be quiet. Or next time I'll slip some rat poison into the food."

"Well, at least it would improve the taste."

Again, Jackie thought her aunt was doing better; Lois almost smiled at this last exchange. But Ted could do that for her, only Ted. He wasn't really Jackie's uncle—he and Lois had never married—but they'd been together for almost twelve years now. And Jackie, after not knowing what to make of Ted at first, had grown to adore him, although her parents still regarded him with a kind of half-benign suspicion. Rose acted like he was a grunting, dirt-caked cowboy, swinging his lasso in their living room, endangering their lamps, and her father, Richard, was more friendly, but still bewildered. The fact that Ted was an engineer for TRW did nothing to improve their opinion of him. They were also displeased with Lois's living situation, especially after Frank moved in (presumably he'd be offended by his daughter's scandalous domestic arrangement), although Jackie couldn't imagine that they'd like Ted much better if he and Lois ever got married.

Now he turned to Jackie and asked, "So did Lois tell you that we're looking at houses?"

"Yes, she did. You have an appointment for today?"

"Yeah, you wanna come? It's a three-bedroom place off of Braddock. We don't know if we can afford it, though. I just bought a computer program that's supposed to help us figure out what we can borrow and what kind of mortgage we should get. I have to install it later. Which reminds me."

"Oh, right," Lois said, pulling the scattered paper out from under the cat, and sounding somber again. "Jackie, can you cancel Dad's online account? Ted couldn't figure it out."

"Sure," she responded, shrugging. "I can try. But I don't know if I can do any better." It amused her that Ted, who understood the inner workings of engines and robots, could hardly find his way around a personal computer. Now, suddenly, she thought of a part of the past she *did* know about and remember. "If you're looking for a house, what about Grandpa and Grandma's old place? What ever happened to that?"

"I'm not crazy about Gardena," Lois said. "Anyway, it's gone—he sold it right after Mom died."

"But the money from the sale . . ." Jackie didn't want to ask what had happened to it, because it brought up, awkwardly, the question of the will, which was going to be read that coming Tuesday.

Lois clearly caught the drift, though. "I don't think he left much, but we'll find out on Tuesday." Now she and Ted exchanged a glance, which Jackie caught.

"What?"

"Actually," Lois said, "the reason I wanted you to come over today has something to do with all that."

Oh, God, Jackie thought. There's going to be a problem. She and Rose disagree about something as usual, and it's all going to explode over the will.

Lois stood and walked over to her desk, where she picked up a spiral notebook. Carefully, she pulled out a folded piece of paper, and then came back over and sat across from Jackie. "I'm wondering about the validity of a will," she said, "written in 1964."

"Whose?"

"Dad's."

"Is that what the lawyer's going to read on Tuesday?"

"No," Lois said. "This is a different one."

Jackie wanted to ask her what exactly she meant, but Lois was acting so strange, looking at Ted again, that she decided to sit tight and wait.

"This one," Lois continued, lifting the paper, "mentions things I'm sure the other one doesn't. And I'm afraid there might be a conflict. Here—I think you should read it." She handed it across the coffee table, and as Jackie took it, she watched the edges dip and rise. The paper was so thin that, even folded, she could make out the dark shapes of her fingers beneath it. The typed words were light, as if the ribbon had been running out of ink. She read:

September 22, 1964

I, Franklin Masayuki Sakai, being of sound mind and body, do bequeath the following items upon the event of my death:
1. *My house and savings shall go to my wife, Mary Yukiko Sakai.*
2. *My car shall go to my wife.*
3. *All of my late father's possessions, including his great-grandfather's kimono and katana, shall go to my mother, Masako Sakai.*
4. *My books and photographs shall go to my daughters, Rose and Lois.*
5. *My baseball cards shall go to John Oyama, Jr.*
6. *My jazz record collection will go to Richard Iida.*
7. *My store, located at 3601 Bryant St., shall go to Curtis Martindale.*

When she finished reading, she kept staring at the page. This will, this random list, was the kind of thing someone threw together in a panic and then forgot once the moment had passed. Lois, who was afraid of planes, made one every time she had to fly, earnestly telling everyone for days beforehand what she'd bequeathed them in the latest version.

"This stuff has already been dealt with, hasn't it? I mean, I don't know about the smaller things, but you just told me there's no house. And I know that there isn't a store."

"Right," Lois said. "He actually gave the cards to John years ago. And Richard Iida died, so Ted and I are going to keep the records."

Ted, behind her, winked and gave a thumbs-up sign.

"You have any idea why he wrote this?" Jackie asked. "He wasn't about to get on a plane, was he?"

But her teasing comment missed its mark entirely. "I just figured this out," Lois said. "He was having an operation to get his appendix removed and, you know, he never trusted doctors after the way they handled his foot." Jackie thought of the smooth, shortened end of her grandfather's right foot; it looked as if the toes had been filed down. She remembered his slight limp, the hitch in his step, which might have passed for a jerky strut if he'd been younger.

"Well, I don't think you have to do anything. Everything in the will is taken care of."

"Not quite," Lois said, and then she gestured in the direction of the bedrooms. "See, I found this will in a box of papers Dad kept in his closet. I was looking for the poem he read at Mom's funeral, because I thought we might read it again. Anyway, there was a lot of stuff in it—old pictures and articles, even his war medals. I mean, all kinds of things I'd never seen before. And there was another box, too, which had 'store' written on it with a marker." She looked at Ted, who turned and disappeared down the hallway. Jackie heard a door open and shut; then Ted reappeared, holding a stone-colored box which was big enough for a pair of boots or a hat. He set it down on the coffee table, and Lois nodded for her to open it. Which she did. And saw more money than she'd ever seen before, so much that her first impulse was to put the lid back on. But then she looked at it again, at all that green, all those Andrew Jacksons. "What the hell?" she finally said. "What's this from?"

"The store, I guess, according to how he marked it."

"How much is in here?"

"Almost $38,000."

"*Excuse* me?"

"Thirty-eight grand," Ted repeated, shaking his head. "Can you believe it?"

"Just sitting in the closet?"

"Yeah."

Jackie put the lid back on, stood up, and walked across the room. At the entrance to the kitchen, she turned around. "But Lois, I can't believe he would have just hidden this money for, what, twenty-nine years? Are you sure it's from the store?"

"I'm not sure, but it seems to be."

"Do we know if it's mentioned in the current will?"

"I don't think so. Like I said, as far as I know, he didn't have much to leave. And to answer your question from before, the money from the Gardena house is gone. He gave that and the redress money to Rose a few years back, in order to pay for your law school." Jackie hadn't been aware of this arrangement. And it was more evidence of what she had taken from Frank—his attention, his money, his time. He was always there to fix her heater, or to build her a set of shelves. She had given him so little in return.

"Well, this is great," she said, trying to shake her guilt. "You want to buy a house, right? So here's your down payment."

"You're missing the point," Lois replied. "He left the store to someone else. And this looks like it's the money from the store."

"Wait. You think the money should go to—" She looked down at the paper again. "—Curtis Martindale? Who *is* Curtis Martindale, anyway?"

"I don't know." Lois leaned back against Ted, who was standing behind her, his big hands draped over her shoulders. "Someone from the neighborhood, I think. The name sounds vaguely familiar. I'm guessing he's pretty young—or that he *was* pretty young back then. Dad *got* the store from someone in the neighborhood, you know, before he married Mom. Old Man Larabie practically gave it to him, almost as a gift. He was probably just trying to pass on the favor." Ted began to rub her shoulders, and she closed her eyes and leaned back. And Jackie remembered how interested Frank always was in her friends and their lives; how good he was with all young people. She thought about mentioning Tony, the security guard, but decided against it; his strong response to Frank's death made her muted one seem even less defensible.

"Anyway, there's no Curtis Martindale in L.A. County," Lois continued. "I checked information."

"Does my mother know who he is?"

"I haven't asked her. I didn't tell her about this."

Jackie nodded. Rose had always seemed a bit resentful of the store; one thing she *had* told Jackie was that Frank had spent most of his time there. Jackie knew her mother would want to invest the money or put it in the bank, and she, for once, would have to agree with her.

"Lois," she said, "you could *use* this money. Why do you want to give it away?"

"Because *he* wanted to. And if he meant it for someone else, it's not mine."

Jackie shook her head; she couldn't believe this.

"I'm wondering," Lois said now, opening her eyes, "if *you'd* be willing to track this guy down."

Jackie stared at her aunt. "Me? Why me?"

Lois frowned. "Because I'm a mess," she answered in a measured voice, "and I don't want to deal with this shit right now. There's so much to do, with the legal will and all of Dad's things, and the business with the house. Curtis Martindale is one loose end I don't really have the time for."

Jackie tried not to pout, or to remind her aunt that she herself was creating the business with the house. It was bad enough that Lois wanted to give away this money, which was sitting in her apartment, in her closet. But to ask Jackie to be a part of it? No thanks. Not that it would be difficult to make a few calls, to check some records. With this kind of money involved, she'd have Curtis Martindales coming out of the woodwork. It was just the principle of the thing, the idea of throwing away that kind of cash. "Well, if I did do this—which I'm not saying I will—do you have any ideas about where I would start?"

"Actually, yes," Lois said. "A couple of people from the funeral. Especially that woman Loda, who caught us right when we came in. She grew up in Crenshaw and I think she still works there. Do you remember her? The older black lady in that dark green suit?"

Jackie did. The woman Lois referred to had been crying herself, she was so worked up about Frank. She was a tall, black-gloved woman with neat marcelled waves in her hair, and she'd hugged them both as they entered the church. She'd told them Frank had once found and sheltered her child when she'd run away from home; said it made sense the Lord had called Frank home when he was giving somebody a hand. She'd insisted repeatedly that they should get in touch with her if they needed anything.

"Yeah," Jackie answered. "I think so."

Lois reached into her purse, which was sitting on the floor, and pulled out a business card. It was one of many they'd both received that day, from people who wanted to document their presence, or to help. They'd also been deluged with *kōden*, condolence money, in small white envelopes with black and silver ribbons, offered mostly by older Japanese. Over and over, the same routine—the checkbook-sized envelope held out with both hands; the offerer avoiding eye contact, bowing low, saying, "It's nothing. I'm ashamed to give it to you."

Jackie took the card reluctantly. It was white, the print black and gold, and it informed her that Loda Thomas was the Adult Literacy Coordinator at the Marcus Garvey Community Center. She dropped it on top of the shoebox as if it carried a disease. "I don't know," she said. Both Lois and Ted looked at her expectantly, and to escape their gaze, to avoid the question, she returned to an earlier topic. "So, do you want me to take care of Grandpa's AOL account?"

Lois looked startled, and then disappointed. "Yeah," she said, throwing her hands up. "Sure."

Jackie fled down the hallway, glad to leave Lois and Ted and the box of money behind. The door to her grandfather's room was closed. It had never been closed when she'd come over before, and she paused now, standing in front of it, fighting the urge to knock. The cat stood at the end of the hallway, swishing his tail, staring at her accusingly, as if he, too, was aware of how much she'd taken Frank for granted. She wanted to shut him out, along with the questions her aunt had raised and the project she'd been given, so she pushed the door open, stepped inside, and closed it again behind her.

It was strange to be in here, and she wasn't sure that she could stay for very long. The room was small and, as always, impeccably neat. The single bed, pushed up under the window, was carefully made. There was a dresser against one wall and a desk against the other, on top of which sat the Macintosh computer. There were two pieces of art in the room—a large painting of a feudal Japanese home with a garden and carp pool in front of it, and a smaller, simpler painting of a single tree, its branches droop-

ing gracefully like the arms of a tired dancer. Both paintings were
the work of Frank's grandmother, Jackie's great-great grandmother,
who had been a minor artist in Japan. Jackie's eyes passed over
these things without really seeing them, but then she noticed something hanging off the back of the desk chair. It was a blue Dodgers
cap, well-worn, the lid bent slightly in the middle. Jackie remembered when he bought it—at a Dodgers game he took her to when
she was seven. He'd bought her one, too, but she'd outgrown it;
she had no idea now where it was. She walked over to the chair
and took the cap off carefully, bringing it up to her nose. It smelled
like him—soap and grass and Old Spice, with a touch of stale
tobacco. Jackie felt a strange sensation in her chest and stomach—
a combination of the warmth she got from a shot of whiskey and
the pang she felt when she hadn't eaten all day. What caused this,
more than the smell of her grandfather, or even the cap itself, was
the casual way it had been thrown on the back of the chair.
Everything else in the room was neat and orderly. But the cap had
simply been tossed there, as if her grandfather had just stepped out
and would return at any moment.

She sat down in his desk chair, thinking again about the
funeral—about all the mourners, like Loda Thomas, and her sense
that the man they were paying respects to was different than the
one she'd grown up with. Or maybe he *wasn't* different with everyone else; maybe she'd just never bothered to know him. Not once
had she asked him a meaningful question—about his thoughts or
experiences, successes or failures, anything. And not once had she
asked about the people in his life, so that the men and women
she'd seen in the church that day, black and Japanese, had been
totally new to her, as mysterious and undelineated as the acquaintances of a stranger. And yet they all knew *him*, and his family. She
remembered sitting in the crematorium after the funeral, the
strange intimacy between all the people there. It was the same
room she and her family had waited in six years before, when her
grandmother died. On that occasion, the staff had brought out a
tray like a giant baking sheet full of still-hot ashes, dotted here and
there with small charred bones, the perfect white kernels of teeth.
Frank had started the ritual passing of bones, picking the larger

fragments out with a pair of special chopsticks, passing them chopstick-to-chopstick to Rose, who passed them to Lois—spirit to body to dust. Once, years before in a restaurant, Rose had violently slapped the chopsticks out of Jackie's hand when she'd used them to offer a piece of fish to her father. She never explained why, and when the connection finally hit Jackie, at Mary Sakai's cremation, it was *that* more than the handling of her grandmother's bones that made her hug herself and rock back and forth. This time, though, there had been no picking through the remains; her mother hadn't wanted it, and Jackie was glad. She sat silently, staring at the wall as if she could see through it, and imagined the glasses melting, the gold wedding band, flames consuming flesh. Her eyes had settled on the odd old man across from her who'd sat through the entire service mumbling to himself, and then, when she and Lois approached him after it was over, had jumped to his feet instantly, spry as a spaniel, and offered a gorgeous, right-angled salute. She'd looked over at Burt Hara, the Buddhist priest from the Tara Estates who Frank sometimes played cards with; he'd just given Lois a thick wooden tablet with Chinese characters, the Buddhist name conferred to Frank upon his death. When the black-tied employee came out and handed Rose a simple bronze urn, Jackie wondered only what had happened to the bones and teeth. Rose handed the urn to Lois, who wrapped it in a purple *furoshiki* and set it down on the table. Burt Hara stood over it and said a few words in Japanese. And then everyone there, even, shockingly, both of Jackie's parents, began to cry in earnest—everyone, that is, except for Jackie. The odd saluting man exploded with great gulping sobs; her mother just covered her face. She felt awful then—for not feeling more; for not sharing in their sorrow; for having been so distant from Frank, by the end, that she couldn't even properly grieve.

But there was nothing, she thought, as she sat at his desk, that she could do about that failure. One tangible thing she could accomplish right now, however, was to grapple with America Online, and so she reached out and switched on the Mac. AOL, she knew, would keep billing her grandfather endlessly unless she canceled the account; her aunt was smart to want to cut them off now. She double-clicked on the AOL icon, double-clicked again. The dialogue box gave her the user's screen name, "FSakai." Now she needed the password. She paused for a moment. Baseball, his biggest love, was the obvious answer. She tried "Dodger," then "Koufax," then "Drysdale." Who else had he admired? She tried "Dusty," "Fernando," and "homerun." She thought about Japanese ballplayers—would he use a player from the Japanese leagues? She didn't think so. Then she recalled a player that he'd mentioned as being half-Asian, whose name she remembered because she thought it so funny, and she typed "Darling" very quickly and hit "return." The modem dialed, whirred, connected. Something flashed on and off the screen. She was in.

A tinny, cheerful voice welcomed her and informed her, "You've got mail!" She'd just intended to log on long enough to cancel his membership, but now she decided to read the new mail. It must have been written around the time he died, and she wondered who it was from. She felt vaguely invasive. Once, when she'd worked for an accountant in high school, she'd had to go through the checkbook of a woman who'd recently died. The barely dried ink there, the woman's belief, in writing the checks, that she'd be around to cover them, had spooked and saddened her, as Frank's mail did now. When she went to open it, though, she found that it was only something from the people at America Online. She was half-disappointed, half-relieved. Then, since she was there already, she decided to look at his file of outgoing mail. The results were boring—the most recent mail had all gone out to her. She felt another stab of guilt—she hadn't answered his last few messages—so to counteract it, she did something worse. Curious about who her grandfather corresponded with, she opened up his address file—the only addresses there belonged to Jackie, Lois, Rose, and Ted. This couldn't be, she thought; these were probably just the addresses he happened to keep on file. She closed that box and pulled up his older mail. The only messages were from her and her aunt and Ted. And there weren't very many. Not, anyway, in comparison to the number of messages he'd sent to *them*—she opened his "sent mail" file again and saw that the list of outgoing messages was about four times as long. She couldn't bear to look at this. She hadn't returned his calls; had forgotten his last two birthdays; had only responded to a fraction of his e-mails. She hung her head for a moment and, looking back at the screen, finally began to sense the loneliness of the man who used to sit where she sat now.

Feeling something strong and definite for the first time since the funeral—shame—she thought that what her aunt wished her to do, while foolish, wasn't really so hard. Maybe Frank *had* wanted all that money to go to the man in the will; who was she to say? Tracking him down was the least she could do—for everyone. And she could spend the day with her aunt, too, like Lois always wanted her to—she could blow off her schoolwork for once and go look at this house with them. Sighing, she turned off the computer and went back out to the living room, where Lois and Ted, red pens in hand, were circling more ads. The business card was still lying untouched on top of the box of money; Jackie picked it up and slipped it into her wallet.

"So I'll give Loda Thomas a call on Monday," she said, as nonchalantly as she could.

Lois smiled, and Jackie knew that *she* knew that something had happened in the bedroom. But she didn't ask about it; she just said, "Thank you."

CHAPTER TWO

LOIS—1994, 1963

S HE SAW him everywhere, at different ages, in different incarnations. It was like the soundless scenes played at the end of certain movies, flashing on and off the screen while the credits rolled. Today the scenes starred Jackie as tiny granddaughter, maybe because Lois had spent the whole day with her, like they used to with Frank twenty years ago, afternoons and outings and dinners at home that her niece didn't even remember.

But Lois did. Small snippets of memory, like cut-up film. Frank handing out cigars when Jackie was born, laughing aloud and then suddenly weeping, as if he already knew she'd be his only grandchild. Frank stomping around the house in Gardena, roaring, pretending he was a monster, waggling his sawed-off foot or half-finger in Jackie's face. Frank and Jackie in the bowling alley, he encouraging her as she squatted behind the heavy ball, pushed it with both hands, jumped up and down as she watched it roll right into the gutter. Frank and Jackie a couple of years later, leaning over the railing at the Redondo Beach Pier. She was riding on his shoulders, legs hooked over his chest, fingers trying to get a hold in his crew-cut hair. He with his sun-browned hands wrapped around each of her legs. Lois beside them getting nervous as Frank leaned over the railing to watch a fish flipping on someone's hook, her niece draped over his head, hanging, tipping out over the water. Lois yelled, "Dad!" and then felt silly as he stood up straight, snapped the child back onto the pier, saying, "What?" And then they'd fished, the three of them, sitting in lawn chairs and holding the bamboo poles that Frank had made himself, nodding them up and down, back and forth, like divining rods. Jackie's mother was in medical school then, her father already a doctor, so it often fell to Frank or Lois—who was slowly finishing college—to take care of Rose's child. To try and show her something different from the gilded, tree-lined world they both knew she was going to grow up in.

Lois remembered the day her family had divided. Looking back, she could see that it had been happening for years, but one Saturday morning in 1963, each member of the family had fallen clearly in one direction or the other.

She was twelve years old, and her older sister was playing for the under-fifteen championship of the Japanese Tennis League. Lois—who was in charge of equipment—had accidentally grabbed Rose's practice shoes before running out to the car; they looked the same as the ones her sister wore for matches. And later, as they pulled up to the tennis court in Gardena, Lois knew her whole family was mad at her. Rose would hardly look at her, hadn't spoken since she'd flipped her ponytail in exasperation and cried, "Lo-is! How could you be so dumb!" Her mother had been tight-lipped, informing her, simply, "This is a very important match, Lois. I hope you didn't ruin it for your sister." Even her grandmother Sakai, who never yelled at anyone, still added to the general air of disapproval. Only her father had refrained from scolding her, trying instead to mollify his eldest, telling her the practice shoes weren't really that much older; their traction should be fine on the nice new court.

Although Lois felt bad about the shoes and wished that someone would talk to her, she wasn't worried about how her sister would do in the match. She didn't care much for tennis. She hated the bright white skirts, the pressed blouses, the scrubbed-clean quality of all the girls who played. And she hated leaving Crenshaw to come down to Gardena, where everyone lived in big, bland houses; where all the boys her age were already talking about college and becoming doctors, and all the girls spoke of make-up tips and Barbie dolls. After their father parked the car, Rose ran off to talk to some girls she knew. Their mother's parents lived here in Gardena now—they'd closed the restaurant in Little

Tokyo and opened another one over on Western—and the whole family came down to visit often enough for Rose to make some new friends. Her sister wanted to move here, Lois knew; every weekend her Gardena friends would pick her up in their cars, and Rose always returned from these excursions sighing and sad, looking out the window for hours.

Lois, her parents, and her grandma Sakai found seats in the shiny aluminum stands. Frank and Mary exchanged pleasantries with some other parents they knew, including Mr. and Mrs. Ikeda, the parents of Stephanie Ikeda, the girl Rose would be facing in the championship. Mary put the red and white cooler of *sushi* on the bench between herself and Lois, and Lois looked at it, stomach rumbling. The big Japanese-style picnic which followed these matches was the only thing that made them bearable.

"I wish you would take up tennis," Mary said. "Or bowling. Something where you'd make some good friends."

"I *have* friends," Lois replied, thinking of Chris, with the gap where his tooth had been punched out, and Janie, with the always-skinned knees.

"Yes, but they're not *nice* friends."

Lois sighed. She'd heard all of this before. At twelve, she was a tomboy, usually outside and almost always dirty. To her, the greatest joy in life was running loose in the neighborhood. She loved the Crenshaw district, and she loved her father's stories about how much it had changed over the years, since the time it was known as Angeles Mesa. It was filled with houses now, and crowded with all different sorts of families. But Frank described a neighborhood of huge, open spaces; of fewer and heartier people. For Lois, going down to Gardena, which was stiff and all-Japanese, was like going to church—something she knew she should do and appreciate, but which bored her to the point of sleep.

After an interminable warm-up period, a short man wearing a golf visor introduced the two players and everyone in the crowd clapped politely. The match began. Rose seemed nervous at first, and Lois feared she was distracted by the fit of her shoes, but then she settled in, as she always did, placing the ball perfectly on almost every shot. It was so quiet that Lois could hear the creak of a swing set on the other side of the park, chain links shifting and straining. Every time Stephanie Ikeda hit the ball, she emitted a small grunt, like she'd been punched in the stomach, and Lois saw her own mother shake her head a little, glad *her* daughter didn't make such ugly noises. The whole crowd cheered when a point was won, and Rose took the first set in half an hour.

At the break, the people in the stands started into a quiet chatter, analyzing the first set, debating a questionable call made by one of the judges. Lois saw the gray clouds moving over them, closing and unclosing like fists, and she wondered if it was going to start raining. Her parents exchanged a few words and then fell silent again, and Lois thought, watching them, not for the first time, that she never wanted to marry. Marriage, to her, meant what her parents had—steadiness, like a small efficient business. Her parents never fought, but they didn't hug either, or talk about anything that wasn't related to the family or work. She knew that love could be more than that—more like Christy Hara and John Oyama from high school, who would vanish into Christy's house in the afternoon and come out an hour later looking happy and relaxed; or like Dexter Coleman's parents, who lived together but had never married, and who still cooked for each other, and sang songs together, and yelled, "Hey, baby!" when they met on the street.

Steadiness, in any form, was stifling to her. She liked the extreme, the inexplicable, the ridiculous and evil. She liked her Grandma and Grandpa Takayas' stories of the hustlers and pimps they served in the old days in Little Tokyo; of the gambling house where they wouldn't let Mary make deliveries because of the desperate, devious men and shady women. She liked their stories of nine-month winters and planting rice on early mornings in Japan, and her grandmother Sakai's tales of surviving on locusts, fried for crispness or boiled for soup. They were citizens now, all of them, transformed into Americans at the mass naturalization ceremony at the Hollywood Bowl in '54, but to Lois their stories of old Japan were like the best kind of fairy tales—fantastical, with familiar elements and odd but recognizable characters.

During the second set, Lois's attention wandered. She looked around at all the well-dressed husbands and wives, the tiny grandmothers with their plain, drab Western clothes and their bright, patterned Japanese fans. She watched a couple of bored-looking wives glance over at her father, who she knew was handsomer than any Gardena man. A better father, too, she believed. He was at the store every night until eight or nine, but then he was always at home, telling stories, teasing his daughters, never going out for drinks or card games like the other Nisei fathers she knew. He even took her to baseball games sometimes at Dodger Stadium, and before that, when the team had just moved out from Brooklyn, right over at the Olympic Coliseum. Rose, of course, wasn't interested in baseball, but once or twice a summer, Frank and his friend Victor gathered a big group of kids and drove them all up to a game. Lois loved being around the men, for any reason—the deep sweet smell of Victor's pipe, the easy way her father laughed when they sat on the stoop of Victor's house, always made her feel secure. The two of them together were a sight to see, especially her father's friend—all the women in the neighborhood, from fifteen to fifty, threw more sway in their hips, more spice and honey in their voices, when Victor Conway came around.

At the break between the second and third sets—Stephanie Ikeda had taken the second set 6-3—Lois asked her mother where the bathroom was. Mary pointed at a small tan building about a hundred feet away from the court. "Can't you wait?" she asked. Lois said that she couldn't. "Hurry back," her mother said.

Lois barely made it to the bathroom in time, and when she was done, she had no desire to get back to the stands. So she dawdled, distracted by a game of volleyball; by a picnic; by a particularly proud and vocal robin. Every so often she looked over at the tennis court and saw the slim white-clad bodies flitting around on the sea-green concrete. When she was about thirty feet away, a small golden puppy came up to her, dragging a leather leash. Lois crouched down to greet her. The dog jumped up, put its front paws on her shoulders, and thoroughly washed her face with its tongue. The owner appeared soon after and disengaged the leash, saying that Lois could play with her for a while. So Lois skipped around, leading the dog in a circle, pretending it was hers. She could hear the announcer over at the court saying the set was tied 5-5. Lois knew she should see the end of the match, so she started back over to the court, but the puppy, ignoring its owner, continued to follow her. Then the dog caught sight of the tennis ball. Rose was bouncing it, preparing to serve, and the puppy, following some ancient, blood-deep impulse, took off toward the court at a sprint. "Wait!" Lois yelled after her, but it was Rose who turned, upon completing her serve, and so she completely missed her opponent's return. Worse, the ball skittered off her end of the court and the puppy pounced on it, growling happily. The entire crowd burst into laughter. Rose went after her, but the dog commenced a game of keep-away, getting close to Rose, then jumping back again, Rose lunging in desperation. The crowd continued to laugh, and Rose to chase, until finally the owner appeared and grabbed the dog by the collar. He pried the ball loose from the puppy's jaws and handed it sheepishly back to Rose. She grimaced at the thing, which was now covered with dirt and saliva, and then glared at Lois, who was standing to the side of the crowd, trying hard to disappear. Rose went back to the court, took out a new ball, and attempted to regain her composure, and the crowd's laughter quieted down to a still-amused titter. The last point had put Rose down 30-40, and now, distracted, she double-faulted. It was 5-6. Stephanie Ikeda had serve, and Rose never recovered. She dropped the last game, love-40, and lost the match in three sets.

On the car ride home, Lois slumped in the back seat and suffered yet another berating from her sister and mother. Rose was almost hysterical, complaining to her parents about how Lois was a brat, and a bad student, and she was trying to ruin her life, and Mary scolded Lois for spoiling her sister's day. Lois felt small, the bad daughter. Even her grandmother refused to look at her. But then, in the middle of this barrage, she caught Frank's eye in the rearview mirror. He'd laughed right along with the rest of the crowd when the puppy went after the ball. Now Lois saw that his eyes were still laughing, despite his immobile face. He looked at her in the rearview mirror, not adding to the din of voices. Then he winked. And in that moment, as they drove up Crenshaw and back toward their house, although she didn't say anything or even return the gesture, she felt the weight of everyone else's fury lift off her, and became her father's child.

CHAPTER THREE

1994

DRIVING INTO her garage that night, after spending the day with Lois, was like walking into open arms. Jackie loved her apartment, a top unit in a four-plex that had been built in the 1920s. All the buildings on this block were old and solid—although her books had fallen off their shelves in the quake and the refrigerator had shuffled out into the middle of the kitchen, the structure itself had withstood the earth's violence. The unit had a refinished hardwood floor; the furniture was simple and elegant. She'd lived in this apartment all through law school, and while she could have found a place much closer to campus, it seemed like too much trouble to move—especially since, in a few more months, she'd be able to afford a much nicer place. The real reason Jackie had stayed here, though, was Laura. It seemed to Jackie that if she moved at all, she should be getting a place with her girlfriend—they'd been together now for almost three years. But something in the strange, shifting nature of their relationship did not make this an automatic choice. For the last year or so they'd been poised at the edge of something—Jackie didn't know exactly what. And any big actions or decisions needed to wait until they fell, decisively, one way or the other.

When she got inside, the first thing she saw was the red light of the answering machine, flashing three times, stopping, flashing again, as if sending out a distress signal. She flopped down on the recliner and looked at her watch. It was just before six. With a feeling that was equal parts anticipation and dread, she pressed the "play messages" button.

The first message was from Laura, at 1:30, checking in. The next was from Rebecca, a friend from law school. She was in Sacramento, interviewing for a public interest job, and she wanted copies of the notes that Jackie would be taking in their Tax Law class on Monday. The third, again, was Laura, this time sounding tired and just short of impatient. *"Jackie, it's me again. It's 5:45. I was thinking you'd be back by now, but . . . I don't know. Anyway, give me a call when you get in."*

Jackie picked up the phone, and as the answering machine rewound she dialed her girlfriend's number. She half-hoped that Laura would be out somewhere; she needed some time to recover. But Laura picked up on the first ring.

"Hi, I'm home," Jackie informed her. "I must have just missed your last call."

"Hi. Where have you been? How's Lois doing?"

"Oh, fine. I ended up staying with them all day."

"What did she want you to do?"

"Just some little stuff. I'll tell you about it later." She wondered how much she'd really tell her, knowing there'd be gaps in the narrative. "What have *you* been up to?" she asked.

Laura didn't answer at first, and Jackie could feel her considering whether or not to press further. "Oh, I just lazed around," she said finally. "Had coffee with people. Went for a run with Marie." She paused now, and Jackie could tell from the texture of the pause—she'd thrown a net around her emotions, but there were holes in the fabric and little bursts of feeling kept wriggling through—that her girlfriend was annoyed. Then Laura added, "Marie and Steven are having a cocktail party tonight. And I know you had a long day, but I was thinking that maybe we could go."

That was it. Marie was one of Laura's friends from work, another young politico, like Laura, who'd been hired out of elite private universities to work in city government. There were about twenty recent graduates who had jobs in City Hall, and they often met for meals or coffee and threw parties for themselves. They believed wholeheartedly that they were the future of the city, and Jackie, privately, hated their self-importance, but also, more privately, envied it. Now, Jackie knew why Laura had been so anxious—she didn't expect Jackie to want to go out with her, and she was right.

"Laura, I'm exhausted," Jackie said. "It's been a really long day and I don't feel up to being social. But why don't you go by yourself? I'll probably just do some reading and hit the sack." There was silence on the other end. "Laura?"

"You never want to spend time with my friends," Laura said.

Jackie sighed and squeezed her temples. "Of course I do. We just went to your friend's dinner party on Wednesday, didn't we? I'm just really tired now. I mean, I've had a lot going on the last couple of weeks. Besides, it's already six o'clock. Why didn't you tell me about this earlier?"

"Because I knew you wouldn't want to go. I know you've had a lot to deal with, but can't you just come and sit there? You do need to eat at least, right?"

Jackie twisted the phone cord around her fingers. "Listen," she replied, "just go. You'll have a better time without me, anyway."

"But I want you to go with me."

For a brief moment, Jackie considered it. The parties weren't terrible. Maybe it would do her good to get out and have a couple of drinks. The food was usually decent and the conversation was interesting, even if the young golden ones tended to forget that there were a few people in attendance who did not breathe the specialized, government-issue air of City Hall. And really, it was a small victory that Laura wanted to take her at all. For her first year in City Hall, she'd been closeted at work, even among the people her age. Jackie had resented being hidden and lied about, but after she'd won this battle—after Laura had told her peers about Jackie (but not her boss), after she'd started taking Jackie to parties and barbecues (but not official functions)—Jackie realized she wasn't missing much. Now, she was in the strange position of not wanting to spend time with people she'd once been furious about not being able to meet.

"I really just want to stay home. I promise I'll go to the next thing."

Laura was silent for a moment. "Fine," she said. And something in her voice frightened Jackie—not because it was angry, but because it wasn't. She wasn't fighting anymore. She'd surrendered. "Fine. You're right. I'm sorry. You've had a hard two weeks. Why don't you just come over? I'll go out and rent a couple of movies."

Jackie put her hand on her forehead and squeezed. "Laura, just because I don't want to go to the party doesn't mean that *you* shouldn't go."

"Forget it, Jackie. It's too late. Just come to my place."

Jackie opened her mouth, then closed it again, biting down on her reply. She didn't want this to go any further—not now, not today. Their fights had been like quicksand lately—if they stepped down in the wrong place, they'd be swallowed up fast, neither of them able to pull herself out, or to reach back and pull out the other. "OK," she said finally. "I'll be there in forty-five minutes."

Jackie took a long shower, fingering the caulk between the square crimson tiles, wondering how she was supposed to deal with Laura. Images of the last ten days kept popping up in her mind. The thin paper of the will. The heavy urn in its flowing *furoshiki*. The black strangers in the church. And she knew she would share none of this with Laura. She felt as guilty and over-whelmed—and as committed to silence—as if she were washing off the evidence of a clandestine liaison that she not only wouldn't admit to, but planned to repeat. She wasn't sure where this secrecy came from—she used to tell Laura everything. And now, as much as she tried to convince herself that she hid things from Laura to keep their relationship pure, to have Laura as an untouched sanc-tuary from all the things that ailed her, she knew she was kidding herself.

The house where Laura lived was only half a mile away. As Jackie left her apartment and stepped onto the sidewalk, she saw that the streets were plugged with cars, full of people who were heading toward the restaurants and boutiques up on Melrose and down on Beverly. Jackie took a detour to a convenience store to buy some Ben & Jerry's—her usual peace offering—and as she walked the ice cream softened, the carton sweating through its paper bag. Jackie loved the Fairfax district and was always amused by it. Their neighborhood was home to many young, hip people trying to break into acting or music, and to elderly Jews who'd been living there for decades. Within walking distance were two large synagogues, several Jewish retirement homes, half a dozen Jewish private schools, and the most famous Jewish deli in L.A. Laura, who'd gone to Hebrew school until she was fourteen, often joked that if she had to be involved with a woman, at least she'd picked the right neighborhood to do it. To Jackie, it was the right neighborhood, period. The seventy-year-old apartment buildings were beautiful and grand, dressed with turrets, gables, red-tiled stairs and roofs, ivy winding up the fronts and the sides. Restaurants, markets, delis, banks, were all within a couple of blocks. Other than driving back and forth from school, she almost never used her car.

Jackie walked at a leisurely pace, enjoying the fresh air, thinking about her girlfriend. It occurred to her that they hadn't been happy for quite some time—maybe not since the summer they met. Although they were both from L.A., they'd started dating in San Francisco, two months before Jackie started law school. Laura had an internship, working for the San Francisco Community Development Department between her junior and senior years at Stanford, and Jackie, who'd just graduated the year before from Berkeley, was finishing her paralegal stint in one of the Embarcadero buildings. They were set up by a mutual acquaintance who'd gone to school with Laura at Stanford and was working as a paralegal at Jackie's firm. Their first date had started over ten-dollar sandwiches at a downtown lunch spot, and hadn't ended until two days later.

They had a perfect, all-too-brief summer of bike rides, big dinners, wine-tasting in Napa Valley, long nights of conversation and sex. Every weekend they'd bike across the Golden Gate Bridge and walk down to Black Sand Beach, where they'd hold hands and stare back at the sparkling city. Then, in early September, Jackie left for L.A., and they'd spent the academic year on the phone. During breaks, Jackie would go up to Stanford or Laura would come down to L.A. Laura would split her home time between Jackie and her mother, who loved that Laura was seeing someone in L.A. because it meant she came down more often. And Laura's mother—and Jackie—were even happier when Laura got the job with the city; she moved back to L.A. right after her graduation.

It wasn't clear to Jackie when things had started to go wrong. But their relationship, on this different turf, had changed somehow, the way a crop that might flourish in one kind of soil struggles simply to survive in another. When Laura first came to L.A., Jackie had visions of their one day moving in together (they both agreed they should live apart initially), having a dog, two cats, and eventually some children. But it quickly became clear that Laura was miserable. Despite the prestige of her job, she hated the stress of it. Despite how wonderful her family seemed to Jackie (Laura's older sister was a second-year student at Stanford Business School, her mother the principal of an elementary school in Beverly Hills), Laura didn't like being so close to them, and Jackie wondered if she resented *her* for also living in L.A. and being part of what had lured her back. But whatever the reason, or combination of reasons, Laura had grown increasingly depressed, and Jackie, who'd been so happy for their first year and a half together, watched with interest, then concern, and then growing despair as Laura slipped further and further out of reach.

Jackie arrived at Laura's door and knocked softly; Laura opened it a few seconds later. She hadn't changed much in the two years and eight months since they'd met. She was thin, 5'4", with dirty blond hair—but her eyes were often watery now, and a little puffy around the edges. She looked very tired these days.

"Hi," she said, moving aside.

Jackie held her bag out. "New York Super Fudge Chunk?"

Laura smiled sadly and took the bag. "Thank you, sweetie."

Jackie stepped inside and Laura hugged her, holding on as if they hadn't seen each other in months. This embrace, Jackie knew, was about her grandfather's death; was meant to show love and support. But it was hard for her to stand through it. Lately all their hugs had seemed out of proportion to the situations in which they occurred—and she didn't feel like she deserved this one anyway.

"Are you sure you don't want to go to the dinner?" Jackie asked as they separated.

Laura nodded. "Yeah. I'm tired anyway."

Jackie looked around. "Where's Rodent and Amy?"

Laura smiled, finally looking just a bit happy. "They're both of out of town."

Rodent—Rodney Adams—and Amy Carillo were Laura's two roommates, acquaintances from Stanford. Amy was a second-year student in the screenwriting program at USC. She was almost always home, working on her screenplay or groaning over other people's, which she read part-time for an agency. Jackie preferred her, though, to Rodney, who wrote music for TV and movies. He had a huge fancy set-up in his bedroom—synthesizer, drum machine, three-foot speakers, and a set of control panels that looked like they could be used to fly a plane. Rodney often had women in his room, watching him worshipfully, as he created the theme song for a new pilot at Fox, or wrote the music for a death scene in a horror movie. He worked off and on from dawn until midnight, and Jackie always felt, when she was there, with Rodney's music in the background, as if she and Laura were trapped in a bad sitcom.

"*Both* out of town," she said. "How tragic."

"I knew you'd be disappointed. Here, come into the kitchen with me. I was just heating up some milk for hot chocolate."

They walked hand-in-hand, Laura pulling Jackie along.

"Wow," Jackie said as she sat down at the kitchen table. "It's so quiet. Wish I hadn't been busy all day." She recounted, then, the more innocuous parts of the day—cancelling the AOL account, going to see the house, which was, it turned out, in horrible shape. "So obviously," Jackie concluded, "it would have been a lot more fun to hang out here with you."

Laura smiled. "I wouldn't have been very exciting. After Marie left, I actually ended up doing some work."

"Work?" asked Jackie. "On Saturday?"

Laura frowned at the pot, turned down the stove, lifted off the thin membrane that had formed across the surface of the milk. "Get used to the idea, honey. In a few months you're going to be working a lot more Saturdays than me."

"Don't remind me. So what were you doing?"

"Some stuff for Manny. He's giving a report next month on

immigration statistics, and on health and education benefits for legal immigrants. He's trying to prove that people who were granted amnesty in '88 are doing better financially since they've been eligible for services. Anyway, he's kind of obsessed with this, which means I have no choice but to be obsessed with him."

Jackie nodded. Manny was Manny Jimenez, the City Councilman from the 4th District. Although he was a lawyer and wealthy entrepreneur, he still lived in one of the seedier parts of Hollywood, the same neighborhood where he had grown up. He'd been elected by an uneasy coalition of mostly poor Latinos from Hollywood and liberal Jews from the Westside, and now, in his second term, many people considered him a potential candidate for mayor. Jackie was suspicious of the man, as she was of all politicians, but she also respected what he'd done; either way, she was impressed by Laura's proximity to him.

"What do you have to do?" Jackie asked.

Laura poured the steaming milk into two green mugs and stirred. "Oh, you know. Research, statistics. Some services are going to be cut, too, and I have to figure out what's practical to fight for."

They went, mugs in hand, into the living room. There they settled onto the couch, with Laura's blanket thrown over them and Rodney's cat, Cedric, curled up somehow on both of their laps. They watched an old movie and then *Saturday Night Live*, getting up between programs to eat leftover pasta, and Laura was asleep by "Weekend Update." Jackie kept watching, though, glad to have something she could laugh at. The stress of the day was finally receding. Her grandfather was dead and accounted for, and she had one final errand to do, after which she could get on with her life. When the show was over, Jackie extracted Rodney's cat, who emitted a sleepy mew in protest, and then half-dragged both herself and Laura to bed. She was so tired that, for the first time in several weeks, she wasn't worried that an aftershock would jolt her out of her sleep; she was unconscious as soon as her head hit the pillow.

At nine a.m., Jackie opened her eyes and listened for the TV music from Rodney's room that normally ushered them into the morning. She felt Laura stir, and they looked at each other.

"Silence," Laura said. "Can you believe it?"

Jackie had noticed this too, but her first thought had been, thank God, no wake today, no funeral, no family obligations. "No," she said. "Maybe we're still asleep."

"We can't be. I have to take my morning pee."

"You're right. They're really gone. For, like, the first time ever."

"So what should we do?"

"Let's celebrate."

They jumped in the shower together, giggling as they soaped each other up, and then made their way back to Laura's bed, not worrying about the noise they made, the roommates. Afterwards, they lay naked on top of the covers, letting the sun and fresh breeze play over their bodies. They were both spent and relaxed now. No matter how heavily their problems weighed on them, Sunday mornings were still inviolate. In the mornings, they hadn't argued yet, they began with an empty slate, and if they spent a few satisfying hours together—in bed, over brunch—it could set the tone for the rest of the day.

Like today. They had brunch at the Farmer's Market and then drove out to Venice Beach, which, on this unusually warm day, was crammed with roller skaters, street performers, barely clad sunbathers, hemp activists, tourists, and dealers. They walked up and down the strip several times, and when the sky began to darken at five, they sat on the beach and watched the sunset. When the last bits of orange and pink cloud had faded back to gray, they headed to Laura's place, picked up her work clothes, then drove over to Jackie's apartment. That night, they ate a light dinner and read on opposite ends of the couch. Jackie settled down with her Tax Law reading, crossing her feet on Laura's lap.

But she couldn't concentrate. She was thinking about calling Loda Thomas in the morning. And she was thinking about all the days she'd spent with Frank when she was little, how she'd been closer to him, once, than to anyone else. And she was thinking about Lois again, how lost she'd seemed lately; how after the funeral she'd sat on the hood of the car and had not known what to do. Ted had wanted to go out to dinner. Lois wanted to go home. Jackie didn't care, but thought they should do *something*, something to celebrate the fact that they were still alive and to put a cap on the miserable day. When her grandmother died, what to do had been obvious—after the funeral, they all drove down to Gardena, where Mary's parents had run a *yakitori* restaurant. The place was under different management then, but most of the employees still remembered the Takayas, their children Mary, Ben, and Grace, and Mary's husband Frank. That night, Frank consumed more *sake* and beer than Jackie had ever seen him drink, and had fallen asleep, mumbling, on the car ride home. He'd taken such good care of Mary, stopping work altogether the last few months of her illness so he could always be at her side, and that night, after Mary's funeral, he had been totally overwhelmed; it was the only time Jackie ever saw him cry. And she'd felt guilty with that death, too; she'd gradually grown accustomed to Mary's withered half-self, so that death, when it came, seemed more like a subtle change than a catastrophe. She'd been young, and her sadness was short-lived and shallow. The night of that funeral, as the rest of her family cried, she'd wondered what was wrong with her.

But this was all too much to contemplate, so she looked across the couch at Laura. And suddenly she found herself distracted by Laura's hair, the shape of her fingers, the three creases that formed between her eyebrows when she read something that displeased her. Finally, with a sigh, she put her textbook down, then reached over and ran her hand along Laura's leg. Laura smiled without looking at her, but she put her hand on top of Jackie's and squeezed. Jackie moved over and touched her face. They kissed, long and slow, and made love again. And afterward, when Jackie drifted off toward sleep, Laura already breathing slowly in her arms, she felt better than she had since her grandfather died; she knew that, at least for this one day, she and Laura had almost been happy.

CHAPTER FOUR

MARY, 1947

INVISIBLE HANDS. That's what Mary Takaya felt like; that was her meaning to the family. She cut the chicken and vegetables into pieces small enough to skewer; she cleaned the tables; she made sure there was always fresh rice. Her parents were the ones that everyone saw, her father talkative and loud behind the grill where he cooked the *yakitori*, her mother friendly and solicitous with the customers. Even her little brother Ben was more visible than her—he'd swoop in and out of the tiny restaurant between school and baseball practice, endure their father's gruff teasing and the questions and affectionate head rubs of the tired clientele. And her older sister Grace was gone now, working as a bookkeeper in Chicago, though both her parents dropped everything for one of her infrequent calls, even shut the restaurant down for a couple of days on her annual trips home to Los Angeles.

But Mary was invisible hands. She did all the back-up work, the thankless work, the someone's-gotta-take-care-of-it work, and she was only noticed when she *didn't* do something, or when her hands were too slow, or inexact.

She couldn't remember if it was better or worse before the war, when Grace still lived at home. In 1940 Mary had been thirteen, shuttling between regular school, Japanese school, and the restaurant where the whole family worked. She was too young to go out with friends the way her older sister did, but old enough to be jealous of her freedom. On Friday and Saturday nights, Mary would sit on the bed in the room they shared and watch her sister get dressed in saddle shoes, a Sloppy Joe sweater, and a short skirt exposing her knees. Then some handsome young Nisei boy would pick her up in his family's car and they would go dancing in Li'l Tokyo, or sometimes, on International Night, the one night they were allowed, all the way up to the Palladium in Hollywood. Grace's life seemed exciting and glamorous to her; it was as if she made short but regular trips to a country that Mary had never seen. She envied even the arguments Grace had with their parents, who objected to her clothes and late hours. She suspected that even when her parents waited up by the window, even when their voices rose so loud in anger that she and Ben both plugged their ears, they felt closer to their older child for the trouble she gave; their grudge had sweetened to a kind of delight.

She would have taken screaming fights over silence. She wanted only to be more than invisible hands—to have made-up eyes and sharp mouth and flailing arms like her sister, churning legs and crew-cut hair like her brother. Her parents, happily married although they'd courted through pictures, remained staunchly Japanese in their ways. The Takayas had been shocked by Grace, plunged into the cold and unfamiliar waters of raising a somehow-American child, and with Ben, their bodies had adjusted to the temperature. But Mary, the best-behaved of the children, the most devoted to them, they couldn't quite manage to see.

And just when she was getting old enough to go to dances herself, just when Troy, from Japanese school, had given her a love letter, the war came and ruined all of her plans. She'd spent the years between fifteen and eighteen at Manzanar, the cramped space and barbed wire a particular kind of torture for a blossoming girl just getting ready to enter her life. It did free her from the restaurant, though, and the mailroom job she took at camp was far better than raw chicken and beef. Her brother didn't mind the confinement so much—he just went to the camp school, then played outside all afternoon—and her sister worked in the administration office, spending her free time with friends from Little Tokyo.

But Grace, camp, her parents, everything, would have been bearable except for her sixteenth birthday. Her birthday fell in July, on one of the days when the heat was so powerful the whole camp was laid flat, and even the lizards were resting and still.

Mary spent the day in the mailroom, cooled somewhat by the government fan, sorting mail for the next day's delivery. A little after five, when she was getting ready to leave, a shadow fell across the doorway. She thought it was one of the workers, who'd all left for the day, returning for some forgotten item. But when she called out, asking who was there, Vince Tajiri stepped into the room. She gasped a bit, in spite of herself. Vince was the best-looking boy in tenth grade, the class vice president as well as the captain of the camp baseball team. He was taller than her father, light and muscular, with bright black eyes and tiny dimples in each of his cheeks. All the girls, including Mary, grew giggly and tongue-tied in his presence, but to Mary's surprise, it was he who seemed nervous today.

"Uh, hi," he said uncertainly.

"Hi," she replied. "Are you looking for someone?"

"Yeah, you. It's your birthday, right? I came to say happy birthday."

She smiled, somewhat puzzled, but pleased. "Thanks."

He took a few steps over and stopped next to the desk, where she was still seated in the straight-backed chair. He held out a small, already wilting wildflower, which she knew he'd gone all the way out to the edge of camp to pick. Two patches of sweat appeared in the armpits of his navy blue shirt, and while she usually thought of boy-sweat as rank and repulsive, she found it almost charming today. "Thanks," she said again, taking the flower and setting it down on the desk. She looked up at him and her own nervousness was calmed by the terror she saw in his eyes. She felt the hair on her arms lift toward him, as if growing toward the sun. Then, just as the heat and closeness of his body were becoming unbearable, he leaned over and kissed her, quickly, on the lips. They both jumped away from each other. Then Mary stood up, shakily, and he moved back over. He kissed her again, and this time they stayed. Mary felt a pleasurable tingling sensation arc up and down her spine. She felt his firm, strong hands on her shoulders, on her back. She couldn't believe how lucky she was—she! Mary Takaya!—and she was so involved in their hands and mouths and just-touching chests that she didn't hear her sister come in.

There was a sharp, high gasp from the doorway. Mary turned, and Grace was standing just inside the door, hand clamped over her mouth. Mary was so startled she forgot to jump away from Vince. She looked at her sister (who'd come to take her back to the barracks, where their mother was going to surprise her with a cake), expecting her to say, I won't tell Mom and Dad, or maybe, I *will* tell Mom and Dad. Anything but what she did do, which was laugh, at first softly, but then the sound broke the surface of her mouth and turned into a full, delighted whoop. "*You?*" Grace managed, between hysterical bursts. "Oh my God, oh my God, it's so funny."

Vince pulled away from Mary, not meeting her eyes. Finally, without saying a word, he squeezed out the door past Grace. Mary wanted to call out to him, but couldn't risk more laughter. She hated her sister then. She hated her so much that she couldn't look at her through the surprise of receiving the lemon cake, which her mother had made from carefully stocked provisions, hidden until her daughter's birthday arrived. She hated her so much that when Grace left the camp to work as an assistant bookkeeper for a church in Chicago, Mary barely opened her mouth to say goodbye.

After the war, the Takayas reopened their restaurant, which they'd been lucky enough not to sell. Mary's father had bought it from money pooled by their *kenjinkai*, and when most other Issei were selling their houses and businesses in the panicked spring of '42, Takaya had flatly refused. Now, in 1947, he had as many black customers as Japanese, but he didn't mind the shift in clientele; money was green no matter what the color of the hand it came out of. Mary worked at the restaurant every day. Her parents promised they'd let her go to college soon, as Grace had done; they just needed to get ahead in terms of money. But as a year passed, then two, then three, college was starting to seem as remote to her as the country her parents had come from.

Then one afternoon Frank Sakai came in and suddenly made her visible. He'd brought his mother, who he accompanied to Li'l Tokyo every week. He sat down and watched Mary, lifting his eyebrows, once, when she looked at him. When she came over to their table, turned his cup over and poured him some tea, he caught her eye and asked softly what was wrong. This boldness was so unusual for a Nisei man that she jerked back and spilled the hot liquid on his arm—a move that would have brought on a scolding from her father if he hadn't known it was caused by love. No harm was done other than a red streak on Frank's nicely muscled forearm, just where the boiling tea had hit, and after many embarrassed apologies and bows by both Mary and her parents, the whole incident seemed to be forgotten. Except that Frank Sakai's steady gaze followed her around the restaurant, and she wondered how he'd known she was depressed. A few days later, her father and one of the customers had a conversation that Mary knew she was meant to overhear. Frank Sakai was a store manager, they made it known, well on his way to establishing himself enough to break away from the man he worked for and start his own business. At twenty-three he was still unmarried, and while his mother had tried to match him up with two beautiful and promising young Nisei girls, he had stubbornly insisted upon choosing his own bride. Mary appreciated her father's efforts, but they really weren't necessary—she had already noticed the young veteran with the slight hitch in his step. Her parents started letting her take breaks when the Sakais were there, nevermind that her mother had to pick up the slack of things left undone by the invisible hands. She and Frank spoke of their families, their hopes and aspirations. She wanted to be a teacher, and when she told him this, his eyes darkened with a sadness that she didn't understand. It didn't matter, though. She was in love. When Frank came in with his mother, he always watched after her, getting her another napkin when her first one was dirty, refilling her cup of green tea. His mother and Mary's parents would bow to each other, smile, and then complain good-heartedly about their American children. In this way, they skipped the go-betweens, the meetings, the formal introductions. All the parents were there when Frank asked Mr. Takaya for his daughter's hand. And as the three parents drank *sake* in celebration, he and Mary sat quietly, just smiling at each other, fingers intertwined beneath the table.

She moved to Angeles Mesa, into the house on Edgehill where

Frank lived with his mother. Frank's mother cleaned houses now, and Frank worked every day at the store. Mrs. Sakai, after years of propositions, suggestions, pleading, and hints, was not joyous so much as relieved that her only son had finally married. She kept her dead husband appraised of the events, filling him in every evening as she paid her respects in front of the *butsudan*, and he seemed pleased with the match as well. The children came quickly— Rose about a year after the marriage, in 1948; Lois just a year and a half later. There was a brother too, three years younger than Lois, but he'd been stillborn, expelled from the womb with the umbilical cord twisted around his neck. For the first few years, Mary Sakai had stayed home with her children; when Lois was five, she went back to school and finally became a teacher. And there on Edgehill Street they had stayed, for seventeen years, until that other conflagration, the war turned inward, of 1965.

CHAPTER FIVE

1994

SITTING IN the lobby of the Marcus Garvey Community Center, Jackie couldn't recall a time she felt more out of place. More like an overseas visitor, scared and clutching her passport. She'd expected something small—a rec room and a couple of offices—not this huge, sprawling facility, room upon room upon room, a layered concrete honeycomb of a building. And people everywhere—mostly women, a sprinkling of men, and a hive of small children, countless bees buzzing and swirling. She sat in her orange plastic chair near the receptionist's window and tried to take everything in. The cowboy-hat-wearing security guard. The teenage boys examining books in the little shop area, busy as an airport newsstand. The auditorium, which had just hosted some kind of meeting and was now disgorging laughing, jostling women. Hers the only face that wasn't black. No, here were a couple of Latino women, speaking Spanish. Hers the only face that wasn't black or Latino. Out of place here. A stranger. A foreigner.

Loda Thomas had told her to come—Jackie had called that morning between classes and run the name Curtis Martindale by her. She hadn't heard of him. But then, an hour later, she called Jackie back and told her that there was someone in her office who might be able to help. A man, younger than Loda, who'd grown up in the neighborhood. She should come down that afternoon, Loda said. He wanted to see her in person.

Jackie had been too embarrassed to tell Loda that she didn't know how to get to the Crenshaw district, and so she'd gotten directions from Rebecca—for a price. That morning, in their Tax

Law class, Jackie had been asked to discuss the long-term effects of Proposition 13, and Rebecca kept puncturing holes in the argument. Jackie knew, from the angle of Rebecca's head and the mischievous teasing lilt of her voice, that her friend was getting her back for not returning her call about the notes.

"So if I give you my notes," Jackie said as they headed to the nearest sandwich stand for lunch, "will you stop attacking me in class?"

Rebecca grinned. "Sorry about that. But you're so much fun to mess with. You look so tormented and mortified."

Rebecca Nakanishi was Jackie's teaser, tormentor, and occasional friend. She was like a smoke-bomb—at parties, at school, she exploded into rooms, as if she knew that someone was about to attack and she looked forward to the challenge. People rarely took her up on it. Rebecca had inherited her glorious black hair and olive skin from her Japanese father, and her green eyes and slender frame from her Irish-American mother. The physical elements worked well together, and she attracted—and appeared to be attracted to—reckless, strong-willed people of both genders. Jackie liked her, but was slightly afraid of her and could only take her in small doses. She couldn't imagine what Rebecca thought of her.

Rebecca jabbered on as they waited for their burgers, about job interviews and their professor's bad haircut; finally Jackie loosened up and had to smile. And when Jackie eventually asked her for directions to Crenshaw, knowing that she'd gone to a reading in Leimert Park the week before, Rebecca was glad to give them—she flattened out a napkin and drew her a map.

The map was perfect. After going home and doing some reading, Jackie traded her backpack for a purse, went down to her car, and set the map and her Thomas Guide on the passenger seat. It was a little after three. Judging from Rebecca's directions, it looked like a twenty-minute drive to Marcus Garvey, but traffic was horrible, the boulevards even more clogged than usual because two parts of the 10 Freeway had collapsed in the earthquake. On Crenshaw Boulevard, just before the 10, there were several blocks of huge, old Craftsman bungalows, which had clearly been stately and gorgeous in some distant time. There was a slow-rolling hill, and from the top, a clear view of Baldwin Hills and Inglewood. The view was surprisingly pleasant, Jackie thought, but misleading—like a glimpse of the ocean that obscured the sandbars and sharks underneath.

As Jackie emerged on the other side of the underpass, she took another breath. She was south of the freeway now, and was decidedly anxious. She locked her doors, and then felt ashamed of herself. But already the streets looked different than they did to the north of the freeway. The large old bungalows were replaced by liquor stores, discount clothing shops, fast-food places. On the left, she saw the Korean Catholic Church, Doug's Wine and Spirits, and a burned-out gas station. On the right, Mama's Soul Food, Victory Guns, two storefront churches, and a store sign that said—she looked twice to make sure—"98 cent Housewives etc." Each place had a black accordion gate attached to the front. It seemed like every other building was vacant or charred from '92, or cordoned off because of damage from the quake.

At Martin Luther King, Jr. Boulevard she took a left, in front of the Baldwin Hills-Crenshaw Plaza. Now she was near her grandfather's old store and old house, although she didn't know exactly where they were. Jackie kept abreast of local news enough to know that this area was undergoing an economic resurgence— but if this was what it looked like when times were good, she couldn't imagine what it was like when things were bleak.

She counted off four blocks and saw the sign for Marcus Garvey. Then the building—the tall windows and glass doors, the wide flat honeycomb she couldn't see the back of. There was a small green lawn in the front with manicured bushes and trees. The whole complex glittered against the tans and grays of the surrounding neighborhood, like a mirage in a desert—an idea that clearly had not been lost on the people who worked there. The sign read: "Marcus Garvey Community Center—an Oasis of Hope."

Now, in the waiting room, she pretended to read a magazine, half-listening to one of the women behind the front desk talk to a young man leaning into her window. Then someone was standing over her, and she looked up and saw Loda Thomas. She had the same grave face, the same stiff-looking waves she remembered from the funeral; when Jackie met her eyes, though, she smiled.

"Thanks so much for inviting me," Jackie said.

"Not at all. It's nice to see you again. And it's always good to have people visit Marcus Garvey."

Loda took her on a short tour, pointing out the library, the classrooms, the dozens of offices, the exercise room, the kitchen, the computer facilities.

"I don't think I've ever seen anything quite like this," said Jackie, truthfully. Laura would love this place, she thought. It was part rec center, part school, part office. The building itself was not as nice as it had looked from outside. Some of the walls were painted a thick industrial lemon yellow, others were naked gray cinderblock. The floors were covered with a faded carpet, puke-orange and worn through in many places. The furniture all looked like garage-sale pieces or hand-me-downs from Staples.

But the building was jumping. Swarming with life. And Jackie, despite her discomfort, couldn't help feeling invigorated.

"Yes, it's quite a madhouse," Loda said as they turned another corner. There were several small children clumped together in the hallway, and they scattered as the women approached. "We run several different programs here—literacy classes, which are my responsibility, a GED course, computer training, after-school, day care. The after-school program is James's baby. He's who I'm taking you to meet. He started that several years ago, along with the young fathers program."

"I'm sorry, who is he again?"

"James Lanier. He grew up a few blocks from here, and he was just a little boy when your grandfather had the store. He seemed very interested in talking to you. Which is something. He usually doesn't make a lot of time for people who aren't connected to his programs."

Jackie didn't have time to wonder what this meant, because Loda had stopped in front of a closed door. She rapped lightly. From inside a muffled voice bid them to enter.

Loda pushed the door open and stepped in. Jackie followed. The man behind the desk was looking down, writing something.

"James," Loda said, "this is Jackie Ishida. Frank Sakai's granddaughter."

"Hi," Jackie said. She was oddly nervous.

The man looked up at them and rose from behind his small desk. He seemed huge in the tiny office, and Jackie had the impression that if he spread his arms, he could touch the walls on either side of him. Lanier was about 6'3", and he looked like the former athlete he was—big biceps, thick chest, and slim, solid hips, with a slightly rounded belly. His clothes were neat but not overly dressy—khakis, a white shirt, a thin black tie. He gave Jackie a quick, undisguised once-over, then held his large hand out over the desk. "James Lanier."

His voice was surprisingly quiet for such a powerful-looking man. Jackie shook his hand firmly, and the solid anchor of his arm made her feel both grounded and unmoored. She felt this man could see right into her, the neat structured piles of her, the lines of her she'd never cross or blur. "Hi. It's nice to meet you. Thanks for seeing me today."

Her voice sounded false to her, and to Lanier as well. He waited a moment before he spoke again. "No problem. Thanks for driving down here."

Loda excused herself, and as she left, Jackie resisted the urge to say no, don't leave, but if you leave, don't close the door. But Loda left, and the door clicked shut. Lanier sat down and indicated that Jackie should do the same.

Jackie sat in a plain brown desk chair. She looked around the office, at the books and folders on the table, the scattered papers on the desk, the pictures and plaques and children's drawings on all the walls. She noticed the baby pictures on the bulletin board above Lanier's shoulder and wondered if any of the children were his. "Nice office," she said, too brightly, and Lanier raised an eyebrow.

"It'll do."

It came out harsher than he intended. But he wasn't sure what he thought of this granddaughter. She was so clearly out of her element here. Different from Sakai, whom he hadn't known well. But who was as much a part of the neighborhood as the eighty-year-old trees in front of his apartment. Rooted deep. Expected there. Permanent. And this fresh cutting, potted in richer soil, producing not nearly as special a plant. A stranger, outsider, even though her beginnings were here.

Lanier, like Sakai, was an insider. It was his business to know the neighborhood, to be aware of which people were harmless; which kids were on a dangerous course he needed to try and disrupt; which kids were already lost. He lived and breathed Crenshaw, always had. Sometimes, as he drove to work in the morning, hearing palm trees rustle and seeing children walk to school and watching the sun start to come into its power, he experienced a joy so perfect and complete that he didn't need anything else. It would pass—kids would get arrested, drop out of school, or die—but this one moment of perfect happiness, of one-ness with the neighborhood, was the thing that made it all worthwhile.

But now, he felt bad for being abrupt with Frank's grand-daughter. He saw Frank's angular face on her, his thin sharp blade of a nose. So he looked at her directly and said, "I'm sorry about your grandfather."

Staring down at her hands, she said, "Thank you." Then, looking up, she saw that he meant it. He really had a good face. His forehead was wide and expressive, and running across it were three long wrinkles, just starting to lay claim in the flesh. His nose was stately, and Jackie noticed that when she said something, it registered not in his eyes but in his flaring, widening nostrils. His lips were full and moist, and his jaw was square and anvil-like; any fist that struck it might disintegrate on impact. The thing that both disturbed his face and underlined its perfection was the deep, inch-long scar just inside his left ear. James Lanier was on the verge of being a beautiful man, and his scar both pushed him toward that distinction and held him safely away from it.

"We all are," Jackie continued. "It's been a crazy last few weeks, with him dying and the earthquake."

Lanier nodded. "Did you have a lot of damage?"

"No, not really. There were some cracks in my walls and I lost a few plates. How about you?"

"About the same. A few plates, a couple of lamps. And we

didn't have much damage here either, so it was real busy for a while—the schools were closed so all the kids were coming here."

"You know, on top of everything else, my poor grandfather had to live through another big quake. He hated them. My aunt told me that after the quake of '71, he slept out in the back yard for a week."

Lanier smiled wryly. "There are people still doing that *this* time," he said. A noisy group of people passed by in the hallway, and he waited until they were gone before he spoke again. "Were you close to your grandfather?"

"No, not really. I used to be when I was younger, but then he moved further away, and I got older, and we kind of, just, you know. Lost touch."

"I didn't know him well, either," Lanier said, which made Jackie feel a bit less judged. "That's why I didn't go to the funeral. Didn't even hear about it, actually, until Loda told me this morning. I was only about eight when his store shut down. But I do remember that he was always real nice—he gave the older boys baseball cards every time they got an A on a test. The kids I hung out with knew him better."

Jackie nodded. "I wish I could have seen him then," she said, and she didn't know this was true until she'd said it.

You could have seen him *now*, Lanier thought, but he kept this to himself. It wasn't his business to chastise her. And he was making her nervous, although this wouldn't have been unusual, even if she wasn't a stranger, and small, and Japanese. Lanier was the kind of man that other men loved—strong, understated, dependable. He gave his life to them, and to boys who had started the journey. And they accepted and admired him, his sternness and discipline. But women didn't know what to do with him. He was like a mountain that provided no avenue for scaling, no trails up through the dense and thorny brush. So it was no surprise to Lanier that this woman didn't know how to approach. Not that men understood him any better. Although they admired his purity, his complete independence, they couldn't see that this strength came at the price of company and comfort. They didn't know that half Lanier's sternness was loneliness, calcified. The empty solitude on top of the mountain.

"Anyway," Jackie said finally, "that's not why I came here today."

Lanier looked at her and nodded, waiting for her to continue.

"I'm looking for someone who would have been a kid in the fifties or sixties, a boy who probably used to go to my grandfather's store."

"Yes," Lanier replied, "Curtis Martindale." He hadn't said the name out loud in years, although he'd thought it, dreamed it, watched it weave and twist and circle around him.

Jackie leaned forward. "Do you know him?"

"Used to. His daddy was my mama's brother. Me and Curtis and his little brother Cory, we used to hang out all the time. Cory was my age and Curtis was older."

"Oh, great." This was easier than she'd expected. "Well, I think my grandfather knew him. He mentioned him in some papers my aunt found after he died."

"That makes sense. He practically lived at your grandfather's store, and he worked there for a couple of years. A lot of the older boys hung out there." He remembered a group of them sitting on milk crates out front. He in overalls, Curtis in his work pants and apron. James—Jimmy—wriggled in between Curtis and another boy, sweater warm and scratchy against his cheek. Anything to be next to his cousin. They were listening to the radio that Mr. Sakai had set up by the door. The Dodgers versus the Yankees, in the '63 World Series. Mr. Sakai handing out ice-cold sodas, beaming, as the Dodgers swept the Yankees in four.

"So why you looking for him?" asked Lanier.

"Actually," Jackie began, then stopped abruptly. She couldn't think of a convenient lie, and she didn't want to mention the money. But a partial truth was probably safe. "My grandfather left him something in his will."

Lanier raised his eyebrows. "Must have been a pretty old will."

"Yeah, it was. So do you know where Curtis is?"

Lanier looked at her, nostrils flaring. "He's dead."

"What?"

"He died in the uprising. The *Watts* uprising—'65."

Jackie wiped her hands on her pants and said, "Shit." She was a bit annoyed at Lanier for making her drive all the way down there; he could have just told her over the phone and spared her the trip. But she was relieved, too—if Curtis Martindale was dead, then her duty had been fulfilled, her task completed. Lois could keep the money and buy a house. When she glanced up, though, she found Lanier looking at her curiously. She'd almost forgotten he was there—she was thinking about getting home and calling Laura—but now he seemed more troubled and interested than he'd been since she had come.

"You don't know about this, do you?" he asked.

She gave him a look. "About the Watts riots? Of course I do. Marcus Frye. Four days of rioting. McCone Commission report."

"No," he said, ignoring her tone. "You don't know about your grandfather's store."

Something in his voice made her pay attention. "Well, I know that it didn't get burned."

"No, it didn't get burned, or looted either. But the day after the uprising ended, four black boys were found dead in the store's freezer. And my cousin Curtis Martindale was one of them."

"*What?*"

"There was a walk-in freezer in the back, where your grandfather kept meat and ice. Someone locked them all in there during the uprising. They would have frozen to death in a couple of hours."

Jackie opened her mouth and closed it again. She couldn't place this information in the same universe with what she'd known about her grandfather. "How?" she finally managed. "Why? I mean, I've never heard . . ."

Lanier nodded. "It was never reported in the mainstream press, since so many other things were going on. Not that anyone would have given a shit about a bunch of dead niggers. But I'm surprised that your family . . ."

Jackie shook her head. She didn't have the energy to explain about how her family didn't talk. None of them, including her grandfather. No words laced together into a chain of intertwined stories that connected her to anyone's past. More than gaps in the narrative; there *was* no narrative. Whole years, like the years of World War II, dropped cleanly from their collective history.

"People thought it was a cop," Lanier continued. "A white cop, Nick Lawson. He had a history of beating up black kids. Anyway, a while later, some other boys in the neighborhood took it upon themselves to shoot him. They didn't kill him, but it got him off the street. I heard he stayed with the police, on a desk job, but no charges were brought against him. No one ever did shit."

Lanier remembered those first few weeks, after. The weariness and sorrow among the people he knew as they tried to piece together their broken neighborhood. The tanks rolling down Crenshaw, through the tense, watchful silence. And Curtis wasn't there to help him through it. Jimmy hadn't understood why his cousin was gone. Knew he was dead, but still expected to see him taking the front stairs of the Lanier house, two at a time, and hear him yelling through the broken screen. When it finally dawned on Jimmy that he wouldn't see Curtis again, or feel his wiry arm around his shoulders and sharp knuckles rubbing his skull, he dove into a thick depression he wasn't sure that he'd ever come out of. It hurt worse than when his father left, because Curtis was dead, not just AWOL, and Jimmy was old enough now to feel it. With an eight-year-old's impotent rage he wanted to kill the man responsible, but instead he took it out on everyone else. Most of all himself. Banging his head rhythmically, obsessively, against his bedroom wall, punishing himself for being alive and for not help-ing Curtis, until his mother couldn't leave him alone. Cutting his arm with razor blades, steak knives, scissors, pens, so he would feel the pain there and not inside him.

"But you're sure it was him," Jackie said.

"I'm sure." Lanier looked down, then looked up again. Uneasiness flickered through his eyes. "There were some people—not a lot, but a few—who believed that your grandfather did it."

Jackie started to stand, and then sat down again. "Jesus Christ."

Lanier put up his broad, squarish hands. "I know he didn't," he said. "Most people didn't even know the kids were murdered in the store. And even the ones who did, just about all of them blamed Nick Lawson. But there were some, you know, who never liked that your grandfather had a business here. Crenshaw was mixed back then, much more than it is today, but there were a few people—white *and* black—who still hated the Japanese. So even though just about everyone knew he wasn't involved, your family still took some flak."

"Which explains," Jackie said, more to herself than Lanier, "why they shut down the store and got out of here so fast."

Lanier nodded. He remembered the "Closed" sign hanging in the window of the empty store for months, the Sakais vanishing like apparitions before the smoke had even cleared.

She looked up at him. "Why are you telling me all this?"

"So you won't waste your time looking for Curtis. And so you'll know." And because I need to share this with someone, he thought, hand over half the burden. He leaned across the desk and looked at her intently. "I want to build a case against Lawson. I want the motherfucker to pay. I've been carrying Curtis's murder, all those murders, around with me for years." He knew his burden, his sense of urgency, were heavy in his voice; he felt accused by the image of Frank there in front of him, for not doing anything until now. Jackie leaned back, away from him, so Lanier eased off a little.

"Well, what about his brother?" she asked. "Or his parents? Where are they?"

"Dead. All of them. His parents both died a few years ago, and Cory was killed in Vietnam. It haunted him, too. I've always meant to do something, but I've just kept putting it off, you know. Didn't know how to start. But when I ran into Loda this morning and she said that Frank Sakai had died and that his granddaughter was looking for Curtis, I knew it was finally time."

"You said people didn't know about it, right? So how are you going to build a case?"

"Oh, they knew the boys were murdered—they just didn't know *how*. There were all kinds of rumors—that they'd been shot, or lynched, or burned up in a fire."

Jackie rocked back and forth, thinking. "But what do I have to do with all this?"

Lanier looked at her and shrugged. "I don't know. As much as you want."

But then doubt settled over him, heavy and uncomfortable as a wet quilt. What the hell was he doing? For one thing, how was he supposed to get information on a cop? He thought of Allen Cooke, the cop from the Southwest Station who volunteered for his fathers group. Southwest was the natural place to ask questions, since that was where Lawson had worked, but it was a tricky thing, he knew, to look for dirt on another cop. The department, when you poked it, tended to close in on itself, and he didn't know if Allen would be willing.

For another, he wasn't sure he'd made the right move by enlisting Frank's granddaughter. Her knowledge of the law—Loda had said she was in law school—might help with legal matters, if they ever got to that point. And someone in her family had to know *something*—maybe they'd even seen Lawson lurking around the store on the day of the murders. But Jackie Ishida was not the same kind of person as her grandfather. Frank was a down-to-earth, blue-collar man. Jackie, on the other hand, had clearly been coddled. She had the air of someone who never questioned her right to anything. Her hands were soft and unlined, her fingernails even and clean; those hands had never seen a day of real labor. Her clothes, though casual—jeans, blouse, light leather jacket—were elegant, cut well, expensive. She was attractive enough—nice face, straight shoulder-length hair, thin athletic figure—but there was something too prim about her, fastidious, as if she didn't swear or sweat. She was a package wrapped tightly with a bright and colorful bow; all the edges of the paper lined up perfectly. Frank Sakai's family, clearly, had moved up in the world—but maybe they'd moved so far that they no longer had use for Frank. Lanier wondered if he should leave Jackie alone and pursue Lawson by himself. But she had been the one to call Loda Thomas; she'd started this entire thing. He believed in omens, and this one was undeniable.

Jackie, sitting across from him, believed in omens too. She

knew that her family was touched by what had happened. Their flight after the murders might have implied something at the time—even if, as she realized, most of her grandfather's old acquaintances had liked him, there would always be that shadow of a question. And Frank would have wanted her to pursue this; he had practically willed it. She looked at Lanier, his probing eyes, his intense and handsome face.

"So what do we do now?" she asked.

CHAPTER SIX

JIMMY, 1962

H E WAS wearing a suit for the first time, skipping south along Westside Avenue, heading toward the church on Santa Barbara. The suit was one of Cory's, fully half of his supply, but his cousin had been happy to wear the other one and lend the scratchy new brown one to Jimmy. Curtis was in a suit too, and suspenders and a hat. Curtis and Cory's mother, Alma, wore a dark flower-print dress that swished and furled around her fast-moving legs. She was a little ahead of them, not looking back, forcing her three ducklings to swim after her quickly, and Jimmy wondered if God always expected his children to come calling in such a hurry.

It was almost nine when they arrived at the church, a plain square building a little short of the corner. Jimmy had never been to this church; hadn't been to church much at all since he was a baby, although his mother came sometimes to get word about jobs. She was working this Sunday—the family she worked for was having a party—but his aunt had insisted that he go with her and her boys. It would be good for him to be there, and his presence was needed. "'Specially today," she'd said. "'Specially today."

People were milling around in the street and on the front steps, touching their hats, picking pieces of lint off their children's shoulders. Jimmy knew from Curtis that several Black Muslims had been shot by the police that week, gunned down just outside of their mosque. He didn't really know what a Black Muslim was, except that Curtis's girlfriend's brother was thinking of becoming one. Now pieces of conversation rustled past him, loose scraps

blown by the wind. "You watch. Ain't none of 'em gonna be punished, neither." "Police be worse than overseers back in
Arkansas." "Those Negroes cause they *own* problems, followin
around after that brother X." "Need to stop hollerin Allah and
come on back to Jesus." "Hush, sister. To the cops, niggers niggers, don't matter what name you tack on to the front of your
prayers."

Jimmy didn't know what any of this meant. But he wondered
if it was related to all the black people he kept seeing on TV, from
Nashville, Montgomery, Birmingham, Jackson. When he was over
at the Martindales', Alma would shake her head at the images on
the screen, and she'd been shaking her head at the *Eagle* and the
Sentinel all week. Now, as they walked through the crowd of people, Jimmy watched her swivel and step, the angle of her head, her
long, elegant neck, the fine hard line of her jaw. She looked strong
and queen-like, and he was proud to be part of her group. The men
tipped their hats and she acknowledged them with nods; the
women, eyeing her suspiciously, laid firm fingers on their husbands' arms. Curtis moved through the crowd more slowly, a man
at fourteen, touching the rim of his hat at the women, shaking
hands with all the men. Jimmy watched his ease, admiringly, and
smiled politely as large women leaned over him and cooed. The
three boys followed Alma at a distance, Curtis with a hand on
Jimmy's shoulder, steering him. They entered the church and sat in
a pew about halfway to the front, Alma, Cory, Curtis, James.
Curtis showed Jimmy where the hymnal was and pointed out some
of his friends from school. Reverend Greene came in then, with his
bible, and the noise tapered down to a hush. He was a tall, skinny
man, all angles, the only rounded parts of him the top of his skull
and the eyes that protruded out of his sunken face.

"My brothers and sisters," he began, "a terrible tragedy
occurred this week on South Broadway." And after that, Jimmy
was lost, words swirling around him that he didn't understand,
Moses and David, Redemption and the Promised Land. He heard
people responding, "You tell it, brother," and "Amen!" and
because Curtis was one of those who called "Amen," Jimmy did
so, too. When it was time to sing, Curtis held the book down for

him, which didn't help because Jimmy couldn't read. But he tried to imitate his cousin as he nodded and rocked. The singing scared and delighted him, the way the voices all flowed together and formed something greater than the sum of themselves, a presence as huge and beautiful to Jimmy as the thought of God. He felt the owners of these voices, the grown-ups in the church, could fight off anything, take over the world.

Jimmy tried to follow the pastor's words for the first twenty minutes. Then his attention slowly failed him and he watched the congregation. He saw a sea of ladies' hats, yellow and green and white, decorated with flowers, and sprays of baby's breath and lace. He saw open faces turned up to the pastor, feeding on what sustenance he offered, and the few people who looked down, refusing to hear, and the others who had drifted off to sleep. He saw the tops of little heads, barely visible over the backs of the pews. He peeked to the left and spied Cory bouncing his knees and twisting his head, dancing to some unheard music. Jimmy started bouncing too, which did not escape Curtis. "It'll be done soon," he said, leaning over.

Outside, Alma stopped to talk to some people she knew—the parents of one of her students, and Miss Vera and Miss Alice, fellow teachers who lived together and didn't have husbands. The boys hung back and Curtis pointed people out to his brother and cousin. "That lady move and belch like a tractor," he said about a particularly large woman, who was grunting with the effort of walking. "That man skinny as a turkey bone four o'clock Christmas Day," he said about a man who made Reverend Greene look fleshy. "That girl got her nose held up so high the birds be flyin into it." The younger boys giggled, although they tried to stop each time one of the grown-ups looked over. Finally, another man approached Alma, a tall, dark-skinned man in a brown suit and black hat. "'Lo, Alma," he said, and there was something about the way she took the veil off her smile that made Jimmy know the man was not trying to take something from her, or approaching out of mere obligation.

"Hello, Victor. Good to see you. How you doing?"

"Fine, fine. And you? Where's your husband this morning?"

"Hmph. Bed, like usual. Didn't get home till 'round three this morning. Got his sister's baby here, though."

The man was alone, which Jimmy thought strange, and in another moment Mrs. Martindale introduced him as Mr. Conway. "Good to meet you, young man," he said, bending over and taking Jimmy's small fingers in his larger ones. He already knew the Martindale boys, and they smiled, looking happy to see him. At the door of the church, the women started to gather; they'd go back inside, cook, trade gossip and recipes, make quilts for the old and the needy. Jimmy wondered why Curtis's mother didn't join them, not understanding that Alma didn't like these group projects and activities; not knowing the other women considered her haughty. And *his* mother was never a part of groups like this, either; the Laniers were one of the families they made quilts *for*.

Alma and Mr. Conway started walking down the street and the three boys fell in step behind them. The sight of her walking beside a man who wasn't her husband seemed odd to Jimmy. They were two puzzle pieces jammed together forcefully, their edges nowhere near matching up. But he sensed somehow that the man didn't *want* them to match; there was nothing sly in his eyes or over-anxious in his step, in the way he smiled and spoke to her. Jimmy couldn't make out their conversation, but he heard the shining, silvery peals of her laughter, the pulse and reverberation. And this unexpected laughter, Curtis's jokes, the warm spring weather, made Jimmy feel—despite the heaviness of the sermon and the pinching of his suit—lighter and freer than he had in months.

A couple of blocks up from Santa Barbara, they saw a man sitting on his porch in a small, plain rocking chair. He was a Japanese man, neither young nor old, and he rocked in his chair and stared out at the street, holding his left arm out straight and making long sweeping motions with his right. Jimmy had seen this man before, wandering around the neighborhood. Sometimes the man seemed perfectly normal. But other times he mumbled under his breath, holding a conversation whose other member was invisible.

"Morning, Kenji," Mr. Conway called out. "How you doing this fine morning?"

"I'm very busy," the man replied. "Trying to keep the traffic under control."

Mr. Conway and Alma both looked at the empty street, then back at the man on the porch. "Don't look like there's too much traffic," Mr. Conway said.

"On *Crenshaw*," the man insisted, pointing. "It's real busy over on Crenshaw."

Jimmy looked at where the man was pointing and saw only a row of houses. Alma smiled.

"Ain't been able to see straight through to Crenshaw for 'bout ten years now, Mr. Hirano."

"That's nonsense," the man said, vehemently. "You're talking nonsense. And this is *God's* day. You all need to get your eyes checked."

The boys were right on the heels of the adults now, and Jimmy heard Alma say under her breath, "It must be one of his bad days."

Mr. Conway smiled. "All right, Kenji," he called out. "You have a good afternoon now."

But the man had already forgotten them, focusing again on the street.

When they were out of earshot, Jimmy shook his head. "That man nuttier than a peanut field harvest morning," he offered, remembering something his mother had once said about a relative. He expected Curtis and Cory to laugh, but instead, Curtis turned and leaned over him, blocking out the sky, face blazing like a too-hot sun.

"Don't you talk 'bout him that way." His voice was low, his cheek muscles working, and Jimmy was so shocked by the anger in his cousin's face that he just stood there, afraid to move. In the ten months since he'd started spending time with his cousins, Curtis had never so much as raised his voice at him. Curtis stood, rocked back, rocked toward him again. "Don't you *ever* let me catch you talkin 'bout Mr. Hirano that way."

Jimmy didn't know what he'd done wrong, or why it had been OK to laugh at the silly people at church but not at this crazy man who couldn't see the houses in front of him.

Alma and Mr. Conway, hearing this exchange, stopped and turned around. "He's a nice man, Jimmy," Alma said.

"That's right," Curtis agreed. "He's just got his own ways, is all."

Jimmy felt so low now that his eyes began to fill, although he couldn't tell whether he was upset because of guilt or Curtis's anger. At least his cousin's anger, though, unlike his long-gone father's, had a reason, a set of rules for things to avoid, and didn't just explode without warning. The boys walked along in silence for several blocks, the grown-ups talking in front of them. Jimmy sniffled and sank deeper into his suit, his chin pressed down into the collar. He wished he could disappear. But just when he thought he was going to cry for real, Curtis took his hand. His heart lifted. He knew, because Curtis still stared ahead and didn't look at him, that he wasn't ready to talk to him yet. But he also knew that he would be forgiven.

CHAPTER SEVEN

1994

THERE WERE so many questions, which she took out in private, unfolded and examined like secret love letters. For one thing, why had no one in her family ever told her about the freezer? That no one talked about history, the internment, seemed a community decision; the entire Nisei generation might have taken a vow of silence. But *this* thing, the death of the boys, was much more personal, unique—and so her family's silence on the matter was more troubling. She had known right away that she'd have to talk to Lois, who was always the best source of family information. Lois, like Rose, didn't tend to offer things on her own, but at least she'd give them up when she was asked.

Jackie called her aunt on Tuesday night, as soon as she got home. They talked about the houses that Lois had looked at, and then discussed the will—the official one—which had been read that afternoon. Frank had left his computer and his savings— about a thousand dollars—to Lois, and to Rose he'd left some old books. Jackie, to her mild and bewildered disappointment, had been willed his box of documents and a bowling ball. As they both expected, there'd been no mention of the store.

After telling Lois that she was in no hurry to pick up her inheritance, Jackie took a deep breath. "Listen. I did some poking around about the kid in the will, Curtis Martindale."

"Oh, really?"

"He worked in the store for a while."

"Oh, right. Of course. That's why the name sounded familiar."

"Yeah. Well, he's not going to be wanting that money any time soon. He's dead."

"Oh," Lois said, deflated.

Why did she sound disappointed? Did she really have no clue? "He died in the Watts riots."

Silence. Something rustled on the other end of the line.

". . . in Grandpa's store," Jackie concluded.

Lois still didn't speak. Jackie could hear her aunt breathing. Finally Lois said, "What are you talking about?"

Jackie stood and started walking, the phone cord twisting around her hips. "You knew about this, didn't you?"

"Knew about what?"

Jackie's mouth fell open. She repeated what Lanier had told her—about the store, about the freezer, about the suspicions concerning the policeman, Nick Lawson.

When she was finished, Lois was silent for a moment. Then she said, very slowly, "I had no idea. Mom made Rose and me leave the first day it was safe. The three of us stayed with Mom's parents down in Gardena until Dad sold the house and the store."

"Well, now you know why."

"Jesus." Lois remembered the frenzy of the days before the looting reached Crenshaw—how she and Rose weren't allowed to wander the neighborhood, or even see their friends. The quick, messy packing of suitcases, the drive down to Gardena, where her mother's parents lived. Lois crying about being plucked out of her house, her school, her life. Her father wild as she'd ever seen him, wide-eyed, in a frenzy. His whipped hair and bloodshot eyes when he came home from the store. How he slept in the garage and avoided the rest of the family, while her mother circled the rooms of the house, tight-lipped and victorious. *I told you so,* she kept saying to him. *I told you this neighborhood was no good for our girls.* "That cop sounds familiar, though," Lois continued. "There was this awful cop in the area who used to harass Dad a lot. He'd come in and knock stuff off the shelves and take cigarettes and soda. He followed Rosie and me home a couple of times, really scared us bad. Anyway, as you can imagine, he was no big fan of black kids, either. I wonder what ever happened to him."

"If it's the same guy, he was shot in retaliation. He didn't die, though, and he was never brought to trial or anything. Anyway, this Lanier wants to bring a case against him. We're meeting again on Friday."

"And you're helping, like the good lawyer you are."

Jackie noticed that she didn't say "granddaughter." "Well, it would be nice if they got him."

"Yeah, I guess you're right," Lois replied. She remembered the ice-chill of fear as the cop walked behind her, humming low, lightly hitting his baton against his thigh.

Jackie put her fist on her hip and looked up at the ceiling, annoyed. "Well, you don't exactly sound enthusiastic, Lois. Do you think I should forget the whole thing?"

"No, I'm just saying you should be careful."

"Is there something you're not telling me?"

"*No*. But it was an ugly time, Jackie. And if everyone knows that a certain person did this thing, but he was still never punished, then think about what you must be up against."

"Right. But it's almost thirty years later now. You'd think that someone would be brave enough to talk. I wonder if there's anyone who actually saw Lawson in the store."

"Well, unfortunately, it wouldn't have been any of *us*. As soon as the looting started in Crenshaw, Dad locked up the store and came home. We all stayed there until it was over." She remembered the four of them in front of the television, staying awake for days. Frank shaking his head and mumbling. Lois crying sometimes. Mary saying *as soon as this is over, we're leaving, Frank. Whether or not you come with us, the girls and I have to go.*

"So Grandpa never left the house."

"Not once the looters came, no."

Jackie was relieved to hear this. She hadn't thought he was involved in the murders, but it was good to know for sure. "But how did Lawson get into the store? Grandpa must have locked the door. Did anyone else have a key?"

Lois thought for a moment. "Yes. There were three boys who worked in the store—no, four. I think they worked at different times, so I don't know who would have been there during the riots. Except, I guess, for Curtis Martindale."

"Do you remember the other boys' names?"

"Let me see now. David. And another D name . . . Derek. I don't remember their last names, unfortunately. And a Sansei boy, Akira Matsumoto, who was a little bit older than Rosie. I remember him—he'd come back and visit even after he went off to college, and he had a really foul mouth. He was one of the original members of the Yellow Brotherhood."

"The what?"

"The Yellow Brotherhood—they were kind of a gang. Not like the ones today. They formed for protection, mostly, and they had a political angle. I don't think they lasted past the sixties."

"Do you know what happened to the boys who worked in the store?"

"I don't know what happened to the two black boys. Akira moved to Japan. He went to UCLA and got his act together, and then took a job in Tokyo. We'd hear about him sometimes because Dad stayed in touch with his parents. They might still be alive—I could look them up."

"Right. But if you called every Matsumoto in the phone book, it'd probably take a year." She paused. "Thanks for the help, Lois. Sorry to shock you with all this."

"It's not your fault. I'll let you know if I remember anything else."

Friday came, slow as Christmas or a birthday, and Jackie drove back down to Crenshaw. Lanier had given her the address for a place he called the "barbecue church," and a little after two, she arrived there. In the corner of the parking lot was a huge, smoking grill, facing several picnic tables which were half-filled with people. Jackie parked her car and made sure all her doors were locked. Then she walked over to the tables.

She was nervous. There were about twenty-five people there, most of them young and all of them black. There were half a dozen older men, sitting together at a table. A middle-aged couple stood behind the grill, apron-clad, he marinating the big sides of beef, she twisting sausages with a pair of tongs. As Jackie approached, she felt self-conscious and not entirely safe. The teenagers looked at her and lifted single eyebrows in calm disdain. Jackie scanned the tables again—where was Lanier? But then he turned—he'd been sitting with his back to her—and waved her over.

"Thanks for meeting me here," he said as she approached. "I needed to touch base with some folks at the church . . ." He gestured toward the building. ". . . and then I thought I'd get some lunch. I hope you haven't eaten already."

Jackie smiled. "I haven't, actually. Once you told me there was barbecue involved, I figured I should wait."

Lanier extricated himself from the picnic table, motioning for her to walk toward the grill. "It's actually an interesting story. Twenty-five years ago, this was just an empty lot. Then the founders of the church started using it to sell barbecue ribs and hot links at lunchtime. Well, word got around and the food sold so well that the founders raised enough money to build the church."

Jackie nodded, feeling encouraged. Lanier still hadn't smiled at her, but he seemed much more relaxed than the first time they met. He wouldn't have brought her here, she thought, if he disliked her.

They had reached the grill now, and Lanier gestured to the couple behind it. "This is Don and Mary Carter. Mary's the daughter of the original church founders. And this," he said to the Carters, "is Jackie Ishida, Frank Sakai's granddaughter."

At her grandfather's name, both the Carters became animated. Mrs. Carter removed her hot-pad glove and held her hand out over the grill, her arm bisecting the waves of rising smoke. "It's a pleasure to meet you," she offered, shaking Jackie's hand. "Frank Sakai's a name I haven't heard in a long time. He was a good man, your grandfather. Remember him well." She paused. "I heard he passed on. I'm very sorry."

Jackie thanked her, and they stood there awkwardly. Again, she had the sense that she didn't deserve such sympathy. The luscious, meaty smells from the grill were making it hard to focus.

"Well, listen, honey, why don't I fix you up a plate? I'd make one up for James there," Mrs. Carter said, looking teasingly at Lanier, "but he's already eaten 'bout a whole week's supply."

"Aw, come on, Mary. That was just one hot link to get me

through my meeting. I'll take a *real* lunch now." He was smiling and his whole face changed. It was no longer a stern mask of angles and stark, immobile lines. He looked boyish and warm, more approachable.

Jackie could feel the eyes of the customers. The Carters' reaction to her, instead of making the other people more comfortable with her, had somehow had the opposite effect. She couldn't remember the last time she'd felt so scrutinized, exposed, and yet, there was a dismissive quality to the teenagers' looks; she wasn't important enough, even, to glare at. Mary Carter handed her a red and white cardboard box full of ribs, black-eyed peas, and corn bread. She waved off the ten Jackie offered and gave Lanier an identical serving. They each grabbed Cokes from the cooler. Then Lanier directed Jackie to the picnic table closest to the fence, away from the milling teens. He insisted that Jackie try her food, which she did—inhaling tangy mouthfuls of the tender pork ribs that tasted even better than they smelled. He started on his own ribs before wiping his mouth with a napkin and asking, "Did you find out anything interesting?"

"Maybe," Jackie answered. She recounted what Lois had told her. How she and Rose hadn't known of the murders. How Frank had reacted, shutting himself away, then moving the family down to Gardena. How three other boys besides Curtis might have had a key to the store.

Lanier stirred his Styrofoam cup full of black-eyed peas. "Any idea who they were?"

Jackie nodded. "Some. They were all teenagers, employees. Anyway, one of them was Akira Matsumoto, a Japanese-American, obviously, who ended up moving to Japan. The other two I only have first names for—Derek and David."

Lanier tapped his fingers on the table. "David Scott. He was one of the other four boys in the freezer."

"Oh. God. I don't think my aunt knew that."

"David and Curtis had just graduated from Dorsey. The other two, David's little brother Tony and his best friend Gerald, would have been freshmen that fall."

Jackie felt dizzy and grabbed the table. "Jesus."

"Derek's last name was Broadnax. I think he might have been there when the boys were found." He paused. "His little sister Angela was Curtis's girlfriend. I don't remember what happened to them, but we could ask around a bit. Some of the old folks around here got memories like books. You think you could track down the Japanese guy?"

"Maybe," Jackie said. "I'll try." She took a sip of her Coke and then, when she felt steady again, she tried the rich, moist corn bread. "Any luck on your end?"

Lanier sighed, waved to a man at another table, then looked back to Jackie again. "Some. I have a buddy who's a detective at the Southwest Station. He grew up around here and he knew your grandpa, and he's been doing some sniffing around." He paused. Allen had not been willing at first. What James was asking was dangerous, too risky. The department was a sleeping monster that it was better not to disturb, and who knew what kind of creatures you'd find if you went digging in its belly. What secrets, half-digested, the twisted guts would offer up. Only after a few days had Allen changed his mind. He had loyalties deeper, he said, than the department. "Most of the cops from Lawson's time have retired, you know, and the few who are still on the force have all moved up and out to desk jobs at other stations. It's hard—no one's gonna speak out against another cop."

Jackie nodded, waiting.

"But Allen heard about this one guy, Robert Thomas. He and his partner worked at Southwest with Lawson, and they were the only two black cops there. Anyway, the partner's gone, but Thomas is still around, up at the Hollywood Station."

"Have you talked to him?"

Lanier took a bite of his ribs. A dollop of sauce got smeared on his cheek, and Jackie pointed at the same spot on her own face. Lanier wiped the sauce off with a napkin. "Tried to," he said. "He thought I was a reporter. I called him at the station, and when I started to explain what I wanted, he interrupted and said he didn't know what I was talking about. Then he hung up on me. I called back yesterday and tried to tell him I was calling at the suggestion of a cop—but he still seemed to think I was messing with him. But this time he remembered 'the incident.' That's what he called it, 'the incident.' Said it was a terrible tragedy and he didn't want to discuss it, why did the press insist on stirring up all those painful things from the past."

Jackie took a gulp of her Coke. "What do you think's going on with him?"

Lanier shrugged. "I don't know. He probably *does* think I'm a reporter. And my guess is, he's gonna retire in the next couple of years and he doesn't want any kind of hassle. The last thing he's going to want to do is dig up a scandal from thirty years ago." Lanier paused, remembering the conversation. Thomas had been curt, self-protective, an old-school Negro. Lanier almost felt sorry for him—what twists, what back-flips he must have had to perform in order to succeed at his job. Thomas was his father's age, and Lanier understood his suspicion, his fear. So many of the old folks had been crushed down and down.

"So what do we do now?" Jackie asked.

"I've got some ideas on that," Lanier said, "but I'll tell you about them later. Let's get out of here before the traffic gets bad."

They threw their trash away and waved goodbye to the Carters. They got into Lanier's green Ford Taurus station wagon, strapped themselves in, and Lanier took a left onto Crenshaw.

"Where we going?" Jackie asked.

"We're taking a drive." They passed Crenshaw Motors, an old building with rounded corners that had clearly been there for decades. There was a string of small offices and stores on the right, and Jackie wondered how all these places remained in business— there didn't seem to be enough foot traffic to support them. When she looked closely, she saw that many of the stores were empty. She thought of the ghost town she'd once seen, driving back from Arizona; she thought of the broken-windowed, barricaded buildings of Northridge, which she and Laura had toured the week after the earthquake. At the first big intersection, several blocks down, Lanier made a U-turn and they headed back north. Looking up, Jackie saw the Hollywood Hills in the distance, the tiny Hollywood sign, which was lovely, but incongruous, like someone had rolled in the wrong backdrop for a movie set.

"This area ain't exactly hopping," said Lanier. "But right up here, by Leimert Park, it's nicer—this is what I wanted to show you. There's a couple of art galleries, coffee shops, jazz clubs. And Magic's new theaters are helping bring people to the mall. You should see this place on Sunday, when they shut Crenshaw down to traffic and the kids all come."

He walked over sometimes, just to watch the show. The young brothers in their souped-up cars, shiny old Pontiacs and Buicks that rattled and groaned like prehistoric beasts. The drug dealers in their Nissans and heavy gold chains. Young men with arms slung out windows, lifting their chins and calling out to the girls, who'd pretend they weren't trying to be noticed. Stereos blasting, music jumping from every open window. The bass lines so solid you could walk on them. You didn't need a ride as long as that bass kept thumping, carried you down to where you wanted to go. Ride this line and it felt so good you knew you were gonna live forever, come back the next Sunday just to keep the thrill going. Young men and young women all looking fine, dressed, and ready. Eyes feasting on each other. Appraising and making offers, rebuffing or rebuffed. Affiliations made and broken. Sex or a hit or even the big prize, love, if the music and the weather were right. Crenshaw on Sunday. Like Mardi Gras. The candy store. Every carnival and holiday packed up into one tight bundle and rolled on down the wide boulevard. The young brothers and sisters cruising Crenshaw on Sunday. Nothing—at least that one perfect night of the week—could ever get in their way.

Jackie nodded as Lanier turned onto Degnan, noting that, indeed, this street was more lively. She saw the galleries and the stores that sold African goods. She saw several older men sitting in metal chairs, playing chess outside a coffee shop. Degnan was only a few blocks long, and soon they were right back on Crenshaw. "What did it look like around here thirty years ago?"

"More open," said Lanier. "The houses didn't look much different—they were nice, and a lot of blocks are still real nice, as you'll see. Although just about everyone has bars on their windows now. There weren't gangs, not the way we have them today. And a lot of these here businesses," he waved his hand in front of

Jackie's face, "were open. This was just a nice, solid, middle-class area, pretty mixed-race even way back then, with a lot of black and Japanese folks. During the '65 uprising, the looting didn't start up here until the third or fourth day. It was a lot less widespread than the mess in '92. But then, things were a whole lot worse in '92."

Jackie nodded, more in acknowledgment than agreement. She'd watched the '92 riots unfold on TV. The rioters had made it to within a mile of her apartment, all the way up to Pico and Fairfax, extending into Hollywood just east of her, along La Brea and Western and Vermont. She'd been horrified and scared, though less certain than Lanier that this upheaval was somehow understandable. But now she remembered the TV newspeople talking about how "it" was coming closer to "us"; telling their viewers—as if they couldn't see and smell for themselves—of the smoke that hovered over the city.

Lanier turned right onto a side street, and then turned left at the second corner. He'd been right—the houses were nicer here, and Jackie was surprised by how middle-class they all looked. The lots were big, the lawns neat, the eucalyptus trees large and looming, the houses well-kept and substantial. The trees that lined the sidewalk reached across the street and tangled their fingers together, so that when they drove down the block, Jackie felt like a child running through a gauntlet of older children in a game of London Bridge. At the next corner they took a left, and then another. Something was different about this block, but Jackie couldn't put her finger on what it was. "Where are we going?" she asked.

Lanier slowed down and pulled over to the curb. He pointed out the window, saying, "Here."

Jackie saw a tan stucco house with a black-tiled, sloping roof. There was nothing remarkable about it. "What's this?"

"Your grandfather's house."

Jackie nodded. She thought, of course. But other than that, she felt nothing—no recognition, no connection. The only thing that struck her was that this house was bigger than the one the family moved to in Gardena. "It's nice," she finally said. She looked a minute longer. And as she looked, certain things became clear to her, the way a stranger's features, once you learn she's related to someone you know, suddenly appear more familiar. Jackie noticed the black tiles, the shuttered windows, the perfectly manicured bushes and bonsai-style trees. "That stuff—the trees, the tiles— that's all Japanese."

Lanier nodded. Jackie looked down the street and saw that all of the houses had the same bonsai-type bushes and trees. Many of the houses also had old Japanese-style doors, black strips of wood criss-crossing the white body of the door, like crust laid over a pie. A few places had window shutters modeled after screens in Japan, and stone lions placed on either side of the entrance. The roofs were black and tiled, some multi-layered and pagoda-style.

"This looks like Gardena," Jackie said.

Lanier nodded. "There used to be a lot more houses like this, but most of them are gone now."

After a few more minutes, he pulled away from the curb, and Jackie realized that she'd seen a picture of this house, of Lois and Rose as little girls, sitting on the lawn with a kitten between them. She stared out the window, feeling like a tourist in her grandfather's life, and when they turned again, she felt a twinge of loss. She didn't pay much attention to where the car was going until Lanier stopped in front of a boarded-up old building. He nodded toward it. "Your grandfather's store."

This time, Jackie reacted. She was afraid, she was curious, she wanted both to flee and to stop and look closer. She got out of the car and stood there for a moment. The store was free-standing— to the right was an alley and to the left, the back of the buildings on Crenshaw. It was bigger than she'd expected, not like one of the tiny bodegas she often passed on Washington or Pico. The building had obviously met with violence and fire—there were boards across the door and the plaster around each window was black and charred. The walls were covered with graffiti, black and inde- cipherable to Jackie. The faded black letters on the rusted white sign read, "Mesa Corner Market." There were several crushed beer cans in the doorway, two or three broken bottles, and a scat- tering of glass vials with green plastic caps.

"Jesus," she said. "How long's it been like this?"

Lanier had gotten out of the car, and he came up and stood next to her, arms crossed. "Since the uprising."

"That long?"

"The '92 uprising. It was open a long time before then. Your grandfather shut it in '65, but he sold it to someone else."

"Has that owner had the place the whole time?"

Lanier shook his head. "No. He sold it again a few years ago to a Korean couple." Lanier kicked at a can in front of him; it went skittering down the sidewalk. "I felt bad for them. The day after the store burned, the wife, Mrs. Choi, was standing out in front, looking at the mess and crying. A couple of the mothers brought back stuff their kids had taken from it—just little things, packages of cookies and cigarettes—and a few others helped sweep up the glass and the ashes. But they never reopened and I don't know who owns it now. It's been empty for the last two years."

Jackie nodded, only half-listening. As she walked forward, getting close enough so that the front of the store blocked out the sky, she was thinking that this place, this shell of a building, was where her grandfather had spent twenty years of his life. She went right up to the door, raised her arm, placed her fingertips on the wood. It was cool and rough, a little frayed. Slowly, so as not to get a splinter, she flattened her hands against the board and closed her eyes. On the other side of that wood, her grandfather had struggled and sweated and laughed. She could almost see him as he'd been then, as she'd seen him in pictures—tan work pants, white shirt that was always slightly too large, crisp white apron, neatly tied and blindingly bright. Tan face, almost as brown as the skin of his field-laborer father, and shiny black hair, slicked back with Pomade. Her grandfather's money had been made and lost here. Four teenage boys had died here. It seemed to Jackie that if she could just get inside, beyond the boards, the answers would all be available to her, scattered among the ashes. Or perhaps Frank himself would be there, sweeping, restocking the shelves, ringing up groceries for an afternoon customer.

Lanier watched her, glad that he'd taken this foolish girl by the head and forced her to look at her past. She seemed nice enough, concerned enough about Frank to be here today, but her parents, clearly, had sent her into the world without the nourishment of her own family history. Her past was like this neighborhood—still there, intact, but she had never bothered to visit. Never driven through its streets, taken in the beauty of its trees and houses. Let it sit there unexplored just down the road from her.

"Can we get in here?" she asked, not turning.

"No. It's all closed up. And there's really nothing to see in there anyway. It was all pretty much burned out."

Jackie nodded. She took her hands off the wood and turned back toward Lanier, who was standing, a bit awkwardly, on the sidewalk. "Thanks," she said. "I'm glad I saw this. It makes every-thing more real, somehow."

Three young boys careened around the corner on bicycles, rode between them, then turned again and darted down the alley. Lanier watched them go. He and Cory always biked over around this time to see what Curtis was up to. "You know, a lot of times at this time of day your grandfather would be sitting outside with his friend Mr. Conway to greet the kids when they were coming home from school."

"You think that's how he met Curtis?"

Lanier shrugged. "Probably. Curtis and Cory lived a couple blocks from here and they would've walked by on their way back and forth from school."

"What do you know about Curtis? Why did my grandfather like him so much?"

"I don't know why your grandfather liked him, but I know why *I* did. He was always there, man. *Always*. He was solid." And he kicked me in the ass when I needed it, Lanier thought. He paid attention to me, and wasn't embarrassed to have me and his brother hanging around with him. With him I felt big, like I mattered. And so much of what I do now is still about him.

"What was his family like?"

Lanier sighed. "Complicated. I'm not sure their parents liked each other much. Bruce—my uncle—was from L.A., but he met Curtis's mom when they were working in Oakland. Actually, Curtis was born up there, and his mother went back up there after he died. Anyway, Bruce and Curtis used to fight something awful.

I don't know what the problem was—Curtis was a pretty good student and didn't get into any trouble. But he did whatever he wanted and hung out with whoever he wanted, and I don't think that sat very well with his dad." Nothing ever did sit well with Bruce, he remembered. Jimmy's own mother didn't, which meant that neither did Jimmy. Uncle Bruce was more frightening than any version of Jimmy's father, drunk or sober. He had a way of making you feel like you were being beaten, even though he never raised a hand.

"Anyway," Lanier continued, "Bruce and Alma, Curtis's mom, used to fight a lot too. Usually about Curtis, I think." But Alma, he remembered, could handle him. Fiercely loving but also aloof somehow, she was Jimmy's first love. And Curtis's. And everyone else's.

"What'd they do for a living?"

"Bruce worked for Goodyear. When I was growing up, there were a bunch of factories and plants in the area. A lot of men walked to work—you could actually hear the five o'clock whistles. And Alma was a teacher. She ended up getting some important job with the Oakland School District after Cory graduated from high school, but back when I knew her, she was a teacher. Before that, she was a factory worker. And before *that*, she worked as a domestic."

"My grandmother was a teacher, too. And my great-grandmother was a domestic."

Lanier laughed. "My great-grandmother was a domestic, too. And my grandmother. *And* my mother. I guess that was the fate of most women of color back then."

Jackie didn't answer. She was surprised and a bit uncomfortable that someone from her family could be lumped together with someone from Lanier's family, and from the Martindales'. Even though she knew that her grandparents, and great-grandparents, had lived in this neighborhood, she didn't really think of them as part of it. Their stay here—and her tour—was only an accident, a fluke. They'd been interlopers, visitors, and now they were gone.

Jackie and Lanier walked back toward the car. Jackie noticed, across the street, more remnants of the earthquake—cardboard covering windows, broken glass sparkling on the lawns. But then, just as she was about to open her door, a string of small children, linked in pairs, came into view on the sidewalk on Crenshaw. There were a good twenty or twenty-five of them, and judging from their organized procession and from the four tired-looking women who walked beside them, they were a class from a local elementary school. The first children were halfway across Bryant Street when one of them yelled, "Look! It's Mr. Lanier!"—and then suddenly children were breaking out of line, sprinting full-speed down the sidewalk. About ten of them streamed toward him yelling "Mr. Lanier! Mr. Lanier!" and they all hit him more or less at once. "We saw a dead squirrel!" one of them announced. "Yeah," said another, "and its head was all bloody!" "Mrs. Davis showed us all different kinds of trees!"

"Whoa, whoa!" Lanier said, laughing. But he'd come back to the sidewalk and dropped to one knee, giving the kids more access to him, and he seemed somehow to be looking at all of them at once, enclosing them all in his arms. The other children were still in the middle of the street, their line depleted and confused, and the women quickly herded them onto the sidewalk, calling to the kids who'd surrounded Lanier: "Shaniqua! Todd! Angelique! Get back here!"

But the children paid them no mind, even when Lanier instructed them to return to their class. They couldn't take their eyes off of him. And as they kept telling him about what they'd seen and done that day, they all managed somehow to touch him— hand to his knee, arm on his shoulder, an elbow linked around his elbow.

"I'm sorry, ma'am," Lanier said to the middle-aged, long-suffering woman who came over to retrieve her charges. "They're in my after-school program."

"I know who you are," she replied. "They talk about you like you're Disneyland."

Because the kids refused to go back on their own, Lanier had to take them. He stood up with one child hanging onto his shoulders, a child tucked under each arm, and the rest of the kids clutching his shirt or pants. Like a many-headed, many-limbed creature, they made their way to the corner where the rest of the class was waiting. After he'd disengaged the last child and safely returned her to her partner, he came back down the sidewalk toward Jackie.

"They *love* you," she said, smiling.

Lanier looked a bit sheepish. "Yeah, well, you know."

But she didn't; she hadn't. The childrens' obvious adoration of him, his tenderness with them, was a surprise, and a recommendation. By the time they reached the parking lot, Lanier's usual face and voice and demeanor had already snapped back into place. But Jackie didn't buy it anymore. She'd seen something that she wished to see more of.

CHAPTER EIGHT

FRANK, 1939

FRANK DIDN'T tell his father, but it was the rabbits and frogs that swayed him. Not that he was sick of going to Little Tokyo, although that was also true. Every weekday that summer he was working at Old Man Larabie's store, and every Saturday he made his own trip to Li'l Tokyo with his sister and the Hiraoka brothers for three hours of practicing *kanji* and bowing stiffly at Japanese school. The last thing he wanted to do on his one day off was to go back again and follow his parents around as they shopped, as they called on their old-time friends. Especially since he'd just seen them all anyway at the big *kenjinkai* picnic in Griffith Park, where all the Issei from Nagano-ken had gathered to feast, play, trade news of home, get red-cheeked and teary-eyed from *sake* and beer. Get intoxicated, too, on their memories of mountains and rice paddies and the plump, juicy apples that his father said made the American kind look like raisins. And he'd see them all again in another three weeks at the Nisei festival, which Frank didn't mind as much because he liked the colorful parade, the red dancing lion with its swirling mane, the women in bright *kimonos*, the men with drums so large you couldn't see their faces. And because he liked the sumo tournament, the powdered sweating bodies and slick tied hair and the small, t-shaped, diaper-like *mawashis*. And most of all, because he was performing in the judo exhibition in the new, still-stiff white uniform he'd paid for with his earnings from the store.

But Sundays were too much. They didn't *live* in Li'l Tokyo anymore—the Sakais had left when Frank was eight, moving into a small house off of Crenshaw Boulevard, a few miles southwest of downtown. His parents still made the trip by train every day, though, to get to their jobs—his father's at the City Market in the Southwest Berry Exchange, his mother's shaping and slicing fish-cakes at the *kamaboko* factory. And his father stayed in town late two nights a week to gamble with his friends, a habit from his bachelor days that years of arguments and marriage had done nothing to change. Frank had worked with his father at the Berry Exchange for the last three summers, sorting the berries, picking out the rotten ones, arranging them in crates for all the grocers who came in from their stores. But he was fifteen now and he had his own job in his own neighborhood, working for Larabie, whom he'd known from his store—the Mesa Corner Market—but also saw downtown on the old man's morning trips for fruit and pro-duce. So as his father was stepping outside to warm up the car, Frank called out to him.

"I don't want to go," he said.

His father whirled around. "Eh?"

"I don't want to go."

"Nani? Dō shite?"

"Because we go every Sunday and you're there every day dur-ing the week. I want a day off. I want to stay around here today."

His father pressed his lips together and pointed out the door at the car. His fingers were nicked and stained crimson and blue, the marks of harvesting, and handling bleeding berries. "You come," he said. "You come Little Tokyo."

"No."

His father let go of the door and approached him. He was wearing the only jacket Frank had ever seen him in and a collaps-ing black hat. His face was dark brown, wrinkled from years in the fields, like the dry cracked earth from which he'd tried to coax life. Frank swallowed and almost gave in. Although Kazuo was almost sixty now, he was still wire-tough, unbreakable. When his ship arrived in San Francisco in 1903, a gang of white thugs were at the docks to greet it. And as Kazuo and the other men walked down the plank and took their first steps on American soil, the white thugs had surrounded them, yelling "Japs!" and "Yellow perverts!" and "Turn around and go on home!" Two of them picked horse dung off the street and flung it at the new arrivals; one of the fresh, mossy dung cakes struck Kazuo in the jaw. But instead of averting his eyes and scurrying as the other men had done, he bent over, picked up a dung cake, and threw it right back. It hit one of the thugs in the temple and he was so stunned that it took him a moment to start after Kazuo. But Kazuo was ready for him and used the throws and deflections of judo he'd pass on to his son, and soon four of the thugs were lying flat on the ground, holding precious parts of themselves. The rest of them took off running. Frank knew that a man who'd scared off a gang of whites within five minutes of arriving in America would never be intimidated by his own son, regardless of the boy's half-foot advantage. He wasn't sure he'd be able to hold his ground. His father stopped right in front of him and looked up into his eyes. "What the hell wrong with you? You come, you be respect."

Just then, Frank's mother came into the room, with his sister Kumiko trailing behind her. She'd heard what had passed between them, and now she approached, laying a hand on her husband's tense and ready arm. "Papa. Papa. Let him stay," she said. Then, in Japanese, "He works hard all week, let him play with his friends."

His father glared at him, still frowning. "You home when we get back. You don't go play the football." Then he, Masako, and Kumiko walked out and shut the door. A few minutes later, Frank heard them drive away.

His plan was exactly that, of course—to go play the football. He was on the junior varsity at Dorsey High, and on Sunday mornings, after church, his friends would gather at the high school field to play. As soon as the chugging of the car had faded and he could hear the *ribbits* of frogs again, he changed into a T-shirt, work pants, and a pair of old sneakers, and skipped down out of the house.

Frank loved his neighborhood. He loved the space of it, the greenery, the view of the mountains, the huge expanse of clear blue sky. There was a scattering of houses, but they were set wide apart, with strawberry fields and walnut groves and marshy lots between them. Just a few blocks away was the swamp where he'd met Victor Conway years before; where the two of them, equipped with Mr. Conway's shotguns, hunted for ducks, and wild pigs if they were lucky. The Sakais' apartment in Little Tokyo had been tiny, dirty, dark, but they lived in a bungalow now, with tan stucco and green trim, and they had their own sprawling back yard. Frank knew his mother loved it in Angeles Mesa, too, despite their rocky entrance. Six months after they'd moved in, part of their roof had collapsed in the quake of '33. And the cold looks and harsh words from neighbors the first few years had not made for an easy adjustment. There was the flooding, too, in the rainy season, water running down from the hills, so much the year before that the milkman had delivered his milk by boat. But all of this was a small price to pay for the space they now had, the lives they led. Masako kept a flower garden in back, with dahlias, sweet peas, snapdragons, sunflowers; she and the children grew most of the vegetables they ate. It was Frank's father who missed the city, the dirt and noise and people, the restaurants and stores stacked side-to-side. His mother, Frank suspected, could live without these Sunday trips; she'd made several friends in the neighborhood.

Frank walked over to Crenshaw, up to Rodeo, then a few blocks west to the high school, which had opened two years before, the same year streetlights were installed on the boulevard. His friends were already there—Victor, David Hara, Steve Yamamoto, Don Styles, Barry Hughes. There were a few other boys he knew less well, including a white boy, Andy Riley, who lived in the hills at the end of Vernon where the Olympic Village used to be, the hills where sometimes Frank would go fishing. All the boys were j.v. players, and the nine Negro and Japanese boys who met that Sunday were the only black and Asian players on the team—a small sprinkling within a slightly larger sprinkling of black and Asian kids who were allowed to do extracurriculars; of black and Asian students in the school; of black and Asian families in the neighborhood. As Frank approached the field, Victor spotted him. He yelled out a surprised and exhilarated "Hey!" and heaved the football in Frank's direction. Frank grinned as the ball spiraled toward him, and he took a few steps up to meet it.

"We're just picking teams," Don informed him. "You make it an even ten."

Steve came over, clapped him on the shoulder. "Your mom and dad let you off the hook today, huh?"

Frank nodded. "Kind of. I think I'm going to pay for it later."

Steve fiddled with the reed he was chewing. "I hate Li'l Tokyo. I haven't been in five years. I'm surprised you've put up with going there as long as you have."

Frank didn't reply, thinking his own impatience with Little Tokyo, with his parents and their friends, was very different from Steve's, who did badly in school, who was drinking already, who was proud not to know Japanese. He turned away from him and listened as Victor and David Hara, the two best players, picked teams. Victor was tall, oak-brown, and handsome—like a movie star, Frank thought, if only movie stars came in his color. He always had girls trailing after him, but restricted himself to one—Janie—who he'd been dating since junior high school. Now Victor chose Frank, and David chose Barry, and all the boys fell in with their teammates. Then the two teams ran to separate ends of the field, and David's team received. Barry, who was a minister's son, returned the kick all the way for a touchdown, without anyone laying a hand on him.

They played for two hours. Frank's T-shirt and work pants got covered with grass stains and sweat but he didn't worry about how he'd explain them, knowing his mother would stuff his clothes into the bottom of the laundry and never mention what she knew to his father. Even then, in July, there was a cool breeze coming off of the ocean and they could hear the palm trees rustle after a particularly strong gust of wind. The score was something like 73-60, and just as the boys were discussing whether or not the game was finished, three rabbits hopped onto the grass. They were light brown, with sharp black eyes and white bouncing tails. "Too many men on the field," Steve announced, and all the boys laughed, taking the rabbits as a sign that they were through. Frank was happy. The laughter, the game, the camaraderie—but even more than that, the breeze, the grass, the palm trees, the rabbits—were why he'd stayed home that day. Nevermind that his old friends in Little

Tokyo called him a country boy now; Angeles Mesa was where he belonged.

The boys parted ways, except for Victor, Frank, and Barry. As they walked to Victor's house on Chesapeake, Victor asked his two friends what they were doing that afternoon.

"Nothing," Frank replied.

"Going home," Barry said. "Got some chores I gotta do." He spat out "chores" like it was a piece of tough gristle.

"No, you're not," Victor informed him.

"Oh yeah?"

"Yeah. You're going to the beach."

"What? The beach? Shut up," Frank said. "How the hell are we supposed to get there?"

Victor grinned, reached into his pocket, pulled out a set of keys, and jangled them in front of his friend's nose. "Got my license yesterday. And my daddy said I could take the car today."

Frank stopped and put his fists on his hips. Barry threw his head back and whooped. And the three of them walked down the sidewalk, jostling and colliding, throwing feet out sideways to trip one another, smacking each other open-palmed on the sides of their close-cropped heads. Victor, at first, managed to avoid his friends' jutting legs and flashing hands. Barry was short but powerful, and when he finally caught up with Victor, he shoved him, like a blocking bag, all the way across the street. Then the two of them came back and picked up Frank, Victor taking his shoulders, Barry his kicking legs, and threw him into a row of bushes. They laughed at, struck, and insulted each other, and the old men who were sitting outside on their stoops thought of friends they hadn't seen in forty years. The young women who were watching, on the street or through the windows, saw the boys' smooth faces, bright teeth, and tight hard muscles, and their bodies relaxed and opened, mouths humming wordless tunes of desire.

The car was parked in the driveway. It was an old Model T that Victor's parents had driven out from Arkansas in 1926, encountering not a single paved road until they reached the Cajon Pass in eastern California. Victor went around to the passenger side and opened the door with a flourish for his friends, ushering

Barry into the backseat and Frank into the front. And they drove, grinning wide and feeling pleased with themselves, through blocks that got longer and longer, and then shorter again, past orange groves, more strawberry fields, and fields of cabbage and lettuce. They went west on Jefferson, up to Pico, then left all the way to Santa Monica. They knew that there'd soon be faster roads to get around on, wide, big roads called freeways; one was already being built between downtown and Pasadena. But the boys were happy to drive along slowly; to feel the sun and wind on their faces; to go someplace they wanted to, and under their own power.

They smelled the ocean before they saw it. Frank had only been there once, as a tiny child, and now, when it finally came into view, he couldn't believe its blue-green color, its majestic rolling voice, the way it flowed and folded endlessly into the distance. The three boys whooped again and could hardly wait to get out of the car. Victor managed to park it, somewhat crookedly, in the crowded lot, and they all jumped out, walking quickly toward the beach. Victor was telling the other two how his feet were sensitive to heat so he couldn't remove his shoes, and Barry was calling him a sissy. But then they stopped, abruptly, because they all saw the sign. It was a dark brown board, attached to a pole that was sunken into the edge of the sand, and it had two arrows painted on it, one pointing right, the other left. Above the left were painted the words, "Whites only." Above the right were the words, "Colored only." They all stared at it, unbelievingly. Then they noticed the fence, which started at the parking lot and extended all the way down to the water. Wordlessly, they scanned the beach and saw nothing but black bathers on the right side of the fence and white bathers on the left. Victor and Barry glanced at each other, and then looked at Frank.

Frank stared. He'd never seen a sign like this, although he'd heard about them in the news, and from Victor's parents, when they told stories about living in Arkansas. He'd never had to think like this, either—for his first eight years he'd lived in Little Tokyo, and then for his next seven in Angeles Mesa, where there weren't enough people of any color to legislate such boundaries. If the beach was divided into two distinct sides, on which side did he belong? Just then, a burly whiteman passed by on the way to his car, his chest burned pink and tender. "Japs go over there," he said helpfully, pointing toward the colored side. His wife swatted him on the forearm. "Oh, honey, no they don't." The couple disappeared and the three boys were left standing in uncomfortable silence. Finally, Frank took a deep breath. "Last one to the water has to walk back home," he said. And then he took off running, to the right.

CHAPTER NINE

1994

THE ENVELOPE that held her family papers was distinct—nine by twelve inches and lime-green—but Jackie couldn't find it for the life of her. She'd been looking for half an hour and was getting impatient, especially since it was Saturday and she'd cut short her time in bed with Laura in order to come home and keep this date with her family. She hadn't been in the mood to stay with her anyway—they'd been awakened by an aftershock, the third that week, and it had left them both too jittery to sleep. Finally, she found the envelope, buried beneath her journals in the back of the closet.

Leaning back against the bed, she poured the contents out onto the rug—the small article about her father being promoted to head of surgery at Cedars-Sinai; a card Lois had given her for her sixteenth birthday; a picture of her optimistic-looking parents and herself as a baby posing in front of the eternal flame at JFK's grave. This photo always made Jackie pause for a moment—her parents had been teenagers at the time of Kennedy's death, and had named her after the president's wife. There was a picture, which seemed about ten years old, of Frank in a coffee shop, wearing a navy blue bowling shirt that said, "Holiday Bowl"; he was sitting next to a man who Jackie recognized but couldn't place. There was a picture of Jackie's father as a teenager, standing with his father in their yard in Palos Verdes, among the fog-shrouded bluffs that overlooked both city and ocean. Jackie found also a few postcards, including one from Frank, who'd written her from San Francisco about ten years before, during the only trip she'd ever known him to make. She remembered the trip clearly—he'd gone, quite suddenly, just after he finally retired, not telling anyone until after he'd made the reservation, and not taking Mary along. The postcard was a standard San Francisco shot, a streetcar pulling out of Union Square. Jackie turned it over and read the fading blue ink. "San Francisco is beautiful," he'd written. His letters were tall and lanky, right-leaning. "I've been to Union Square (picture on front), Fisherman's Wharf, Telegraph Hill, Chinatown, Nihonmachi (Japanese food better in Gardena). I miss LA, though. Not enough space here, and too much fog. See you soon. Love, Grandpa."

Jackie finished looking through the pile of family memorabilia, and felt distinctly let down. There was nothing here of value or interest. She picked up an old brown-tinged portrait of Frank, as a baby, with his parents, the only picture of her family from before the war. Her great-grandfather—she didn't know his name—was wearing a dark suit with his tie pulled out slightly between the lapels of the coat. Her great-grandmother, who was younger, wore a simple white dress. Both of them looked oddly uncomfortable— dressed up, as if for a costume party. She saw elements of Frank in each of them. There, on his father's face, was Frank's slender nose, and there, on his mother's, his generous, gentle eyes and the strong square jaw bequeathed to all the Sakais. But it was the man's stance that Jackie recognized most clearly—it was humble, unassuming, shaped through habit and years of hard labor. Humility didn't disguise, however, the resilience and pride beneath it.

That evening, after she'd read for a few hours and gone for a run, she and Laura drove over to Beverly Hills to have dinner with Laura's family. Laura's sister, Sarah, was down from Stanford Business School for the weekend, and so their mother had invited everyone over. Laura had not been looking forward to it—she always grew tense and close-mouthed around her older sister—and the evening turned out to be as difficult as she had feared. Despite the attempts on the part of Laura's mother to draw Laura out, Sarah hijacked the conversation, telling everyone in excruciating detail about her job offers, her professors, the apartment she and her boyfriend were hoping to buy, only pausing to field a question or to stuff food into her mouth. Every time Jackie looked over at

Laura, she seemed to be sinking further down into her chair.

As they drove back to Fairfax a few hours later, Jackie tried to cheer Laura up. "Hey, come on," she said, putting a hand on Laura's shoulder. "Listen, why don't we go to The Palms or something? We could have a couple beers and put dinner behind us."

Laura shook her head and fought back tears. "I want to go home, but you go on ahead."

Jackie gave her a look. "I can't go there without you."

"Sure you can. Just go. I know you want a drink."

She did. "Do you want me to come back to your place after?"

Laura shook her head. They turned the corner onto her block, and she waited until they'd straightened out before she answered. "No. I'm sorry. I don't think I'm going to be very good company tonight."

They pulled up in front of the house, behind Laura's car.

"OK," Jackie said. She kissed Laura goodnight and watched Laura disappear inside the house.

Jackie sighed. She was relieved to be rid of Laura, but also saddened—they used to be so much closer. There'd been a time when a night like this, a hard family scene, would have sent them into a frenzy of lovemaking. But those nights seemed to have occurred in a different life. Jackie started her car, sighing, and drove back to her apartment. But as she approached her building, the darkness in her windows made her unbearably lonely, and she knew she needed to be someplace that was noisy with people. She swung around the block and got back onto Fairfax. At Santa Monica Boulevard, she took a left and drove a mile to The Palms.

After showing her ID to the butch, overweight bouncer—she'd reached the age where it was a compliment to still get carded—she removed herself from the flow of people streaming in and out, and stood to the side, trying to spot someone she knew. The place was hopping that night. The two bartenders were running back and forth behind the long bar, surrounded by a flurry—which clung to them like rain clouds to a mountain—of glasses, and ice, and bottles of liquor. To the right, in front of the mirrored wall, were a half-dozen tables surrounded by women. At the end of the bar was a small tiled dance floor, full now, on a Saturday, with dancers. Jackie could not make out the individual people, but she could see the way the crowd moved as one gyrating, sexual, strobe-light-spotted mass. People were laughing and greeting each other with big, theatrical hugs, and Jackie wondered if this was still the euphoria she'd seen in the month since the earthquake, the uncomplicated relief of being alive. She spotted a few familiar faces, but no one she knew well enough to approach, so she weaved her way through the crowd and up to the bar, and ordered a pint of beer.

She needed this drink; she'd needed it all night. As the bartender filled the glass, she watched with anticipation, and just as she reached out to receive the mug, she felt a hand clamp down on her shoulder.

"The drink's on me," announced a big, happy voice from behind her. She turned around: Rebecca.

"Hey," Jackie said, smiling, genuinely happy to see her friend. She had to yell to be heard over the music. "How you doing?"

"Great." Rebecca tossed a five on the bar, telling the bartender with a little smile to go ahead and keep the change. Then she turned to Jackie and gave her a different kind of smile. "What are you doing out? Don't you know that law school students aren't supposed to have any fun?"

"Well, I'm not having fun yet. And you're a law school student, too."

"Yeah, much to the law school's horror."

Jackie smiled. It was true that some of the faculty were less than thrilled with Rebecca Nakanishi. In the hallowed halls of the law school, where even the liberal students wore ironed pants and buttoned-down shirts, Rebecca stuck out like a drag queen at a Rotary Club meeting. She was irreverent, colorful, and disrespectful of convention, but she was brilliant—third in her class. She stood there now, one foot on the rung of a stool, waving her hair and conscious of the eyes that watched her. She wore Levi's, loose-fitting, which made you wonder at the shape of the legs inside, and a low-cut tank top, black. Jackie noticed the fluid muscles of her arms, the strength and vulnerability of her collarbone.

"I had another interview yesterday," Rebecca shouted. "With Legal Aid, in Westlake."

"How'd it go?"

Rebecca rolled her eyes and launched into a loud monologue of complaint. It was a bad time to be doing public interest, she said—no one in the public had any interest. And the field she wanted to go into—immigrant health—was especially tough, since no one in California seemed to give a shit about immigrants, except for thinking of better ways to keep them out. Legal Aid was doing the best they could, but they only had sure funding for two lawyers, and weren't certain they could take on another. "So who knows?" she concluded. "Maybe I'll just end up at a firm, like you. Maybe this isn't the time to try and save people."

Jackie teetered on the edge between guilt and annoyance—she always felt a bit accused, a bit defensive, about Rebecca's commitment to public interest law, when she herself was on track for corporate riches.

Rebecca took a sip of her drink, a gin and tonic. "Speaking of saving people, where's your Other?"

Jackie took a gulp of her beer. "Home. Alone. Depressed."

"What a surprise. You know, I was talking to Albert Stevens the other day and he told me that your last two girlfriends at Berkeley were just like Laura. What's the deal with you, anyway? You're like a reverse missionary. Rescuing the lost white children."

Jackie smiled wryly. "Yeah, well, somebody's got to."

"So what's the occasion for her sadness today? She break a fingernail?"

"Shut up. No. We went over to her mom's place for dinner, and her big bad older sister was there."

"Her mom's cool with you though, right?"

"Very cool."

"Good. Maybe *she* could tell your parents about your deviant sexual practices."

"Oh, be quiet."

"Well, *somebody's* got to." Rebecca grinned.

Jackie shook her head. "Be fair. It isn't that simple. It's not just that I don't want to tell them I'm gay. My parents don't want to talk about *anything*." It was true. Jackie's parents lived with the luxury of an innocence that Jackie didn't totally believe in.

She'd taken Laura home or out to family dinners, and her parents had accepted Laura's presence without question. Jackie wasn't sure whether this acceptance meant her parents knew what Laura was to her and were all right with it—like Lois; Lois always asked after Laura, and invited her to things—or that they simply had no idea. When she was in high school, they'd remarked sometimes on the intensity of particular friendships, but after a certain point, the remarks and questions had stopped. Laura didn't understand why Jackie didn't just tell her parents, since everybody, *everybody* (including them, she said) knew. And Jackie couldn't explain to her that she didn't tell her parents about her sexuality for the same reason they never asked her: If she told them, it would be out there, and then they would have to talk. And considering how poorly they all did discussing *anything* of substance, she couldn't imagine how her parents would deal with *this*. "I mean, come on," she said, half-pleading. "*You* know how it is with a Japanese family."

Rebecca raised an eyebrow. "Oh, so now you're Japanese?"

"What the hell is that supposed to mean?"

"Nothing, nothing," Rebecca replied. "Anyway, Laura. Does she know you came to this lesbian lair without her?"

But Jackie was still stuck on her friend's last comment, and couldn't answer right away. She didn't really know what Rebecca was referring to, but she suspected that it had to do with Laura, and with the place where she grew up, and with the fact that, except for Rebecca herself, Jackie didn't really have Asian friends. "Yeah," Jackie said, finally. "She trusts me. She knows I won't pick anyone up."

Rebecca laughed. "Yeah, you're kind of boring that way."

Jackie raised her eyebrows. "Look who's talking. When's the last time *you* took anyone home?"

"Touché. I've been celibate for so long I can't even find my own twat anymore. Not that I've ever been into the bar scene." She looked troubled for a moment, and Jackie leaned in closer.

"What?"

"Well, I did go out on a few dates a while back, with this med school student from Hawaii."

"Boy or girl?"

"Girl. And I mean, *girl*. Eyebrow waxing and manicures and shit."

"So what happened?"

Rebecca shrugged. "She vanished. Stopped calling. Presto. Gone."

"Wow," said Jackie, standing up straight again. "You mean there's actually someone who doesn't want to sleep with you?"

Rebecca looked at her dismissively. "What are you talking about? There's plenty of people who don't want to sleep with me. Heather doesn't," she said, indicating a woman behind them who they both vaguely knew. She turned back to Jackie. "*You* don't."

She looked at Jackie and smiled, and Jackie looked away. She *didn't* want to sleep with Rebecca—she wasn't really attracted to her—but there was something between them, a challenge or a question. She was suddenly even more glad that Laura hadn't come along—Laura didn't like Rebecca and was threatened by her. Jackie assured her that there was no reason to be—she'd never go for Rebecca, girlfriend or not, despite, or maybe because of (as Laura said) "the things they had in common." It wasn't that she didn't find her friend attractive or appealing. But Rebecca was half-Japanese, and despite her green almond-shaped eyes and wavy brown hair, she looked Asian enough to turn Jackie off; to make Jackie think of her as a mirror she didn't want to look into. Kissing Rebecca would be like kissing a sister, if she had one—unerotic, strange, slightly creepy. But it was more than that. Rebecca, with her brains, her looks, and above all, her panache, made Jackie feel stiff and boring in comparison. Jackie wasn't used to feeling inadequate, and it occurred to her, suddenly, that part of what she got out of being with Laura was that she felt so strong and able in contrast.

A table opened up behind them, and Jackie and Rebecca sat down. After the brief moment of discomfort at the bar, they smoothed down to normal again, gossiping about the students they knew, complaining about school, checking out the women who passed by. Jackie contemplated telling Rebecca about Curtis Martindale and Lanier, then decided against it, for now. Things were easy between them. Rebecca had come with a couple who

SOUTHLAND

didn't leave the dance floor all night, and she seemed as happy as Jackie to have found someone to talk to. They had a few more drinks and watched the happenings in the bar. Rebecca kept up a running commentary on this woman's hairdo, on that woman's jeans, on the other woman's girlfriend flirting too eagerly with the DJ, and had Jackie laughing as she hadn't laughed in weeks. Jackie felt the difficulties of the evening receding, the memories of Laura's misery lifting off of her. She wondered, for a moment, what it would be like if she could do this all the time—go out, not while leaving her girlfriend at home, but not having a girlfriend at all. She liked the feeling of sitting at a table, with good beer and good company, having nobody's tears to go home to.

CHAPTER TEN

FRANK, 1942-1948

D
URING THE last week of April, 1942, the Japanese of Los Angeles awoke to find that evacuation orders had sprouted, overnight, from trees and poles all over the city. They had a week, the orders said, to prepare for their departure; they were being moved inland, away from the coast. All over L.A.—all over the coast—Issei and Nissei rushed frantically around their homes and neighborhoods. They didn't know if they were coming back, so they had to get rid of everything. Houses and farms were sold to white men wearing soft felt hats and hard smirks. Furniture, and boxes of books, dishes, plants, clothing, were dragged out to front lawns for emergency sales. Some neighborhoods were so choked with beds and tables and clothes that it looked like Japanese America was simply moving outside. Old photographs and letters from Japan, paintings, records, *kimonos*—anything with a whiff of Japanese about it—were burned or buried, so no arrogant young soldier who'd just started to shave could come and claim they were in league with the enemy.

Frank's father wasn't there to see his family depart. The night after Pearl Harbor, as the Sakais were burning pictures in a trash bin near the shed, three large *hakujin* in dark suits appeared at their door. Frank was never sure whether they were from the police, or the state, or the FBI. They led Kazuo into the kitchen and asked him many questions—none of which made any sense to Frank, who was listening from outside the door. Do you know so and so, what were you doing on such and such a night, isn't your gambling group really a cover for strategic war meetings?

Then they took him away—largely, it seemed, because two of the men he gambled with were Junichi Murau, the head of a Japanese-language school, and Minoru Kanazawa, vice president of the Vegetable Growers Association. Frank stayed up all night, sitting with his dumbstruck mother. The next morning, she made a round of phone calls and discovered that Steve Yamamoto's father and David Hara's father had also been arrested. No one knew where they'd been taken. Over the next several months, the remaining Sakais received two letters from Kazuo—one from Fort Sill, Oklahoma, and the other from Camp Livingston, Louisiana. They were written in English, which Frank found strange, but then he realized his father had been forced to write in English, for the censors. Even so, the letters had large sections blacked out of them, or cut out all together. Frank gleaned only that his father missed them, and that he didn't like the food he was served.

The Sakais spent the winter and spring of '42 in a strange, suspended limbo, mother working, children going to school, thinking of their father every day. Frank had been going out that summer and fall with Victor, frequenting the jazz clubs over on Central, but they stopped now, for Frank's safety, and because of the blackouts. Every evening, Frank and Kumiko did their homework by candlelight while their mother cracked open the curtains and looked out at the street. When they awoke on New Year's Day to find the city covered with snow—enough for Frank and Victor to make wet, sloppy snowballs and slip and slide on the white-slick sidewalks— Masako mumbled and prayed, certain that the first snowfall she'd seen in America did not bode well for her family. The *L.A Times* and the radio newsmen warned that the Japs were going to parachute into the streets and engage in face-to-face combat; Mayor Bowron snarled that each of the little so-called American Japs in the city would know his part in the coming invasions; the Chinese and Koreans took to wearing red, white, and blue buttons to distinguish themselves from the enemy. The Sakais caught people's glances in the hallways and on the streets. It seemed to them that this fear and hatred was like a huge, invisible cobra that was slowly encircling them, poised over them, waiting to strike. When the rumor, and then the order, of evacuation came, Frank felt beneath his anger some parcel of relief. At least now there was an answer, a conclusion.

Frank's mother didn't know how long they were going, or if they'd return, but she refused to sell the piece of land that she and Kazuo had struggled for so many years to buy. Even after they'd had enough money (pieced together from their harvesting earnings, plus money lent by the pooled fund from their *kenjinkai*), they'd had to wait until Frank was born—because of laws barring Issei from owning property—so they could place the new land in his name. And it was Frank, finally, who arranged for someone to watch over it while they were away—his best friend from school, Victor Conway. The day before they were supposed to leave, the Sakais arrived home from buying underwear and socks to find several of Frank's friends and their parents assembled on the lawn.

"What are you doing here?" Frank asked Victor, who came down the walkway to greet them.

"We figured you could use some stuff out there in the desert."

Frank looked around at his friends, noticing for the first time that they'd all come bearing something. Victor and his mother brought two heavy coats that their father still had from World War I. Barry Hughes and his family, who were originally from Cleveland, brought heavy sweaters for everyone, including Kazuo. Old Man Larabie brought some canned fruit and the wool socks his wife had knitted. Andy Riley, the white boy from Boston, brought three pairs of long underwear. The Conways also brought a basket of fried chicken for the next day's journey, and Victor presented Frank with a football. Finally, Old Man Larabie's wife unwrapped a huge chocolate cake, which everyone ate inside off paper plates from Larabie's store, since the dishes had all been packed away or sold. Masako, who didn't know her son's friends very well, was completely overwhelmed by their kindness. Although she had not shed a tear in front of her children through the imprisonment of her husband; through the rumors of internment; through the selling of their car and possessions, now she sat crying in the one remaining chair and refused to take her hands from her eyes. Kumiko, whose own friends had quietly been supplying her with magazines and make-up (no stockings, though, since nylon was needed for parachutes), tried in vain to comfort her. After an hour or so, people started to leave, hugging Frank and his family and wishing them luck, and Frank tried not to wonder if he'd ever see them again. When everyone else had left and Victor got up to go, he and Frank faced each other, lower lips trembling.

"You watch your back now," Victor instructed. For the next three and a half years, he would remove the trash that was dumped on the Sakais' wilted lawn; board up the holes left by bricks and rocks that people heaved through the windows; check the house every month, even after he'd moved to Watts, to make sure no one had taken up residence inside.

"I'll try," Frank said. "And you watch yours, my brother."

The Sakais spent six weeks at the Santa Anita racetrack, living in the stalls that had been emptied of horses to make room for this different brand of livestock. Then they were taken to Manzanar in the height of the summer, on a day so choked with dust that when the guard pointed toward what he said were their quarters, Frank thought he was directing them into the desert. They shared their room with a family of five, the space divided by a string of blankets, but they knew they were luckier than most. Their room was on an end, and when Frank went to sleep on his cot near the wall, hay in his mattress rustling as he turned, he heard not voices on the other side of the thin tar paper, but the wind—whistling between the barracks, rattling the trees, weaving and howling through the mountains. The wind slipped under the barracks too, and up through wide gaps in the floorboards he could thrust his hands into. Frank didn't think about this, though; he simply tried to get through his days. His sister, who was enjoying the freedom and proximity of so many young people, made a new set of friends in the camp high school and spent most of her time away from their room.

Masako worked in the camp mess hall, and at seven she returned with left-over eggs and stale bread, sometimes only slightly spoiled fruit, so that her family would not have to eat the runny piles of gray, limp slabs of brown she prepared for everyone else. This saved Frank and Kumiko from having to stand in line at the mess hall, although there were still lines for everything else—the bathroom, the shower, their mail. The food—the bologna, the canned spinach, the bug-seasoned oatmeal—would get worse, and the portions smaller, the longer they stayed.

The heat Frank could handle; it was a dry heat, unoppressive. But the wind and dust he couldn't get away from. The wind pressed the dust into every crack of skin, every fold of his clothing; he nailed soup can lids against the holes in the wall in order to keep it out. When the winter came, sudden and harsh as judgment, everything got worse. The wind relinquished its dust in the winter, and instead blew snow and pieces of ice against the side of the barracks. The ice hit hard, a freezing assault, and when Frank opened the door, the cold air slapped his face; the wind sucked the water from his eyes. Frank's mother stuffed rolled paper into the door frame to shut out the air, but the cold still rose from the ground. At night, Frank lay huddled and shivering under his green army blanket, while the voices of the young ones on the other side of the room all rose in a chorus of complaint.

Frank wore a long-sleeve shirt, an old army jacket, and the same pair of gray work pants every day. Frank's mother, who was always cold, had to dress in men's clothes—the sweaters and long underwear she'd received from her son's friends, khaki trousers and peacoats and green earmuffs left over from the first World War, black boots and knit caps the officials handed out after three people died of exposure; huge ugly clothing everyone had to take because they had nothing else; because they had only been allowed to bring what they could carry. In the mornings and evenings, Frank went with his mother to the bathroom, helping carry the folding cardboard refrigerator box he had given her to bring. There they waited half an hour to catch a glimpse of the overflowing toilets, and Frank waited another ten minutes while Masako sat in silence, the cardboard box her only means of privacy.

When spring came, after they had been there for nearly a year, Frank's mother made a small clearing in front of the barracks, three tufts of bush next to the stairs, the whole space bound by rough white stones. There she sat and wondered about her husband. They were both from farming families in Nagano Prefecture, and in America he'd become a *buranke katsugi*, a shoulderer of blankets, a man who followed the crops through Northern and Central California. Masako had married him sixteen years later, on the evening she arrived in America; she was twenty on their wedding day and he was thirty-seven. She traveled with him, cooking for the roaming gangs of workers, until— because they could, and because of their son—they bought the house in Angeles Mesa and found jobs in Little Tokyo. Their original intention of saving money and returning to Japan had changed as soon as their daughter was born. Both children seemed so happy here in the Land of Rice, less cramped than *they'd* been as children, in a larger world with more opportunity. But now, in the camp, Masako wondered if she and Kazuo had been foolish. Look at them—jailed like criminals, like animals, and the children now lacking their father. Many of the Issei men who'd been whisked away the night after Pearl Harbor had been spirited back to their families after five months, eight months, looking gaunt and sad and exhausted. But a few men, like Kazuo, the government still required. The people inside the camp heard rumors of them, along with whispered accounts of how the war was progressing; of the legal cases of the reckless few who'd challenged the evacuation; of the Negro soldiers in Arizona protesting the internment— because of principle, and because they knew it could happen to them.

Frank would stay and talk to his mother sometimes, but other times, to get away from her sadness, he would go walking by himself. He walked around and around the barracks, past the hundreds of families boxed inside, past the leafless skeletons of trees that reached out with their spindly, skinny fingers, through the shadow of the guard tower that stood a few hundred feet away from the barracks. He walked past the Buddhist church, a tar paper-covered building like every other except for the sign on the top and the white doors flung open like the arms of a loved one. Beyond the church he reached the edge of camp, the barbed wire, the long strings of metal with teeth. He looked out at the brown land and the mountains; saw the endlessness of California, ground and sky opening into each other.

Since they had come to camp, they'd received two more letters from Kazuo. The first time he'd written from a prison in North Dakota, and the second time from another prison, in Santa Fe, New Mexico. Frank kept talking and writing to the camp officials, who said there was a good chance that his father would be allowed to join them. But then, in April, almost a year after they'd been evacuated, they received a telegram one night after dinner. It said that Kazuo Sakai had died that morning, and instructed the family to advise the officials in Santa Fe by eight the next morning about what they should do with the remains. Kumiko sat on her cot and wept quietly. Frank stared at the words. Masako lowered her head for several minutes, and then looked at her son, eyes lit with anger and pain. She told him to tell the camp officials that she wanted her husband sent there, so she could look at him again, so they could bury him.

Frank took this message to the Administration Office, and by eight the next night, after almost a year, his father was finally brought into Manzanar. Frank got word that he should go identify the body. Without telling his mother, he went to a room beside the jail. A body lay on a table under a dark gray blanket. The shape seemed odd, and when the official pulled the blanket back, Frank saw why. His father was lying on his side, his arms pulled behind him. When Frank walked around the table, he saw that his father's wrists were swollen and red from whatever had been used to bind them. On the side of his head, just behind his ear, was a fresh wound, the huge bump discolored and caked with blood. Walking around to the front again, Frank looked into his father's face for the first time in sixteen months. The lower lip was cut and swollen. There were lacerations all over the cheeks and forehead. And near the hairline, a thumb-sized dent. Frank reached forward, touching the place where the skull had been crushed. It felt like ice-cold clay. He stood back and felt no tears, just a slow, rumbling anger, a fast-sinking sorrow, a hard pride that his father's face showed no signs of fear or pain; that he'd been strong and impassive to the end.

"That him?" asked the official, disinterestedly.

"Yeah," Frank said. Then, looking the official in the eye, "What did he die of?"

The official lit a cigarette. "Heart attack."

Kazuo wasn't their only loss that spring. For the next month, Frank and Masako were so busy with burial and mourning that they didn't see what was happening to Kumiko. She had been getting plumper and sicker for weeks; only when a camp nurse put a hand to her belly did Frank figure out what was wrong. After several days of tears and arguments, angry words volleyed back and forth between Kumiko and her mother, Masako began to accept the circumstances surrounding the birth of her about-to-be grandchild. But then three months before the child was due, Kumiko woke up screaming, and Frank carried her to the camp hospital. She died there giving birth, the blood draining out of her, the baby stuck and smothered between her small, unyielding hips. She was buried next to her father in the camp cemetery, when his grave was only seven weeks old.

The *hakujin* soldiers had come around a few months earlier, distributing questionnaires to separate Japs from Americans, in order to determine who was still a loyal citizen. And when they came again, after Kazuo and Kumiko died, asking for young men to volunteer for the army, Frank signed up right away. His mother, who still remembered the green hills of her homeland and longed to see her brothers and sisters again before she died, begged him not to fight for the country that had claimed her husband and daughter. But Frank, despairing, needed simply to move, to be free. And he knew he was trapped. If he didn't fight, he'd be branded, excluded forever, lose what little chance he still might have for making a life in his own country.

Frank packed what few clothes he had and took a train to Mississippi, to the boot camp full of Nisei from all over the western half of the country. And there, the west coast men, who were used to dry heat, sweated and suffered in the swamps and marshes that seemed to extend into the sky, making the air as lush as water. They trained for months and gradually, incrementally, Frank lost the last few traces of boyhood that were left after the deaths of his father and sister. He prepared for battle physically and mentally, talking to men who'd seen action already, reading everything the army gave him—including a small booklet entitled "The Jap Soldier," which told him of the secrets, odors, and linguistic limitations of Japs in the Imperial Army. He and his new friends made up the 442nd, the all Japanese-American regiment, which was drawn almost wholly from the camps. They were quickly stripped of the illusion—if they had it at all—that their uniforms changed the way the *hakujin* saw them. When Frank's company was finally shipped abroad on the Queen Mary, they slept in the crowded open troop berths below sea level while the Italian POWs being returned to Europe were given luxury cabins upstairs. If they were angry, if they were unhappy at being packed like prisoners while the enemy was treated like guests of honor, none of them ever complained. They knew what was at stake. Although they never talked about it, even amongst themselves, they all knew the reason they were there.

Frank's unit—the American Japs—moved up the boot of Italy, fought at Anzio and Cassino, struggled up the long and treacherous road to Rome. They broke through the German line of resistance at the battle of the Gothic Line, accomplishing with four thousand men in half an hour what 40,000 "regular" American soldiers hadn't been able to do in five months. Not that they got the credit—at least, not then. Later, Frank heard that Steve Yamamoto's company had liberated a Nazi death camp, only to be shunted aside for the army cameras while *hakujin* soldiers walked through Dachau as if the credit was theirs. A few times, when they were on campaigns with other companies, *hakujin* soldiers called them dirty Japs, and Frank, and Kenny Miura, and Tom Kobayashi went after them, decking men who outweighed them by seventy pounds. *Listen, motherfuckers,* they would say. *Who do you think is man enough to get the* real *work?* And the *hakujin* couldn't argue, because they knew it was true. Roosevelt, who had no love for the Nisei when they were still living in their homes, suddenly couldn't get enough of them now, and the 442nd was asked to carry out the most difficult assignments; to take on the tasks that everyone knew were impossible or crazy. Kenny and Tom took pride in this, and Frank did as well, but he didn't tell them what he suspected was the reason they were chosen—they were Japs, after all; they were expendable. The boys swallowed their fear and kept marching and tried not to cry when their flesh was ripped by bullets or land mines. They wrote faithfully to their families back in the camps; worried more about them than themselves. One morning, Frank read an article denouncing the 442nd, claiming that they were treacherous, but that they might be good soldiers because everybody knew the Japs could fight. And the editorialist was right, although not in the way he thought. Frank and his friends were such great American soldiers, ironically, because they were Japanese—because of their sense of duty, and integrity, and faith in each other. Because they knew that somebody always had their back; that if they got hit, their brothers would come in after them. Because the worst thing that they could imagine wasn't death, or injury, or permanent disfigurement, but bringing shame upon their families. For the sake of their families, they would never be less than heroes.

Frank's war ended in France, when his battalion was sent to save a group of cowboys. The 1st Battalion of the 36th Division, from Texas, had gotten caught in a tangle of forest in the Vosges Mountains—there were a little over two hundred men up there, surrounded on all sides by Germans. The 36th Division general, a graying cattle-rancher with a John Wayne accent, kept urging Frank and the other Nisei soldiers on, anxious to reach his own men. But the task was impossible. Suicidal, and everyone knew it. With the trees, and the bushes, and the fading light, Frank could only see a few feet in front of him. Fire came from all directions, guns stuttering and popping, bullets ricocheting off trees. The 1st Battalion had left their machine guns behind as they scampered up the mountain, and the Germans had picked them up; so now the Germans were shooting with American guns, and you couldn't tell who was shooting at what or where it was coming from. The soldiers, too, were mixed up and intertwined. There was no line of attack or retreat, the armies bumping surfaces, then merging, hundreds of soldiers shooting in all directions.

Frank and his buddies were supposed to go nine miles. Frank's eyes jumped and shifted everywhere, trying to fix on something.

He occasionally caught a flash of white face, and that's when he fired his tommy gun—other than the general, he knew all *hakujin* faces were German. To his right, Frank saw Tim Nakagawa go down without a sound, brains exploding, slow-motion and almost pretty, out into the smoke-filled air. He spotted the sniper who'd shot him and ducked behind a tree just in time to avoid his fire. Then he saw the sniper crumple and fall. He moved to another tree, stumbling over three bodies—two American, one German—grabbing the bark as if he could somehow crawl into it. "Push on!" he heard the general yell, and he did, catching glimpses of other Nisei sprinting and shooting, crouching behind bullet-torn trunks. Frank's ears hurt and he smelled his own funk, and he was itching all over with fleas. A tank rolled past him, slowly, picking its way through the forest, and he ran over to it, bent double, and banged on the side. It groaned to a stop and the hatch slammed open, a dirt-caked hand emerging to drop .45 ammo into his palms. Kenny Miura, a farm boy from Northern California, had materialized by his side, and he held his hands out, too, cupped and together, as if waiting for Halloween candy. The soldiers in the tank, who had a periscope, warned them about two Germans behind the tree at ten o'clock, and Frank and Kenny dove back behind another tree, firing in that direction as soon as the tank moved out of the way. They stayed there, wrapping a quarter-way around the tree and firing, until they were sure the two Germans were dead. They moved on, slowly, from tree to tree, firing forward, behind, to the right, to the left, talking to each other all the time: *You got it, man. You're golden.* But then, during one particularly long sprint between trees, Kenny Miura went down, and Frank reached the other tree before looking back. Kenny's arm was about twenty feet behind the rest of him, but he was twitching and alive. He was losing blood rapidly, the dark red fluid pouring over the leaves and soaking into the earth. Frank got down on his belly and crawled over to where Kenny lay moaning. He reached him and pressed his shirt against the torn, bleeding shoulder. He started to drag him over to the second tree and heard someone yell, "Watch out!" And then there was an explosion that carved out his ears, and Frank saw nothing more for five days.

When he first woke up, he saw two people hovering over him. They were in a flapping tent and the voices and artillery were loud. Then a needle in his arm, and he was out.

When he woke up again, he was in a different, larger tent, and he heard no noise outside this time, just the moans of the people around him and the cheerful chorus of male voices from a nearby radio: *"And we'll have those Japs down, on their Jap-a-knees!"* He felt an odd, all-over pain and tried to move. Then he looked down and saw that he was coated in plaster—he had casts on both legs and a body cast up to his armpits. A nurse walked by and he called out to her.

"What happened to the 36th?"

She came over to the bed, smiling at him. "The Lost Battalion," she said. "You boys saved them. No one quite knows how you did it."

"The 442nd," he said. "Did we have a lot of casualties?"

She nodded. "About eight hundred."

He felt hot and nauseous and dizzy, and faded out again. Only later, after he'd been shipped to the hospital in Rome, did he think about that figure. Eight hundred casualties. Eight hundred men sacrificed to save a battalion of two hundred.

In Rome, a doctor told him that he'd been thrown against a tree by the force of the grenade and had broken both his legs and three ribs. He had shrapnel wounds all over his arms and back, and he'd lost part of his left middle finger. But he was lucky. Kenny Miura had gotten the brunt of the explosion, and there was nothing left of him to ship home. Frank contemplated this information. The nothingness where once there was Someone. The sheer luck that had determined that *he* should survive.

Frank slept on and off for two weeks. Ate. Dictated a letter to his mother. Shifted in his body cast to try and relieve his itching back. When he was strong enough, when the fever was lower, he talked to his fellow patients. He tried to get word of others from the 442nd and learned that most of his friends were dead. At one point his body cast was removed with a saw, although he was too weak to enjoy the new freedom. At another, a doctor came in and noticed that his big toe was turning black, and that the others looked gray and dull. He instructed the nurses to prepare for immediate surgery to stop the progression of the gangrene, which was advancing up Frank's foot like an enemy army. When they lifted him off the bed and onto a litter, he saw why his back had been itching and uncomfortable: on the bed was a swarming mass of maggots, their bodies inch-long, white, and wriggling. A wave of nausea swept through him, and he didn't feel any better when the nurse told him that the maggots had been put there intentionally, to eat the dead flesh on his back. He went out again, and when he came back to, a third of his right foot was gone. He stayed there in the hospital for three more months, healing, brooding, learning to walk. Hearing by word of mouth—because it wasn't mentioned in the papers or on the radio—how the 442nd was doing.

By the time Frank was finally flown home—through Florida, then San Diego—he thought the gangrene had progressed to his heart. He felt numb and spent whole evenings just staring at the walls. His mother had just been released from Manzanar, and together they stayed in the old house in Angeles Mesa and waited out the end of the war. Frank went to the VA hospital for pain killers and physical therapy, and he was there, on August 14, 1945, in the waiting room full of maimed Nisei veterans, when the doctor burst in, beaming.

"It's over!" he shouted. "The war's over! Japan surrendered!"

The doctor was a kind man, one of the few white military men who believed that the treatment of Japanese-Americans had been unjust, and he was glad to be able to pass on such happy news. But to his utter surprise, not a single man cheered. Not a single man clapped his hands together or laughed in exaltation, or even spoke at all. Frank wanted to lower his head, but he refused to let it sink. He didn't hide the tears, though, that had been building for months. He thought of all the friends—Kenny, Steve Yamamoto, Tom Kobayashi, so many others—who didn't live to see that day. And as he saw the trembling lips, the falling tears of his fellow veterans, he knew that they were thinking of their friends, too.

The next year, when the Nisei soldiers were invited to

Washington, D.C.; when they marched around the Mall and then gathered on the ellipse in front of the White House, Frank did not go with them. He did not hear—although he read about—President Truman's words of praise and thanks for the 442nd, the most decorated unit in American history. He couldn't listen to the man who'd allowed atomic bombs to melt and disintegrate the long lost cousins and siblings, parents and grandparents, of the soldiers he now deigned to honor. Frank's mother was concerned about her son's injuries, his silent brooding, but she was ecstatic over the simple fact that he was alive. All over the country, old white men with stripes on their uniforms were pinning medals on the mothers of dead soldiers. The year before, at Union Station, she had watched the Yamamotos meet the coffin of their only son.

The Sakais slowly got used to their house again, which seemed so empty now without Kazuo and Kumiko. It had received some abuse the three years they were gone—broken windows, a little graffiti—but nothing was stolen, and Victor had kept the lawn mowed. Because it was just the two of them; because they needed the money; because the neighborhood was starting to fill, Frank sold all the land except the plot where the house stood. He opted not to sell the house itself because he wanted to stay in Angeles Mesa, thus avoiding the humiliation of the Yamamotos and the Haras, who tried to buy houses in the South Bay and Westside and were turned down by thin-lipped realtors. When his wounds were healed—at least the ones on his body—he went down to the Mesa Corner Market. Old Man Larabie welcomed him back, knowing he was doing a kindness not just by paying Frank, but by keeping him busy. And Larabie needed the help—business was booming, local people had money, and others were driving into the neighborhood every day to work at the new stores and offices on Crenshaw. Frank took classes at UCLA on the GI Bill, but after he got not one callback from his interviews for summer jobs, he quit school and started working full-time. He and Larabie worked side by side for three years, Frank making the daily trip to the wholesale fruit and vegetable market and thinking of his father every time. And when Frank informed his boss that he was planning to marry, the old man told him he was retiring and offered to sell Frank his store.

"How much you going to charge?" Frank asked.

"How much you get for your land?"

"Not much. About four thousand dollars. But we only have about fifteen hundred left."

"Well, the store is fifteen hundred dollars, then."

"It's worth a lot more than that, Mr. Larabie."

"I want you to own it, son. Can't put no price on that."

And so although the Sakais had lost so much, something, too, was given. Frank took the store and made it his own. It had always been, by accident, a gathering place, a place where women bumped into each other in front of the vegetables and traded recipes for chicken; a place where tired men bought beers at the end of the day and drank them outside in the sunset. And Frank encouraged this gathering, enabled it. He set up milk crates on the sidewalk so the men could sit as they drank, and huddle the crates together, plastic scraping on concrete, or line them up and watch the people go by. He put a little table up front, near the counter, where he placed flyers for bake sales and church socials and the benefit for the high school. Where he placed, also, three folding chairs, so the women tired from working in other people's houses could rest their swollen feet. He rewarded children who made good grades with single sticks of licorice and baseball cards (the Jackie Robinson cards he saved for those who got straight As), and gave them pocket money sometimes if they'd help him bring in the latest load of vegetables, tiny hands dragging the boxes. He even got a downtown distributor to start delivering tofu and fish, *miso* and *nori*, so that the Japanese in the neighborhood wouldn't have to go all the way to Little Tokyo (the chitterlings and black-eyed peas had been delivered since Larabie's time), even using his car sometimes to make Sunday deliveries to the farmers in Gardena. It was Frank's place. But it was Larabie's, too. Through the flowering of the business, the decline and death of Old Man Larabie, Frank never forgot that his store had a reason; that his good fortune had been someone else's gift. And because of the store, the children, the company of people—even without surgery or minor amputation—his gangrened heart was beginning to heal, the grayed flesh to beat again with color and life.

CHAPTER ELEVEN

CURTIS AND ALMA, 1961

ALTHOUGH IN the end the police weren't involved, Alma still felt no relief. It was the principal who called, informing her that Curtis had been implicated in the mess at the junior high school. A kind man who'd supported her own teaching application at Carver five years earlier, he sounded apologetic about the news: someone had broken in through a classroom window at Audubon, and had gone around spray-painting graffiti on the lockers and doors. It wasn't gang-related; it was more childish fare: "Mr. Adams is a stupid fuckhead" and "Mr. Doolan likes to touch girls booties." But the school had called the police in, and between the school officials and two officers from Southwest, they had questioned a hundred students. Finally, someone said they'd heard a couple of boys bragging, and three eighth-graders—Tyrone Cooper, Jason Buford, and Curtis Martindale—were fingered for the crime. It was clear right off that Curtis wasn't one of the main perpetrators. He'd just tagged along, both the other boys said; he hadn't broken any glass and had only used the spray can once. But that was far too much for Alma. As she and Curtis drove out of the school parking lot the day they met with the principal, she saw the two cops watching from their squad car. Although they'd been called in to help with the questioning, they were not asked to make the arrests, because the school had declined to press any charges and had opted to punish the boys itself. Now, the cops stared at Curtis from the window of their car, angry at being denied the quarry they'd been summoned to flush. And Alma was nervous—because of her son's flirtation with the law, but also because of the start of the larger romance it might imply.

Curtis was sullen on the car ride home. When Alma had first walked into the principal's office, where Curtis had been left alone to contemplate his crime, she'd whacked him on the head and yelled at him for being a fool. Now, she breathed and fumed and sucked down her words, afraid of what might come out of her mouth. Finally, though, she burst.

"What the hell did you think you were doing, Curtis? Breaking into school like that?" Her voice was touched lightly with a west Texas accent, the most obvious souvenir from her birthplace.

Curtis crossed his lanky arms, which were so angular and skinny, and with such sharp elbows, she was surprised he didn't hurt himself. "I didn't mean to, Mama. I didn't know that's what Ty and Jason was gonna do."

"Oh, you didn't *mean* to, huh? When they busted the window and went inside, you didn't mean to follow? When they stuck the spray can in your hands, you didn't mean to paint that mess on the walls?"

"I didn't know what to do."

"Well, you got two strong legs. You should have walked."

"I'm *sorry*."

"Yeah, you sorry. You sorry now, just wait till I get you home."

She was afraid for him. Afraid of the effects of his age, his friends, the neighborhood. She *taught* kids his age over at Carver Middle School, and they reminded her of the litters of pups her family had raised near Lubbock. If you didn't make them work, let them run, provide them with structure, they grew restless and bored and destructive. Most of the trouble her kids got into was of the minor variety—fist fights and truancy and shoplifting—but a few of them fell harder. Several of her former students were in prison now, a couple of them were dead. She'd seen wide-eyed kids worn down into nothing. And she'd seen other kids turn, like milk, into something sour and spoiled, the change sudden, final, complete. The change happened so much faster in the city than it ever had out on the plains. Crenshaw hadn't even *been* city when she first arrived, years before, and lived in a house next to a sprawling field of barley. But it was city now, or getting there, crowded and teeming with tension. Already two of Curtis's classmates had been arrested for robbery, and his break-in buddy, Jason, had spent six months at a boys' detention camp for assaulting another boy.

She wondered, just briefly, if she'd done the wrong thing by becoming a teacher. She was gone in the afternoons and worked on lesson plans most evenings—had she not paid enough attention to her two young boys; had they been changing in ways she hadn't noticed? But no, she thought—in the end, it was good that she was teaching. Alma was from a long line of women who had refused to accept the status to which their color and gender threatened to confine them. Her great-grandmother, Alice, was born into slavery, but after Emancipation, she had taught herself to read and opened the first school for colored children in east Georgia. Her grandmother, Eve, had whipped barehanded the whiteman she and her husband sharecropped for, who'd tried to shortchange them on their yearly payment of grains and chickens, and whose shame and fury they avoided by fleeing to Texas. And her mother, Alene, had been a member of the Negro Victory Committee during the war, which pressured the defense plants to hire black men, and which responded, when the U.S. Employment Service said black women weren't interested in defense jobs, by getting black mothers and daughters and sisters and aunts to flood the agency with applications. No, her mother's side of the family was never in question—not like her father's side—and she had to live up to it in her own small way; she had to keep helping children. Increasingly, the parents of Curtis's friends were unemployed, or barely making it, or vanishing altogether, and he needed to see adults with steady jobs. Both of his parents worked. Both had respectable jobs. He had two good examples. He was lucky.

But that didn't solve the immediate problem of what to do about him now. The school had suspended all the boys for two weeks, which created another dilemma—how to keep track of Curtis during the day. She sighed deeply, and at the next stoplight, glanced at her oldest son. He was still staring out the window, looking grim. He'd always been a thoughtful child, curious and yearning. At five, he'd quietly bombarded her with so many questions—about everything from the making of ice cream to the shape of her eyebrows to why the seasons changed in Montana—that it nearly drove her crazy. He'd always been more reserved, though, than his younger brother, who now, at five, rushed head-long and happy into every new experience. While Cory jumped up on her lap to hug and kiss her for no reason at all, not caring if other people saw, Curtis would surreptitiously take her hand or gently lean against her, and move away if anyone—including her—remarked on it. Or at least he used to. In the last couple of years, something had changed. He'd turned away from her, out toward his friends, and toward whatever appealed to them on the street. As of recently, he even looked different. He'd shot up six inches—overnight, it seemed—like one of her sunflowers when she didn't check it for a month. His body seemed stretched, all long limbs and liquid joints. And he sounded like someone else, some lower man's voice burrowing through the boy's voice she'd grown so accustomed to. She was afraid she was losing him, and she wasn't going to let him go. Not after what had happened to so many other boys she knew. Not after the way she'd lost her brother, Reese.

When they pulled into the driveway, she saw Bruce's Dodge and swore under her breath. She'd phoned her husband at work to tell him what had happened, but had specifically asked him not to come home early. Pushing Curtis in front of her, she walked through the front door, and they didn't even make it to the living room before Bruce appeared, loud and tornado-like, and knocked Curtis against the wall.

"Boy, you better give me some good kind of reason why I shouldn't beat your ass. Why you got to act so ignorant?" He was breathing hard, raising his hands and dropping them again. A big, hulking man with a slight afro and a mustache, he was still dressed in his gray work uniform, streaked with dirt and grease.

Curtis just touched the place where his shoulder had met the wall and moved past his father into the kitchen. He opened the refrigerator, pulling out a carton of milk. Bruce followed him, yanked him around, and knocked the carton out of his hand. "Don't you walk away from me when I'm talking to you." Milk splattered and bubbled all over the counter and floor, the carton landing in the corner by the trash can.

Alma came into the kitchen. "Bruce," she said. She shot him a look. He raised both hands and stepped back against the sink, conceding, crossing his arms while Alma cleaned up the milk.

After she'd thrown the sponge into the sink, she tapped the table with her index finger, indicating that Curtis should sit. He did. She circled around him, wanting both to hit him again, and to hold him and not let go until he was twenty-five, thirty, grown-up and away from the dealers and hoodlums, and relatively safe. "You're damned lucky you only got suspended," she said. Curtis nodded. "And I don't need to tell you that this is a terrible way to end junior high school. You're done in one month, Curtis. And you're going to high school in September. And what the teachers at Dorsey are going to think from your record is that you're a discipline case and a vandal."

"That's right," Bruce concurred, pointing at him. "And you disrespected your *mother*, painting up that school. Don't matter that she teaches at another school. Those teachers are people she *knows*."

Curtis flinched but didn't look up, treating his father as if he were simply an intrusive noise. Then he turned to his mother. "I'm sorry," he said, sitting up. "I know I messed up, all right? But that's not the only thing people at Dorsey gonna think about me. You know my grades are good."

Alma stopped on the other side of the table. "Well, we'll see how good they are *this* semester, since you can't make up the work you're going to miss."

Curtis rested his chin on his hand, looking miserable. "Well, I'll do extra credit, then. And I'll study real hard for my finals. I can do all that in the next two weeks, when I'm not going to school."

"That's right," Alma answered, sitting down. "And that's not all you gonna do."

And so she told him her punishment, which she'd concocted in the car on the way home. His little cousin, Jimmy, needed someone to look after him. Jimmy's mother, Bruce's sister Estelle, was working two jobs and didn't get home until late at night. And at Grandpa Martindale's house a few days before, Estelle had told her that the woman who usually took Jimmy in the afternoons was going to see her family in Georgia for a month. Jimmy's sister would be fine—she went to another woman now, who only took care of babies. But Estelle still hadn't found anyone to look after her son. He got out of kindergarten every day at 12:15, and now that Curtis was suddenly free, Alma figured, he could pick him up at school and keep an eye on him until she and Bruce got home from work. And since Cory was in the same class, he could take care of his little brother, too.

Curtis squinted in distaste. "Aw, Mama. They five years old. I don't wanna be no babysitter."

She stuck an index finger in his face. "You gonna be whatever I *tell* you to be."

"But all my boys gonna laugh at me and stuff."

"They would have laughed even harder if you'd ended up in jail."

He argued and whined and pleaded his case, but Alma remained unmoved. It was impossible to change her mind once she'd set it to something, and Curtis knew he was flailing uselessly. The news kept getting worse—he wouldn't be allowed to leave the house or see his friends the whole two weeks he was suspended. And that was all for now. He could go to his room.

With a final "Aw, man," Curtis pulled himself up from the table and left the kitchen. Alma sat. Bruce, who'd been growing increasingly tense throughout Alma's sentencing, now circled her as she had circled Curtis.

"That's a messed-up punishment," he said.

"Why?"

He ignored her, sidestepping into another topic. "It's 'cos you're never here, you know. With your teaching and your meetings and all the rest of that shit. Curtis don't get enough guidance."

If she'd been in a lighter mood, she might have smiled, for Bruce had never complained about her hours when she was working as a maid or at the paper factory. And she said nothing now about his nights out bowling or playing cards—she herself had no recreation anymore, never did things for fun, although she used to bowl, and go for walks, and take in movies with her friends. "I'm here more than you are," she responded. "It's not anybody's fault the boy's got nothing to do."

"We got to be harder, Alma. We got to take things away from him. Maybe don't let him run track in high school if he screws up again."

"He *needs* to run track. If we don't let him do that, we take away the only outlet he has."

"Fine. If you want your son to turn into a punk, then don't punish him. Just let him be." Bruce leaned back against the counter again and stared at her.

"I am punishing him," she said. "Or maybe you didn't hear what I've been saying for the last twenty minutes."

"What I heard is that you helping Estelle out, which you're probably doing just to aggravate me anyway. You making him *babysit*. Why? You trying to make a woman out of him?"

"No, I'm trying to make a man."

It wasn't her intention, but it *was* a nice perk, that Bruce was so annoyed about Jimmy. She'd never understood why Bruce and Estelle got on so badly, and once she saw them together at Grandpa Martindale's house, she knew it was Bruce's doing. That day in the back yard, Estelle kept offering him food, smiling at him, asking about his job, and Bruce had been sullen, uninterested. Alma knew he saw his sister as just another single woman with a couple of babies, which offended him in ways she never understood. But what Alma saw was a hard-working mother who was trying to do well by her children—a mother not unlike the ones who dropped her students off at school every day. Bruce had two other sisters he ignored, Nellie and Florence, who had both moved to Riverside with their families. She had never understood this, either. And when she saw the cousins together at their grandfather's house, her displeasure with her husband only deepened. Little James, the quiet, handsome boy whose eyes took up his entire face, was lonely and still, with a hurt so big it was visible. He and Cory were wonderful together, tearing around their grandfather's yard, wrestling and laughing and chasing each other. But Jimmy's eyes grew wide when he first saw Curtis. His whole face opened, and bloomed, unself-conscious as a flower. From that moment on, he was attached to Curtis's elbow as if by a string, and he started imitating his cousin's gestures—the slap of fist against palm when he was making a point, the sweep of hand over head when he was thinking.

It was a crime that the cousins lived three blocks apart and yet never spent time together. But Curtis clearly didn't think so, at first. When Alma came home the first day of his suspension, dragging in the extra chair from the garage, Cory and Jimmy were trying to build a model plane on the living room floor, two sets of hands in a festival of plastic and glue. Curtis was watching television, sulking and ignoring them. The next night, the two younger boys were stirring up ant hills with long sticks (Alma quickly put a stop to it), and Curtis was sitting on the back stairs, looking bored and grim. Both nights, he hardly spoke at dinner and ignored the worshipful glances from Jimmy, who still copied him, putting napkins on the ends of his ears of corn to keep from burning his fingers, eating all of one thing—the greens, the cornbread, the chicken-fried steak—before moving on to the next. The third evening, though, as Alma came in the front door, she heard three voices, together, like smoke rising and mingling off of three separate fires. When she entered the living room, she saw the parts of the model plane again, except this time Curtis was sitting with the two younger boys, holding the square instructions card in his hand. "No, that part goes there, little man," he said to Jimmy, and then he laughed when his cousin tried to jam the wheel on upside down. When Jimmy finally got it right, he looked up at Curtis hopefully. "That's *it!*" Curtis exclaimed, reaching over to rub his head, and he was rewarded with a huge, happy grin. Alma smiled, and, not wanting to disturb their play, she tip-toed into the kitchen.

For the rest of Curtis's suspension, the three cousins were inseparable. Curtis stopped complaining about not seeing his friends, and instead found new ways to entertain the boys. They built a small platform tree-house, crooked and holey and not strong enough to support all of them at once. They constructed another plane. They worked on their fastballs, Curtis acting as catcher as the little ones heaved pitches from a makeshift mound. Alma watched Curtis grow almost physically to become the older boy the younger boys needed. Even Cory seemed to look at him differently. The brothers had always been a bit removed from each other, unwilling or unable to span the nine years that separated them, but now Cory, seeing Curtis through the eyes of his cousin, was tagging along after his brother like a puppy.

The two weeks were over in a flash. Then Curtis went back to school, Cory back to his normal babysitter, and Jimmy to another babysitter, who Alma had found for Estelle. At first, Curtis talked of how relieved he was to have Jimmy gone, and to be able to forget about Cory. But after a couple of days of seeing his friends again, he surprised Alma by declaring them "tired." He stared at the empty space at the table where the extra chair had been, remarking that it now seemed kind of quiet. The next afternoon she came home and found Jimmy in the living room wrestling with Curtis and Cory. Her oldest son looked up at her sheepishly, tugging his shirt back into place.

"I went and got 'em," he said. "Ain't no use having 'em stay at someone else's house if they can just hang out here."

Alma smiled and went into the kitchen to start their dinner. Then she went out to the garage for the extra chair.

CHAPTER TWELVE

1994

HIS FATHER'S generation. That was the way he thought of men that age—fifty-five or sixty. They belonged to his father's generation. The phrase both less powerful than it should have been, and more powerful, too, because Lanier didn't know his own father. Hadn't laid eyes on him, in fact, since he was four. So he took his knowledge and ideas of the older men around him and tried to construct an image of his father. Most of the men he knew of that age were either bitter or resigned. They were already grown by the time the Movement came along, many of them crushed, dry and fine, like powder. The bitter ones hated all their dealings with the white world, and abused themselves or their loved ones to forget it. The resigned ones shuffled in the shadows of their lives, looking up only to see the step directly in front of them, or to find the mouth of the bottle. A few stayed optimistic, like Carrier, the finance man at Marcus Garvey, by dint of will or God or just plain foolishness. And the even rarer men who really succeeded; who made their way in the world without anger or alcohol, Lanier could only wonder at. Where was Marvin Lanier in this spectrum? The one place he knew for sure Marvin wasn't, was with them.

Robert Thomas was a man of his father's generation, and on Tuesday evening, after all the kids had gone, Lanier drove up to Hollywood to find him. Thomas, he thought, might know something about Nick Lawson and the murders. It made sense that none of Lawson's brethren had ever come forward to turn him in, but maybe what Thomas wouldn't do on his own, he'd do if somebody asked him.

Lanier wondered how Jackie was doing. He hadn't talked to her since Friday, when they'd driven around Crenshaw together. He wondered what she'd done with the weekend, whether she was as busy with school as she claimed to be; or whether she had something fun to divert herself with—a hobby, or a man. His own weekend had been uneventful. On Saturday he'd tried to get his house in order—cleaning, doing laundry, paying overdue bills— and searched his drawers and his own memory for anything related to Curtis or Frank. That night he sat in front of a rented movie that he hardly paid attention to, drank three beers, and went to sleep. On Sunday he'd gone to his friend Carl's house to watch football. Although he didn't like to admit it, he was always happy and a bit relieved when Monday came and he could go back to work, where there was always something to do and where he didn't have to think about himself. Yesterday, also, he'd asked Allen to pull up Derek Broadnax's name on the police database. Allen had discovered a string of drug convictions and petty crimes dating all the way back to 1966. Then the record stopped abruptly in 1984. There seemed to be no record of his death anywhere, so he'd either moved away or cleaned up his act.

After Lanier reached the Hollywood Station and parked his car, he walked into the receiving area, where about a dozen people, mostly Latino, were sitting quietly on green plastic chairs. He went to the front desk, cleared his throat to get the attention of the young desk sergeant—the man's name tag said "Davis"—and asked to see Captain Robert Thomas. The desk sergeant called Thomas's extension.

"Yes, sir," said Davis. "A man here to see you, sir. A James Lanier. I don't know, Captain Thomas, but . . ." Lanier saw the man's eyebrows lift, wiggle, and settle down into a troubled furrow. "Certainly, sir. I'll send him right in."

He hung up the phone, mumbling to himself, and Lanier wondered what Robert Thomas was like, to instill such fear in burly young men.

Davis gave Lanier directions to Thomas's office and Lanier walked down the hall. The station was bustling with men and women on phones, shuffling people being led along in handcuffs.

Lanier reached the door that Davis had directed him to, turned, and stopped at the doorway.

It was a small, cramped office, not much bigger than his own. The desk was large and wooden, faced by two nondescript metal chairs. Behind it sat a middle-aged black man. He was on the phone and he waved Lanier in. Lanier sat in a chair and set his briefcase down, and while the older man took notes on a pad of yellow paper, Lanier tried quietly to study him. Robert Thomas, he knew, was in his late fifties, but he looked about ten years older. The lines on his face were long and deep. His large, round eyes were baggy and pink-tinged. His hair was almost completely white, which made his rich brown skin look darker. Even sitting he was obviously tall—his chair seemed entirely too small for him—but his movements were slow and seemed to take great effort. Lanier wondered if he'd ever run across Thomas in Crenshaw. His voice on the phone was strong and stern, business-like, not-quite-pleasant. When he hung up, though, he stood, held his hand out across the table, and offered a friendly smile. "Bob Thomas," he said. "You must be James Lanier."

Lanier shook his hand—Thomas's grip was firm and strong. "Yes," he answered. "Sorry to barge in on you like this, but after our conversation last week, I figured I'd have to show up in person to convince you my intentions were good."

Thomas waved him off and sat down. "No problem. *I'm* sorry. You get the strangest calls sometimes, people trying to get information for articles, college term papers, Lord knows what else. But then I guess I should expect it, considering how strange the job is." He pointed at the phone. "That call was about a complaint we have, a guy taking deposits for a rental. He told people he needed a twenty-five-dollar deposit in order to run a credit check, and then they never heard back from him again. Turns out he didn't own the place. He'd just broken in and he was using the deposit money for crack. What a bunch of gutter slime we have to deal with these days. You civilians out there don't know." He shook his head, and Lanier said nothing. "Anyway, I asked about you a couple of days ago," Thomas continued, "when I talked to Captain Ray at Southwest. He told me his division deals with your office and he had a lot of nice things to say."

Lanier nodded. "He's a good man. He volunteers for us. But how do you know him? He didn't come to Southwest until a couple of years ago."

Thomas picked up a mug of coffee; it left a luminous ring on his desk. "We were at Rampart together for about ten years. That was the one pit stop I made between Southwest and Hollywood."

"How long were you at Southwest?"

"About seven years. I started there in '59, right out of the Academy. It was called University then." A fly buzzed around his head and he batted at it absently. "It was a rough seven years, though, I'll tell you that. I can't say I was sorry to be transferred."

Lanier nodded. "It must have been tough, especially back then."

"It was," Thomas answered, but he was watching the fly, which flew straight up, bounced off the ceiling, and circled around the room.

Lanier paused for a second. "And you didn't have a choice but to work at Southwest, did you? Didn't all black officers have to work in black neighborhoods?"

"Yep," Thomas said. "And that area, as you know, was already pretty much black by the sixties. My first few years on the job, there was no way a white man could be arrested by a black man. Or even *work* with one, for that matter—we were all paired off together, you know." He pushed his chair back and pointed to a framed picture on the wall behind him. It was a black-and-white photograph, tinged yellow by age. In it, two black officers, in cap and uniform, were standing in front of an old-time, box-like police car. "This is me," Thomas said, "back in 1964. And this here's my partner, Oliver Paxton."

Lanier stood up and leaned across the desk to get a better view. In the photograph, Thomas's face looked much the same as it did now—except it had no lines and his hair was still black. His body, however, was tight, lean, and powerful. The man beside him was slightly smaller, and fairer-skinned. Thomas's features were not totally discernible in the picture's bad light, but Paxton's were clear—the bright eyes, the high cheeks, the large square jaw. Oliver Paxton was smiling at the camera. Robert Thomas was not.

"That's a great picture," said Lanier, sitting down again, and as soon as his pants made contact with his chair, he knew he'd seen Thomas in Crenshaw. When or where, he couldn't recall. But the face—he'd seen that face, he'd seen this man walking around the neighborhood. He wasn't sure the memory was good.

Thomas nodded and threw back the rest of his coffee. "Ollie's wife took it in front of the station one morning. The department wasn't about to pay, you know, for some picture of its nigger cops."

Lanier looked at him. The older man's words were bitter, but the tone of the voice was calm. "Y'all went through a lot," he said.

Thomas half-smiled. "We sure did. Had to work ten times as hard as the white cops to get any kind of respect. And then the recognition was grudging, you know, like we were a necessary evil. I tell you, there were a lot of racist cops back then, but on the other hand, some of the first few black men on the force didn't do much to change their views. Some of those Negroes were so ignorant I don't know how they got through the Academy. They came from nothing, you know, and acted like it. Made it real hard on the rest of us." Thomas took a sip of his coffee. He'd thought he was escaping them, blacks like them, by joining the department. When his father—his respectable, college-educated father—moved out to Los Angeles and couldn't get a machinist's job, the Thomases had to live in a small apartment off of Central, among the Southern migrants they found course and uncultured. There they stayed for all of Robert's childhood, his father dazed by the one-two punch of Jim Crow and the Depression, piecing together odd lawn and rail-laying jobs to keep food on the table. And Robert, rather than hating the white men who were too offended by his father's skills to hire him at the work he was trained in, had instead despised the Southern masses with whom his family was lumped together. He swore that some of the kids he'd grown up around were the same ones he saw later, on the street.

Lanier heard what he said, as well as the bitterness behind it, and tried not to judge him. This man had gone through things, he reminded himself, that he could only imagine. He'd been a pioneer, Jacques Cousteau, first man on the moon. A success who'd had to twist himself to get as far as he did, like so many members of his father's generation.

"This is my wife," Thomas continued, pointing at a picture of a proper-looking woman who was so fair-skinned that Lanier had to look twice to confirm she was black. "And these are my children. Robert Jr. is an entertainment lawyer and Cassie is in international development." Thomas couldn't help but smile. He was proud of his wife, one of the first black women to get a graduate degree from Pepperdine; and of his children, who never felt constrained by their color. When they'd first moved into their all-white neighborhood years before, none of the other children would play with them. But he hadn't played with the local children, either, when he was growing up. They were unkempt and wild, his parents thought, the products of adults who were loud and whiskey-soaked. Sometimes, when he watched the children play with the crude wooden toys that their fathers had fashioned; or heard their shouts during stickball; or watched them chase each other across his front lawn, he regretted the division of the living room window, and wondered what it would be like to be out there with the children, who still carried Alabama, Georgia, Mississippi, Texas, in the lilt of their beautiful voices. But this wondering only lasted a second.

"Nice," Lanier said politely, still looking at the picture. Then, "What happened to your partner? Is he still on the job?"

Thomas sat back in his chair. He picked up his mug and set it down again. "No. He quit and moved back east somewhere. I think he became a schoolteacher."

The fly settled on Lanier's left knee. He let it sit there for a moment before shooing it away. "Second career," he said. "He must have left pretty young."

"I think he was in his twenties. It was some time in '66 or '67."

"After Watts."

Thomas nodded. "After Watts."

Lanier tried not to look too eager. "Do you think that had anything to do with it?"

Thomas shrugged. "Who knows? It could have. That was a pretty bad time, you know. Worse than '92 'cos it was such a surprise."

"Was it?"

"It was to me. Although I guess it shouldn't have been. Ollie said he'd been expecting it for years. But it was rough, all right." He leaned forward. "That's what you're here about, right? Something related to Watts."

Lanier nodded. "There's an incident I'm trying to look into. I thought you might know something about it."

"There were a lot of incidents during the riots. What makes you think I would know about this one?"

Lanier leaned forward a bit more. "Because people did. Cops too. But not a lot of them are going to want to talk."

"What's the story?"

Lanier took a manila folder out of his briefcase and placed it on the desk. "You ever heard of Frank Sakai?"

Thomas thought for a moment. "No."

"He owned a little store on Bryant, off of Crenshaw." He opened his folder and took out a photograph of the store in its present condition. "This is what it looks like now—but the damage is from '92."

Thomas took the photograph. He wrinkled his brow and then nodded. "I remember now," he said. "The Jap with the grocery store. What happened, did somebody kill him?"

Lanier struggled to keep his face impassive. "No, but someone *did* kill four black boys. Locked them in the freezer. Two of them worked there in the store and the other two were younger. They weren't found until everything was over."

"Who found them?"

"The owner. And maybe one of the other employees."

"And you think a cop was involved?"

Lanier nodded. He took another picture out of his folder, one he'd gotten from Allen, and handed it across the desk to Thomas. "I think it was this guy. Nick Lawson." Lanier hated to look at Lawson, even through the medium of photography. The face was older, filled out from when he had known him, but the particulars were the same—the thin nose, tight lipless mouth, the brows that came together in a flat and angry V. Lawson must have been in his fifties in this picture, but he still had the crew cut he'd worn when Lanier had spent his days avoiding him; had watched him taunt and hassle his friends.

Thomas's eyebrows shot up, and after a moment he dropped the picture as if it would burn him. "I know who Nick Lawson is. What makes you think he had anything to do with it?"

"He hated black people. Used to rough folks up pretty good. And he was shot right after the uprising—probably because of what happened at the store."

Thomas stood up and walked around his desk. "What makes you think the Jap didn't do it?"

Lanier collected himself for a moment before he replied. "It wouldn't make sense. He loved those kids."

"What about the other employee? You said one of them was there when they found them? Maybe they caught him stealing or something. People take advantage, you know. You should have seen all the looting after the earthquake."

"I doubt it. The boys who were killed were his buddies. The people in the neighborhood—the ones who knew about the killings—were pretty much sure it was Lawson. He had a history of going in there and, well, making his presence felt."

Thomas began to pace, looking thoughtful. He lifted a hand and stroked his billy club, palm around the base of it, thumb lightly brushing the tip. "Well, he did have a heavy hand. Everybody knew that. And you're right. He was no friend of black folks."

Lanier tightened his hold on the folder. "Did you ever hear him brag about what he did during the uprising?"

Thomas shook his head, walked behind his desk, and sat down again. "No. But it wasn't like we were friends. The most we ever did was nod at each other. And he wasn't about to tell me about murdering someone. What I heard about his beating on folks I heard from other people." He paused. "So what are you up to, anyway? What are you trying to accomplish?"

"I'm trying to prove he did it. If it's true, I want to bring charges against him."

Thomas was silent for a moment. "It's going to be hard, you know. Maybe impossible. Even if he did do it, and talk about it, no one in their right mind is likely to rat out another cop." He looked at Lanier. "I wouldn't."

Lanier met his eyes, and was suddenly frightened.

Now Thomas gave him a look that was somewhere between sympathy and warning. "You watch yourself, son," he said.

Tuesday was an alone night, the one night a week that Jackie and Laura always spent apart. Jackie worked on a brief all afternoon and didn't think of her girlfriend until seven, when her stomach began to grumble. She resisted breaking the agreement and calling Laura, but Laura wouldn't be there anyway—she was spending the evening with her friend Kristine, a fellow Stanford grad who was visiting from out of town.

Jackie had just leaned back in her chair, pondering what she could make for dinner, when the phone rang. She picked it up and heard the swoosh of traffic in the background. Then Lanier's voice: "Hey, Jackie, what's up?"

"Lanier? Hi. Where are you?"

"I'm at a gas station down the block from the Hollywood Station. I just talked to Robert Thomas, and I was going to call you tonight anyway, but since I'm kind of in your neighborhood, I thought I'd call from here and see what you were up to."

"I'm just doing some work," she said. "I've got an assignment due tomorrow."

"Oh," Lanier replied, and in the brief silence that followed, Jackie heard the moving traffic again. "Well, then I guess you wouldn't want to grab a bite to eat."

Jackie hesitated. They'd never done something on the spur of the moment like this; it had always been orchestrated, planned, contained. But what the hell—she could meet Lanier for dinner. It would solve her food problem, she needed a break, and she was curious about what he had found. "Actually, I'd love to."

"Great," said Lanier. "Where should we go? I don't know your neighborhood very well."

Jackie felt a blip of panic travel through her chest. Where

could they go? She couldn't take him to one of her usual dinner spots, like the French Market Place or Stan's; they were either crawling with gay people or with straight people she knew, who would be too friendly to her and ask after Laura. She suggested an Italian place, which Lanier vetoed, and then a Thai place, which he agreed to. She threw on some jeans and a long-sleeve shirt, and drove over to the restaurant.

They were meeting at Thai Cuisine, a small free-standing building on Fairfax where Jackie sometimes went with Laura. Across from it was the Farmers' Market and the square white monstrosity of CBS Studios, which always looked to Jackie like a gigantic piece of tofu. The studio was the only thing Jackie knew of that hadn't lost its power during the earthquake. In the early morning of January 17, after the first jolt of the quake had tossed Jackie clear from her bed and she'd crouched beneath her desk, praying and bargaining, as the house bucked and rolled, she'd run straight outside as soon as the ground stopped moving. There, for the first time in all her years in L.A., she saw stars spread out all over the sky. There were millions of them, trillions, and she couldn't believe that they had always been there, waiting to make themselves visible. She looked around then and saw people running into the street, screaming; people holding each other; people heading instinctively to their cars and driving—anywhere. She looked to the left to see the reassuring lights of the Hollywood Hills, but there was nothing but a huge black hulking emptiness. The hundreds of houses, the hills themselves, might never have been there at all. This, more than anything—more than the screaming people, the exploding transformer boxes, the fire alarms, the still-bucking ground—made her realize the magnitude of what was happening. She didn't know yet about the freeways falling down; about the collapsing apartment building in Northridge; about the hundreds and thousands of houses and buildings that were half or completely destroyed. Her neighborhood, with its old solid houses, was fine. But she took off anyway, for Laura's house, seeing more people crying, running, screaming. She passed by someone with a radio and heard snippets of a DJ's voice—*Oh, God,* he said, *it's starting again. Hold on. Oh my God, oh my God*—and imagined him trapped in the top of a thin skyscraper, swaying back and forth above his devastated city. When she got to Laura's house and found her outside, they just stood there on the street and held each other. And it was as they walked back to Jackie's house to get her wallet and phone that Jackie looked over and saw that the CBS studios were still lit up, as if nothing had happened at all.

After Jackie had clubbed and locked her car, she went inside and found Lanier sitting at one of the benches by the door. "Thanks for sacrificing some of your study time," he said, standing. He'd wondered, at the phone booth, what exactly in hell he was doing. And now he was surprised by the simple pleasure he felt at seeing this woman he hardly knew.

"It wasn't a sacrifice, believe me. Thank *you* for saving me from it."

The waitress seated them at a small table in the back. All the tables were covered with white tablecloths and topped with candles; the lights were dim and the music was low. They ordered their dinner—Pad Thai, yellow curry with chicken, spring rolls, sticky rice—and then looked at each other for a moment, as if surprised to find themselves at the table together. All things being equal, Jackie thought, she could have done worse for a dinner date.

They filled each other in on the minutiae of their days—classes, meetings, drives against traffic. Finally, Lanier took a big gulp of the pint of beer that had just arrived, put it down, and looked at the five oval spots his fingers had left on the frosted glass. "So Bob Thomas was pretty interesting," he said.

"Helpful?" Jackie asked. "Or just interesting?"

"Both, I guess, but not because he wanted to be. I'm sure he knows more than he's telling. He was friendly enough, but it seemed like he was holding something back. He knew, though, that Lawson used to beat people."

Jackie nodded, taking a sip of her beer. "Maybe they're friends," she said. "Maybe he's protecting him."

"That's a good possibility." Then he related everything about his visit, and Jackie just listened, chewing slowly on the spring rolls that were placed in front of them. "So I think another thing to do," he said, "is find his old partner, Oliver Paxton. Since he left the force, I'd assume he's not as true-blue as Thomas."

In another few minutes the waitress came again, bearing a platter of food. They both watched silently as she set down the Pad Thai, the curry, the rice. Then she left, and Jackie reached first for the rice, spooning two big clumps onto her plate.

"Anything new on your end?" Lanier asked as he served himself some food.

"Not really. I went through some old family pictures over the weekend, but there wasn't anything interesting. What I *should* do is go through my aunt's box of stuff."

Lanier looked up, fork suspended halfway to his mouth. "What box of stuff?"

She met his eyes; she'd forgotten how much he didn't know. "This is how this all got started, for me. After my grandfather died, my aunt found an old boot box full of papers, including the will—the one that mentioned Curtis. It was written some time in the sixties."

"Which reminds me," said Lanier. "What did Frank leave Curtis, anyway?"

"I can't believe I never told you this. The store."

"What?"

"The *store*. And it was sold, you know, but he put the money away in his closet. Thirty-eight grand in cash."

"In his *closet*?"

"Yeah. My aunt found it in another box, right behind the boot box. And that's why I started looking for Curtis."

Lanier picked up his fork again. "Jesus. What else was in the box—the other one?"

Jackie shrugged. "I don't know. I haven't seen it. Obituaries, I think. Articles. Various letters and notes. And a bunch of old pictures, Lois said. I'm going to see it pretty soon—he left me the box. That and, believe it or not, a bowling ball."

Lanier hit the table lightly. "A bowling ball. The Holiday Bowl. Of course."

"The Holiday Bowl—in one of the pictures that I have, my grandfather's wearing a T-shirt from there."

"It was a big hang-out place when I was little. Still is. I can't believe I haven't thought of it before. Your grandpa used to go down there a lot. Maybe some of his friends still go."

"You think I should check it out?"

"Absolutely. You never know what those old-timers might remember. They might even know what happened to Derek Broadnax. And his sister." He related then what he'd found out from Allen, his friend in the department.

"Any chance that either of them went to the funeral?" Jackie asked. "We got a bunch of business cards from people."

Lanier pointed at her, happily. "Yeah."

They ate quickly, almost breathlessly. Finally, Lanier stabbed a shrimp with his fork, ate it, and looked back up at Jackie. "So what happened to your family after '65, anyway? I know they moved to Gardena, but . . . I mean, two generations later there's a lawyer in the family. That's quite a step up from a shopkeeper and a domestic."

Jackie smiled. "Some people wouldn't think so."

"This is true."

Jackie gave a brief summary of her family's history, or what she knew of it: how Frank stayed close to the food business for another few years, and then trained to become an electrician. She told him about her parents being doctors; her aunt Lois and Ted; the small apartment where Frank had spent his last years.

Lanier, in turn, told Jackie the story of his own grandparents—how they'd moved the family from Louisiana because of the war jobs, his grandfather entering an apprentice mechanics' program at Douglas Aircraft in Santa Monica.

"He used to work the night shift," explained Lanier, "and then sleep on the beach during the day. He always said he didn't mind it—the lifeguards were all women, 'cos the men had all been drafted." His mother and uncle Bruce had been grown then, he said, and his aunts Nellie and Florence little girls. The family was lucky, though—his grandfather kept his job at Douglas Aircraft even after the war, and bought the house in Carson where his mother still lived.

"What about your father's side of the family?" Jackie asked.

Lanier shrugged and looked her square in the eye. "I don't

know. I don't know much about him. All I know is that he was from Mississippi, and that my mama met him when she was serving food in the cafeteria at the VA hospital. He stuck around long enough for me and my sister to be born, but then he left before my sister's first birthday."

Jackie didn't know what to say, so she didn't say anything. Lanier's face changed, and she noticed his scar again, the clean, dark line that marred his cheekbone.

"I don't hardly remember him," he continued, "but I do remember that he was cold, and not real affectionate with us. Our mama said it was because of what had happened in Korea." The waitress passed by and Lanier waited until she was gone. "He was a medic, and he worked in this medical facility a few miles off the front line. He was the only black man there except for the wounded soldiers who came through. Anyway, one day this middle-aged Korean guy's brought in, a civilian, just a peasant who'd been accidentally shot. Marvin, my father, worked on him, but he died pretty quick. And when Marvin left the table, he saw this little girl standing at the doorway, just staring at the dead man. Turned out it was her father." He scraped his fork against the plate and furrowed his brow. "Her mother had been killed by a land mine a couple months before. She had no other people and they didn't know what to do with her, so my father took her in." He paused. "Eight-year-old girl. No one in the camp would talk to him, you understand, and he needed some company. He loved that girl. He ate and breathed for her. He spoke some Korean and she knew a little English, so they'd sit up talking about her old farm or America or whatever. She'd seen so much, you know—she'd seen her whole family die. He was going to adopt her and bring her back to the States." He looked at Jackie, and then away again. She wanted to take a drink, but was afraid to move. "Anyway, about three months after she came, there was a real bad battle nearby and a lot of casualties were brought in. My father didn't get back to his tent for two or three days. And when he finally got back there, the little girl's throat had been cut. She was naked, and she'd been raped, and someone had carved 'nigger whore' into her stomach." Jackie bit her lip, and Lanier made a fist on the table. "My father lost it. He didn't report what happened, because he knew it'd be pinned on him; he just took her out and buried her. And when enough time had passed for people to forget the girl—they thought she'd just vanished into the hills—he started to take his revenge. One night he caught one of the soldiers who'd called him nigger to his face and slit his throat in the outhouse. A couple weeks later, he strangled one of the officers in his bed. A few weeks after that, he killed a medic who he knew had been letting Koreans die. The whole camp was up in arms, you know, but they thought it was a North Korean who was doing it, sneaking in from outside. Eight white men, my father killed. One for every year of the little girl's life. There were people who might have suspected, but he never got caught. And according to my mother, after what happened there, after what they did to that little girl, he never let himself care about anything again. I don't think he gave a shit about us, or my mama either. She raised us by herself, on a maid's salary."

Jackie still didn't know what to say. Everyone, it seemed, had something awful in their lives—some death or misfortune that shaped them. But she had nothing; her life had been flat and tex- tureless as a starched white sheet. And while she'd always consid- ered herself lucky to be so blessed, now she felt that she was some- how not real. She couldn't bring herself to comment on what Lanier had just told her, so she tried to take their thoughts in another direction.

"So you have a sister?"

Lanier looked at her in disbelief. He'd told her about his fam- ily and this was her response? But he managed to answer her, in a much colder voice than before. "Alice. She's three years younger than me. She manages a Sears out in Riverside County." He looked away, and Jackie followed suit. In the silence that followed, Jackie became aware of the conversation at the table just behind them, of the rustle of a skirt as the waitress walked by. She looked up at Lanier again and tried to pull herself together. "Lanier," she said. "James." He raised his eyes. "I'm sorry about your dad." She didn't know if this was the appropriate thing to say about a man who'd killed eight people, but Lanier smiled. His anger faded. He was back with her again.

"Thanks." And as they sat there looking at each other, silently, Jackie felt something shift. She didn't have time to ponder this, though, because just then, from behind her, she heard Laura's voice.

She spun around and saw Laura turn the corner with Kristine, both of them a step behind the waitress. Laura spotted her right away. Jackie watched Laura take in the scene; watched confusion fill her face. The waitress led the two women past the table, but they stopped for a moment, and Jackie and Kristine exchanged hellos. Then Kristine went on to their table, and Laura stood there, looking at Jackie, her lips pressed tightly together. "Hi," Laura said. "What are you doing here?"

Jackie saw the red spots of anger rising in Laura's cheeks, and it occurred to her how intimate this scene must have looked. But Laura knew—Jackie knew she knew—that she had no reason to worry.

"Laura," she said, before the silence got too uncomfortable, "this is James Lanier. He works at the Marcus Garvey Community Center down in the Crenshaw district. James, this is my friend Laura." She was afraid, briefly, that Laura would jump in here and make a crack about just what kind of friend she was. Laura didn't, though. She nodded at Lanier without speaking to him; her attention was all on Jackie.

"I called you a little while ago," she said. "I thought you were staying in tonight."

The words were accusatory. Out of the corner of her eye, Jackie saw Lanier glance up at Laura and then look down at his plate. "I was," she replied. She tried to look her girlfriend in the eye and assure her that there was nothing to worry about, but she knew it was precisely this, the consciousness of her effort, that made it appear like she was lying. "I was just sitting there reading, when James called. He was in the neighborhood on business, so . . ." She was just digging herself in deeper. "Anyway, I'll be home in a little bit. Can I call you later?"

Laura pressed her lips together. "I won't be home. Kristine and I are going to a movie after this, and then we might meet Marie for a drink. So who knows what time I'll be back."

"Well, then, do you want to call me when you get in?"

"Oh, I wouldn't want to bother you. I'm sure you'll be busy."

They just looked at each other, Jackie half-annoyed and half-amused at Laura's jealousy. Finally, she said, "All right. I'll talk to you soon."

"Bye," Laura threw at her, hostilely, and then she went on to her table. Jackie watched her sit down and lean toward her friend; watched Kristine look over at her and Lanier, then turn back to Laura and whisper. She was afraid to look at Lanier, so she stared at her fork as it pushed noodles around on her plate.

But Lanier's mind wasn't totally on her. He felt slashed open by what he'd said about his father. He so rarely thought of him, was only sometimes aware of a series of vague half-images from a time that was almost pre-memory. A pair of large hands hoisting him over a shoulder. The faint hint of bitter smell from the thick, conked hair. The face he couldn't conjure, but he remembered the way it clouded over, the way a man's deep yelling shook the house. The enveloping, stifling silence when he was finally gone for good. "She seems pretty attached to you," he finally said, cautiously. He wasn't sure what he'd just seen.

Jackie looked at him and saw the bewilderment, and something else, in his eyes, and wondered how much he suspected. "Yeah, well, she's pretty intense."

Their plates were empty, and the air had shifted again; they got the bill and paid up quickly. They walked out of the restaurant together, and when they reached Jackie's car, they just stood there, not knowing what to say. Finally, wincing at the awkwardness of the gesture, Jackie stuck out her hand. Lanier smiled a bit and shook it. They agreed to talk in a couple of days, and Jackie suggested that they meet over the weekend—after she got in touch with Lois—so she could show him the contents of the box.

Less than an hour later, just as Jackie was finally losing herself in the reading she'd been trying to do all night, the phone rang and made her jump off her chair.

"What the hell was that all about?" Laura demanded without saying hello.

"It wasn't a date, Laura."

"Well, I know that," said Laura, although Jackie wasn't convinced that she did. "But who was he, and what were you talking about? Seems like you were pretty comfortable with this person, and I don't even know who the hell he is. It would be nice, *honey*, if you could let me in on a little of your life."

Jackie sat down in her desk chair, spun around, and watched the phone cord wrap around her ankles. "I'm sorry. You're right. He's just . . . We're both . . . I mean . . . He's from the Crenshaw district, where my mom and Lois used to live, and he's helping me find someone who worked for my grandfather."

"What are you talking about? What's going on?"

Spinning herself around again, Jackie gave Laura a brief, selective summary of the family's history in Crenshaw. She mentioned the store and the kids who used to frequent it, and the family's move to Gardena. She told Laura that her grandfather had willed some money to one of the kids. Listening to herself cut, edit, censor, distort, she wondered why she wasn't telling the truth. There were plenty of things she didn't share with her girlfriend, but those were just silences, acts of omission. This was a flat-out lie. Even the summary she was giving, though, she began to regret. What little she revealed to Laura now was already too much.

"Why didn't you tell me about this?" Laura demanded. "Why'd you keep it a secret? Now I know why you've been so preoccupied the last couple of weeks, and I thought . . . well, you can imagine what I thought. I would have been understanding, you know. It's great that you're doing this, but why don't you ever share things with me?"

Jackie thought, *this is why*, but what she said was, "I'm sorry." Laura was appeased for now, and after a few more minutes of catch-up and chatter, they said their goodnights and hung up. Jackie turned to the clock: it said 10:40. She hoped that James had made it home safely.

CHAPTER THIRTEEN

FRANK AND CURTIS, 1963

FRANK WAS sitting behind the cash register when he heard the noise at the back door. It was late afternoon, about five o'clock; Victor would appear in a minute for their afternoon smoke. The noise was light and clattering, as if a sudden gust of wind had blown the screen door against the frame. He lowered the paper he'd been reading, listened for a moment, and then looked back at the *Times*. But then he heard it again, a light *bang bang bang,* someone appealing very gently. He put his paper down and walked to the back door, thinking about the new shipment of ice cream that sat in the back freezer, which he needed to move to the smaller freezer out on the floor.

It was the blood he saw first, a cascade of red against the bright white shirt, wide as a tucked-in napkin. The boy was resting his head on his forearm, which was pressed flat against the door frame, and when Frank approached, he pulled his head up to reveal the smashed face. The jaw was huge and purple, like some overripe fruit. The upper lip was split open and his cheek was cut. One eye was swollen, swirled in purple, and there was blood everywhere, obscuring his face.

"Curtis!" Frank managed. "My God, what happened to you?"

He pushed the screen door open and pulled the boy in quickly, as if the attacker might still be out in the alley. He took him into the office, sat him down on the couch, and retrieved towels, ice, a basin. The boy who was working that day, David, was out at the moment, delivering groceries to a neighborhood widow, and Frank was glad for this; his immediate instinct was to keep Curtis hidden.

He dropped ice into a plastic bag and wrapped the whole bundle in a towel. He filled the basin with warm soapy water. Then he made the boy strip off his shirt, so he could determine that the dark caked blood had come from his nose and mouth and not from a hidden wound on his neck or chest. Frank knelt before the boy, mumbling to himself, dipping a cloth into the basin and dabbing the boy's cheeks and forehead. By the time he finished, the liquid in the basin was as pink as cherry smash, each touch of the cloth sending swirls of red through the water. Frank examined the cleaned face now—the black eye, the cut cheek, the bruised but not broken jaw, a few abrasions to the forehead and nose. There were other, not visible wounds—the bump on the back of the boy's head, the bruised leg Frank only knew about because of the way the boy had limped. Looking at Curtis's face, he thought of his father, lying sideways, bruised and beaten on the gurney. He felt that old anger fuse with this newer one and coil through him, twisting and twitching.

"Who did this to you?" he asked finally, after giving Curtis the cold pack to hold against his jaw. "If their parents don't punish them good for this, I'm . . ."

"Nobody," said Curtis.

"What do you mean, nobody?" He thought of the flat-eyed young men who huddled together on corners and in alleys, beckoning people over to exchange bags for money, or keeping them at a distance with their glares. He thought of the knife the boy always carried, and was thankful he hadn't used it.

"I mean nobody, all right? It's no big deal." His voice was getting fluttery and high.

Frank, who'd been leaning in close to the boy, now sat back on his feet. He stood, walked over to the desk, and hit the side of the bookcase, hard. Several books fell off the shelves, and bills and papers fluttered down to the floor. He bit his lip, clenched and unclenched his fists, and wondered if he and Victor still had it in them to take on a group of punks. He leaned in toward the boy and beckoned softly: "Come on, Curtis. Tell me what happened."

"They kicked me in the back of the *head*, man," he said, voice quivering. "And in my thigh, and in my face. And they punched me a couple times, and I was just scared they were gonna kill me. I don't know why they were trying to mess me up like that, I wasn't doin nothing, we were just hanging out." With his other hand, he covered his eyes, and Frank heard the low, pained sobs. Frank felt like a fist had plunged through his chest and thrust its nails into his heart. He sat on the couch and put his arms around the boy, who collapsed against him, crying. They stayed like that for several minutes.

Finally, Frank spoke again. "We have to call your mother."

Curtis shook his head no against Frank's chest. "She'll do something stupid. She'll start a damn protest or something and get me into worse trouble."

Frank was torn. Curtis was right about his mother—there was no way she'd sit still on this. And if she *did* go after the punks who'd done this, or after their parents, they'd do nothing but laugh—or worse, take their displeasure out on Curtis. "Well, what do you want to do?" he asked. "You can stay here until you feel a bit better. But you've got to go home sometime."

"I just wanna lie down for a while," Curtis said. "And I don't wanna go home until my mama's asleep. Can you tell her I'm working late?"

"She's going to see your face sometime. It's not going to be much better tomorrow."

"I just can't talk to her now. Not yet. All right? You go on back out to the store, Mr. Sakai. I'm sorry to be bothering you like this."

Frank stood looking for a moment while the boy lay down. Then he reached behind the door, pulled out a clean white shirt, and placed it on the arm of the couch. Finally, he went back out to the store, shutting the door behind him.

The boy was asking him to lie. He needed Frank to back him up with Alma, to not call her, to pretend he didn't know what had happened. It was a strange position to be in, especially since he'd given Curtis the job in the first place as a favor to his mother. Alma had been concerned about Curtis, and had told Frank about the suspension during his final year in junior high, about the more complicated messes his friends had gotten into. She'd been less worried in the last year or so, since he'd started watching his brother and cousin, but she still thought he needed structure, useful things to fill his time, and to keep him away from the flat-eyed boys, who were aging fast and growing in number. Curtis liked Frank, it was obvious; he always brightened on seeing him and started dropping by the store on his own. So it was only a matter of time before Alma asked Frank if he needed another boy to help out. And he did, since Akira Matsumoto was gone, starting college at UCLA.

This job was for Alma, a favor to her. But it was also true that Frank had always kept an eye on the boy from afar; had worried over his slips and rejoiced at his triumphs. By having Curtis work there, he could see him more often. Curtis worked three days a week, and David three, and Derek Broadnax two, overlapping one day with each of the others. Frank loved being at the store, preferred it to his house, his tense, accusing wife and older daughter. Sometimes, on Sundays, he and Victor would collect all the boys—along with Lois if she was willing, and Kenji Hirano if it was one of his good days—and take them to a Dodgers game, or bowling, or fishing up in Baldwin Hills.

Curtis had been there for six months now, and was already the best worker that Frank had ever had. Like his mother, the boy was totally focused. She was right about him—he needed things to do. So Frank kept him busy—unloading shipments, stocking shelves, cleaning the freezer, running the register. He even started showing him how to keep books, the invisible skill that kept a business afloat.

Frank had not given him, though, the gift he had for people. At fifteen, Curtis Martindale was a boy who appealed to everyone. Men liked him because he was about to become one of them—funny, cocky, and roughnecked, but too young to be a threat. Women liked him because he was considerate, a listener, a well-reared boy, but with something sly and flirtatious in his manner. Boys liked him because he was good at getting over with adults but still knew the latest baseball scores and dance steps. Girls loved him because of his sleepy eyes, his big, articulate hands, his taut body, which was not much bigger than their own. They would follow him through the aisles of the store, throwing their sass, and Frank would tease him, asking how he ever got anything done. And he had the magic with children, who watched him, big-eyed and admiring, until he flashed them his radiant smile. His cousin Jimmy worshipped him, but every child might have been his cousin, his nephew, his niece. A couple of times he'd caught kids stealing things—candy or yo-yo's or gum—and he'd always coax them gently to put the things back and then go apologize to Mr. Sakai.

Frank loved the boy, detecting in him both the drive and caring of his mother, but also a humor, an ease that she lacked. He saw how she looked at her son with worry, and with a love so intense it was almost crushing. And he saw how the boy wanted so much to please her, and how impossible she was to live up to. He sympathized with both of them, but was glad that Curtis had come to him when he was hurt. There was no question he'd be loyal to the boy.

When David returned, Frank told him Curtis was lying down in the office because he didn't feel well. Then he asked David to watch the store for a while, and to tell Victor he would be right back.

Frank walked over to Crenshaw, then paced the street for twenty minutes. He patrolled one side of the boulevard, crossed, walked back down the other. Then he turned onto Rodeo, moving toward the still-high sun. He wondered if he'd gotten his timing wrong, but then he saw it—the squad car, inching down Rodeo, looking for trouble and usually finding it.

Frank stepped off the curb, flagging the squad car down. It slowed, stopped, and a *hakujin* got out. It was the wrong one, though. Not the friendly Irishman who always waved at him, who'd caught the perpetrators the one time the store had been robbed, but the other one. The green-eyed blonde who came into the store sometimes and knocked things off the shelves. Who only sometimes rode with his partner, which only sometimes curtailed his actions. Who told him leeringly how nice his daughters looked.

The cop recognized him. Stomach shaking, fully aware that it was probably useless, Frank waved him over. Lawson, looking bored, sauntered up onto the sidewalk. "What's the problem, grocery man?"

Frank looked up at him and met the hollow eyes. *Hakujin* in uniform always reminded him of Europe and the war. "I want to report an assault," he said. "A boy named Curtis Martindale was beaten up by some other boys."

Lawson looked at him, barely interested. "What do *you* care, grocery man? He's just a little nigger punk."

Frank glared. "I know him. He works for me."

The cop shrugged. "So? What do you want from me? Worker's comp?" He laughed.

Frank stepped up to him, felt the cop's bitter breath on his forehead. "Well, why don't you do something about it? Instead of driving around doing nothing all day."

The cop looked down over his long, slender nose. Then he started to laugh mirthlessly, wrinkles creasing the skin around his eyes. "You telling me how to do my job, grocery man?" He touched Frank lightly on the forehead, one cool round fingertip against the heat of Frank's skin. "Well, don't. I don't tell you how to arrange your fucking vegetables." He glared at Frank for a moment, holding his finger in place. Then he walked back over to the squad car and drove away.

Frank watched him go, arms twitching with rage, his forehead still burning where the *hakujin* had touched him. He thought of Europe again, the place he'd been allowed, no, *instructed* to kill. And he wondered, not for the first time since he'd come back to the States, if he'd defeated or even recognized the enemy.

CHAPTER FOURTEEN

1994

T HE INVIOLATE was violated. And this was now the second time. The previous weekend, Jackie had left Laura in
bed, unsatisfied, in order to go home and look at her family
file. Now, she was up even earlier—eight—and Laura didn't stir as
she dressed next to the bed. They'd had a good night, dinner out
at their favorite Italian restaurant, and Laura seemed to have gotten over the scene with Lanier, believing that Jackie had filled her
in on everything. She hadn't. That morning, for example, Laura
thought that Jackie was getting up early to study with Rebecca, but
she was really going back down to Crenshaw. It was mornings,
Lanier had told her and Lois had confirmed, that all the old folks
gathered down at the Holiday Bowl.

The streets were almost empty this early on a Saturday, the air
was still foggy and cool, and as Jackie drove south on Crenshaw,
passing Adams and Exposition, she wondered what she'd find at
the bowling alley. There it was, on the left side of the street next to
Ralph's, just as Lanier had described: a circular orange sign with
curved white letters that said "The Holiday Bowl—Coffee Shop and
Bowling Alley." The entire west side of the building was made up
of windows, with thick, protruding white and orange beams. The
edge of the roof was orange and rippled, like a conch shell, and it
extended out over the sidewalk. There were tables set smack
against the window, and as she drove past, Jackie saw that the
place looked full. On the far end of the building was a red neon
sign which promised, "Always Open." She made a U-turn at the
first light and found a parking space directly in front.

Once she stepped inside the coffee shop, she stood there for a moment before going to the only free spot in front of the window. The yellow Formica table was speckled and chipped; the chairs had creaky metal legs and orange vinyl cushions. Jackie put her bag down on the chair beside her, looking around self-consciously, certain that everyone there could feel how nervous she was. Before she even had a chance to pull a menu out of its little metal perch, a Japanese woman in her sixties came over and poured her some coffee. She took a few sips to try and calm down. Then, trying not to be too obvious, she began to look around her.

What struck her immediately was that the coffee shop was filled mostly with old people, about equal numbers Asian and black. She had seen gatherings of elderly Asian people; she'd seen gatherings of elderly blacks; but never before had she seen the two in one place. It was such a surprise to her, so visually inconceivable, that it was as if someone had taken footage of two senior citizens' groups and then skillfully spliced them together. There, in front of her, a table full of Japanese grandmothers. Two tables behind her sat three older black men. There were a few tables where old couples sat together, including a squat and hawk-eyed woman who looked at her closely, certain she had seen her before. One large table held three Asian couples. And here and there, interspersed with these single-race groups, were groups of Asian and black people together. Then Jackie became aware of a loud, hollow striking sound, and realized she was hearing people bowl. When she looked to the right, she saw another door, which led to the bowling alley. Listening more carefully, she could make out the low rumble of bowling balls and the buzz of conversation from the other part of the building. She remembered her grandfather, during a rare thunderstorm one summer, telling her that thunder was the sound of the gods bowling. She'd have to go investigate when she was finished with breakfast.

She pulled the menu out now, opened it, flattened it on the table. Here, more hodge-podge: hot links, *donburi*, jambalaya, *ramen*, hamburgers, corn bread, *sashimi*. For breakfast, there were omelets with home fries or rice. She looked up, slightly dizzy from the oddness and variety of her choices, and saw that the Sumitomo

Bank clock read 9:15. She wondered if anyone here had known her grandfather.

When the old waitress wandered back to her table, Jackie ordered two fried eggs and sausage. Then she took out the newspaper she'd brought and pretended to read until the food arrived. Although she wasn't very hungry, she shoveled it down, and when the waitress came back to take her empty dishes away, Jackie thanked her. Then, after clearing her throat, she asked, "Did you happen to know a man named Frank Sakai?"

The woman looked startled. "Frank Sakai," she said. "Yes, a very nice man. I'm sorry, but he died a few weeks ago."

"Yes, I know. I'm his granddaughter. I came down here because I knew that he met friends here sometimes."

"His granddaughter!" The woman looked so surprised that Jackie was afraid she'd drop the plate. Now she leaned forward, peering at Jackie more closely. "I'm so sorry," she said. "Your grandfather was a wonderful man."

Then she turned quickly and walked away. Was the woman so overcome that she had to flee? But no—she was headed toward another table, the one with the hawk-eyed woman, half of a couple about the waitress's age. The waitress stopped right next to them and said a few words. The man looked up at her sharply, and even from twenty feet away, Jackie heard him say, "Granddaughter!" The waitress turned and pointed at Jackie, and when the man spotted her he grinned and waved her over. Jackie hesitated a moment; then she stood and walked over to the couple's table.

"Frank Sakai's granddaughter," the man repeated as she approached. "The law school student, right?"

"Right," Jackie answered. She turned to look at the waitress, but she was already gone.

"Bradley Nakamura," the man offered. Then he nodded toward the woman. "And this is Christina, my wife."

"Call me Tina," the woman said. Mr. Nakamura reached behind him and pulled another chair over, the legs squeaking across the tiles. Jackie sat. Nakamura was a short, squarish man, with sun-browned skin and cheeks split with deep creases from smiling. His wife was stockier, with thick curls of silver hair. Behind her glasses, her eyes were sharp and watchful. "I thought I recognized you. Bradley and I went to the funeral. We're very sorry about your grandfather."

"What brings you down here?" Mr. Nakamura asked. "Want to check out your grandpa's old haunts? From what he used to say, you usually stay locked in the library."

Jackie shifted in her chair. It bothered her that this man knew the outline of her life when she hadn't even known he existed. "Kind of," she responded. "My mother grew up around here and I've never seen it. No one ever brought me around."

"Your grandfather did," said Mrs. Nakamura quietly, and the other two turned to face her. "When you were little. Brought you in here for breakfast, even."

Jackie cocked her head. "Really? I don't remember that at all."

Mrs. Nakamura put her coffee cup down. "Well, it was a Saturday, if I remember correctly. And your grandfather always came here on Saturdays for breakfast and bowling, even after the family moved to Gardena. He just stopped coming regularly a few years ago, in fact. Anyway, I think he was babysitting that day. Later he told us that your mother got mad at him for bringing you here." She laughed. "I guess she didn't think it was safe."

"I don't think that was the problem," Jackie said. Suddenly she felt a rush of anger—why didn't her mother want Jackie to see the place that her grandfather loved? Why would she deny her daughter this connection to her past? How many *other* things— stories, people, places, histories—had Rose denied her daughter? After a few moments, Jackie remembered the Nakamuras, who were looking at her curiously. "How long did you know my grandfather?"

"Almost all my life," Mrs. Nakamura replied. "I was born in 1940, right before the war, and I spent most of my first few years in the camps. And after we came back to Angeles Mesa, we always shopped at your grandfather's store. He was such a compassionate man. My brother Harry was a No-No Boy, and Frank was one of the few people who didn't treat him like he had a disease." She paused, thinking about her brother. When the loyalty questionnaires were circulated at Manzanar, Harry, who was fighting age, had answered *No, No*. It wouldn't have been so awful, maybe, if he'd done this out of principle. But he didn't appear to be either protesting the internment or signaling allegiance to Japan. He had simply said no. As a result, he was sent to Tule Lake with the rest of the No-No Boys, and Tina's family was shunned. And when the family moved back to Angeles Mesa, Harry was refused jobs by whites *and* Japanese. Eventually, tired of the shame he was bringing on the family and the harassment of Nisei vets, Harry left without leaving a note. "You don't know how unusual Frank's attitude was," she said, "especially for a military man."

Jackie was half moved and half uncomfortable. "Do you know anything about his years in the army?"

"Not because of him, of course—he never talked about the war. But I met someone once who fought with Frank, and he said your grandfather was the best soldier in his battalion. It always struck me, because he seemed like such a peaceful man to me. He was a small man, you know, and so mild. He had none of the swagger of some of the other Nisei vets."

Jackie felt slightly queasy now. It disconcerted her to know that her grandfather was capable of killing someone. She had known in theory that being a soldier meant having to hurt other people, to kill them, but she hadn't actually thought about the more brutal aspects of her grandfather's service. Her own war, the Gulf War, hadn't seemed quite real—so sudden, and over as soon as it started. Her strongest memory of the war came not from any of the protests she witnessed, or the images she saw on TV, but from a perfect summer day the August before President Bush set out to liberate Kuwait. She was at the beach with Laura, among thousands of other people, all laughing, splashing, smoothing on lotion, playing volleyball, tossing footballs and Frisbees. Then, from the east, a buzzing, which grew louder and nearer, until they saw the first planes, small and flying low to the ground. Soon the sky was thick with them—thousands it seemed, as far as the eye could see, so loud Jackie covered her ears. She stared up at the planes, which went on and on and on for ten minutes or more, and after they were gone, the last of them shrinking to small points on the horizon, Jackie noticed how quiet it was.

She looked around her then. And all down the beach, the swimmers, the sunbathers, the tossers had stopped. All of them—thousands— were standing there, stunned, still staring off into the sky.

She looked at Tina Nakamura now, trying to keep her expression neutral. "Are any of these men still around? Do any of them come here?"

"Not really, no. And a lot of your grandfather's friends have passed."

"What about Kenji Hirano?" asked Mr. Nakamura. "Isn't he still around?"

"That's right," she replied. "He is." In fact, he was around that very day, which Tina knew, because she'd glimpsed him in the bowling alley when she'd gone to the restroom. But she didn't want to set Frank's grandchild on that particular path—not without thinking about it, not without warning, although she wasn't sure who she was trying to protect.

"Kenji Hirano's been in the neighborhood forever," her husband said. "Knew your grandpa a lot better than we did. He'd be a good person to talk to, if you've got the patience for it."

"Does he come here?" Jackie asked.

"Yes," answered Mrs. Nakamura. "But he's old, you know, and he's not always completely coherent. He and his friends still meet on Tuesday mornings to bowl."

"Maybe I'll come back and talk to him," said Jackie. Then, worrying that she was pushing too much, but unable to stop herself, "Do you know Akira Matsumoto or Derek Broadnax? I found their names in some of my grandfather's papers."

"Akira I know," said Mrs. Nakamura. "He worked for Frank at the store. A real hot-head, if I remember. I think he ended up going to Japan to write for an English-language newspaper, didn't he, Bradley?"

"But you don't know Derek Broadnax?"

"Well, there was a Derek who worked for him, too, but I don't know what happened to him. Everyone seemed to scatter so fast, you know, after Frank shut down the store. It was a real shame, I'll tell you. The neighborhood was never the same after your grandfather left."

Jackie tried not to look at her too closely. Before, she'd wondered if the Nakamuras were just being considerate in not mentioning the murders, but now she was starting to think they didn't know about them. Why were so few people aware of what had happened? And if people didn't even know about it, then how were she and Lanier going to find anyone to corroborate his theory? She finished her coffee, made some final small talk, and decided she'd had enough for the day. She was excited about her leads on Akira Matsumoto and this older man Hirano, but she was starting to feel her schoolwork looming like a pile of unpaid bills. And it was only later, after she'd paid for her meal and was driving home to Fairfax, that she realized she'd never gone into the bowling alley.

As soon as she left, Bradley looked at his wife and sighed. "You think introducing her to Kenji is such a good idea?"

"I don't know. I don't know how helpful it would be to either of them." And she thought about Kenji, the old shell of a man in the next room. She remembered how he had changed after the Sakais left Crenshaw; how his comments, more and more, were directed only to God, and how even his rare moments of lucidity grew fewer and further between, until they'd disappeared altogether. She had known this man, too, for most of her life. Finally, Tina got up and wandered back into the bowling alley. Kenji and his friends—Aaron Bennett, Trace McKinney, and the Third LeRon Johnson—had finished bowling, and the old man was sitting at a table behind the rail, nodding at his paper cup of coffee. "Kenji," she said, stopping in front of him.

He raised his head quickly. "Yep, bowled a 285 today. Jesus was watching over me."

"That's great, Kenji." She wondered, not for the first time, what it was like to be inside his head; to go home to an empty house for forty years. No one really knew what was wrong with him—he'd been functional enough to work as a gardener for most of his life, and he kept himself immaculate and organized. He had friends, Frank among them, people who didn't question the odd swayings of his mind; who accepted his crooked readings of the world. "Listen, Kenji," Tina said. "I just met Frank's granddaughter."

Kenji kept looking at her for a moment, the fine lines in his eyes getting darker. Then he looked over at the lanes. "Yep, 285. Not bad considering I only had one cup of coffee this morning."

Tina felt her heart sink. She didn't know if he understood. "She wants to talk to you, Kenji. Not today. But she wants to know some things about Frank."

The old man stared at the lane and slid his cup back and forth, paper scraping softly over wood. His voice, when he spoke, sounded pained. "It's so cold in here. So cold." He crumpled his cup and left it on the table, then stood and walked stiff-legged to the door. And Tina, looking after him, wondered at his head. She picked up the scorecard he'd left behind to fan herself absent-mindedly, fighting off the stifling heat.

CHAPTER FIFTEEN

KENJI, 1955

K ENJI HIRANO was closer to Jesus than most people, so when He advised him to take up bowling as a way to occupy his hands, Kenji went down to the Holiday Bowl that very day. It was 1955, and Kenji had just turned thirty-six. His father Seiichi, who was suspicious of all forms of sport, had to defer to the Lord in the case of his son. It was Seiichi, after all, who had written the bishop in Japan back in 1912 and asked if he could confess his sins—and be pardoned—through international mail. The horrified bishop, realizing the dire situation of the tiny flock in Southern California, arranged for the formation of the Catholic church in Little Tokyo. Seiichi Hirano was and continued to be one of the most influential members. A cheerful, rugged man, he'd made his trip to the Land of Rice on faith alone. Denied a visa in Japan, he'd taken a ship to Mexico, fighting off heat, snakes, sandstorms, starvation, and a pack of masked bandits (Catholic, so he believed they wouldn't hurt him) on his way up the bent elbow of Baja, California. Once in the City of Angels—he chose Los Angeles over San Francisco because it sounded more holy—he spent several years at the mercy of the sour-breathed labor agents who took huge cuts from his pay and lied about the nature of the backbreaking jobs they found him. Finally, he joined up with another laborer and started a gardening business. He'd never worked as a gardener before, but this didn't concern him—he was from a farming family and knew how to grow things. Gardening was just a matter of water and balance and what you did with your tools, plus a few rocks you dragged down from the mountains. So with the help of Jesus, whom he asked to bless his shears, truck, and lawnmower, he and his partner prospered.

Seiichi eventually saved the money he needed to send for a picture bride. Noriko, the young girl who became his wife, was from one of the few Catholic families in Wakayama Prefecture. Once she got over her fear of the crowded American sidewalks and the sputtering of cars, she found a job at the orphanage on Alameda Street for abandoned and homeless children—many of whom had been deposited there, it was rumored, by the women engaged in shameful work near Chinatown. Kenji, the couple's only child, spent his early years going to church twice during the week and all day on Sunday. But by ten years after the second world war had ended, Jesus was less a distant deity the Hiranos went to church to worship, and more like a member of the family. The wisest member, though. So when Jesus instructed Kenji to start in with the new craze of bowling, all the Hiranos paid attention. Especially after what happened the one time that Kenji had ignored his advice.

Kenji defied the Son of God in the fall of 1942, soon after the Hiranos had been evacuated to Heart Mountain. He became convinced that he and his new wife, Yuki, should have a baby, because of the rumor that all Nisei men would soon be sterilized. His wife did not believe the rumors—the government, she knew, would never resort to such measures—but she liked the idea of having a baby. And besides, there was very little to do with all their leisure time but try. But then, one already-cold evening, as Kenji took a walk along the border of the camp, getting as close to the fence as he dared to with the snake-like rifles sniffing his way, Jesus fell in step beside him. He was wearing a government-issue peacoat just like the internees so as not to draw the guards' attention, but his flowing beard, the bleeding scars on his hands, his limp from the wounds on his feet, were unmistakable. "It is not time, my child," He said.

Kenji didn't want to seem disrespectful, so he folded his hands together and nodded. "But the rumors," he said, not looking his Lord in the eye.

"Nevermind them," said Jesus. "Wait awhile. Your child is not yet ready to enter the world."

Kenji nodded, but didn't pay the words much heed. Jesus

couldn't understand such earthly matters. Besides, he and Yuki were enjoying themselves, sneaking brief, clutching moments in their barracks when his parents were out; and in the mess hall after lunch; and in the closet of the supplies office where she worked afternoons, boxes of bandages falling down on their heads. Their marriage had been arranged by their parents and negotiated by two *baishakunin* who were also members of their church. And while the two intendeds had liked each other—they were both good-looking and educated, and very devout Catholics—they'd been shaped just enough by the country of their birth to regret not marrying for love. So when they found themselves, a year into their marriage, starting to grin and blush and shiver in each other's presence; starting to feel like it was Christmas morning every day, they knew that they were the luckiest couple alive. Yuki finally missed her period in November, and they celebrated with two rare, fresh oranges that a friend had smuggled out of the camp kitchen.

A few months later, when the recruiters came, Kenji signed up for the army. He was sent to Camp Shelby for boot camp with the other Nisei men, but allowed to come back to Wyoming for the birth of his child. When he stepped into the barracks he'd left five months before, he hardly recognized his wife. She was puffed up all over, her features bloated and exaggerated from the salt tablets the doctors had prescribed to fend off dehydration. He had never seen a woman look this way—pillow-like, almost comical—and worry settled in his gut like a pile of stones. A few days after he arrived, Yuki went into labor. Kenji took her to the camp hospital, where they were shunted into a corner, shut off from the rest of the patients by a hanging brown blanket. A nurse came once to talk to Yuki and take her temperature; then she disappeared. But Yuki's contractions, her pain, her moaning went on for hours, and Kenji, between prayers, finally emerged from behind the blanket to ask the nurse where the doctor was. The nurse looked uncomfortable. She finally informed him that there were only two doctors capable of delivering a baby, and that one of them, a Nisei woman, had been suspended for treating—and thus endangering—the white employees of the camp. The other, the *hakujin*, was not in the hospital, and she didn't reveal her suspicion that he was being entertained by a certain large-busted Nisei woman who'd been given a private room. They stayed there—nurse, Kenji, Yuki—through one sunrise, one sunset, and part of another sunrise, Kenji pleading and praying, catching snippets of sleep between his wife's contractions. Finally, the nurse determined that the baby could not emerge through the normal avenues, and she ran off to the Nisei woman's barracks to fetch the doctor. Kenji held his wife's hand and looked into her sweating face—the rounded cheeks, the pert but now-spreading nose. "If it's a boy," she said, "we name him Timothy, after my brother."

And although Kenji didn't like this name, he nodded and smiled, anything to bring a moment of pleasure to her eyes. "And if it's a girl?" he asked.

"Same thing."

They laughed and squeezed hands and began to pray together, and then they heard the doctor come in. Kenji pulled the blanket aside and saw a big, red-faced man shuffling toward their corner.

"Hello, Mack!" the man called out cheerfully when he caught sight of Kenji. "You know, I've never seen a yellow belly in a uniform before."

The nurse, who walked behind him, lowered her eyes, and Kenji decided it would be best to say nothing. As the doctor reached the side of the bed, though, Kenji caught a whiff of liquor, and he looked at the man uncertainly.

The doctor touched Yuki's stomach and then moved down between her legs, his hands huge and clumsy as two-by-fours. "Looks like this one's stuck in there pretty good." He was going to have to perform an operation, he said, but the nurse reminded him that there was no anesthesiologist in the camp. He swore, and sighed, and reached behind him, producing a long needle from a cart the nurse had brought over. "This here's a local," he informed the Hiranos as he administered the shot to Yuki's belly. They waited a few moments. Then the doctor pulled out a knife. He placed it against the dome of Yuki's stomach, and at the precise moment that the tip broke through her skin, Kenji felt a piercing pain in his own flesh. Yuki did not feel it, though, even as the *hakujin* doctor pulled the knife downward, a bit crookedly, a path of blood springing up where the blade had cut. Kenji crossed himself and muttered. He had accidentally caught a small shark once, off the pier at San Pedro, and when he split its belly, the wound had looked something like this. Now, the doctor hooked both his thumbs in the incision and pulled Yuki's flesh apart like a loaf of bread. Kenji felt sick. Yuki couldn't face the doctor or look at her own numbed stomach, so she stared instead at her husband's face. Kenji tried to hold his expression together. Then the doctor put the knife down and the nurse handed him a huge pair of forceps. He wriggled them in through the wound. He seemed to strike something, because after a few more grunts and adjustments, he braced himself against the table and started to pull. His face was even redder now, and the smell of whiskey was rising out of his pores. Kenji tried not to look too closely at the procedure, saying under his breath, "Please, Jesus, take care of them, please." He watched his wife's eyes grow wider. The doctor seemed to be yanking very hard, as if pulling a stubborn tooth. The nurse looked at him in alarm, inquired, "Doctor?" But then, with a final yank and grunt, the doctor pulled the big tooth free. Kenji saw immediately that the baby, red and slick, was very still. Its head was crushed on both sides between the forceps. Then, to his horror, he saw that the stubborn tooth had brought its roots with it; the gaping mouth in Yuki's belly was pumping blood. She screamed at the sight of it, since there wasn't any pain, although she began to feel something tugging at her chest, her legs, her arms, her heart, something pulling hard from inside. The doctor swore again and pressed towels to her stomach, one after the next, but the blood bloomed through them all and oozed and bubbled between his fingers. Kenji looked past the doctor at his wife, and her eyes were bright with comprehension. He'd been holding her hand and now he brought his face up to hers, touching her softly with his fingers, whispering into her cheeks, her ears, her eyes, her lips, until the yawning mouth in her belly was silenced forever.

Twelve years later, Kenji didn't know what to do with his hands, which still shook from not strangling the doctor. They quivered and jumped all the way back to Camp Shelby, and then over to Italy, where the *hakujin* they *did* kill didn't satisfy his rage. They shook through the year his family lived in a government trailer in Lomita, where they were sent after the war because their neighbors in Boyle Heights, upon receiving word of their return, promptly set fire to their house. And they shook for eight years after Kenji's parents bought the new place in Angeles Mesa. The only way he could keep them still was to give them occupation, which was why he had so enjoyed holding guns, and then his father's gardening tools. Jobs that didn't require his hands weren't appealing to him, and not useful anyway, since it took hard labor and constant pep talks with himself to keep from going after each burly *hakujin* he saw with flushed cheeks and cheap whiskey on his breath. Sometimes his gruff pep talks alarmed the people he passed on the street or the families he gardened for, but they didn't mind because he *did* do such a beautiful job on the lawn, honey, don't you think? Even if he is a bit odd. And he was even starting to learn what to do with his hands when they weren't holding a pair of shears or pushing a mower. He took up smoking, buying a pack every other day from Frank Sakai's store, even though, three years later, his father would die of lung cancer. And then one afternoon outside of Frank's store, Jesus came up to him again, dressed in his normal white robes this time. He looked at Kenji and pointed over toward Crenshaw Boulevard. "You must bowl, my son," He said. "Fill your hands with the nourishing weight of sport." Then He disappeared into the store, where Kenji was sure He was going to buy some fruit. Kenji followed, but when he got inside, there was no one there but Frank.

"Did you see Him?" he asked. "The Son of God. He was here."

Frank didn't lift an eyebrow. "No, I must have missed Him."

Kenji stared, eyes wide. He looked hard at the fruit bins, and then turned back to his friend. "Nevermind," he said. "Tell me, Frank, could you teach me how to bowl?"

CHAPTER SIXTEEN

1994

REBECCA, ON Monday, practically skipped into class, and her mood was so different from her usual nonchalance that Jackie knew something wonderful had happened.

"What's up?" Jackie asked when Rebecca sat down beside her. "You get laid last night?"

"No," she answered, plopping her bag down. "I got a job."

"Are you serious?"

Rebecca nodded, looking pleased with herself. "Yep. Remember that Legal Aid office in Westlake I interviewed with?"

"The place off Alvarado, with two lawyers for like five hundred clients?"

"Yeah, that one. Well, the funding they'd been working on came through last week, and they just called me about an hour ago and offered me the job."

Jackie pounded her lightly on the shoulder. "Get outta here! You got probably the only public interest job in the country this year."

"Yeah, well, they're going to make me suffer for it, too. Salary's thirty-two grand a year, and with all my damn loans, I'm still going to be living like a student."

The professor cleared his throat a few times, signaling that he was about to begin, so Jackie bent in close to her friend and lowered her voice. "Well, let's celebrate. What should we do?"

"Get drunk, of course. But you're buying, girl, 'cos I'm about to increase my debt."

Their professor made a few announcements about moot court

results and speakers coming to campus. They both half-listened for a moment, and then Jackie leaned over again. "Hey, you know," she said, "There's something I want to talk to you about."

Rebecca turned toward her with her eyebrows raised. The tone of Jackie's voice suggested that something out of the ordinary was about to be imparted. And Rebecca's obvious interest suddenly made Jackie self-conscious. She'd toyed, half-seriously, with the idea of telling her friend everything—about the store, James Lanier, Curtis Martindale, the will. But she hadn't known she might really do it until that moment. "Later," she whispered, turning back toward the front of the lecture hall. She stared straight at their teacher's neat blond hair for an hour and did not take a single note.

That evening, Jackie drove down to Hawthorne. She was meeting Lanier at a Winchell's there, and together they were going to see Angela Broadnax. Jackie's hunch had been correct—among the cards that Lois had collected at the funeral were ones from Angela Broadnax and Bradley Nakamura. According to her card, Angela Broadnax was a supervisor at the DMV office in Hawthorne, and Jackie had called her on Monday. She'd mentioned James Lanier, hoping that Angela would remember him. She did. Then Jackie told her who *she* was, and what she wanted from her brother. There'd been a long silence on the other end of the line. Then Angela Broadnax had said, "Listen. Derek's dead. He OD'd on heroin ten years ago. I don't think he ever got over what happened to Curtis and David. But there are some things about that time that you should know about." Jackie had waited, holding her breath, for Angela to continue—but Angela wanted to talk to them in person.

When Jackie pulled into the Winchell's parking lot, she saw Lanier sitting at a table by the window. He was wearing a jacket and tie, and he looked more business-like than usual. She was thrown slightly off-kilter, her discomfort reminding her that she really didn't know this man at all. As soon as she walked in, though, and he raised his head and smiled, he became familiar again, James Lanier, a man who was becoming a friend.

"Hey," he said when he saw her, voice muffled by a donut. "Ready to go?"

"I guess so," she replied, sliding into the booth. "Are you? You're all dolled up tonight. What's the occasion?"

He glanced down at his outfit. "Oh, this? I had meetings with possible sponsors all day. Besides, I think I'm a little nervous. At least in my jacket and tie, I feel more grown-up."

"Why are you nervous?"

He broke out into a shy, boyish grin. "Well, she remembers me, right? And what I remember most about *her* was that I wasn't all that nice to her. As far as I was concerned, girls just took Curtis's attention away from me. Besides, she was older and I was just a little kid. Who knows what kind of trouble she saw me get up to?"

Jackie laughed. "What—you think she's not going to respect you because she saw you crash your tricycle when you were three?"

"I *never* crashed my tricycle. Let's go."

Lanier drove, and they talked about meaningless things—the weather, city politics, the new 105 Freeway, which they'd both ridden, the day it opened, like an amusement park ride. At one point Lanier mentioned the dinner they'd had, and then asked, "How's your friend?"

Jackie didn't know whether he meant "friend" innocently or as the euphemism it sounded like. "Fine," she said, wishing Lanier would change the subject—which he did, moving on to his opinion of who should win that year's Oscars. They covered a dozen topics in their five-minute drive, discussing everything except the task at hand, the woman they were going to see. Jackie didn't know whether this silence had to do with Lanier's nervousness or with the possibility that they were about to learn something definitive.

Angela Broadnax's apartment was in the back of a small building on Ramona Avenue. The walkway was bisected by a long, deep crack, clearly fresh, caused by the earthquake. Through the open window Lanier and Jackie could hear loud voices—not angry, just raised, as if the people were talking to each other from separate rooms. The voices both belonged to women, or girls, and when the door was pulled open after Lanier's firm, three-point knock, a striking, dark-skinned woman stood before them, looking harried, and behind her stood a smaller, younger, smoother-skinned copy, who was unquestionably her daughter.

"Hi," the woman said, making room in the doorway. "You must be Jimmy Lanier and Jackie Ishida."

Her voice knocked Lanier over. Dragged him back thirty years. And before his mind fastened on what her face had looked like, he remembered the low, gravelly voice. Asking Curtis *What you want, honey?* as she leaned toward the open refrigerator. Singing along with the radio as they sat on the porch at dusk. "Yes," he responded. "And you're Angela Broadnax."

Angela shook their hands before moving aside to let them in. She was Jackie's height exactly, but Jackie felt smaller in her presence. Although she was in her mid-forties, she looked a decade younger—her hair was shiny and black, and her skin only wrinkled—and then only lightly—around her eyes and her tense, tight mouth. She wore a blue sweatshirt, but her pants were dressy and gray; it looked like she'd come home from work and only half-changed to cook. And cook she clearly had—the house smelled, luxuriously, of chicken and spices. At the table sat a young boy of eleven or twelve, who was reading while he ate.

"Thanks for coming," Angela said, indicating that they should sit on the couch. "As you see, I've got a handful here, and I don't like to leave them at night."

"Mama," said the girl, suddenly and loudly, "I'm going over to Rhonda's." She stood there defiantly, thin arms crossed, as if she and her mother were alone.

Her mother just looked at her, fist on hip. "Renee, this is Jimmy Lanier and his friend Miss Jackie Ishida. You say hello to them now, and don't act like they're not here. And you *ask* if you can leave. You don't announce it."

She didn't mention that she knew Lanier—Jackie wouldn't have thought she did if she hadn't kept calling him Jimmy—and Jackie liked her for this.

Lanier, though, was focused on the fist. The womanish, stubborn fist propped up on the hip, hard close-to-the-skin bone against bone. It was a gesture he'd seen her make a hundred times, and from the axis of that stance a world of memory spun out, the girl whose body framed the fist against the hip. He remembered her soft, lanky arm over Curtis's shoulder. The face lit and laughing when Curtis kissed her on the forehead. The hard languid stride that both challenged and beckoned; and suddenly Curtis was sitting beside him again, jostling and winking, showing Jimmy, who was still too young to really understand, the way her ass moved when she walked.

That long-ago girl's daughter looked sullen now, and seemed to be thinking of talking back. But she must have decided against it, because she uncrossed her arms and looked at the guests. "Hi," she said reluctantly. Then, to her mother, "Can I go to Rhonda's place? I'm gonna do some homework tonight."

"Yes," her mother replied. "You can go. But be back by ten. And I'll expect you to show me what you've done." Her voice was stern, not angry, but the girl rolled her eyes as if she'd been dealt some major injustice. She gathered her things and stomped out the door without saying goodbye, and her mother looked after her, silent. Then she turned back to her guests, trying to smile. "That's my headache. Sixteen and moody from morning to night. Ricky," she said, nodding toward the boy at the table, "never gives me any trouble."

The boy was so engrossed in his book that he dropped a piece of chicken and ended up with a forkful of air.

"I worry about him a little," Angela continued. "Twelve years old and he doesn't really have friends. But I'd rather he keep to himself than have friends like Renee's. Some girls now rougher than the boys I knew when I was coming up."

"Renee and Ricky Broadnax," said Lanier, trying it out. And he remembered Derek now, the flat broad face, the ever-ready grin.

"Drake," Angela corrected. "They have their daddy's name, even though they've seen the man maybe six or seven times in the last five years. I took my own name back when we got divorced." She nodded toward the doorway. "That one started to get wild as soon as he left. She was always full of the devil, but she was never out of control until their dad was gone. And Ricky just got quieter. Ricky," she said now, raising her voice, "are you done eating?" He looked up at her and nodded, glancing with curiosity at Jackie and Lanier, as if noticing them for the first time. "Come over here, sugar," she beckoned, and he obeyed.

When Angela introduced her guests, Ricky shook their hands gravely and said, "Nice to meet you." Lanier grinned at him, eyes softening. Then Angela instructed the boy to put his dirty plates in the sink and to go to his room and read. She watched him while he carried the dishes, turning her attention back to Jackie and Lanier only when his door had clicked shut.

"You want something to drink?" she asked. "I have coffee, juice, maybe a couple of beers."

They both protested, saying that they'd just drank, just eaten. Angela leaned forward in her chair, taking stock of Lanier. "You know, you look the same," she said. "You still got that worried expression." She remembered him clearly, the quiet boy who was her boyfriend's appendage, and she saw, like a ghost that hovered behind him, the texture and shape of his loss.

Lanier placed one hand flat against his knee and put the other right on top of it. "Well, Ms. Broadnax . . ."

"Oh, honey, stop it with that 'Ms.' stuff. Just call me Angela."

"All right. Well . . . Angela . . . You look pretty much the same, too." He paused. "I'm sorry about Derek."

"Yes, well. It's been such a long time now." She turned to Jackie. "I'm sorry about your grandfather. He meant a lot to me when I was younger, and to my brother and Curtis, too."

"Thank you," Jackie said.

"It was a lovely service. Your family did a nice job." She sighed, looking older now, as if the exhaustion she'd been fending off all night had finally begun to catch up with her. Now she turned back to Lanier. "Anyway, thank you about Derek. We still miss him so much, you know."

"When did he start using?" asked Lanier.

"In the sixties. After Watts. That messed him up in ways he never recovered from."

"He worked in the store," Jackie ventured.

"Yes," said Angela, looking at her now. "He worked in your grandfather's store."

There was a strange, pained expression on her face, which Jackie couldn't interpret. "Oh, honey, I *know* he didn't do it. There was some talk that it was him, but the people who said that didn't know your grandpa."

Lanier leaned closer now. "Do you know who *did* do it?"

Angela rocked back and forth on the edge of the couch, looking thoughtful. "Well, Derek saw them, you know, right after your grandfather found them. He was afraid that something was wrong, since he didn't hear from Curtis or David for so long. He'd been at the store with them, just before the looters hit Crenshaw. Mr. Sakai sent them all home, and then he went home to his family." She paused. Her eyes welled up. "I don't know why they went back in, unless somebody made them. And then after Derek saw them . . . you know . . . in the store, he came back home and told us. He was crazy that day, ready to kill someone. He scared us all. I mean, I was crazy too—but my brother, it's like he never came back."

Lanier spoke again, his voice gentle. "Did he say anything else?"

Angela brought herself back, and met his eyes. "He said, 'It was that motherfuckin cop. It was that motherfuckin cop.' Over and over and over." And she remembered the abyss that had opened in his eyes, a yawning space that couldn't take in any light. Curtis and David and eventually her brother had fallen into that abyss, and were consumed there.

They all let Angela's words sink in. Jackie noticed the pictures on the bookcase, Angela's children at an earlier age, and a picture of the three of them with a large, smiling man. She wondered what Curtis's children would have looked like—and what Curtis himself had looked like. Finally, Lanier broke the silence.

"So Derek went over the edge because of what happened to David and Curtis?"

"Basically."

Jackie said, "Well, I guess that's understandable," and Angela snapped.

"*Why* is it understandable? Why? He's not the only one who suffered. Mr. Sakai didn't lose his mind, and he loved Curtis and David, too. *I* didn't lose my mind, even when I saw him laid out that first day at the funeral home, and I was going to *marry* the boy."

Jackie looked down at her hands, sorry she'd spoken. She could feel Lanier's eyes moving back and forth between her and Angela.

Angela slumped a little. "I'm sorry. It's hard to think about, even now. Curtis was my first boyfriend, my first real love. We were so young when he died, and it just shouldn't have happened, you know?" She paused, looking down at her hands. "I don't know how I would have gotten through it without Mr. Sakai. He was always real quiet and stoical, but I think the murders tore him up as much as they did me."

Lanier sat back, suddenly feeling very tired. It occurred to him that he'd been selfish all these years, even more selfish than he'd been when his cousin had died. As if he were the only one that Curtis had left behind. "No, no," he said. "*I'm* sorry."

"We were together all through high school," Angela continued. "All those years and my parents never knew. My folks were real religious, you know, and my father didn't approve of me dating anybody. But Mr. Sakai was always good to us. He understood. Even though you'd think he wouldn't, 'cos he was such a straight arrow, he always understood."

"Do you remember when he hired Curtis?" Lanier asked. "Was it before or after Derek?"

"After. He'd just started working there when we got together. And he loved it. He loved all the stories Mr. Sakai told him, about when he was a boy and about the war, and he wanted to run a place like that someday, a little corner market. And he'd talk about how I was going to help him out, how we'd live in the house next door."

Jackie suddenly felt a little jealous of this long-dead boy who heard things Frank wouldn't talk about with her. Or maybe he *had* talked about them and she simply hadn't listened.

Angela patted down the corner of a cushion. "His dad was never crazy about him working there. I'm sorry," she said to Lanier. "I know he was your uncle, but it was true. He wanted Curtis to concentrate on school instead of working. Problem was, the more he didn't want Curtis to be at the store, the more Curtis wanted to be there."

Lanier scratched his neck. "How did they feel about you?"

"Well, Mrs. Martindale was real sweet about it. My parents were a lot like hers, I think—religious and strict. I don't think she liked having to keep our secret, but she was good to us." Angela stopped talking, and remembered. It had always surprised her that Curtis's mother, who was so rigid about so many other things, approved of her son's relationship with her. Angela feared Alma, respected her, and felt honored, always, that Curtis could even see her against the backdrop of the woman who made all others seem frivolous and weak.

"And what about my uncle?" asked Lanier.

Angela thought for a moment before answering. "Well, he was different. I wouldn't say that he disapproved, but he wasn't nearly as nice as Curtis's mom." She looked down and fussed with a string that hung loose from her pants. "But I don't think it was personal; it wasn't about me. It was more that nothing Curtis did was ever good enough. That was part of why Curtis liked the store so much, why all the boys did—because Mr. Sakai made them feel like men."

"Did my uncle know Mr. Sakai?" Lanier asked.

"You know, I really couldn't tell you." She paused, scratched her temple, and looked up at Lanier. "It's amazing how little I know about Curtis's dad, considering how often I saw him. I just remember Curtis saying he wasn't too happy they were living in L.A."

"That's right," Jackie said. "His parents met up north, didn't they?"

Angela nodded. "Curtis's mom was living with her sister up in Oakland, and I guess she met Curtis's father through work. They lived in Oakland for a while, and they moved down to L.A. when Curtis was four." She paused. "Your grandfather was so good to them, you know, after. He always made sure they had what they needed."

Angela looked down at her hands, and then up at Jackie. It took a great effort for Jackie not to turn away. "I was sad to see him go. He was such a big part of my youth, and I don't think I could have made it through that time without him. We'd just sit up somewhere—outside, or in a coffee shop, 'cos I couldn't stand to be in the store—and he'd let me talk to him, let me cry. He was always willing to take on other people's sadness, even though he had so much of his own." A few tears spilled down her face. "I think he did that for Curtis's mother, too, at least at the funeral. I remember that everyone was crying during the service, grieving real loud. Mr. Martindale was falling apart. But Curtis's mother was quiet up there, she was being so still, like she was in shock or something. But after the service, she was walking back through the aisle and Mr. Sakai was there, and he hugged her. I remember it so clearly—it happened right in front of me. He put his arms around her, and at first she tightened, you know, but then you could see her let go. She just gave in, and she let him hold her, and she cried and cried."

Jackie felt something snag in her chest. The scene that Angela had just described seemed viable, not unusual—but in all of her grandfather's dealings with people, Jackie had never seen him touch anyone.

"Is there anyone else still around from that time?" Lanier asked. He didn't want to hear anymore about the funeral, which he had not been allowed to attend. He was too young, his mother had said, so he'd sat in his room, rendered silent by grief and guilt, slowly and methodically hammering to pieces all the planes he had built with his cousins.

"What about Curtis's aunt?" Angela said. "Mrs. Martindale's sister? She might be able to help."

"The one in Oakland?" asked Jackie.

Lanier nodded. "Yeah. I forgot about her. Cory used to go up and visit her, but that was years ago. I think I heard she was in an old folks' home. I don't know which one. And shit, I don't know her married name."

"I'm sorry, I can't help you there," said Angela.

Lanier looked at her. "You've helped us a lot."

He and Jackie got up to leave and they all exchanged phone numbers, work schedules, pleasantries. Angela shook Jackie's hand and then turned and offered her hand to Lanier. He looked at it for a moment. Then he took it, stepped closer, and hugged her. They stood holding each other and there was such intimacy in this gesture, such mutual sorrow, that Jackie looked away. Lanier didn't speak on the way back to Winchell's, and Jackie felt, once again, as she sat hunched in the passenger seat, like a visitor in someone else's grief.

CHAPTER SEVENTEEN

CURTIS AND ANGELA—1962, 1963

A SANTA ANA wind blew through the region in the last week of April, leaving everyone in the city restless and lusting for water. All the people who could walk, drive, take a bus, or hitch a ride headed toward the ocean, and the beaches were as crowded as they'd be on any August Sunday. But Curtis and his friends, landlocked, didn't bother to go—the weather was too exquisite to endure the endless stuffy bus rides, or the cold stares that dark faces on the sands inevitably inspired. And they couldn't swim, either, in the pool at Exposition Park; Negroes were allowed only one day a week, right before the water was changed.

The Catholic gardener, Kenji Hirano, saved the day. Hearing Curtis complain to Frank about the lack of relief from the heat, he went "Hmph" and beckoned Curtis with his gnarled, callused pinky. He led the boy next door to his house, both of them followed by Derek's little sister, Angela, who'd started tagging along on everything Curtis did. There, in the garage, amidst all the tools and mowers and potting soil, was a huge pile of clear green plastic. Curtis used his knife to cut where the old gardener pointed, and then Hirano rolled up a big strip, ten feet wide and thirty feet long. Curtis and Angela carried it, awkwardly, to the Martindales' house, where Jimmy and Cory, who'd been sitting on the steps, watched closely while they spread it out across the lawn. Curtis smoothed it like a sheet and then turned on the hose, covering the plastic with water. Setting the hose down so the mouth opened on a corner, he backed almost into the neighbor's yard and then sprinted toward his creation. At the edge, he dove head-first, gliding across the slick, wet plastic like a base runner sliding into third. The boys didn't need an invitation. They ran back to the edge of the lawn and flung themselves toward the plastic, sliding feet-first, belly-down, and sideways. Curtis put bricks on each corner to keep the plastic from moving. He kept soaking it with water, and sometimes he turned the hose on the boys and on Angela, the cool streams hitting their bodies and then exploding out like liquid fireworks. Other kids, attracted by the laughter and the water, appeared to take their turns. David and Derek showed up from the store, released by Mr. Sakai so they could go out and enjoy the weather. For hours they stayed out there, darkening in the sun, exhilarated by the water and the yielding plastic, which was as slippery and smooth as a dolphin's skin. Frank and Victor appeared at dusk, bearing paper buckets of hot links and ribs from the barbecue church; the kids ate ravenously, quickly, and then went back to their play. And the hose leapt and twisted like a living thing, moving from one hand to the next, everyone shrieking in shock and delight when the water hit their bodies.

The next time Curtis saw hoses was on the evening news, from Birmingham, Alabama. There, during a peaceful demonstration, the police had set dogs and fire hoses on the crowds of black marchers. Sitting next to his mother in the living room, Curtis watched unbelievingly the images on the screen. A young black man smashed flat against a wall by the hurricane force of water. A mother losing hold of her child, the stream prying it loose, as invasive and precise as an ice pick. Two children, sitting down, being beaten by three policemen, their batons rising and dropping with a steady, sickening rhythm. A young girl of maybe six caught and shaken by a police dog, her arm enclosed in the shepherd's huge jaws. The big, intimidating cops made him think of the ones in his neighborhood who sneered at him out the windows of their squad cars—even the black one, Thomas, who'd towered over him in the office at Audubon, and who scared him as much as any of the others. Alma kept saying the Lord's name, softly, under her breath, and soon she went to the phone, where from her low mumbles and familiar manner Curtis could tell she was talking to Miss Vera and Miss Alice, who she always called when there were Negroes on TV.

He swallowed hard, watching the hoses, and felt a chill like an ice cube applied to his spine, completely at odds with the still-steaming weather.

The next day in class, he was moody and distracted, not hearing when Mrs. Anderson called his name for roll. And he barely acknowledged Angela, who he usually met at her locker before the first bell rang, or at least smiled at and touched on the hand before they sat down—both gestures as necessary to her morning well-being as the coffee she had with her breakfast. She was a freshman, he was a sophomore, both assigned to the gloom and boredom of pre-algebra. Angela had first met Curtis the previous spring, at the store where her older brother worked, and while she'd noticed his smooth, tight, caramel-colored skin; his soft, sleepy eyes; the four bottom teeth that overlapped like a quartet of friends bent over a joke, she'd remained unmoved, her eyes compelled to follow him but her stomach and her heart left safely behind. But then, three moments that added more to her measure of him. Late that summer, she passed by the baseball field at the high school and saw him playing catch with two five- or six-year-old boys, who she learned later were his brother and cousin. The younger boys stood about ten feet apart, with Curtis facing them from a distance of perhaps twenty feet, the vertex of their V. He was throwing them grounders, and she watched while the boys let the ball go through their legs or bounce sharply off their shins. Once they crashed into each other. But Curtis, offering ball after ball, didn't laugh at their mistakes. He instructed them calmly, telling them to pull their legs together and lay the glove down in front, so that the ball could not get past. Angela saw in his confident stance, his light flicking of the ball, his patient attention, a hint of manhood that made her pulse jump.

On that same field, but a hundred feet over, on the track, the second moment occurred. It was a month and a half later, one of the first days of school, during try-outs for the cross-country team. Angela was walking toward the field with two of her new friends when she caught sight of Curtis rounding the far end of the track. He was sprinting all-out, shirtless, looking more like a 400 man than a cross-country hopeful. With his long, streamlined legs; his huge strides which gulped up yards at a time; the way he didn't seem to notice any of the people he passed, he looked like a strong young antelope running across sun-dusted plains. The display only lasted another thirty seconds or so, until he completed his lap. But his intensity and concentration—not to mention the beauty of his body as it hurtled through the warm afternoon, the washboard stomach she wanted to press her face against—unleashed an awe-tinged desire in the pit of her womb. And when Curtis showed up in her pre-algebra class the next morning, having been shuffled over from another classroom, Angela felt a wave of heat go through her as all-consuming as the strongest Santa Ana.

Then the third moment, in that very same classroom. Curtis strolled up to Mrs. Anderson, handed her his note, and fixed on her the most bold, playful smile that Angela had ever seen a student give a teacher. Mrs. Anderson shooed him toward a seat, but she smiled a little, tolerant in the way that teachers sometimes are of bright but irreverent students. Curtis turned back toward the class and grinned, both aware of the effect he had on the girls, whose titters and giggles swarmed the room like butterflies, and subtly making fun of it. There was something about the way he sauntered back to the one empty desk, shoes sliding deliciously across the linoleum, that made Angela know that this most serious of boys didn't take himself too seriously. And his physical presence—the beautiful, tapered, long-fingered hands; the close-cropped, always-moving head; the slim graceful waist that drew her eyes down and down—was almost more than she could bear.

That afternoon, at try-outs, he repeated his blazing 400 performance, and Angela waited for him at the finish line.

"Why you sprinting like that, fool? Track season ain't till spring."

He walked back and forth a couple of times, trying to catch his breath, running his hand over his finely-shaped head. "I like to push myself," he said. "See how fast I can go."

Angela examined her fingernails. "Waste of energy, if you ask me."

"I *didn't* ask you, far as I can remember."

"Those some ugly-ass shoes you got on, too. Tell your mama she should get you a new pair."

"Aw, girl, leave me alone. Why you hassling me?"

She continued to hassle him—on the track, in class, at the store after school—until he had no choice but to do something about it. He finally did about a month after school began, on an October afternoon so unusually hot that they had to sit under the bleachers to get some shade. Angela was chattering on and on about Mrs. Anderson and the test they'd just taken when Curtis leaned over and kissed her. When he pulled back, smiling, she straight-armed him. Elbow locked, hand flat against his chest, she said, "Boy, what makes you think I want your mouth all up in my face?" They looked at each other. Then she curled her hand around his neck and pulled him toward her.

She chose him. As much as her mother had chosen to leave their lying, thieving daddy in Cleveland for the straight-laced man they now lived with; as much as her oldest brother, Gene, had chosen—or been chosen by—heroin, and then had chosen the Muslims to help him kick it, she chose Curtis Martindale, and kept choosing him through all their years of high school. He delighted her with his teasing; with his sudden hugs and kisses; with his tenderness toward his brother and cousins. And he enraged her with his total refusal to listen to her, about school, or clothes, or the fact that his strides were too long when he ran. She both loved, and was annoyed by, how much he lived in his life—how a clear view of the snow-capped mountains on a January morning could make him happy for the rest of the day; how a snapped pencil or a blister on his foot would instantly ruin his mood. But despite his brooding father and the tense air in his house, Curtis seemed oddly, immeasurably happy. He had her, he had the boys, he had track and the store. He had his mother, whom he loved fiercely, and who always had his back. All of these elements made up the universe for him, which Angela gladly entered. There was no one else like him, the mischievous, beautiful, always-tender man of a boy. And he was hers, he was hers, he was hers.

CHAPTER EIGHTEEN

1994

D OWNTOWN L.A. seemed incomplete to Jackie. Whenever she saw the skyline from the freeway or a plane, she always felt a bit of a let-down. The several dozen skyscrapers, the shorter office buildings, were paltry compared to the glass and steel of downtown San Francisco; would fill a single block of midtown Manhattan. To Jackie, they were like the abandoned beginnings of a more vertical city, except Los Angeles had grown sideways instead of up.

Jackie's new job at Turner, Blake & Weinberg would be downtown, and the Tuesday after she and Lanier visited Angela Broadnax, she skipped her afternoon classes to go there. In the two-hour meeting for all the first-year associates, she learned her official starting date and her payment schedule for the summer, when she'd be studying for the bar. She'd always liked coming down to the firm; seeing all the people dressed in expensive suits, working in big plush offices with beautiful desks and soft, plump leather chairs. She liked to envision herself there. The thought of the paycheck was pleasant, too—her starting salary was $71,000—but it wasn't the primary attraction. When she started to work here, when she was no longer someone fresh out of law school but a regular part of the landscape, she'd feel like she'd finally become someone, like she had finally arrived.

After chatting with some of the other incoming associates, she took the elevator down, with the intention of going directly back to her car. But when the elevator stopped on the first floor, one level above the garage, she let herself be disgorged with the people who were headed out into the street. She walked east, down the hill, past the museums and City Hall. She watched the faces change from white to black to brown, saw the signs on the buildings go from English to Spanish. At the corner of 1st and Main, right before the New Otani Hotel, she saw her first sign in Japanese. She crossed one street, and then another, and now all the signs were in Japanese, or Japanese and English. She passed a bookstore, several noodle shops, a candy store. All the buildings on the north side of the street were old and cramped together—small storefronts, with apartments above. And the people—there was not a white face here, nor a black or a brown, and somehow Jackie felt more conspicuous on this street, as if everyone could sense how out of place she felt. Two old women, dressed in cardigans and clutching their purses, met and bowed to one another on the sidewalk. Three young men walked by, ties flapping in the wind, talking in loud, cheerful voices about the Lakers. She saw a couple of older men in dark, stiff suits, and something about their manner made Jackie think they were visiting from Japan. She passed a small restaurant, out of which drifted the sweet pungent smell of teriyaki. She thought about stopping—she hadn't had lunch that day, and she couldn't remember the last time she'd eaten Japanese—but then decided against it, at least for now. There was something that she needed to do.

She walked through an imitation Japanese village and then passed a large Buddhist temple. She saw two thirty-story apartment buildings and learned, from the signs in front, that they were retirement units for Japanese-Americans. Jackie was shocked to see that so many people still lived in this area. Just south were empty warehouses, drug-clogged parks, skid row, but here, Little Tokyo remained.

Going down another block, she found a large bookstore and went inside. Near the magazine section she saw what she was looking for, the English-language versions of the *Asahi Journal,* the *Tokyo Shinbun,* and the *Japan Times.* She picked up a copy of the *Asahi Journal* and looked at each of the articles; most of the reporters' names were Western. Then she turned back to the masthead, examined it, and returned the paper to its pile. She went through the same procedure with the *Tokyo Shinbun,* and then picked up the *Japan Times.* Finally, on page seven, she saw an article written by Akira Matsumoto. She pulled a pen and paper out of her bag and wrote "Matsumoto" and "Japan Times." Then she flipped back to the masthead, and found his name under the heading of "contributing reporter." She copied down his title, and the paper's address and phone number. Then she walked out of the bookstore, satisfied. Probably, Akira Matsumoto's parents were still around, and she could get in touch with them. But Lois had been right—there were dozens of Matsumotos in the phone book, and why work so hard to find someone who could lead her to Akira when she could get in touch with him directly herself? And she wanted to talk to him as soon as she could. He was the only living employee of her grandfather's store, the only other boy with a key, the only other person who might have been there that day, the last day of Curtis's life.

Feeling proud of herself, and eager to tell Lanier, Jackie walked back through the imitation village. She came out on 1st Street again, at a different angle this time. And as she stood there facing the old wooden storefronts, bits of memory fell into some prepared, waiting place, and something in her mind clicked and whirred. She'd been to Little Tokyo maybe three or four times, most recently a couple of years ago, when Lois had dragged her to the Japanese-American National Museum. But the time she remembered now was from twenty years before, when she'd come to the Nisei Festival with her grandfather. They had stood, the two of them, right here on this corner; Jackie remembered the shape and shadows of the building across the street, the way City Hall loomed in the distance.

She couldn't move. The traffic light changed from green to red and then back again, while Jackie stood there wondering how that trip had come about. The festival day came back to her in snippets. The children in the crowd, hoisted on shoulders and sitting on curbs, many of them dressed in *kimonos.* The smells and tastes of food—*soba, yakitori, donburi, sushi, mochi*—that she only came across during events like these, or when she went to her grandparents' house. The strains of music, plucked and pristine, played on instruments she didn't recognize. The signs written in two different languages, one business-like, direct, one more flowing and beautiful. And her grandfather! So handsome, so proper, his hair still mostly black, his body still straight-backed and lean. He walked proudly, chin up, hand clasped around his granddaughter's. They kept running into people whom her grandfather knew. Too young to understand about war or sex, Jackie still registered how people responded to him—the pleasure in the eyes of the women he talked to, the camaraderie and respect of the men. Everyone seemed to look at him, everyone—and as his smile got wider, his stance more erect, Jackie felt a simple, overwhelming pride that she had never felt for her parents.

Jackie walked up 1st Street now, remembering how much bigger Little Tokyo had seemed, how much more vibrant and full of people, when she was younger, and with her grandfather, and still able to be impressed. Both sides of her family had started here, in places she'd never seen. She knew, without knowing how she knew, and realizing it had to be from Frank, that his father, the first Sakai, had stayed in a Little Tokyo boarding house between planting and harvesting seasons. And that her father's family— one generation longer on American soil, more deeply rooted, wealthier—had owned two boarding houses just off of 1st Street. Jackie's other grandfather, Thomas, got his degree in landscape architecture from UCLA, and, when the war came and the Ishidas were evacuated to Postom, Arizona, he couldn't serve in the army because of his clicking knee. When they returned to L.A., Thomas dipped into family money—which had multiplied during the war—and joined up with Greg Miyamoto to start Ishimoto Landscaping, kicking off a business in the one field where their names didn't hurt them. People's lust for tasteful lawns and gardens—along with the perception that the Japanese were better with plants—had quickly made both men wealthy. Jackie remembered how uncomfortable Frank always seemed around this other side of her family—how out of place he looked among the Ishidas' well-dressed friends at the party they threw for her parents' silver anniversary; how her grandfather Ishida spoke to Frank in the cordial but dismissive tone he always used with the people who worked for him. And everything—the Ishidas' fortunes, the Sakais' struggles—had started right here in Little Tokyo, on the tiny piece of land a mile away from where Jackie would spend her future.

The next afternoon, Jackie drove down to Culver City to take Rebecca out for drinks. Rebecca was on the phone when she answered the door; she waved Jackie in and then walked into the kitchen. Jackie shut the door behind her and looked around. The stereo was on, a sad singing woman; when she picked up the open CD case, Jackie saw it was Nina Simone. That week's reading from their Entertainment Law class was laid out on the couch, half marked up with green and yellow highlighters. There was a small stack of folded laundry on the floor in front of the stereo, next to a basket full of not-yet-folded clothes. Rebecca, in the kitchen, walked back and forth with the phone, taking bites of a microwaved burrito while the other person talked. Jackie sat down on the couch and flipped absently through the reading, which she hadn't even looked at yet. Finally, her friend got off the phone.

"Hey," Rebecca said, walking over. She was wearing baggy sweats and a T-shirt, and she looked like she'd just gotten up.

"Hey, you don't look ready for a drink just yet."

"Why?" Rebecca asked, sitting down on the floor. "Are you?"

"Very," Jackie said. She closed Rebecca's book and tossed it away from her. "I didn't do the reading for class today, so of course Professor Hinchey calls on me, and I didn't even know enough to bullshit."

"God forbid you should ever not be in total control."

Jackie grabbed a pillow off the couch and threw it at Rebecca's head. "Fuck you."

Rebecca blocked the pillow away and grinned up at her. "You're cute, but no thanks, honey, you'd probably try and run the whole show."

"I'd *have* to—it's been so long since you got any you probably don't remember how to do it."

"You might be right—but I wouldn't trust *you* to reacquaint me. God knows what three years with Laura have done to your natural skills."

"Ooh," said Jackie, "Ouch."

"Speaking of such matters," continued Rebecca, "I think I have a date."

"Really? Who's the lucky person?"

Rebecca waved her hand dismissively, but Jackie could tell by the self-consciousness of this gesture that Rebecca was looking forward to it. "Oh, this architect babe I met at a meeting last week. She's a little older than us, early thirties I think, talkative, cute, seems cool."

"Is that who you were just talking to?"

Rebecca glanced over at the kitchen, as if some version of herself was still pacing there, telephone glued to her ear. "Yeah," she said. "Dinner Friday. We're doing Ethiopian."

She went into the bedroom to change, and Jackie looked at the television. Chevy trucks were moving in slow motion across the screen and, although the mute was on, her mind filled in the Bob Seger song the ad was shamelessly abusing. She knew even without asking that the architect babe was Asian. Rebecca had found many more gay Asian women than Jackie had known existed—whole organizations full of Chinese and Japanese, Thai and Filipina, Indian and Pakistani dykes. With men, for some reason, she was far less restrictive—she considered all men of color as potentials, and her last relationship had been with a Chicano lawyer. But out of all of these possibilities, nothing. Rebecca was stubbornly single, and as much as she liked to talk about people, check them out, catalog and flirt with them, she didn't follow up on these looks and flirtations, they were like window-shopping for her, a hobby totally removed from the real task of finding and loving someone. And that she had not been able to do. Jackie wondered, suddenly, who Rebecca was beneath her cauterized, careful exterior. She had the disconcerting feeling that she knew less of Rebecca than Rebecca did of her.

A few minutes later, Rebecca emerged. "Do I look presentable?" she asked.

"Always," Jackie answered, and she did. She was wearing faded Levi's, an olive shirt, and black boots. She'd reapplied her make-up, gelled her hair. "You look great," Jackie said, meaning it; she was almost, *almost* attracted to her. But the Asian qualities of her face—the flatness, the roundness, the slight slant to her eyes—were hurdles she could not clear.

They took Rebecca's car, the ancient, boat-like Pontiac. They drove down Overland and when they reached Jefferson Boulevard and passed the Tara Estates, Jackie thought about her aunt and all the things she needed to tell her. Rebecca chatted on and on about a paper they had due in their Tax Law class. She continued to talk as they arrived at the El Torito, as they chose a table by the bar, as they were served huge, white, frothy margaritas. Finally, after taking a large sip from her glass and wiping the salt off her lips, Rebecca gave her friend a funny look. "What's up with you, girl? You've been in another world the last few weeks."

"Have I?" Rebecca gave her a look. "Well, yeah," Jackie said. "I guess you're right." She took a big gulp of her drink and set her glass down. Then, for the next fifteen minutes, Jackie told Rebecca what she had been doing. She stopped and started, drank from her glass, cracked and played with the overdone chips. And while her friend sat there, silent for the duration of the monologue, Jackie watched her face change—the lips parting, then pressing together, the eyebrows lifting, the lines deepening around her eyes and on her forehead. But she listened, she stayed there, and Jackie felt something lift off her; it reminded her of how she felt when she came out to her then-best friend, Michelle, the day after their high school graduation. When Jackie finished with the part about Angela Broadnax, she just stopped; in the silence between them, they heard dance music from the speakers, a college basketball game on TV, the whir of the bartender's blender. Jackie watched her own fingers twist the stem of her empty glass, and looked across the table uncertainly. Rebecca let out a long breath.

"Damn, Jackie," she said. "Your poor grandfather."

"Those poor *kids*." Jackie waved over their waitress and ordered another round of drinks. "But you're right," she continued when the waitress was gone. "I understand a lot more about my grandfather now. And this explains why my family left Crenshaw."

"It explains some stuff about your mother, too. No wonder she cut herself off from the place."

Jackie pressed her lips together, feeling a defensiveness about her mother that surprised her. "You may be right, although I'm not sure she ever knew about the murders. My mother was always kind of uncomfortable with my grandfather anyway."

"Did she hang out at the store when she was growing up?"

"No. And neither did my aunt or my grandmother. It was very much a man's world, with no girls around, really. Except Angela Broadnax, I guess."

Rebecca jiggled the basket of chips. "So you think this cop did it? How exactly you going to prove it?"

Jackie sighed. "I don't know. I have to get in touch with this Sansei guy from the neighborhood who was one of the employees. And Lanier's trying to track down some cops from that era, to see if anyone will talk about Lawson."

Rebecca cocked her head and gave Jackie a wicked grin. "You had dinner with him, huh? And Laura saw?"

"Yeah. It was a pretty weird scene. Lanier had no idea who Laura was, and she was acting kind of crazy."

"What was she worried about? Did she think you were going to fuck him?"

Jackie shrugged. "Lord knows."

Rebecca leaned forward. "Well, would you?"

"Would I what?"

"Would you fuck him?"

"*No.* Jesus. Of course not. I'm not remotely interested. And I don't know why Laura was tripping."

"Well, you don't need to be interested in *him.* You could just be interested in what he could do for *you.*"

"Hey, come on—you're the one that's bi, girl, not me."

"So what? Guys are useful sometimes, even if you're not really into them. It's like masturbating, but better, 'cos you have to do less of the work. Just think of a man as a dildo with a really big base."

"I know," Jackie said. "I remember." She'd dated a few boys in high school, and had even, on a couple of drunken occasions, slept with men in college. But the experiences had been unnoteworthy, pleasant but mechanical, without the shiver and risk, the loss of control, she always felt with women.

"I think you might be missing out."

"Well, *you* can have him, then," Jackie snapped, but realized she didn't really mean it. She started on her second margarita. Her vision was blurry at the edges and the music seemed to press on her head. She wanted to stop talking about Lanier and her recent project, so she looked at her friend now and assumed a cheerful expression. "Anyway, enough about me and my family crap. What's happening in *your* life, besides the architect babe?"

Rebecca brightened. "Well, I went down to Legal Aid yesterday to meet the other associates and get a feel for the place. It's nuts in there, but I like it. You can tell the place is running on a shoestring—the office is really bare and the furniture's falling apart. And they told me, as I feared, that they couldn't pay me this summer while I study for the bar. So I'm on my own until I start in September, although I might just volunteer—because of what's happening with the garment workers, they're really overloaded. I don't know what I'm going to do to support myself—maybe I'll have to start waitressing *here*."

Jackie nodded, feeling fortunate and guilty about being paid for the summer. "What garment workers?" she asked.

Rebecca gave her a look. "The Thai women, the indentured servants," she said, as if Jackie should know. And she realized she did know, a little. It had been all over the news the last few days. Jackie had gotten the general shape of the story—the INS, acting on a tip, had gone to arrest several illegal Thai immigrants at an apartment complex in Westlake. And what they found were twenty-odd Thai women and girls in front of sewing machines, watched over by a man with a gun. Rebecca told her now that this first raid had led to discoveries of other dark and windowless sweatshops; all in all, the INS found over one hundred Thai women held captive by a group of smugglers who had contracted with a downtown manufacturer. Jackie hadn't paid much attention to the story and now she felt inadequate, out of touch. But this was always how it was. Rebecca would make sarcastic, pointed comments about something in the news—the Baton Rouge shooting, on Halloween, of an unarmed Japanese boy, and the subsequent acquittal of the killer; the recent bombing of the Japanese-American Community

Center in Norwalk. Jackie never followed these things too closely, but Rebecca seemed to take them all personally.

"What's Legal Aid doing?" Jackie asked. "Are you taking them on as clients?"

"Kind of, but it's difficult, because we're trying to figure out who to sue. Probably it'll be the manufacturers who hired the smugglers in the first place. We might go after the smugglers, too, but it's not clear what's going to happen with them—they might get deported and that might be their only punishment. At least the motherfuckers are in jail, though. I wish something bad would happen to them in there and save us the trouble of going to court. Shit, where are corrupt policemen when you need them?"

As Jackie sat there listening, she felt not angry and excited, as Rebecca clearly did, but increasingly ashamed. Although she'd heard about the Thai workers, she hadn't paid much attention, because their plight hadn't really concerned her. She made a mental note to follow the news more carefully.

"Anyway," Rebecca continued, "no matter how the lawsuits turn out, we're going to make a big stink about what's happening to the women."

"What's happening?"

"Well, this hasn't really hit the papers yet. The women have gotten a lot of sympathy from the general public, but the ironic thing is, they're probably being deported."

"*What*? You've got to be kidding me. Why?"

"There are only a few reasons why illegal immigrants are granted asylum, and the INS doesn't think these women qualify. Religious persecution is a reason for asylum, and political persecution, and physical danger—but not simple, plain-old poverty."

"But these women were essentially slaves."

"Yes, but in *America*, not in Thailand. And remember, they were indentured servants—they chose to come here. Now, I personally think that they *do* qualify for asylum and that they should be allowed to stay. But the INS thinks differently, and they've been getting a lot of pressure from the mayor and the city council to resolve this as quickly as possible." Rebecca twisted her glass around a quarter of a turn. "There are a couple of council members who are pushing to let the women stay." And she mentioned three names, strong Democrats. Laura's boss was not among them.

"What about Manny Jimenez?" Jackie asked.

Rebecca shrugged. "I don't know what he thinks about it. He hasn't said shit. Why don't you ask the woman who's got the inside scoop?"

"But I can't believe he'd stay silent about this. He's always been a champion of immigrants."

"*Legal* immigrants," said Rebecca, "except for Mexicans. And Mexicans don't really count, he thinks, and he has a point there, since the land once belonged to them anyway."

"But if the conditions were as bad as you say, the situation seems pretty cut-and-dried."

Rebecca shrugged again. "One would think. But remember we're discussing politicians here, not regular human beings. First of all, it's not exactly the time to be Mr. gung-ho immigration. And the other three council members just got re-elected, so they have nothing at stake. But maybe Manny's making a statement, because, well, you know. Everyone thinks he's going to run for mayor."

"But I don't see how this would help him. I mean, this case is sympathetic."

"All the better. It'll show that he can be tough on the issue and put some distance between him and all the teary-eyed liberals."

"Jesus," Jackie said. Looking down, she noticed that her napkin was in shreds. She wondered why Laura hadn't talked about this, not remembering her own continents of silence. And she realized that they hadn't been saying much about anything lately, even though they still spent most of their nights together. She looked up at her friend's face to find that the intensity was gone. Rebecca was grinning widely. "What?" Jackie asked.

"I think you might actually agree with me on this one. What's the matter, girl? You starting to get a bit soft?"

"I *must* be getting soft—in the head."

Rebecca continued to grin. But then suddenly, she leaned across the table. She slipped her left hand around Jackie's neck, cupping the base of her skull, and rubbed her knuckles against the top of Jackie's head. "It *is* a bit soft," she said, smiling.

On the drive back up to the Fairfax District, Jackie wondered about Laura, about her job, about the secrets they kept from each other. She realized that she had always kept things from Laura. Little things, like her occasional flirtations with other women; things she should have shared, like her near-constant worries and doubts about their relationship; personal things, like what she thought about her family, and how thrilled she felt over her success at becoming a lawyer. Most of these things she refrained from telling not because she didn't want Laura to know, but for the simple idea of *having* things that Laura didn't know. By keeping so much to herself, by having this secret, private storehouse of her own memories and thoughts, she kept Laura outside of her, and made herself safe. And she *wanted* to be safe, or at least she thought she did; she wanted someone to stand at the edges of her and never really enter. But now it occurred to her that Laura had secrets, too.

On Oakwood, Jackie turned right past the newsstand, then passed her own street and kept driving. She drove down to Sierra Bonita and turned left. Laura's car was parked in front of the house and Jackie pulled up behind it. The lights were on in the house and Jackie could see the way the room changed colors, subtly, reflecting what was showing on the television. Jackie sat there for ten minutes, waiting for the calmness, or courage, to go in and face her girlfriend. Finally, she was startled by headlights in her rearview mirror. It was time to make a move. But she couldn't muster the energy to deal with Laura now, and so she started her engine up again and drove the six blocks home.

Later, on her couch, as she floated somewhere in the no-man's land between sober and drunk, it wasn't Laura or their problems she thought of. Her mind went back to something that Rebecca once said—that Jackie's being gay had saved her. She wasn't sure what her friend had meant by this, but she knew Rebecca was surprised by, and approving of, Jackie's sudden new interest in her family. She kept returning, also, to the moment in the restaurant when Rebecca had reached over and rubbed her head. And it wasn't really her friend's strange gesture that troubled her. It was that when Rebecca loosened her fist, when she let the still-curled fingers of her now-relaxed hand rest right at Jackie's hairline, Jackie hadn't pulled away from her friend's warm touch, but instead, for just a moment, pressed into it.

CHAPTER NINETEEN

FRANK, 1976
(WHAT JACKIE DOESN'T REMEMBER)

FRANK WAS Brownie leader for the morning. He was standing outside the entrance of a Safeway in Torrance, where five seven-year-old girls from Jackie's troop were selling Girl Scout cookies. One of the girls was sitting at the card table, which held neat stacks of red, green, and yellow cookie boxes and a gray metal box for cash. Next to the table were much bigger cardboard boxes, which contained the reserve cookie supply. The girl at the table handled people who approached on their own, wisps of brown hair catching in the corner of her mouth as she explained the different kinds, and the other four hit up customers as they entered and left the store. The parents worked in shifts, and Jackie's mother was supposed to be there, but she'd been called away for an emergency, so Frank had driven over. The other girls had reacted to his presence with interest. "Where did you come from?" one of them asked, when he introduced himself as Jackie's grandfather.

"Gardena," he'd replied, and they'd looked at him, confused.

"No, where did you *really* come from?"

That awkward beginning an hour past now, he watched with pleasure as his granddaughter worked, running excitedly to customers in her neat tan uniform, Brownie button shining on her lapel. She was so confident, Jackie, and in her the seriousness of his older daughter met his younger daughter's capacity for joy. Jackie was his only grandchild, and although he worried about the long hours kept by both of her parents, he was happy about the result—more time with him. He'd missed out on these years with his own daughters—the childish, open years, before self-consciousness or cynicism, when each shade of pleasure or sorrow showed so clearly on their faces. And he was making up for it with Jackie, a fact which hadn't been lost on his daughters, and was resented a bit, he was almost sure, by Rose. They'd had words a few times about where Frank took Jackie, what he did with her. But he wasn't trying to shape her, as Lois was. He just took Jackie to the places where he liked to go himself—downtown, bowling, fishing off the pier—and because she lit up like a sunrise when she watched the waves roll in, or sent the bowling ball rumbling down the lane. There was nothing else he'd rather do than what he was doing— watching the child run about, at peace with the world. His reverie was broken by the arrival of Lois, whom he'd enlisted to help him handle the girls.

"You look like a natural," she said. "You could start your own troop."

"Well, I've had some experience in sales."

"Aunt Lois!" Jackie shouted, running over and giving her a hug. "I've already sold seventeen boxes!"

"That's great, sweetie."

"Actually," Jackie said, looking suddenly grave, "I've only sold fifteen, but I knew you and Grandpa would buy a box."

"Now what would make you think that?" Lois asked. Her question went unheard, though, because all four of the miniature salesgirls had swarmed around a middle-aged couple who had just come out of the store. Through the clamor of childish voices, Frank and Lois heard the woman's "Oh, my!" The couple looked taken aback, and then delighted. Frank smiled. What a brilliant capitalist organization the Girl Scouts of America was. While the woman reached into her purse, Jackie and one of her troop mates suddenly sprinted to the other exit, where another likely victim was emerging.

"Why didn't I ever do Brownies or Girl Scouts?" Lois asked.

"You were never interested. Your sister did, though, remember?"

They talked about Rose's hectic schedule—she'd just started her residency, and so Frank and Lois were taking Jackie more often. Both of them had easier schedules than Rose. Frank was still working a forty-hour week, but he'd been his own boss for the last seven years, since breaking away from Richard Iida, and now he set his own schedule, wiring new restaurants and businesses with lights and electricity, providing them with conduits for life. And Lois, at twenty-five, had finally finished college; she was working part-time as a teacher's assistant while she tried to figure out her next move. They were discussing what to do with Jackie after the sale was over, suggesting and then deciding against McDonald's and Chuck E. Cheese.

Then another woman came out of the store. She was dark-haired, wearing a navy blue suit, thirty-five or forty. She had two paper bags of groceries, which she set down on the ground while she fiddled with the strap of her purse. The strap readjusted and her groceries collected, she started to walk away, and Jackie broke ranks with the rest of the Brownies to run over and give her pitch.

"Would . . . you . . . like to buy . . . some . . . Girl Scout . . . cookies?" she managed to get out between breaths. Her cheeks were flushed pink from the effort of her sprint, and a few sweaty strands of hair were stuck to her forehead.

The woman wrinkled her nose and looked at Jackie as if she'd just offered to sell her dog shit. "No, I would not," she said, and she started to turn away, but then another Brownie appeared. And when this other girl made her appeal, the woman put down her bags and bought two boxes of thin mints.

Frank and Lois were stunned. Jackie looked puzzled for a moment, not knowing how she'd been insulted, and then ran back toward the store, unconcerned. But her grandfather stood there, fuming. Lois looked at him incredulously, and his ears were beet red. He didn't return her look, though, because he was staring at the woman, who was briskly striding out to the parking lot. He clenched and unclenched his fists a few times as the woman moved further away. And then he commenced the slow, deliberate walk of a man who is trying to keep himself from murder.

The woman was getting into a white Volvo station wagon, which was parked back-end first, and she didn't know that she was being followed. She placed her purse and grocery bags on the passenger seat, buckled her seatbelt, and looked up to find Frank right in front of the car. Frank didn't know what he intended to do. But when the woman started her engine, he didn't move. He just glared at her, and finally, after glaring back for a moment, the woman honked her horn. He still didn't move, but drew himself up and curled his hands into fists. The woman tossed her own hands up in annoyance and disbelief, and then rolled down her window and leaned out.

"Could you move?" she said loudly. The hostility in her voice was sharp and undisguised; it seemed to come from something more than the inconvenience of someone blocking her way.

Then Frank realized what he wanted. "Not until you buy a box of cookies from my granddaughter."

The woman stared at him, and it took her a moment to make the connection. "You've got to be kidding. Get out of my way."

"You go back there and buy a box of cookies."

Frank was vaguely aware that normal life carried on around him. A few spaces to his left a car pulled out and drove away. A teenage girl walked by and looked at him quizzically. In the next aisle of cars a store employee was collecting shopping carts, pushing each new one into the collapsing back of the one in front of it. The woman revved the engine a few times, as if firing off warning shots. When Frank still didn't move, she put the car into gear and inched forward. The car drew closer to him, closer, and he felt the bumper touch his knee. Frank and the woman glared at each other through the windshield, and for a brief moment he thought the woman would run him over. Then, finally, she put the car back into park. She leaned out the window again. "Get out of the way, you idiot, or else I'm going to call the police!"

But there wasn't a cop in sight, and Frank knew it. Moving again without thought or intention, he pulled his keys out of his pocket and held them up in the air. The sunlight glinted off the metal.

"No, *you* get out," he said, and his voice was steady. "Get out of the car, go back over there, and buy a box of cookies from my granddaughter."

The woman laughed. "Or else what? You're going to jingle your keys at me?"

Frank took the largest key, the one to his office, and held it like a switchblade, and he made a long, deep gash in the hood of the car. He did it slowly, firmly, deliberately, and the sound was excruciating, like fingernails scraping a blackboard.

The woman stared in disbelief. "What the hell are you doing?"

"You go over there and buy a box of cookies." He stood up straight and picked the paint out from between the teeth of his keys. He felt very calm now. The woman didn't speak or move, so he leaned over the car again and started making another gash. He could see the silver metal beneath the coat of white paint, and he took pleasure in what he was doing.

"All right, all right," the woman said, getting out of the car. She walked briskly toward the entrance, and didn't look at Frank as she went by. Frank followed her from maybe ten feet behind. He saw Lois standing next to the card table, giving him a look like he was crazy—and maybe he was, but he didn't care. The woman went straight to Jackie, who was flitting about between customers, thrust a five into her hand, and said, "Here." Then she yanked away two of the boxes Jackie was holding, turned, and started back toward the car. Jackie, who'd missed the whole conflict, and was still nonplussed by the woman's rudeness, went to the card table to hand over the money. Frank was standing at the edge of the lot, and as the woman passed he gave her a bow. He knew there were things he should worry about—whether the woman would file a complaint; whether the girls had seen what he'd done; what it meant that he'd surrendered to his anger. But right now he didn't want to consider them, because he felt vindicated and good. After he bowed, though, the woman spun toward him, just as Jackie came up to say hi.

"You fucking asshole!" the woman yelled. "I bought the cookies, all right? I mean, what the hell else do you want from me?"

Frank put his arm around Jackie and looked the woman in the eye. "Please," he said, "don't swear in front of my granddaughter."

CHAPTER TWENTY

1994

THE WEATHER was clear and perfect that Saturday morning, not unlike the morning, a month before, that Jackie had first gone over to Lois's house and laid eyes on the will. When she arrived at the Tara Estates, Lois and Ted were already dressed and prepared for the day. Ted said hello to her, kissing her on the cheek as he headed out the door to meet a friend for a game of paddle tennis. Lois ushered Jackie in and sat her down on the couch. The box—a Timberland boot box—was on the coffee table already; the dull black bowling ball sat cannonball-like on the frayed reclining chair. In front of Jackie there materialized a cup of coffee and a bagel. After several minutes of catching up—Lois's job, the mid-sized aftershock that had awakened them all in the night, the house in Blair Hills that Ted and Lois had made an offer on— they both ran out of words and let their eyes wander over to the box.

"I don't *have* to take it," Jackie said, feeling suddenly awkward. "I mean, do you want it?"

"No, no. He left it to you. And it's not like I want to look at it anyway. Actually, I'll be glad to have it out of here."

Jackie pulled the box toward her and removed the lid. She was met with a collage of documents and half-obscured pictures. On top were two velvet boxes, which she found, when she creaked them open, contained war medals dulled with age. She set them aside and reached into the box again. The documents seemed alive to her, and when she picked up her first handful of papers and photographs, she felt something like a pulse beat through her. This was where her search for Curtis had started, and also, in a sense, her search for Frank. And she was sure, without quite knowing why, that her searches would end here, too. She set the documents down on the coffee table and spread them out, like a fortune teller arranging her tarot cards. How to read them? How to string together the story they might tell her? She picked up the thing that jumped out at her first, a picture of Frank as a soldier. He was flanked by two other young Nisei in uniform. All three of them were kneeling, right knees on the ground, left elbows propped up on their other legs. They held their guns gently, like breakable things, the butts against the ground, the barrels pointing up at the sky. The men were weighted down with mysterious belts and pouches. Their helmets were on but the straps hung loose, and all three men were grinning widely. Behind them was a beautiful, empty, rolling field that looked untouched and deceptively peaceful. Off in the distance, though, above some hills, were white billows of clouds or smoke.

"Kenny Miura," Lois said, pointing to the man on the left. "And Tom Kobayashi. Dad's best friends in the army. That picture was taken in Italy, although I don't know exactly where."

"Grandpa was kind of a babe here, huh?"

"Looks like he knows it, too."

"I never heard about these guys. Did Grandpa lose touch with them after the war?"

"They both died. Kenny was killed not long after this picture was taken, in the same battle that Dad got wounded. And Tom was killed a few weeks later."

Jackie shook her head.

"Dad was the one who wrote both their parents, from the hospital." Lois shuffled through the papers on the table and pulled out a newspaper clipping. There was a picture of a stern-faced white military man, standing on a porch with a dazed-looking young woman. The caption read, "War Widow Presented with Husband's Distinguished Service Cross."

"This is Kenny Miura's wife," Lois said, "at their house up in Tustin. She sent this clipping to Dad. What the picture *doesn't* show is that her windows were smashed, and that 'Japs Go Home' was painted on the side of the house."

"How thoughtful. Is there a clipping about the other guy?"

"No, but he had an equally heart-warming response to his death. He was from a small town up in Washington, and his name was carved into a stone monument with the names of a bunch of other soldiers who were killed in action. But then the American Legion came and chipped it off."

"Lovely." Jackie uncovered a few more photos—Frank, her mother and aunt as children, some pets she didn't recognize. Then she came upon a wallet-size portrait of her grandfather in uniform. She realized she'd seen it before, a larger version of the very same picture. And then something came back to her. She'd remembered the result of it, the final remark, but the event itself had been obscured until now.

She was six years old, and spending the weekend at her grand-parents' house. It was raining, so she was playing in the garage, digging through a chest of old clothes. About half the clothes were out, strewn around on the floor, when she found a framed black-and-white newspaper article with a picture of a young Japanese-American soldier. She pulled it out and read the headline: "Southland Soldier Receives High Honor." The caption said something about war and a medal; the soldier was handsome and smiling. There was something in the sharpness of his cheeks and the thinness of his nose which reminded Jackie of her mother, and then she just burst out with it: "Grandpa!" Although she knew that Japanese-American men had fought in some long-ago war (there were always uniformed men in the Nisei Week Parade, old-timers popping out of their faded jackets), she'd never known her grand-father was one of them. Excited by her discovery and impressed by the image of her grandfather in uniform, she'd rushed into the house. She hoped that, when she showed him the article, her grandpa would get misty-eyed and offer tales of how he beat up on the enemy. But when Jackie held it toward him, as proud as if she were offering a report-card full of As, something opened in his eyes, and then closed again, and he took the frame away. Jackie, not understanding, tugged on his pants. "Did you fight in the war, Grandpa? Why didn't you ever tell me that you fought in the war?"

And Frank was silent for a moment before he looked at her and said, "Because it didn't make any difference."

Now, at Lois's, Jackie set the tiny picture down and looked at the other one again, the shot of Frank and his friends in the fields of Italy. She heard again her grandfather's answer, which she'd remembered all this time: *"Because it didn't make any difference."* For almost twenty years, she'd assumed he meant that the army, or his part of it, hadn't done anything of consequence. But then she looked at the faces of Miura and Kobayashi. She thought of broken glass, black spray paint, hammer and chisel applied to stone. She thought of the expression on the face of Kenny Miura's young widow, and suddenly realized that this wasn't what he meant at all.

Lois touched the box again. "There could be something in there that might help you, you know. Have you found out anything new since the last time I talked to you?"

Jackie took a moment to snap out of her memory. "Yes and no. Derek Broadnax apparently saw the cop around the store the day of the murders. But he's dead now—he OD'd on heroin. And I found out where Matsumoto works; I just have to get in touch with him. I talked to someone at the Holiday Bowl, too, who told me about this guy Kenji Hirano."

"Kenji. Of course. He might be able to help, if you can get a complete sentence out of him."

Jackie nodded, and then realized she didn't want to say anything more—nothing about what she was hearing of Frank or learning about Curtis and Lanier. It all seemed like something private, something shared between her and her grandfather. She cared now, very deeply, about putting closure on the murders, but it wasn't just Nick Lawson she was after anymore. And she couldn't say, either, that she wanted to learn about Curtis, except in the ways that he affected her grandfather's life. Nick Lawson, Curtis Martindale—they were the catalysts, but no longer the reason. For Jackie, the search had come to mean something else.

She pulled out another handful of documents, and a piece of soft paper fell out of the pile. It was brown elementary school writing paper, with wide blues lines to contain the loose, childish script:

MY Momy said I shold thank you for the crayns so thank you. I like to color and blew is my favorit. I filed up half the coloring book alredy I can do picturs real fast. Also I like the candy you gave me do you hav any more?
See you soon
Love, Curtis

Jackie showed the page to her aunt. "This is interesting. Do you think it's the same Curtis?"

Lois read the letter. "Could be. I don't know."

"When did Grandpa meet him?"

"I'm not exactly sure."

"But he must have known him before he hired him, right? I mean, this looks like it was written . . ." she read it again, "by a seven- or eight-year-old kid. Curtis was four when the Martindales moved to L.A., so Grandpa—if this is the same Curtis—must have met him in the next few years."

"Do you think it means something? Dad knew a *lot* of little kids."

"I have no idea—although if he did know Curtis for that many years, leaving him the store would seem a bit less crazy."

"Speaking of the store, look at these." Lois reached into the box and pulled out two pictures. One showed her father, in his early twenties, with Old Man Larabie—young man and old man, Japanese and black—standing in front of the market in their matching white aprons. Frank's hand was curled around the handle of the broom and he was grinning at the camera, bright-eyed, stiff-backed, confident. The other was a shot of an older Frank, in the doorway with a smiling, aproned boy. There was something about the tilt of the boy's head, the space between his eyes, that looked familiar to Jackie.

"This must be Derek Broadnax," she said.

She looked through some more papers—envelopes, clippings, pictures—until she discovered a black-and-white photograph of seven young people in a bowling alley. They looked around college age and they were all dressed in white shirts and dark skirts or trousers. The three young women stood arm in arm, smiling widely at the camera. The four young men were crouched down in front of them.

"I think they're a team," Lois said, craning her neck to see the picture. "That's definitely the Holiday Bowl."

"Are any of these the boys from the store?"

Lois took the picture and squinted at it. "I don't know. This could be Curtis here, but I just don't know."

Jackie continued to dig through the box while her aunt tilted and frowned at the picture. Something was here—Jackie didn't know what, but she could feel it. Maybe it was in the picture that Lois held, or in the papers that she'd gone through at home. But she was excited—whatever it was, it was slowly coming into her reach. Now, beneath some envelopes, she discovered a pile of obituaries. Her grandmother's was here. And many names she didn't recognize—Richard Iida, Steve Yamamoto, Andy Riley, Barry Hughes. Her great-grandmother's obituary, but not her great-grandfather's. A slew of Japanese names Jackie recognized from her stays in Gardena. And then both of Curtis's parents, Bruce in 1992, Alma in 1985. She handed the stack to Lois, who went nostalgic over some of the people and began to tell stories about them.

But Jackie was feeling impatient now. She wanted to leave. She wanted to look at the box in private and then show the relevant things to Lanier. He'd be able to tell her if Curtis was in the picture at the Holiday Bowl, and he might know some more of the dead. So after setting up a coffee date for the following week, getting the cards from the funeral, and lugging the bowling ball and box out to the car, Jackie drove back up to Fairfax, singing all the way, happier than she'd been in forever.

CHAPTER TWENTY-ONE

JIMMY, 1963

THEY WERE three—Curtis, Cory, and Jimmy—playing in the alley behind the store. Jimmy and Cory were six years old, and Curtis fifteen. Jimmy was the quietest, even in his own house—it was his sister who laughed raucously or screamed in displeasure; who made loud demands of their mother. He'd wanted brothers, boys to play with, and then he'd met Cory a year earlier on the first day of kindergarten. And he saw Cory more often, almost every day at school, but it was Curtis who'd turned out to be the prize. Curtis was the older cousin, a big brother, a half-man. That day, they were excited because Cory had found an old guitar in a dumpster, and they'd brought it immediately to Curtis—partly because Curtis had learned to play in music class at school; partly because Cory always showed things to his older brother. Now all three of them sat, with Curtis in the middle, on the old brown couch at the end of the alley behind Peterson's Garage. Curtis bounced the guitar lightly on his knees, running his hands softly over its worn brown surface. With his left hand, he traced the slender neck of the instrument, all the way up to the knobs. These he took between his thumb and finger, coaxing, twisting lightly, while the fingers of his right hand touched the strings. Cory, who was sitting to the right of him, kept up a running commentary.

"Make it tighter, that don't sound right," he instructed as his brother tried a note. Or, "You think we can fix that crack down there at the bottom?"

Jimmy, on the other side, watched silently. He watched

Curtis's long, graceful fingers as they coaxed coherent sound from this collection of old wood and wire. He loved his older cousin. Curtis was gentle with him, quiet, but more stubborn than you'd think just by looking at him. When Mr. Martindale yelled at him—Jimmy had seen this—Curtis would just shut down, become unreachable. This impassivity only seemed to make his father even angrier; he never yelled at Cory that way, even though Cory did so much more to warrant scolding. And Cory, at least, looked like he could take it. He was sturdy and square, a box-shaped boy; nothing could knock him over. Even his afro grew out at right angles, squaring his large, blunt head. Curtis, on the other hand, was thin like his mother, but also like her, steel-tough, unbendable.

"It's more tuned," he said now to Cory. "Y'all sure this don't belong to nobody?"

Cory nodded vigorously. "We found it in the dumpster behind the barber shop. You gonna teach us how to play?"

"I only know a couple things, C. You gotta find someone plays better than me."

He brought both his hands underneath the guitar, supporting its two soft curves. Then he held the instrument out sideways toward his brother. Cory stared and then took it gently, as if his brother were handing him an entirely new guitar. He set it on his lap, with difficulty; he could reach barely halfway up the neck.

"Try it," his brother encouraged.

Cory gripped the neck tight with his left hand and raised his right uncertainly. Then he plucked a string so loudly that the twang made all of them jump. He looked startled, uncertain what he'd done.

"No, let me show you," Curtis said, laughing. He took the guitar back, repositioned it on his knee, and strummed gently with the side of his thumb. The sound that came out now was synchronized, sensical, not like the awkward low complaint produced by Cory. Curtis handed the guitar back over again, and Cory tried to imitate his brother's hold on the chords. Then he ran his thumb down along the strings, causing, instead of one loud twang, six smaller ones. He looked frustrated, and Curtis laughed again.

"Do it softer," offered Jimmy, and Cory glared at him.

Curtis spread his legs and patted the small tan triangle that opened on the couch. "Come here," he said. Cory looked at him uncertainly, and Curtis patted again. "Sit here."

Cory stepped over and sat between his brother's legs. Curtis lifted him up onto his own leg and then guided Cory's arm under the neck. Small hand in larger one, Curtis showed him how to hold it, fingers pressed lightly to the strings. Then Curtis shaped his right arm to Cory's. He took his brother's right hand and held the small thumb, like a pick, between his own thumb and first finger. Then he strummed. And when the sounds lifted off the strings, converging in the air, Cory's mouth opened wide. Curtis brought their hands back up, then down again, sending out six more notes to join the others. The third time he brought their hands back, he pressed his brother's against the wood, and then pulled his own hand away. Cory turned his head, questioning, and Curtis nodded. Cory moved his hand uncertainly, but then, gently, he ran his thumb over the strings, drawing out sounds that made sense. And now he smiled widely, and Jimmy rocked on the couch, aching to cradle the sound that strumming produced.

He was just about to ask if he could have a turn now when he heard something at the end of the alley. He turned and saw a man walking toward them, a whiteman in a dark blue uniform. Jimmy saw metallic blond hair, the flat V of light brown eyebrows. The cop leaned forward, his fists clenched, and he moved toward them very quickly. He was maybe twenty feet away now, and Jimmy saw, behind him, the parked police car, which was blocking the end of the alley. He looked to the left then, reconfirming what he already knew: there was no outlet on that side, just the back wall of Peterson's Garage. Curtis and Cory had seen the cop, too; Jimmy felt Curtis's hand on his back and heard him say, "Go." Before the cop had taken another step, the boys were up, looking around for a way to escape. There were no easy walls to scale, just blank garage doors. Then Curtis said, "There," and Jimmy saw where he was pointing. Between two of the garages was a tall wire fence with a bottom corner loose. Cory ran to it, pulled it back. "Go on," insisted Curtis. He yanked the fence aside and held it open just wide enough for the boys to scramble through. Cory went first, butt and legs wriggling, and Curtis shoved Jimmy in after him. Then they both turned around to help Curtis. He held the fence open with his right arm and pushed his head through the space; the two younger boys saw him, then watched him vanish, as the cop dragged him back into the alley.

Cory yelled out his brother's name and started to dive under the fence, but Jimmy pulled him back and held him.

"Run!" they heard Curtis yell. "Get outta here!"

But while they didn't go back out to the alley, they didn't run, either. The fence was covered with black plastic, and Cory pushed it aside, and the two boys peered out into the alley. The cop had dragged Curtis out near the couch and stood him up again. He held him by his T-shirt, the white fabric balled in his fist.

"Who'd you steal that guitar from?" asked the cop.

"Nobody," Curtis said, and Jimmy could not believe how calm he sounded. "We found it in a trash bin."

The cop yanked on Curtis's shirt. "Bullshit. That guitar's in good shape. Even you people aren't stupid enough to throw out something new." Curtis did not remove his eyes from Lawson's face. Lawson shook Curtis again. "What are you looking at, nigger?"

"I didn't steal anything," said Curtis, calmly.

"Bullshit!" yelled Lawson, and he pushed Curtis back so hard he fell to the ground. Curtis sat there, knees bent, arms supporting his weight, looking at Lawson as if interested in what he'd do next. Lawson stepped toward Curtis as if approaching a football, and kicked him, hard, in the thigh. Curtis made a noise, and Cory gasped.

"Ssshh," said Jimmy, tightening his grip on Cory's shoulder. He pressed hard against the fence, feeling and ignoring something sharp against his cheek.

On the other side of the fence, Lawson pulled Curtis up with both hands. "I know you, boy. You're the punk who broke into Audubon. My fellow cop was *real* upset he didn't get to punish you himself." He laughed. "I'll have to tell him that you've moved on to robbery."

"I haven't."

"Shut up." Then he leaned back for leverage and punched

Curtis in the cheek, and then once more in the jaw. Curtis's head jerked back again, and spit and blood flew. Quietly, in Jimmy's arms, Cory began to cry. Jimmy banged his head against the fence in frustration.

"You just try to tell me again," said Lawson, "about how you didn't steal anything. What do you have to say for yourself now?"

Curtis's mouth was swelling and there was blood all over his chin; he just turned to Lawson and looked at him. The V of Lawson's eyebrows got steeper and he grabbed Curtis's shirt again.

"Say something, nigger!"

But Curtis still did not respond.

Lawson's face grew redder and his lips pulled back into a snarl. "You fucking smart-ass coon," he said. "You think you're too fucking good to talk to me?" Then he let go of the shirt just as he pulled his fist back; it was like he was tossing up Curtis's head to smash a serve. When he hit Curtis this time, the blow was much harder, and Curtis's body swiveled a quarter of a turn before falling dully to the ground. He landed heavily and grunted, then brought his hands to his head. He pulled his legs up and curled into himself.

"Yeah," said Lawson, shaking out his fist, "you're not looking at me *now*, boy, are you? Don't think I'm so funny now, do you?"

He stepped up to Curtis and kicked him three more times—twice in the legs and once in the back of the head. Then he leaned over, as if he were about to spit on him, but just glared, enjoying his work. And it was then, as he stood up straight again, that he looked over to the fence. He couldn't see Cory and Jimmy—they were obscured by the plastic—but the boys both saw him clearly. They saw the thin, sharp nose, the tight lips and narrowed eyes, as the cop yelled out a warning. "Next time, boys, I'm not gonna let you get away!" Then he walked back to the end of the alley and drove off.

When he was gone, Cory and Jimmy scrambled out from behind the fence and ran over to where Curtis was lying. His lips and nose were bloody, his right eye was starting to swell. There was a growing stain of blood on his T-shirt and spots of blood on the concrete beneath him. He lay very still, and breathed slowly and hard. Cory and Jimmy kept touching him, laying hands on his shoulders, knees, hands, head, less to comfort him than to convince themselves that all of him was there. They were so concerned with Curtis that Jimmy didn't notice his own blood, dripping from the gash on his cheek where he'd sliced his face on the broken fence. No tears escaped their eyes now, but Jimmy felt them welling in his throat; with the slightest noise from Curtis, he knew he would break. But Curtis did not complain. He didn't groan or cry. And when, twenty minutes later, he finally pulled himself up into a sitting position, what he said was, "Don't tell Mama and Daddy what happened."

Cory looked him, puzzled. "Why?"

"Just don't," Curtis answered, holding his side. "I'll say I got into a fight or something."

"Well, what are you gonna do?"

"I'm gonna go see Mr. Sakai," Curtis said. And slowly, wincing, he made himself stand, and limped off to the end of the alley.

CHAPTER TWENTY-TWO

LOIS, 1965

BEFORE THE gunshots, before the looting, before the radio and TV newsmen said they'd better stay inside, Lois knew something awful was happening because the sky was filled with smoke. It wasn't their sky yet, but the sky southeast. And it wasn't an isolated plume, as if from one small fire, but a thick, gray blanket over Watts. It had started to form on Thursday, the second night of the riot. And by Friday, when the National Guard came, the whole city smelled of smoke. The people who dared to go to work at all left their jobs and stores early, eager to get home before dark.

Lois slept fitfully on Friday, because of the unusually hot night, and because she feared what would happen tomorrow. By dusk, it was clear to everyone in the Crenshaw district that the smoke was moving closer. On Saturday morning, the Sakais awoke early and the whole family gathered around the kitchen table. Frank, who was baggy-eyed from getting no sleep, instructed everyone to stay in the house.

"We're almost out of toilet paper," Mary informed him. "And milk." She seemed irritated, whip-folding towels as they talked, as if Frank had cooked up the riots to inconvenience her.

"I'll bring some from the store," he said. "I've got to go make sure everything's locked up safe, and I'll be back within an hour. Just keep the door locked and the TV on, and wait for me."

Lois didn't want her father to leave. Although both her mother and her sister looked sober and alert, she was downright scared. Would the looters just do what they'd done so far—rob and burn the stores and businesses, abuse the cars that crossed their path? Or would Crenshaw be the place where they finally went further— off the streets and into the houses? Would the boys from the neighborhood jump into the fray or defend themselves against it? And if anything happened to their block, to their house, how would they be able to stop it? No, she didn't want her father to leave them, so as he walked through the door, she went outside with him and into the hot, hot day. It was so humid the Japanese shutters wouldn't close. It was so sultry the manicured bushes were drooping, heavy with the weight of themselves.

"You've got to stay here, Lo," her father said, using the shortened version of her name he only did when they were alone.

"Let me come with you, Dad," she pleaded. They were on the walkway in front of the steps.

"No, honey, I'll be right back."

Then came a low, booming voice from next door. "I'll protect them," it said. They turned and saw Bill Acres, a thick red-faced man who looked like the Indiana farmer he once was. He was sitting on a chair he'd pulled out to his porch, a rifle propped up on his knees.

"What are you doing, Bill?" Frank asked. He looked from Acres' gun to his face. Lois, frightened, just stared at the gun, fighting off the urge to run inside.

"I bought this yesterday," Acres replied. "An M-1 Carbine. Ain't it a beaut? Hell if I'm gonna let some punk-ass niggers run roughshod over my neighborhood." He didn't say the rest, but Lois knew what it would be—*bad enough they live here already.* Lois could remember a time when he wouldn't talk to the Sakais and forbade his daughters from playing with her and Rose. But their stock had risen considerably, in Acres' eyes, once the blacks began to move there in earnest.

"Well, thanks," said Frank. "But I'll be right back. Don't go pointing that thing at my house."

"I've got another one inside. You want it?"

"No, thanks, Bill. I'll be fine."

Lois watched her father walk across the street, his quick, slightly forward-leaning stride. After giving a fake smile to Acres, she went back in the house, where her sister and mother were sitting in front of the news.

"There's looting over on Western," Rose informed her.

"As soon as this is over," their mother said, "we're getting out of here. We're going to Grandpa and Grandma Takayas'."

Lois nursed a cup of tea and sat with her family. Just as she was worrying about the time he'd been gone, her father came home with the items that Mary had asked for. He walked into the living room looking grim.

"The boys were there," he said to his wife, "wanting to protect it. I had to send them home."

"Why? Why not let them be useful for once?"

He didn't answer, knowing he'd helped create some of the bitterness he despised, and Lois wondered if he was sorry for trying to talk about the store, which almost always brought such a response. Now he leaned forward and looked at the screen. "Anything happen since I left?"

"No," Mary said. "It's getting closer."

This was like a storm, Lois thought—everyone knowing, vaguely, that it was approaching; people locked inside, away from the elements. Her family watching the news to track its progress and destruction, knowing they weren't going anywhere. Except. Except this storm was personal—it burned buildings and dragged people out of cars. Except this storm recruited, maybe boys that Lois knew. Lois understood the rage, or thought she did, but not the way it was playing out. The problem wasn't just the lack of jobs, the hunger. It was, as the Yellow Brotherhood always complained, the sense that people were being threatened, watched—even her, even her sister. The police were like an army, and acted that way. In Crenshaw, only the straw-haired Irishman was cordial—the rest, especially Lawson, who'd taunted her sometimes, and even the black ones, trying hard, at the expense of those they policed, to make themselves feel like men, were frightening, and always to be avoided. After another hour or two of near-silent watching, they heard the first whoops on the boulevard. And then the sounds of breaking windows, of people running, of guns fired into the air. They were only two blocks from Crenshaw, and the wind brought it all—the voices, the textured and complicated laughter, bats and crow bars against glass and steel. And the smoke was now filling *their* part of the sky, too, and the neighborhood was covered in gray. From next door they heard gunshots, and Frank shook his head. "That fool's shooting into the sky."

They weren't watching the news now, just listening to the street, and Lois began to cry. All the businesses she walked past, the stores where she shopped. She was sure her father's store would be hit, too.

When Frank closed the curtain and turned from the window, his face looked pale and blood-drained. He wouldn't meet Lois's eyes—he wasn't looking at any of them—but she knew how he felt. The place where he'd lived since he was a boy. Their neighborhood, their streets, were in chaos. At least her grandmother wasn't here to see this—she'd passed away the year before—but Masako's son wasn't taking it any easier than she would have. He was hurting almost physically, while Rose just looked scared, and Mary, something else entirely. She seemed to be taking a certain pleasure in the fact that this place she so disliked and wanted desperately to leave; this place that had changed so much the last ten years, was falling apart all around her. But Lois felt more like her father. And when he sat down heavily in his upholstered chair, she wanted only to be a little girl again so she could sit in his lap, with her head beneath his chin and her ear against his chest, while he rocked her fears away.

They didn't eat dinner that evening—no one was hungry—and the fires burned on through the night. The whole house smelled like smoke, but they hardly noticed anymore. Mary and Rose eventually went to bed and Lois stayed downstairs with her father, who was pouring himself drinks from a bottle of whiskey he'd produced from the back of the linen closet. They watched the news, switching channels, and Frank occasionally looked out the window. All the street lights were out and it was quiet now—on the boulevard, looters might be picking through the dark, but the shouting and shooting were over. Lois was drifting off to sleep around one in the morning when she heard her father speak.

"You don't think we should leave here, do you?"

Lois shook herself awake. "No."

"Your mother wants us to leave."

"I love it here, Dad," said Lois, but he didn't seem to hear.

"Maybe the store is gone now."

"You could call Mr. Conway or Mr. Hirano."

He shook his head. "Maybe the store is gone and we'll have to leave."

Lois looked at him—his face seemed strange in the TV light, odd colors and shadows crossed his cheeks and eyes. And as he sipped from his glass, it occurred to Lois that he was drunk. "Dad, don't talk like that. The store will be OK. You'll see. We won't have to move."

"Maybe your mother is right," Frank said. "But a man can't leave his family."

"Dad. You're right here."

"A man can't leave his family," he repeated.

He was scaring her, but she stayed there, and the next thing she knew it was morning. Her mother shook her awake—she had slept on the couch, her father in his chair—and the newsmen were saying that the riot was controlled, the raging fires finally contained. They were just finishing breakfast when someone knocked on the door. Frank went to get it, and when he pulled the door open, they all heard Kenji Hirano.

"It's over, Frank. It's all over. You better come quick."

And so he left, and he was gone for several hours. Lois again watched the news. They were reporting damages now—property losses, dozens of deaths, the beginning of clean-up efforts. She called a few friends to make sure they were all right, exchanged stories of fright and adventure, heard a firsthand account of the tanks on Crenshaw, rolling armed and silent down the boulevard. But then her father burst in. And he was wild-eyed, unhinged, his hair sticking up in tufts as if he'd been pulling it. He gestured and paced and wouldn't talk to anyone, and when Lois tried to approach him to ask what was wrong, he whipped around and yelled at her.

"Everything! Everything! Every Goddamned thing in the world!"

And since Frank was a man who neither shouted nor swore, Lois was shocked and began to cry. He didn't notice or acknowledge the rest of his family, and he stormed out the back and slammed the door, going straight into the garage. They didn't see him for the rest of the day. And although Lois was terribly lonely, and worried, and confused about what was happening, she didn't have much chance to work on getting Frank to come inside, because by morning she and Rose had packed most of their things, and their mother drove them down to Gardena.

CHAPTER TWENTY-THREE

1994

WITHOUT BEING totally aware of it, and without knowing why, Jackie avoided Laura for several days. They talked on the phone every night, though, and Jackie was curt; she could hear in the silences that Laura felt this but tried to ignore it. On Friday, she finally ran out of excuses. She walked over to Sierra Bonita a little after six, feeling grim and pessimistic.

Laura answered the door quickly, as soon as Jackie finished knocking. "Hi," she said, hand anxiously turning the knob.

Jackie considered her from what seemed like a very long distance. Even when she stepped through the door and felt Laura's arms around her, she didn't feel any closer. Still, out of habit, she raised her arms and embraced Laura—but awkwardly, as if unused to her contours and shape. When Laura pulled back and brought her mouth up to Jackie's, the kiss felt like something dead against Jackie's lips.

"What's wrong?" Laura asked, pushing a bit of hair off Jackie's forehead. "Are you mad at me?"

"No."

"Just tired?"

"I guess. It's been a really long week."

"I've missed you," said Laura. "It *has* been a long week. My bed's seemed so empty without you." She leaned into Jackie, tightening her embrace.

Jackie kept her hands on Laura's hips, lightly, conscious of the texture of her jeans. "Where are Rodent and Amy?"

"Amy's staying at her boyfriend's tonight. And Rodney and

Lisa, his latest woman—Holly's upset, didn't I tell you?—went to Tijuana for the weekend."

Above them, Holly, one of Rodney's girlfriends, was playing the piano beautifully. She was a classical pianist, and now, in the angry, mournful notes that floated down through the ceiling, Jackie heard how Holly felt about the trip.

"So the place is all yours," Jackie observed.

"All *ours.*"

Laura squeezed again and then started kissing Jackie's neck. She tugged lightly on Jackie's shirt until it came untucked, then slipped a hand beneath the fabric and touched her back. "I've missed you," said Laura again, between kisses. Jackie felt Laura's hands move over her skin, felt them cup her shoulder blades, touch her sides, trace the hard line of her backbone. But all of these sensations seemed remote, barely real, as if someone were tapping lightly at a thick wooden door on the other side of a very large house. Laura parted Jackie's legs with her knee and pressed into her. She ran her hand up roughly to Jackie's breasts. And it was when she pushed aside Jackie's bra and took the nipple between her finger and thumb; when Jackie failed to respond even to this, that she finally asked, again, "What's wrong?"

She was looking into Jackie's face now, worriedly. And Jackie, from her considerable distance, experienced her lover's hand on her breast like a cold, wet reptile. "Nothing," she said. "Let's just . . . not now."

Laura pulled away completely. She walked across the room and then turned to look at Jackie. "What is it? Tell me. What's bothering you?"

Jackie looked at Laura. It would be so easy to say that everything was fine; that she was just tired and feeling moody, and until a couple of months ago, that was what she would have done. Then her anger would fester inside her with all the other, older angers, eating away at her stomach, driving her to the medicine cabinet for the chalky white liquid she always used to neutralize her rage. And she didn't exactly know what was troubling her, anyway—or she knew what it was, but didn't know why it should matter, when such things didn't normally bother her.

"Why isn't Jimenez standing up for those women in Westlake?"

Laura looked at her as if she'd just spoken in a foreign language. "What do you mean?"

"The Thai workers, the indentured servants. I heard they might be getting deported. Why isn't Manny trying to stop it?" She knew she sounded ridiculous, and was too angry now to care.

Laura laced her fingers together behind her neck and exhaled. "It's not as simple as you think," she said. "There are a lot of factors—home country situation, certain criminal records. The press has made it sound like a case of slavery."

Jackie stepped into the middle of the room. "It *is* that simple. Those women might be getting deported, and other council members are making a stink, but your boss is too concerned about his *own* selfish ass to speak out about it, isn't he?"

"He's not—"

"*Isn't* he?"

Laura backed away and looked down at the floor. "You really don't understand what you're talking about."

"You're right, I *don't* understand. Manny Jimenez, of all people. I mean, give me a fucking break. If those women were Latino, he'd be having a press conference on the steps of City Hall every day, and you know it. But then again, he's a politician, so I guess it's not surprising that he's going back on everything he's ever stood for. But what I *really* don't understand," she paused and glared at Laura, "is how you can go along with this."

Laura's cheeks filled with color. "Well, *I* don't understand why you care so much. Since when are *you* concerned about what happens to those women?"

"Since now. And what really bothers me is *why* Jimenez is doing this."

"What are you talking about? You should *get* this, Jackie. Sure, those women were in an awful situation. But that doesn't make them any less illegal. I'm not saying that Manny wants them to get sent back to Thailand. He's just taking a second to think about it."

"Right. And this would have nothing to do with his wanting to run for mayor."

Laura narrowed her eyes. "Jackie, that's a horrible thing to say."

"Well, it's not as horrible as what he's doing."

"He's not doing anything. He's just waiting to see how things develop. People shouldn't take a position on such a controversial issue until they have all the facts."

Jackie looked at Laura as if she'd never seen her before. "Jesus, you're quoting right from the manual. Just listen to yourself. It's crazy."

"What the hell is *that* supposed to mean?"

"*You* figure it out."

"I can't believe you're talking to me like this," Laura countered. "I mean, you're the one who encouraged me to take this job in the first place, and now you're jumping on me for supporting the man I work for."

"That's before I knew that supporting him would mean going back on yourself."

Laura stared at her, mouth open. "Fuck you," she said calmly. "Just fuck you." She paced back and forth, and then turned back to Jackie. "You know what I think this is *really* about? It's about the fact that I don't tell you what I'm working on anymore. I mean, God forbid I keep anything from you. Since *you*, of course, tell me everything that *you* do."

"Oh, Jesus. This isn't even *about* me."

"Of course it is," said Laura, "Isn't everything?"

They stood there now, not moving, just glaring at each other, Jackie feeling the pull of the door. She remembered the sensation of Laura's hand on her hip, on her breast, and she stepped backwards, away from the memory. Now, looking at Laura—at her red cheeks, her tense mouth, her blond hair and milky skin—she felt a repulsion so strong it made her shudder. "I've got to go," she said, and then she walked out the door and slammed it behind her. She half-hoped that Laura would follow her, but the door didn't open again. And as she walked down to Oakwood and headed toward home, she remembered what Laura had been like the first year she'd known her, when she was still in college, and even the first few months after she'd moved to L.A. She'd been so full of conviction then, so strong in her faith in government; in her belief that it could be used to help people. Jackie had been half-amused by Laura's idealism, but also more than a little admiring. She couldn't believe that the same person she knew back then could rationalize the current situation. She couldn't believe that she herself was so upset about it. And what scared her, more than anything, wasn't that Laura was going along with what Jimenez was doing, but that she didn't even seem to see it clearly. She wondered if Laura really believed her explanations; whether she was honestly that far gone. And if she was, Jackie thought, then she was turning into someone that Jackie didn't want to know anymore.

When Jackie reached her own place, she sat on the couch and turned on the news. There was a piece about the workers, further details of what their captors had made them endure. Then a story about the murder of a young Asian man in Orange County whose killer had been caught because of letters he'd written, bragging about murdering a chink. Then a story about white parents in Cerritos who were upset about the influx of Asians. One woman, despite her child's junior high being one of the top-ranked schools in the state, announced, "I haven't paid taxes for twenty years for my daughter to be a minority in her own school." Jackie shook her head, not believing what she heard. Had it always been like this? Had she simply failed to notice? Because she was thinking such things, she picked up the phone and called Rebecca. Her heart beat with an anticipation which surprised her; please, she thought, let her be home. When Rebecca answered on the fourth ring, Jackie sighed in relief. "Wanna get drunk?" she asked without saying hello.

Rebecca paused for a moment, and Jackie could feel her smiling. "Sure," she said, "I'll be right over."

The phone woke Jackie up in the morning. It was a wrong number, and as she fumbled with the receiver, trying to hang it up again, she wondered why anyone would call so early on a Saturday morning. Then she looked at her bedside clock. She felt dizzy and weak, but even through the haze of her hangover she could make out the blurry red numbers: 11:36.

"Shit," she said aloud. When she tried to get out of bed, it was as if a giant, flat hand was holding her down. She sank back into her pillows, closed her eyes, and cursed herself for drinking so much. Rebecca had come over a little after eight, and they'd walked up to Santa Monica Boulevard, had dinner and drinks at the French Market Place. They'd only had appetizers—nachos and potato skins—but their favorite waiter, Dennis, kept bringing them beers and vodka shots until they could barely keep their heads off the table. Wincing now, Jackie tried to recall how they'd gotten back, and wondered if Rebecca had made it home. But then she remembered, hazily, that she'd set her friend up on the couch. She dragged herself out of bed, put on a robe, and staggered out to the living room. Rebecca was twisted in blankets, fully clothed, and when she saw Jackie, she groaned.

"Are you living?" Jackie asked.

"Barely." She waggled her brown boots in Jackie's direction. "Bitch, why didn't you at least take off my shoes?"

"You think I was doing any better than you?"

"Well, you managed to get yourself undressed."

"Yeah, but I've had years of practice."

Jackie sat down on the end of the couch and Rebecca propped her boot-clad feet on her lap.

"God," Rebecca said, "Are you as hungover as me?"

"It's not too bad. My head hurts, though. Does yours?"

"I don't know. I'm lost in such a haze right now that I can't even tell where it is."

For the next ten minutes they did a postmortem on the evening, pausing now and then to hold their heads.

"Listen," Jackie said finally. "You've got to go soon."

"Wait. You get me roaring drunk, painfully hungover, and now you're just kicking me out?"

"You have to. I'm sorry. I'm having company."

"Laura?"

"No. The guy from Crenshaw—James Lanier." She'd almost forgotten—he was coming over at 12:30 to look at the things in the box.

"Oh," Rebecca said, sounding way too interested. "You mean, I don't get to meet him?"

"Well, see, no. I—"

"When's he coming?"

"In like half an hour."

"Well, we'll just have to see if I'm ready by then."

She smiled, and Jackie rolled her eyes, knowing that her friend was staying put. Jackie needed coffee, water, a shower. She still had to straighten up the apartment and she didn't want Rebecca to answer the door, so she just started a pot of coffee and postponed her grooming. She gathered her notebooks and papers and stuffed them into her schoolbag. She fluffed the pillows on the couch and placed them back neatly, working around Rebecca, who was dressed now and watching with amusement. A few minutes later, the doorbell rang.

"Hey," Lanier said when she opened the door.

"Hey," answered Jackie. "Come in."

She moved aside to let him pass and shut the door after him. He was dressed casually today, in Saturday clothes—worn jeans, sneakers, a faded blue sweatshirt, a beaten old cap that said "Long Beach State"—and he looked decidedly boyish.

"You a fan?" she asked, indicating the cap.

Lanier touched the lid self-consciously. "No. Well, kind of. I went there."

"Really?" said Rebecca. "So did I."

Jackie and Lanier turned toward her. She was sitting on the couch, made-up and smiling, and she looked like she was waiting for a date.

"Uh, James," said Jackie, "this is my friend Rebecca, from law school. Rebecca, this is James."

"Hi," Rebecca said. She stood and crossed the room in what seemed like one huge step and held her hand out for Lanier. He shook it. "So when'd you go there?" she asked.

"Where?"

"State."

"Oh. Well, a long time ago. Way before you, I'm sure."

"It couldn't have been *that* long ago."

"I graduated in '80."

"Really. Well." She lifted an eyebrow. "You look great for such an old man."

Lanier laughed a bit nervously. She kept smiling at him, head cocked to one side, and Jackie could see what Rebecca thought about Lanier, and didn't like it at all, and couldn't figure out who she was jealous of.

"Anyway," Jackie said, "Rebecca was just leaving. Right, Rebecca?" She gave her friend a look.

Rebecca nodded at Jackie. "Catch you later," she said. Then, to Lanier, "It was a pleasure."

When she was gone, Jackie didn't know what to say. "Long night," is what she came up with. "Too much to drink."

She indicated that he should sit, and went to get him some coffee. She was definitely jumpy this morning. Lanier wasn't helping matters, either. He was paying attention a little too closely, which made Jackie feel scrutinized. Now, when she came back to the living room, he was standing up again, looking at a picture of her and Laura at Laura's birthday party the year before. They had their arms around each other and they looked happy. Lanier turned when he heard Jackie enter, and she could tell by the smile on his face, by the way he looked at her, that he understood. She expected him to ask about Laura, but instead he asked, "Is this your family?"

He was pointing at another birthday party picture, her father's, from several years ago. Jackie said that it was. She pointed out her mother, her father, her paternal grandparents—Frank hadn't gone to this party. She showed him another picture of Mary and Frank in front of their house in Gardena, and then another, of her college graduation. But Lanier was there to see other pictures, the ones in the box, so she retrieved it from her bedroom and carefully handed it over. They both sat down on the couch. Lanier gently lifted the lid off and picked up one of the velvet boxes. He opened it, and his eyes grew wide.

"Wow," he said finally. "This is a Silver Star." He opened the other one and whistled. "And this is a Purple Heart. Did he ever show these to you?"

She shook her head. "No. I never saw them before this week."

Lanier put the medals down and started sifting through papers, smiling at an article about Jackie's moot court victory at the law school the previous year. He held this up, along with several pictures of her. "This man loved you," he said, and Jackie couldn't tell if the odd, low tone in his voice was scolding. He shuffled through the news clippings, flipped over a couple of postcards. There were several envelopes, but Jackie had found nothing interesting in the letters, so Lanier just set them aside. He looked at the obituaries and then the letter from Curtis, and he seemed to age years right in front of her. He pressed his lips together and then shook his head slowly when he saw the pictures of Frank at the store. "This is him, that's exactly what it looked like." He held up the shot of Frank and Old Man Larabie, and then the second one, which he tilted to get better light. "And this is Derek Broadnax, you know."

"Yeah, I figured."

"They look exactly like I remember them. This couldn't have been too long before Watts." His voice was shaky and he was rocking a little. Instead of laying this last picture on the coffee table with everything else, he placed it next to him on the couch. "Is there a picture of Curtis?"

"I think so," Jackie said, pointing into the box. "At the bottom. There's a picture of a bunch of people at a bowling alley and I'm sure it's the Holiday Bowl."

Lanier looked into the box, pushed some papers aside, and fished the picture out of the bottom. He held the photograph up at eye level. Jackie watched him examine it, saw his mouth twist and his eyebrows furrow. "I don't see Curtis here. I don't recognize these boys at all."

"Really?" said Jackie. "Are you sure?"

"Yeah," Lanier replied, tilting the picture this way and that. He shook his head. "Curtis isn't in this picture. I don't know any of these—" He stopped. "Wait—holy Jesus."

Jackie leaned forward. "What?"

He brought the picture in closer, and then lowered it and looked up at Jackie. "This is *Alma*."

She stared at him, confused. "But she's, those people . . ."

"Look here," Lanier said. He held the picture out and tapped the image of the girl on the end. The girl was elegant and thin and straight-backed. She was wearing a simple white v-neck blouse and a long dark skirt; her hair was held back by a clip or a tie. She was smiling at the camera easily, and Jackie thought she was beautiful—deep brown skin, strong nose, generous mouth, and the expression on her face was confident, direct.

Jackie looked at Lanier, whose face was closer now, leaning over the picture. "Are you sure that it's her?"

"Yes. No doubt."

"How old do you think she was?"

Lanier shrugged. "I don't know. A lot younger than when I knew her. Late teens, early twenties, maybe."

"How do you think he got this picture?"

"I don't know," Lanier said. "Maybe he asked her for it."

Jackie looked at it again and wondered if Alma had, in fact, given Frank a picture of herself. The questions flew at her from all directions, impossible to handle all at once. Why would Frank have had this photo, and what could it have meant? Exactly how well had Frank known Curtis's mother? She met Lanier's eyes, not saying a word, and they just sat there and stared at each other.

CHAPTER TWENTY-FOUR

CURTIS—1963, 1965

SIXTY-THREE was the year Curtis started to change. That was the year of police dogs and firehoses, the year a bomb killed four girls at a Birmingham church. Every night there was a story of violence or resistance in Alabama, Mississippi, Arkansas. But despite his mother's attempts to link the Movement with their lives, despite the lectures from Angela's oldest brother, Gene, about white devils and separate existence, despite Akira Matsumoto's denouncing of cops whenever he came into the store, all the politics and protest had seemed distant to Curtis—as far away as news of war in Europe. The day after Bull Conner let German shepherds loose on children, Curtis and Alma were watching a second night of television commentary. Curtis shook his head at one of the people talking, an organizer for the Ku Klux Klan. "Man, I'm glad we live in L.A. It's messed up down there."

His mother looked at him sideways. "Down there?" The way she said it made him know that she meant, "and it's not messed up out here?"

"Well, the white people in California ain't *that* bad," Curtis said—except, he thought, for one.

"They worse," said Bruce from the dining room table, where he sat polishing a pair of shoes. "Here, the white man smiles when he's got murder in his heart. Down home, he don't act like he likes you, so at least you always know where you stand."

"You really think it's that bad out here?"

Bruce put his shoes down on a newspaper. "Curtis, every day I got to answer to this skinny young white boy who never once in his life has got his hands dirty. He couldn't run a machine if he had to, yet he pays me less than the white men who got easier jobs. A foreman's no different than a master, far as I'm concerned. Ain't no mistake people call this place the Southland."

There was something about the hoses, his mother's sad and bitter comment, his father's description of the foreman, that made Curtis look around him. He started noticing things that were happening right there in L.A. The demonstrations down at City Hall because Negroes were locked out of city jobs. The protests over the white policeman, unpunished for shooting and killing the Negro minister. The college students integrating the lunch counter at Woolworth's, right there in his new western city. And things closer to him, too, less definable or documented. His junior high buddies Jason and Ty, who were now doing sentences at detention camp. How much smaller his junior class was than his freshman class had been, as they lost kids to inertia, or jail, or pregnancy, or the lucrative trade on the street. His own incident with Lawson, which in the light of these other events, seemed less random, less a matter of chance.

"People dropping, just disappearing everywhere," he said to Angela one day. Then he pointed to Cory and Jimmy, who were playing with a toy truck in the yard. "It's getting worse. Don't know what's gonna happen when *they* come up."

"They got you to look up to," she replied. "And to keep 'em in line."

He recognized the truth in what she said, but suddenly it wasn't enough. There were so many other kids like Jimmy and Cory—needy and willing, their eyes not yet dulled by the knowledge of what the world had in store for them. Curtis wanted to help them all. He started tutoring at Audubon once a week, he and Angela both, on one of the days he wasn't working in the store.

Alma was thrilled. Up until that point, despite her best efforts, her son had remained blissfully ignorant of what was happening around him, the stagnant quality of their acquaintances' lives. But now, independent of her, he'd suddenly woken up; there was a new air of purpose about him.

"Mr. Sakai offered me a full-time job after I graduate," he told her one night at dinner. It was just Alma and the boys—Bruce was still at work, and Curtis tried not to speak of the store when his father was around. "And if I work eight to four, I can go to night school at the City College."

Alma looked up from her plate of red beans and rice. "You serious about wanting to run a store?"

"Yeah. It pays all right, and you can keep an eye on folks." He didn't add—although they were both aware of the debt that Curtis owed—that the man who ran the store had probably saved him.

Alma wasn't pleased with the plan, but she didn't try to discourage him. There wasn't much she could say about his choice of school—she wanted him to go to a four-year college, but his ninth and tenth grade marks had been mediocre, his junior year marks, now, a little better, but still sufficient only for junior college. Besides, she and Bruce didn't have much money stored up. His plan—full-time work and part-time school—made sense.

But then, March of his senior year. The big track invitational at El Segundo High, Dorsey and five other schools. The track itself was beautiful, sunken and green, surrounded by a neighborhood of small, neat houses. Five lily-white track teams, including the hosts, and then Dorsey with its mix of all the colors. Curtis placed second in the 200, and then won the 400 going away. He'd beaten two runners from El Segundo to do so, the top two boys in league. And he was so thrilled and surprised by his unexpected win that as he broke the tape, he turned to face the boys behind him—and, running backwards, punched his chest in triumph. They both looked daggers at him, but he didn't care; there was no feeling better than what he felt, running as fast as he could through the warm spring air swept clean by the breeze off the ocean.

After he'd cooled down and put his sweatpants on, he climbed into the stands to watch Angela win her races. They sat together for the rest of the meet, cheering on their teammates. Then, as the sun was lowering and the meet drawing to a close, Curtis went to the boys' locker room to use the restroom. When he walked in, he almost tripped over the feet of an El Segundo runner, one of the boys he had beaten.

"Well, look what we got here," the boy said. Then he and another boy slipped between Curtis and the door. Curtis turned around and realized that he was cut off, then turned again and saw half a dozen more El Segundo boys, in various stages of undress.

"Isn't that the nigger who taunted you, Kevin?" asked a shirtless boy who was sitting on a bench.

"That's the one," answered the boy he'd almost tripped over. He stepped closer to Curtis, and Curtis could feel the other boys rise and circle him. "You think you're something else, don't you, boy?"

Curtis gave a little laugh. "Come on, man. It's just a race. Shit. You'll probably kick my ass the next time."

"What makes you think you can come in here and disrespect us like that?" said another voice.

Curtis looked toward the showers and saw the second boy from the race; he beat his chest now, just as Curtis had done.

"Aw, man, I'm sorry I celebrated on you. I was just excited, is all. It was stupid."

"Stupid isn't the word for it, you little black punk."

A hand shot out from nowhere, striking the side of his head. Then another—a slap, open-fisted but hard, landing just below his right temple. Curtis reeled in one direction and then another. "Hey, come on!" he said. But the world seemed to be closing in on him and his guts curdled with sudden fear.

Kevin stepped forward and grabbed him by the front of his sweatshirt. "What are you gonna do about it, nigger?"

Something about this grab, the menace in Kevin's voice, touched off a memory and a knee-jerk rage he didn't know was in him. There was no way he was going to take another beating off a whiteman. Without thinking about the consequences, Curtis pulled out the knife he always carried and quickly opened the blade. Kevin stepped back, but Curtis moved toward him, flashing and slicing, not caring if he cut every boy in the room. But the whiteboys scattered like birds at the first shot of a hunter, scrambling all over each other in their effort to escape. One of them passed close by, and Curtis swung, sweeping sideways, aiming for the thick white neck. Fortunately for both of them, he missed, the tip of the blade just opening the front of the whiteboy's jersey. They were gone in an instant. Curtis sat down on a bench and looked at the open blade, and then his hands shook so badly that he dropped it.

The next day, the coach from El Segundo filed a complaint. Curtis tried to tell their school's officials, and his own principal, that he'd been acting in self-defense, but no one believed the word of a black boy who had once vandalized his school. When Alma told Curtis that he was being suspended and dropped from the team, he punched the kitchen door so hard he cracked the wood. Alma had never seen him react to anything with violence, and in another situation she would have scolded him, but she didn't say anything now because she was so relieved he wasn't hurt, and because she knew how he felt. If he weren't there, she'd put a crack in the door herself.

A week after Curtis was allowed to return to school, he and Angela were sitting in the bleachers at Redondo Union High School after she'd completed her events. Curtis had been moody and irritable for days, and he sat in silence now, staring angrily out at the track he was no longer allowed to compete on, even though he still attended all the meets. Then he turned to Angela and said, "I'm gonna try and find a store."

She looked at him. "What?"

"I'm thirsty. I want a soda. I'm gonna try and find a store."

"Come on, Curtis. You know that ain't what I mean."

"You comin with me or what?"

It was crazy, what he was saying. Redondo Beach was wealthier than El Segundo, and equally as white. And they had never pressed this particular envelope; had never even thought about it, really. But Curtis was looking at Angela as if their entire relationship hinged on her decision. So she zipped up her bag and went with him.

As they walked out of the gate, she thought of Adam and Eve, taking their first steps out of the familiar confines of Eden and into the wider world. They went a couple of blocks in silence, and she felt naked, exposed. As they crossed an intersection, a man in a business suit leaned out of his car window. "How you doing?" he asked, but the tone of his voice, the curl of his lips, were nothing close to friendly. Angela fought the urge to grab Curtis's hand.

Further on, they found a market, smaller and not as nice as Mr. Sakai's. Inside, it was brightly lit and cold. Curtis pulled two Cokes out of the cooler in front and set them up on the counter. The proprietor, a thin, balding man in his thirties, didn't even look up from the back of the store, where he was sweeping.

"You got customers," Curtis informed him, and the man continued to sweep.

"You got *customers*," Curtis repeated, more loudly this time, and now the man stopped sweeping and looked past him.

"I'm busy," the man said, slowly, as if Curtis didn't understand. "You'll have to wait until I'm through." And he resumed his sweeping, straw bristles rearranging invisible dirt.

Curtis glared. The man ignored him. Angela pulled on Curtis's arm. "Let's go," she urged. "Let's try another store."

He shook her hand off and crossed his arms, never taking his eyes off the man. Minutes passed, and Angela looked out the door, watched people walk by on the sidewalk. Finally, almost ten minutes later, the man set his broom against the wall and strolled slowly up to the front. Curtis handed the man a dollar and opened his palm for the change. The man slapped the coins on the counter. They stood frozen like that, Curtis with his hand extended, palm upward, the whiteman's palm down against the counter. "Thank you," Curtis spat.

"Any time," the man replied.

They went out into the neighborhood of every school where the team competed. They drew glares, or curses, or refusals of service, from a bookstore in Torrance, from a hamburger joint in Venice, from a market in Beverly Hills. They did this so regularly, with such purpose and care, that the walks after the meets seemed more the point of these trips than the events of the meet itself. Angela wasn't sure if Curtis was driven by anger or pain or recklessness; she herself was scared with every step they took. But a few of their teammates, noticing, began to come along. Her brother Derek was one of them, taking her left side, always, while Curtis walked along on her right.

They didn't tell their parents what they were doing. And they didn't discuss the walks amongst themselves, except to say, *Let's try this place,* or, *That chicken stand ain't open,* or, *The bus gonna leave in ten minutes.* They didn't talk about the danger they were putting themselves into. They were foolish and brave and haphazard and young, not organized and huge in number like the students in the south. Curtis knew their actions were tiny, even pathetic, in the very different landscape of Southern California. And he didn't like the idea of angering and maybe provoking so many ignorant whitepeople. He'd be relieved when track season was over, so these excursions could stop, but for now, for reasons he didn't fully understand, he knew that they had to continue. Then one day when he and Angela were walking home, a squad car cut them off at an intersection. Two Negro officers got out, the younger one, whom they'd never seen before, hanging behind, the older coming up into Curtis's face.

"I hear you been causing trouble," he said, and his voice was low and threatening.

"Well, you heard wrong," Angela shot back.

"What do you mean, officer?" Curtis asked. And he fought the urge to bolt, because he knew that this cop didn't like him. It was this cop who'd towered over him in the principal's office until Curtis finally admitted to the break-in. And it was this cop who glared in anger when the boys were let off with just a suspension; this cop who parked outside the store every few months to show Curtis that he knew who he was.

"You've been trying to go places," Thomas said, "that you got no business showing your face in. My son runs track for University. You got the stores up that way all riled up." He knew about this punk—the break-in back in junior high, his latest trouble now. Knew, and wouldn't tolerate it.

Curtis tried to sound brave, for Angela. "Your boy can go in those places, but we can't?"

The cop's eyes narrowed. "My son's got nothing in common with you and your two-bit hoodlum friends." And he believed that he didn't. Thomas and his wife had worked so hard to get beyond these people, who still had, to him, that stench of poverty and long-ago plantations. They'd been the first black family in their neighborhood in West L.A., and even though they'd had to pose as a white friend's maid and chauffeur just to get a look at the house; even though a cross was burned on their front lawn the first week they moved in; even though realtors slid flyers under their white neighbors' doors advising them, "You need to sell *now*," they were undeterred, determined to stay. They didn't worry that no one would talk to them or play with their son and daughter; they would endure anything, everything, to live where they did, and not someplace like Crenshaw or Watts. But the tolerance they'd earned was provisional, and they didn't need anyone messing it up. Especially not a bunch of young idiots one step away from being hoods.

"All right," Curtis said. "I get the message."

"You watch yourself, boy."

But Curtis didn't. They had work to do. And no scared-ass Uncle Tom was going to keep them from doing it, no matter how he made Curtis feel. He continued to go to stores, to cause trouble. And Angela was there—despite how much she hated the walks, she went with him every time. She wasn't going to let Curtis go anywhere without her, especially not into danger.

CHAPTER TWENTY-FIVE

1994

ON TUESDAY morning, Jackie skipped class and drove back down to the Holiday Bowl. She immediately spotted the Nakamuras and walked over to their table. Mrs. Nakamura saw her first and tapped her husband.

"The granddaughter of Frank Sakai," he said, as if announcing her at a ball. "Sit, sit." He pulled a chair over from the table next to them. "How are you doing this morning? Aren't you supposed to be in school?"

"Fine, thanks. I do have a class this morning, but it's not important if I miss it. And you told me that Kenji Hirano comes here on Tuesdays, right? I wanted to see if I could find him."

Nakamura leaned back in his chair and slowly wiped his mouth with a napkin. Jackie looked from him to his wife, who was using a piece of toast to soak up egg from her plate. "Well, he's here," said Mrs. Nakamura, "but you missed his breakfast time by a couple of hours. He's back there bowling now. He's probably just about finished."

"Do you think he'll stop in here before he leaves?"

Mrs. Nakamura shrugged. "Maybe. But you should probably just go back there and look for him. He always bowls in lane eight. He's a big man with white hair, and I think he's wearing a gray sweater today." She leaned forward. "Be very polite to him. He's old, you know. And he's also a bit . . ."

". . . odd," her husband finished.

Jackie looked at both of them, suddenly wanting not to leave. "Well, thanks. If you're still here when I finish, I'll come back and say goodbye."

When she went through the doorway and into the bowling alley, the sight before her was so different from where she'd just been that it was as if she'd walked through the wardrobe to Narnia. She stared out at the endless array of lanes, all new-looking and shiny. The brilliance of the lanes contrasted with the antiquated scorers' tables. These tables, like so many other things here, were straight out of another era; their chairs and lamps predated Jackie by a decade or two. Across the huge tan wall at the end of the lanes were the words "Holiday Bowl," written in archaic black cursive. Beneath them, the racks of pins broken violently by the hurtling balls were sent scattering backwards and out of sight. Jackie watched wooden arms come down and pull the remaining pins into the blackness, the way a gambler encircles the chips on the table and rakes them into his lap. She looked up at the side walls and saw banners: "Veronica's Beauty Shop—Ladies' champions, 1958"; "Crenshaw Motors—Mixed Champions, 1973"; "Goodyear—Midnight League Champions, 1949." Hanging over the lanes themselves were newer signs announcing an upcoming tournament. The floor shook from the rolling of the balls.

And now, looking down, she saw the people. There were swarms of them—every single lane was occupied and the bowlers filled up the scorers' tables. Behind them, on the raised floor where Jackie now stood, were linoleum tables which held family members and spectators. Jackie noted again the advanced age of the people; how surprisingly mixed the groups were. The noise was already getting to her. After just a couple of minutes here, she was already feeling a headache take root in her neck. She hoped that Kenji Hirano was almost done with his game and that he'd want to go someplace quieter to talk.

She approached lane eight, where four men stood huddled around their scorers' table. One of them wore a gray sweater and dark gray pants; his hair, too, was gray, touched with white. His shoes were the most colorful parts of him—bright red and blue, like children's sneakers. Peering down, she saw that all the men wore them. Jackie walked up to the railing and curled her hands around the iron. She cleared her throat and called out, "Mr. Hirano?"

Four faces turned toward her, distracted, annoyed, and she suddenly felt very young, a little girl who'd interrupted a meeting. One of the men held a large piece of paper, and she realized they'd been debating the score. The way they turned to her in unison, the way they stood so close to each other despite their momentary quarrel, made her think they'd all been friends for a long time. The man dressed in gray, the only Japanese man, said, "Yes?"

"Mr. Hirano," she repeated, standing up on her toes. She recognized him, but didn't know from where. "I'm Jackie Ishida. I was wondering if I could talk to you about—"

"Yes," he said. The three other men turned back to the sheet of paper. Hirano wasn't looking at it, but neither, Jackie realized, was he planning to move any closer. "Tina told me you were coming. Do you bowl?"

Jackie looked at him. "Do I . . . what?"

"Do you bowl?"

"Well, no," she said. "I—"

"Get some shoes on," he said, and then he put his head back into the huddle.

Jackie stood there, bewildered. And then she remembered where she'd seen this man before—at her grandfather's funeral, giving the salute, and then sobbing at the crematorium. And it was him, too, in the picture with Frank, the one where Frank was wearing the navy blue bowling shirt. She couldn't believe it—*this* was the man that she'd been sent to? What were the Nakamuras thinking? He was nuts.

The four men began to nod now, and then three of them patted the shoulders of the man to Hirano's right, who appeared to be the winner.

"Mr. Hirano," Jackie called out, louder. "I don't—"

He looked up. "Didn't you bring the ball?"

"What?"

"Your grandfather's ball. Didn't you bring it?"

She shrugged and looked at her empty hands. "No."

"You've got to come *prepared*, girl. You can rent shoes over there." He pointed to a booth behind her, where a middle-aged black woman was whipping out shoes like a barkeep slinging bottles of beer. Jackie looked at the booth and then back at Hirano. She was annoyed now, and a little embarrassed. What *was* this? What was he doing? But she was here, and, as strange as he was, he might have useful information, so she let go of the railing and began to walk toward the booth. From behind her, she heard Hirano yell, "And get yourself a ball!"

At the booth, she gave the woman her shoe size, relinquished one of her flats, and received a pair of blue and red bowling shoes. Then, tucking her remaining shoe under her arm, she walked over to the ball racks. She tried several balls that she could hardly lift, then chose a lighter purple one from the rack below. Holding her one shoe in her armpit and cradling the ball, she walked back to lane eight.

When she stepped down onto the alley floor and dropped her shoe, only Hirano was still at the scorers' table. The three others were milling around the chairs beneath the railing; they nodded to her as she passed. Jackie set the ball down in the ball-return and moved over to where Hirano was standing, staring down the lane, as if at a distant horizon. And he was much bigger now than he'd seemed from behind the railing—about a foot taller than she. Just as she was about to address him, he said, without turning, "The floor's fast today. Throws my timing off. Burt needs to polish it more often, so we get used it, or don't polish it at all."

Jackie didn't know if he was talking to her or to himself. "I've never bowled before," she said. "In fact, I've never even been in a bowling alley before."

"Yes, you have," replied Hirano, turning to face her. "Frank brought you here a couple of times. You sat right up at those tables."

She looked at him, surprised, but didn't respond, because she was distracted by his face. It was tanned and deeply lined, but still looked younger and more vigorous than its seventy-odd years. His hair was gray and white, but there was a lot of it. His features were large and definite—he had thick, dry lips, a squarish nose, and extraordinary eyes, which seemed, like the rest of him, unexpectedly vibrant and slightly off. Face-on, too, she saw how large he was—as broad across the shoulders as Lanier.

"You're a lawyer," he said, and it was a statement, not a question.

"Yes, almost."

She saw him consider her clothes—in black pants and a green silk shirt, she was overdressed for the occasion—and she expected a comment, but what he said was, "You've got to keep your wrist straight."

She looked at him, confused. "Excuse me?"

"Your wrist," he repeated impatiently. "The ball's heavy and if your wrist moves, it'll go into the gutter. Keep it straight and follow through, so that when the ball leaves your hand, you're pointing at the pins."

She glanced over her shoulder at the ball-return, unsure of what to do. But Hirano was done with her for the moment. He picked up a ball as easily as if it were a baseball, walked past her, and stopped a dozen feet from the line. Then he took several quick steps, swung the ball back, and let it go. His arm was extended out toward the end of the lane, and he kicked his right leg up behind his left one, like a dancer. The ball hit right of center and flirted with the gutter, but then it shimmied back to the middle of the lane and appeared to pick up speed, striking the head pin square on the nose and knocking down the set.

Hirano walked back to her, and his expression hadn't changed. "It's in the wrist," he said again. "And when you get good, you can learn how to put on some spin." He gestured toward the lane with his thumb. "Go on. Plant your left foot, remember the wrist, and pray."

Jackie just looked at him, not sure he was serious. "Mr. Hirano, I was hoping we could talk."

He waved her off. "Go on."

She didn't want to do it. What was Hirano thinking? *Was* he thinking? Why was he putting her through this? She looked around at the people in the other lanes. Surely they would watch her and whisper to each other. She felt uncertain and scrutinized, and when she picked up the ball, it seemed to have tripled in weight. But it was clear she had no choice in the matter.

She stepped past the ball-return and onto the runway. After checking on either side of her to make sure no one was watching, she took a few awkward steps, pulled her left hand off the ball, and brought it back behind her with her right. It felt huge and unwieldy, like she was swinging a suitcase. When she let the ball go, it hit the floor by her foot and skidded straight into the gutter.

"No, no, no," said Hirano from behind her. She turned to face him, chastised. "The *wrist*. Keep your wrist straight and follow through so you're pointing at the wall. As if you're offering the ball up to Jesus."

"Mr. Hirano, I don't think I—"

"Nonsense," he interrupted. "Let me show you." He picked his own ball up again, approached the line, and let go. Again, it was a beautiful roll, knocking all the pins over but one. Hirano just stared this last pin down, as if he could will it to fall. He couldn't. A few seconds later his ball reappeared, and he walked by and retrieved it without a word. He went up to the line again, sent the ball flying, and knocked over the final pin. "The wrist," he said, when he turned back to Jackie. "The wrist, and concentration."

When the pins were reset, Jackie picked up her ball. She was determined this time not to embarrass herself. She swung the ball back, and then forward, with a bit more control, and when she let go, she tried to keep her wrist straight. The ball trickled down the lane—weakly, but in line. Near the end, it veered left and caught just three pins in the corner. Still, she felt exhilarated. She turned back to Hirano, expecting a smile or a nod of approval. Instead, he pointed toward the ball-return.

"You've got one more."

She walked back and stood next to him silently, until her ball came back. Then she took her second roll and it moved to the right this time, but again, it clipped a couple of pins off the corner.

"Five," Hirano said. "Not bad." He scribbled something down on a large piece of paper, and Jackie realized that he was keeping score.

She wanted to say something, to stop him, to explain that this was all a mistake. Instead, she asked, "How often did you bowl with my grandfather?"

Hirano was silent so long she wasn't sure that he'd heard. Finally, though, he answered. "Not that often. Your grandfather was at the store all day. When he came, he usually came after work, and I was at home by then. We only bowled together on his days off."

"This place was open that late at night?"

"Of course. People came after their swing shifts and night shifts." He stood, picked up his ball again, and began to walk away. "But I didn't know Frank through bowling. I met him at the store. Moved next to it eventually, in '62. Yup. Me right next to him, Victor Conway across the street. We saw each other every single day."

"Really?" Jackie said to his back.

He went up to the line and let fly. The ball hurtled down the lane and knocked down all the pins except the one in the far right corner. Hirano nodded, then came and stood next to Jackie. His ball spilled out of the ball-return and he picked it up, approached the line, and threw. The ball looked like it was headed directly toward the pin, but somehow it managed to miss. Hirano put his hands on his hips and shook his head. "Frank taught me to bowl," he said. "With a little help."

He pointed up, which Jackie took to mean, with a little help from God. She tried to imagine this strange man in the same scene as her grandfather. As soon as their eyes met, Hirano pointed at her ball. "Your turn."

She retrieved her ball, just wanting to get her roll over with so they could get back to her grandfather. Because she was hurrying, she wasn't mindful of her wrist or her footing; her ball went into the gutter.

"You're not concentrating," Hirano shouted over the noise of crashing pins. He stood there with his arms crossed, and Jackie felt, once again, like a misbehaving child. They didn't speak while they waited for the ball to reappear, and this time, when she retrieved it, she paid closer attention. She was careful about her wrist and concentrated on the spot on the floor where she wanted the ball to land. The roll was a good one—it stayed in the center of the floor and hit the first pin squarely. Eight pins fell, leaving just the two corners standing. She returned to the table and saw Hirano recording her score. Without looking at her, he spoke.

"It was cold in there. Very cold."

She looked at him. "What? Where?"

"The *freezer*," he said. He hit the table with his fist. "Big white policeman in front of the store and dead black boys in the freezer."

"How do you know it was cold?"

He stood up and hovered over her. "I was there! I was there when Frank found them!" He was staring, eyes wide. Two deep furrows split his forehead, his cheeks had gone red, and his eyes looked like something was boiling.

"You were?"

"I was outside," he began, "just looking around on Sunday, when everything was over. I had a bad feeling and went to Frank's house and told him to come to the store. There was some broken glass, you know, from one of the windows, and we kicked that around before we went inside. We thought the place would be looted but it wasn't. Frank was relieved because he thought it was just the windows, and then we went back to the freezer so he could check on the meat." He paused, and his eyes grew wider. Around them, Jackie could hear the sound of balls on wood; of people laughing and calling out to each other. "He saw that the door was locked, and then we knew something was wrong. Someone took a padlock from off the shelves and the key was on the floor. Frank unlocked the door and opened it, and that's when we saw them. They were sitting on the floor in a corner, all huddled together. The two older boys had put the smaller boys between them, and they had their arms around each other. Frank saw them before I did. And his face." Hirano's eyes got wider, and he crossed himself. He leaned closer to Jackie, but she could tell he wasn't looking at her; he was seeing the boys in that freezer. "His face, I hadn't seen a face like that since the war. He ran right over and started touching them and shaking them and laying his hands on their heads. Their eyes were open and they were covered with frost. And he knelt down in front of Curtis and took his face in both hands and pressed his forehead against the boy's forehead. And he started to shake, and when he pulled away, I saw that his tears had fallen onto the boy and melted tracks on his face. And then Frank just knelt there and put his head on his knee, and I went back out into the store." He paused again. "I just walked around and around in there. Didn't know what to do. Frank finally dragged the bodies out of the freezer. He wouldn't let me help. He pulled himself together and he called his wife then, and I tried not to listen but I couldn't help it. He said, 'They're dead. He's dead, my love. They murdered him.' And I stayed there with him while he called some other people. The morgue. The other boy Derek came in and he ran away crying, and then Frank made me go home and the store was closed down, and then he and his family moved away."

Jackie felt sick. She found it difficult to breathe. When she spoke, her voice sounded thin. "Didn't anyone call the police?"

Hirano looked at her incredulously. "What's wrong with you?" He put his head in his hands for a moment. "I never told anyone. Never. The boys were dead and that policeman was never, ever punished. Nothing ever happened to him. I saw him take the boys in and I didn't think he'd kill them. I didn't think the Lord would let that happen."

He stood up now and found his ball and set himself to roll. He took four big steps, swung the ball back higher than before, leaned forward, and let it go. It hit the wood so hard that Jackie thought it might break through the floor. Then it bounced, and barreled home, and smashed into the pins. They broke violently and flew over the edge. Not one was left standing. Hirano remained where he was, staring down the lane.

Twenty minutes later, Jackie was standing in front of the store. She'd come straight to Bryant Street after her talk with Hirano, who'd promised to testify, and who'd also given her the where-abouts of Frank's old friend, Victor Conway. She wasn't sure what she was doing here, but her hands had practically steered of their own volition. Once again, she left the car at the curb and stared at the store—the boarded-up windows, the crumbling walls. She tried to picture this place as it had been when Frank ran it, and also on the day he'd found the bodies. The bustle, the activity, the sorrow. Now, the sidewalk in front was cracked and uneven, whole chunks of concrete sticking out of the earth. And the store itself looked desolate—not just old and closed, but dead. She saw that more graffiti had been painted across the boards; that more trash had collected in the doorway. She saw the green stucco house to the left of it, Hirano's, and Conway's, the tan frame house across the street. She saw the dry brown grass and bare earth in the yards, the fractured walkways, the barred windows and doors. And looking at all of this, she felt the sinking sensation of loss—not just for Frank, but for this neighborhood, and for the boys who'd lived and perished in the store. She wanted to rest somewhere, and glancing down at her hands, she noticed they were shaking. She'd known all along that Frank had found the boys, but hadn't pictured the scene until now. This was enough to think about, but there were also her grandfather's words. *"They're dead. He's dead, my love. They murdered him."* And she'd known immediately, when she'd heard this, that the first person her grandfather had called, the person he'd addressed as "my love," had not been her grandmother, but Alma.

CHAPTER TWENTY-SIX

1963

THE BELL rang as someone entered the store. The man had been sitting behind the counter filling out order forms, but now he stood to greet whomever was coming in. He'd expected a customer, but it wasn't; it was her. From the shadowy light of the three uncovered bulbs he could see that she was tired. Her steps were slow and dragging; her eyelids looked heavy. But her chin was up, her neck and back were straight, as always.

She approached and said hello to the man and then inquired about her son. Normally the boy was there at that time, but he'd complained of a headache coming on and so the man had sent him home early. The man explained this to the mother and she nodded, looking around her. There was no one else in the store just then. The air was thick with unsaid words.

The man told her that the boy had left a notebook for school; he had it in his private office. He invited the woman to step around the counter and come into the room to retrieve it. The door was open and he walked straight to his small, tidy desk, where the green notebook lay on a stack of white paper. The woman took two steps into the room, glanced at the man, and looked away. The man stood still for a moment. Her glance was both accusing and sad. She hadn't been in there since he'd changed it around, and he'd forgotten she knew it before, and the office he used now held little relation, for him, to that other place, which existed only in memory.

The man picked up the notebook and handed it to the woman. She thanked him, and they spoke about the boy's progress in school, about his various responsibilities at the store. The man inquired after the woman's other, younger son, and she said that he was well; he'd just started playing little league baseball. The man nodded and smiled, genuinely pleased. He couldn't bring himself to ask about her husband.

They fell silent for a moment and looked at each other. He saw in the woman of thirty-five, the younger woman she had been when he met her. But he, to her, looked totally different. Family or work or the neighborhood had roughened his skin and bent his back. His hands, though, were the same—long and graceful. Now, he folded those hands in front of him and cast about for what to say. After a moment, she told him she had to go.

They walked through the store together and to the front door. He noticed useless things as they moved down the aisle—that the cereal boxes were crooked; that the chicken noodle soup was almost gone. Finally, at the door, she turned. She was about to extend her hand to him, but then appeared to change her mind. "Thank you for everything. We both owe you a lot."

"You owe me nothing," said the man, and he watched her walk away, down the street and around the corner. When she was gone, out of sight, he put the "Closed" sign up and went back into his office. He sat there in the dark until it was time to leave.

CHAPTER TWENTY-SEVEN

VICTOR, 1942–1955

V ICTOR CONWAY knew about returns. Not homecom-
ings, which imply that somebody notices, somebody cares,
somebody raises a glass, maybe, to mark the occasion, but
quiet, unspectacular returns. He'd left Angeles Mesa, too, a few
months after Frank, and when he returned, a dozen years later;
when he bought a house a mile away from the house he'd grown
up in and just across the street from his old friend's store, most of
the faces he remembered from his childhood were gone. New
houses had spread like wildfire and new businesses had sprung up
on the boulevard, but all of these places were full of strangers. The
whites he knew had left, and the ones who remained seemed more
private to him, more defensive. The Japanese of his age had vanished too, although he saw in a few of the older ones a dimple, or
a stance, or a tilt of the head, that he connected to the kids he grew
up with. And a lot of black families had moved out as well—some
trading up to better neighborhoods, some dying out like his parents, and others resurfacing in Watts. It was Watts that he'd
returned from, swimming upstream against the flow of people
down into the ghetto.

He'd moved there in the summer of '42. Graduation took
place in June, but the event was pointless without Frank and David
Hara and Steve Yamamoto, and the other Japanese kids who'd
been herded away that spring. In July he married Janie, and the
two of them moved into the one-room cottage behind her parents'
house in Watts. Janie's parents had lived in Watts since it was
Mudtown, a country village with dusty wagon paths and hoot

owls sitting on fence posts. It had been mixed then, still was, although the scales were being tipped by the influx of Southern blacks, who were mostly settling south of 103rd. A week after the wedding, Victor went down to the shipyard in Long Beach, where the bosses who'd been shaking their heads no for so long were finally, because of the war, nodding yes.

Like most of the other black workers the shipyard hired during the war, Victor was assigned to the night shift. Getting home was no problem—there was an 8:30 Red Car from Long Beach to Watts, and even though the train broke down regularly or stopped to let freight trains pass, he could usually count on getting home by 9:30 or 10:00. But getting *to* the shipyard was another story, a new puzzle every day. The Red Car didn't run that late at night, and Victor didn't own a car. So every evening, before his shift, or during cigarette breaks, he'd have to arrange a ride for the next night. Finally, Pipes Sullivan took care of this problem. Sullivan was his leaderman—their gang welded and riveted gun emplacements—and he lived on 104th Street. He and his brother Horn restored an old Buick they'd bought from the junkyard and charged a nickel a ride to be part of their car pool. So every night, seven young men would crowd into the seats, long lanky arms and legs all jockeying for room, the men laughing, smoking, passing a bottle around, the car chugging through the streets of L.A. Although their shift started at midnight, Victor left about 10:30 every evening. The trip took forty minutes, and they had to pick up all the others at Imperial Courts and Nickerson Gardens, the housing projects built to accommodate the war workers. And the Sullivans and Timmy Grace would wash up at the shipyard since the tiny apartments in the old split-up house where they lived were not equipped with bathing facilities. They washed at night, because the foreman who came on in the morning objected to seeing Negroes in the showers. And Timmy and the Sullivans had to be clean; they had women to see in the morning.

The hours were long and the pay was low and Victor barely saw his wife—just between 8:00 p.m., when she got home from cleaning the Burns house, and 10:30, when they heard the honk of the Buick. Victor and Janie had time only to eat a quick dinner, which was usually made up of the cheapest cuts of meat—the ham hocks, the neck bones, the tongue. They would catch up on their day and then lie down for a while on their mattress if the mood arranged it. But it was fine, they were making it, until the swing shift started letting out early.

While Tim Grace and the Sullivans were inside washing up, Victor stayed out in the yard with Bill, Harris, and Colter, having a final cigarette, a final joke before their shift. Usually, they punched in as the swing shift was ending, and they nodded at the occasional colored men mixed in with the hordes of white women and the few white men who'd been rejected from the fighting. But in the fall of '43, without warning or explanation, the swing shift started getting out at a quarter to twelve. Rumor had it that the foreman had lost his senses over a whore who could only achieve orgasm if he entered her precisely at midnight. But whatever the reason, the crowd of four-to-twelvers began to pass through the doors while Victor and his friends were still out in the yard. Some of the just-released women would gather on the other side of the entrance, smoking and laughing, complaining loudly that the war had thinned out the pool of available men, leaving them precious few to pick between. Victor and his friends ignored them, resenting their presence, hushed their voices and tightened their circle. But one night about a week after the women had started to gather, one of them left the group and walked over. Victor watched her approach—he couldn't imagine what she wanted—noting the white cotton shirt which was now smudged with grease, the denim pants, the fake leather shoes. A few tufts of red hair poked out from beneath the white rag on her head, and as she got closer, she removed the cloth, shaking out the thick hair that reached down to her shoulders. The men went instantly stiff and swept their eyes around the yard. But the woman seemed not to notice, and she made a bee-line for Victor.

"I'm out of smokes," she said when she reached them. "You got any?"

Victor glanced at his friends, who shrugged, and then over at the group of women, who were watching him closely.

"Yes, ma'am," he answered, careful to avoid her eyes. "But it seem like your friends already got some."

The woman smiled, exposing teeth that were crooked and yellow. Despite her stylish haircut and just-applied rouge, she looked aged and worn, thumbed-over. "They do, honey, but they're sick of me asking. Why don't you be nice now and give me a smoke?"

At "honey," all the men looked around again, with more urgency and fear. Their hands fiddled with cigarettes, with loose strings on their shirts, with the suddenly itchy skin on the backs of their necks. Victor looked down at the woman's shoes, debating whether it was safer to give her a cigarette and maybe overstep his bounds, or *not* to give her a cigarette and appear disrespectful. Finally, he pulled a pack out of his front shirt pocket, tilted it, tapped it against his palm, and offered the pack with a single cigarette sticking out of the top.

"Thanks, sugar," said the woman. And when she reached over to take the smoke, her hand closed lightly over Victor's and lingered a moment. "My name's Peggy," she told him as she pulled her hand away. "It's good to make your acquaintance, Victor. I'll pay you back tomorrow."

And as she returned to her friends, Victor was so shaken by the way she'd touched his hand that he didn't realize she'd somehow known his name.

All the men were relieved when it was time to punch in. Victor spent his whole shift looking over his shoulder, and on the Red Car the next morning, Harris and Colter told what they had learned from their fellow tackers—that this whitewoman named Peggy liked her men young, strong, and black; that she'd noticed Victor her first night smoking outside with her friends; that she'd asked some of the colored men who worked in the copper shop with her if they knew the tall oak-brown boy with the dimple in his chin.

That night, as they smoked, she came over again, talking more, staying longer, trying to engage the other men. All of them, including Victor, said as little as they could, but the whitewoman didn't seem to notice. By the third night, Victor felt more capable of standing his ground, but then, a week later, Peggy asked if he had a girlfriend.

"No, ma'am. I got a wife," he said, and his voice swelled with pride.

The whitewoman tilted her head a bit, considering him with mock disapproval. "A wife? A handsome young boy like you? Now what'd you go and do that for?"

"We been together a long time, ma'am. Since we was fourteen."

"Your little wife, does she work, too?"

"Yes, ma'am. She cleans house for a family up in West L.A."

The woman smiled a bit now. "So you don't see much of each other, do you? You must get real lonely." And her mouth did something with "lonely" that made it sound like something else. Victor just kept staring at her hand, where she rolled a cigarette between her fingers. The other men looked around again, their eyes settling on a couple of whitemen standing off in the distance. They didn't want to be there, but they weren't about to leave Victor alone with this hungry whitewoman who didn't seem to notice or understand or care what kind of danger she was putting him into.

It was almost a relief to find the cat in his locker. At first, Victor thought it was alive, despite the strange position (propped up on its hind legs with its front paws pressed against the wall), because of the open eyes, which looked up at the shelf where his extra shirts lay folded. But then he noticed how flat the green eyes were, like calm, dirty water, and when he lifted the little body out, it was rigor mortis–stiff. He lay the cat on top of the bench and looked it over—it had dull black hair, a thin body, a long skinny tail, and no mark to tell him how it had met its death. He felt no revulsion, only sadness, and a strong, sudden current of fear. But he'd been waiting for something to happen; had not gone anywhere—not the bathroom, not outside, not over to catch the Red Car—without taking at least two other men with him, and he felt justified now, corroborated. He wrapped the cat in a dirty towel and dropped it in the trash. Then he changed into his work shirt and blue denim overalls and walked over to the outfitting dock.

There were other, smaller signals, which Victor tried to ignore. The sneers from the whitemen as he moved around the shipyard. The way some of the larger men, like Trip Stevenson, bumped him as he passed them on the gangway, once clipping him so hard that he was knocked to the floor. The loud conversations during breaks about black and white babies being even worse than regular niggers.

Through those weeks, Peggy kept bothering Victor, first outside, and then, when he and his friends stopped smoking there in
an effort to avoid her, inside, on the outfitting dock, even following him onto the ship. The Sullivans, who usually visited their
Long Beach women in the morning, stopped seeing them so they
could drive Victor home. The previous winter, eight black men had
been beaten in separate incidents outside the shipyard, two so
badly that they never returned—and that was simply for having
the audacity to work there. No telling what would happen with a
whitewoman in the mix.

Throughout those few weeks, the air at the shipyard seemed
thin, dry, sharp enough to cut. Every evening, when Victor left his
house, he kissed Janie and pulled her close, and kissed
Christopher, their new son, and his wife laughed at his intensity,
not knowing where it came from.

He felt like a man waiting out his execution, and then one
night, Peggy sat down on a bench beside him.

"You want to have breakfast with me tomorrow?" she asked.
"I could pick you up at eight." She punctuated her question with
a light touch on his arm, three fingers hovering and alighting like
butterfly wings. He felt a shudder go through him that he knew she
mistook for excitement. Their backs were to the group of whitemen lounging by the rail, and Victor felt the air go even sharper,
the collective suck of breath, at Peggy's question, at her butterfly
touch. He didn't dare to look behind him, but he said, voice shaking, loud enough for the whitemen to hear, "No, thank you,
ma'am. I got to get on home."

That touch was the final insult, and he knew it. All the next
week, his friends surrounded him, always, men covering his left
and right, his front and back. But they didn't protect, didn't think
to protect, the one place where he was vulnerable. On Monday
afternoon, Victor woke up around five and went up to his in-laws'
house to play with Christopher. Janie wasn't there at eight, which
was when she usually got home. Nor was she there by eight-thirty,
or nine or nine-thirty. They waited, Victor and his in-laws, with
growing concern, until finally, Victor decided to go and look for
her. He walked quickly to the bus stop where she usually got off,

but nobody was there. Then he started home, slowly, listening and looking, and as he passed Cordelia's Beauty Shop, he heard a quiet moan. He stopped and waited. Another moan—from there, in the alley. He ran around the corner and saw his wife on the ground. Her shoes and purse were scattered, her sweater was ripped, her white domestic's dress shoved up around her hips. She was curled against the wall, as if asking it for comfort. Victor heard a sound come out of him that was not quite human; he rushed over, knelt down, and rolled her over. Her lip was split, her eye was swollen, there was a golf-ball-sized welt on her cheek, and dried specks of blood covered her chin and forehead. Victor choked back his own tears and tried to sound strong. "I'm here, baby, it's all right. They won't hurt you no more." He carried her home, yelling to her parents as he reached the door that they should put the baby away. All that night he and her parents stayed with her—cleaned her off, put her in bed, pressed ice packs to her head. He thought of work only once—at ten-thirty, when the Sullivans honked—and then shoved the thought out of his mind.

By morning, it was clear she'd be all right, and she did not lose the baby that was three months inside her. After crying off and on through the night, Victor felt empty and dazed, and when the Sullivans picked him up the next evening, all the men in the car stayed silent, but they kept touching him, laying hands on his head, on his still-shaking shoulders and arms. In the locker room, as Victor got dressed for work, one of Mr. DeMarco's men said that the boss wanted to see him. Victor knew what was coming. When DeMarco fired him for missing a day of work, Victor didn't even try to explain. And out on the dock, when Trip Stevenson and the other whitemen sneered, confirming what he already knew, he felt too lost and tired even to conjure up rage. The whitewoman wasn't there that night—maybe they'd gotten her, too—and Victor never saw or heard of her again.

It only took Victor a few days to get another job—at Bethlehem Steel, which was right there in Watts. And he was assigned to a day shift, nine to five, so he saw a lot more of his wife. It had taken her six days to feel well enough to get out of bed, but her employers were more sympathetic than Victor's, and welcomed her back when she was ready. At first, Victor's extra time at home seemed like a good thing; Janie had nightmares almost every night and would start shaking uncontrollably during the day. But slowly, over the next several months, everything started to burden him. He didn't like the dull weight of Janie beside him in the bed. He couldn't stand to sit at the table with her and eat another meal in silence. He couldn't endure the wails of the just-born baby girl. But most of all, he couldn't bear to look at his wife, to see the face and lips and dull sad eyes of the woman he had failed to protect. Several men from the plant lived there in the neighborhood, and Victor began to go out with them after their shift, having a drink or two over at the Downbeat on Central, or playing cards at Penny's Barbershop on 103rd. When he'd get home late, smelling of whiskey, Janie would fix her eyes on him and ask where he'd been. And because he couldn't stand hurting her, he began to get angry and yell that he was just relaxing after a hard day's work. They fought over his hours, over money, over the perfume she once detected on his collar. And then one night, exasperated after yet another fight, he threw his hands up and walked toward the door.

"Where you going?" Janie demanded, fist on her hip.

"Friend's place. I can't sleep in the same house as you."

"You going to see a woman?"

"Naw, girl, don't be foolish." But he was already thinking of the perfume woman, how glad she'd be to see him, how *her* eyes didn't measure him against some silent expectation and decide that he came up short.

"So you just gonna walk out of here and leave me with your babies?"

"Well, I know the *first* one's mine, anyway." He didn't know why he said this; he didn't believe the thought behind it; knew she was pregnant when he found her in the alley. But a canyon cracked open between them now and he could barely make her out on the other side. She just stared at him and nodded, as if understanding something, and then walked over to the crib and picked up the baby. The space she created that held herself and her children no longer had room for Victor. He knew it. Without saying another word, he turned and walked out the door.

Victor moved into a room above a liquor store in the only place besides Watts and the Mesa where Negroes were welcome—Little Tokyo, renamed Bronzeville, which had been emptied by the war. Where just two years earlier every face had been yellow, now every face was black. Negroes were running businesses with names like "Yamashita Clothing" and "Ushimoto Dry Goods." They inherited, too, the cramped and crumbling apartments, the lack of plumbing, the roach-infested quarters carved out of any empty space—a storefront, a storage room, a dirt-floor garage—that are the fate of all unwanted people. Victor's room had only a bed, a chair, and a shelf for all his clothes. Janie accepted money from him every month to help care for the children, but after a few failed attempts to bridge the deepening canyon, she refused to see him again. And the night life that had been so attractive when he was married held no appeal for him now; he stayed in, read the *Sentinel* and the *California Eagle*, and saved and saved his money. He felt both odd and comforted as he walked through the streets where his best friend's family had first settled in this country. Occasionally, he made the acquaintance of a woman he liked, but all of them were painful reminders of the woman he had loved and let down. Finally, he decided to go back to the Mesa, in order to try and have some kind of life again. And so he used all the money he had set aside over the years and bought a house a mile away from the house he'd grown up in. It wasn't intentional, but it did seem fitting, that the house was right across the street from his old friend Frank, whom he hadn't seen since right after the war; who seemed, like himself, quiet and reduced; who'd also made an inglorious return.

CHAPTER TWENTY-EIGHT

1994

JACKIE GOT home from the Holiday Bowl and called Lanier before she even put her bag down. "I think we got him," she said when he picked up.

"Who?"

"Lawson. I think we got him. I went back down to the Holiday Bowl today and talked to Kenji Hirano, and it turns out he saw Lawson on the Saturday of the riots in front of my grandfather's store."

"Really? Doing what?"

"Just standing out there with the boys. And then while he was watching, he saw Lawson make them go inside."

"That's beautiful. A witness."

"Not only that, but Hirano was there when my grandfather found them."

"Shit. We've got him. Do you think he'd testify?"

"Yeah, but I don't know how much help he would be. I think he's a little bit senile."

"Always was. Why didn't he say something before?"

"Who knows? I didn't ask. Maybe he thought it was useless. But at least he's saying something now, right? So what do we do from here?"

"I don't know, girl. You're the lawyer."

Jackie laughed. "OK, I guess we call the District Attorney's office. I have a professor who's good friends with him, and that should make it easier to set up a meeting. We should try and get the funeral home records, to prove the boys died and were buried."

"I can do that," said Lanier. "It was Ferguson's Funeral Home, on Adams. It's still there."

"Good. And I still want to contact Matsumoto in Japan, and there's one other person we should talk to—Victor Conway. Hirano mentioned him, and my aunt's brought his name up, too."

"Of course. Mr. Conway. He lived across the street. Did you find out anything else?"

Jackie paused. "Well, I'm not sure. But when Hirano was telling me about the day they found the boys, he mentioned that my grandfather made a phone call. And he assumed it was to my grandmother, but I'm pretty sure it was to Alma."

"Why?"

"Because from what Hirano quoted me, he talked specifically about Curtis."

"Well, that would make sense, wouldn't it? To call the parents first?"

"Yes," Jackie said, "except he called her 'my love.'"

"Shit. Do you think—"

"Yeah, I do. And my question is, could Lawson have known about it, and could it have had anything to do with why he murdered the boys?"

"You mean, like, did he have something against the two of them together? Or something against Alma?"

"That, or maybe something *for* her."

"Right. But if there *was* something going on between the two of them, do you think anyone else would have known about it?"

"I don't know. And the thing is, we can't really ask." She paused. "What I don't understand is how they did it. I mean, she worked and he never left the store, and there were always other people around. How'd they ever see each other alone?"

"I don't know. But people manage. People can be real secretive about love when they need to be. And even when they *don't* need to be."

Jackie didn't answer. She knew this last comment was in reference to her, and although she appreciated his effort, she wasn't prepared, just then, to talk about Laura. She was finding it hard, recently, to think about her at all, and so she let his ball lie where it had landed.

Two days later, Jackie was standing on a sidewalk in front of an elementary school, waiting for Lanier to show up. Here, she'd learned from Hirano—this neglected-looking school in the Westlake district—was where Victor Conway spent his days. Beige paint was chipping off of the sides of the building; half the letters on the sign had dropped away. And the schoolyard looked like a ghost town—the unraveling cloth swings swayed lightly in the breeze; the metal rings on the jungle gym clanked together for-lornly; what little grass there was on the soccer field was brown and patchy. If a child was shy of stepping on cracks, she'd never be able to play here—the cement was full of them, large and small, intertwined and crossing; it looked like a net had been laid flat on the ground, waiting to entrap all the children. Jackie glanced at her watch again—it was a little after three. Lanier was late and she was getting nervous; she didn't want to face Victor Conway alone.

In front of the entrance, women were starting to gather. Jackie didn't pay much attention to them and moved further down the block to keep her privacy. Then the clanging, reverberating final bell—the sound so engraved in her that she felt the blood-deep urge to run away from school and home for the day. She turned to watch the children pour out of the entrance. Which they did—run-ning, jumping, screaming children, dressed in bright sweaters and pants, some of them hugging the women who waited, some of them moving in clumps down the sidewalk. And she noticed, now, that while a few of the children were black and Latino, most of them were Asian. Largely East Asian, Korean and Chinese, a few others who looked Thai or Filipino. She heard them talking to their mothers and amongst themselves in lively, private languages she couldn't understand. And looking closer, she saw the marks of poverty—the slight, unsturdy limbs on both the women and the children; the poorly made and threadbare clothes; the bags and shoes that seemed older than the children themselves. She thought of herself at their age, the only Asian child in a well-off school where everyone had new clothes. She thought of the Thai workers, locked inside for months on end, the trials they'd overcome and had yet to face. And she wondered for the first time what it had been like for the original Ishidas and Sakais, the desperate or brave ones who'd left their home country to try their luck in this new, wide land. She wondered about the battles they'd had, amongst themselves, against others; she wondered how they struggled and suffered. And she knew, unmistakably, that while they'd acquired and achieved; while they'd cut ties with their old land and dropped anchor in this new one, the cost had been high, the losses massive. She was where she was, her parents where they were, because of what Frank and the other elders had been through. But the original Issei had been like the mothers on the sidewalk, and Frank and the second generation like the children—poor, lost, enclosed in themselves, not yet ready for their struggles with the larger world. The swarms of children looked to Jackie like a deep, slow river, which she wanted, now, to enter and be a part of, but which she needed just as deeply to avoid.

As the last of the children finally trickled away, Lanier walked up in front of her.

"Hey," he said. "Hello? Anyone home?"

She turned to face him, with great effort, dragging herself out of the current. "Yeah. Hi. How are you?"

"You OK?" he asked. "You're looking a little lost."

You have no idea how lost, she thought. But she just frowned at him. "You're late."

He apologized, citing traffic, and together they climbed the steps and entered the building. Inside, the school was more cheerful—pictures and drawings decorated the walls and the floors were clean and shiny. They wandered the hallways until they came upon an elderly man mopping outside of a classroom. Lanier cleared his throat to speak, but the sound made the man look up. His movements—his handling of the mop, the time it took to straighten—betrayed his age, but his face was still strikingly handsome. His skin was dark and smooth, barely wrinkled. He had a full head of gray hair and glasses which made his eyes look larger and warmer than they already were. They widened when they settled on Lanier.

"Jimmy?"

And Lanier, under Conway's stare, was transformed into a boy again, struggling to be worthy of standing in front of a man. "Yes, sir."

Conway's eyes moved over to Jackie and widened more. "Good Lord," he said. "You look like Frank. Are you Jackie?"

"Yes, sir."

"I used to bounce you on my knee, girl. Remember?"

Jackie looked down at her feet. "No."

Conway ran a hand over his head, then carefully placed the mop back into the bucket of dirty water. The boy who always followed after Curtis. This girl with his best friend's face. They'd walked through several decades to see him, but he wasn't surprised; the past never stayed in the past. Nodding, he indicated that they should step outside and into the schoolyard. He pulled out a pack of cigarettes, which he offered to Jackie and Lanier (they both declined), and Jackie saw that his hand was shaking as he lit the match. After one puff, two, he looked at them. "They're bad for you, I know. Doctors keep telling me I've got to stop, but I'm too old to be breaking bad habits."

"How you doing, Mr. Conway?" asked Lanier. He remembered the old man more clearly now—his ready, side-splitting laugh; he and Frank sitting together on the crates in front of the store; the way all the women, including his mother, always brightened in his presence.

Conway took a drag and raised his eyebrows. "Well as can be expected at my age, I suppose. Broke a hip a couple months ago, had to have an operation—slipped right there in the hallway. That's why I missed Frank's funeral," he said, looking at Jackie. "I'm real sorry about that. I was still in the hospital then. Just started back to work this week." He didn't say the rest of it, which was that he'd felt relieved, spared the difficulty of bidding Frank goodbye. The closest thing to a brother, Frank Sakai. The ranks of Conway's friends were thinning out anyway, and he didn't like to think that Frank was gone.

"Why are you working?" asked Lanier. "Why not just take it easy at home?"

"I retired from Bethlehem Steel in '86. But after a year of sitting up in the house, I was about to lose my mind." He couldn't explain about the heavy hours staring out the window, mind always chewing on the past. The only things he'd looked forward to were his monthly breakfasts with Frank and the visits from his children, who'd finally started speaking to him after thirty years of silence. "Mrs. Choi, she ran the store after Frank sold the place, she had a sister who was a teacher's assistant here. The paycheck adds a bit to my social security, and it's good to be out of the house."

A little girl ran across the schoolyard. She found something in the grass, retrieved it, and dashed back to the sidewalk, where a man took her hand and led her away.

Conway held his half-smoked cigarette in the air. "Used to take smoke breaks with your grandpa," he said to Jackie. "Every day in front of the store. Way before then, too, in high school. Back then, they had smoking areas for the students."

Jackie turned. "You went to high school with my grandfather?"

"Yep, Dorsey High, class of 1942. Although Frank didn't graduate with us, you know."

Jackie looked at Conway differently now, and so did Lanier; neither of them had known the men went back so far. She wanted to get a better sense of this man—his shaking hands, his sad eyes— and through him, a better sense of her grandfather. "I can't imagine him as a boy," she said. "What was he like back then?"

Conway stubbed the cigarette out against a pole and lit another. He thought of Frank at seventeen, the rigor and responsibility bred into him by his parents, the joy he took when he could be with people and forget about himself. "Very serious, very focused. I always liked to try and loosen him up."

"Did you always live across the street?"

Conway shook his head. In the distance, they heard a siren, coming closer and moving away. "No. I bought that house in 1955. I'd been living down in Watts a few years. Didn't see Frank for a long time, you know. Just right after the war, and then not again until I moved back to Crenshaw. But it was me that took care of the house when your family was sent to the camps." And the time of the war seemed to age them as much as the fifteen years that followed. All the marks of boyishness pressed out of them by violence and loss. He thought briefly of his family; of the childhoods he'd missed. He thought of old friends from the shipyard and their deteriorating lives, spent almost wholly, after the war, in the once-temporary projects which had fast become permanent, hulking, unsafe.

Jackie didn't know if she was supposed to acknowledge Conway's caretaking, but he cut off her train of thought.

"You're here about the murders, aren't you?"

"Yes," Lanier said. "My cousin . . ."

"Curtis," interrupted Conway. "I know. I know who did it, too—a cop who worked in the neighborhood, Nick Lawson. I don't know if you remember him, Jimmy, but the day your cousin died, I saw him take the boys into the store."

"Did you see him leave?"

"No."

"Did you see anything else?"

"Not really. Just a bunch of kids running back and forth. Kenji Hirano out in front of his house, testifying. You've got to remember—there was a lot of craziness that day. I was trying to stay away from the windows. And I didn't think Lawson . . . well, I just didn't think. Some other cops passed by—the Irishman, the nice one. The two black ones, too, the partners."

"I talked to one of them, Robert Thomas. He wasn't very helpful. Basically told me to mind my own business."

"Sounds like Thomas," the old man commented. "He always was the white man's pet, and he had no love for black boys. If he knew anything about the store, I'm sure he wouldn't tell you." Conway remembered Thomas, the loud bluster that was so easy to see through, but still intimidating to the kids. It was different now, but there was something about being a cop thirty years ago that made certain weak-willed black men act like white men.

"So that day outside the store was the last time you saw the boys?" Lanier asked.

Conway nodded. But he had seen them again. On the floor, in front of the counter, after Frank had dragged them out of the freezer. After Derek came in and left again, clutching his head. The two men standing there, Victor's arms locked tight around Frank's wiry chest, trying to keep his friend from falling over.

They were all silent for a moment. A gust of wind blew through the schoolyard, rattling the chains and the rings on the jungle gym.

"Did you know the boys at all?" Jackie asked.

Conway nodded again. "I knew the older ones, Curtis and David Scott. I tell you—what happened to them, it made me want to kill somebody. Might have been the worst single thing that happened in that mess, but no one knew about it, and no one did a Goddamned thing. It tore your grandpa up, girl. Tore him up. He was always real close to those boys."

Something else occurred to Jackie. "Mr. Conway, do you know how my grandfather met Curtis?"

"Sure. Through his mother, Alma."

"So he knew Curtis through Alma—it wasn't that he met Alma through Curtis?"

"No, no. Frank and Alma were friends for a long time."

"She'd always been a customer, right? Since Curtis was little?"

"Well, yeah, I suppose, but they went back further than that. Her family moved to Angeles Mesa before the war. Had a house right over on Olmsted."

Jackie tried to keep her expression from changing. She heard Lanier breathe in sharply. When she spoke again, she did so slowly, making sure she had control of her voice. "But I thought the Martindales lived in Oakland. I thought they didn't come down to L.A. till after Curtis was born."

"The *Martindales*, yeah. I'm talking about the Sams. Alma lived in Oakland and met her husband up there, but both she and her sister Althea grew up down here. They came out from Texas to live with their aunt, and their parents moved here just before the war got started. The girls didn't go to Oakland until *after* the war. Althea was in school with us and Alma was in middle school, I think." And she was a fireball, he thought. Salt and vinegar. Trying so hard to make up for her brother. Tried after her boys were born, too, and after they died. And he'd liked

Alma, admired her even, but he couldn't see how all that trying was going to save her.

"Are you sure they were here that early?" Jackie asked.

"Yeah, I'm sure," Conway answered. Then he looked at both of them and lifted his eyebrow. "Why, does it make some kind of difference?"

"No, no," Jackie said, shaking her head. She looked at Lanier now, saw the same alarm in his eyes, and the same need to play things down.

"No, not really," Lanier concurred, looking back at Conway. "But it does help shed some light on why Frank was so attached to Curtis."

Conway nodded. He didn't know why they were all in a fuss about how Frank met the boy, but he could see that they had questions about Frank and Alma. So did he. The way Frank looked at her. The way he said her name. His reaction when she moved back to Oakland again, after both of her sons had died. "Oh, yeah," he said. "He loved that boy. And he would have done anything for Curtis's mama."

Jackie couldn't sleep that night. She sat on the couch and looked at the photo of her grandparents standing side by side, not touching, in front of their house. They were smiling in the picture, though; they always seemed happy to her. But how much of their lives, of her grandfather's life, was not as it appeared? His constant dealings with the public, his openness, had created a smokescreen for him, behind which he might have had an entirely different existence. Had he known Alma Martindale since she was a teenager? Had he been secretly involved with her? And if he was, when did it happen? When did Alma move to Oakland? And why did she leave L.A. in the first place?

Jackie finally fell asleep around five a.m., but got up three hours later to go to school. There she filled Rebecca in on all the sightings of Nick Lawson—but not about her suspicions regarding Alma and Frank, she somehow felt protective of that. She and Laura had a strained but civil night—neither of them wanted to make up from their fight, but they also lacked the energy to continue it. After a night they each spent safely on their own sides of the bed, Jackie drove home to wait for Lanier.

He had gone to his mother's place in Carson on Friday to see if he could dig up any information on Alma and Bruce. He showed up just after noon, and Jackie let him in, sat him down, and poured him a cup of coffee before she finally gave in and asked if he'd found anything.

"Part of something. Maybe." He opened a manila folder and showed her a clipping. It was from the *Sun-Reporter,* an old black newspaper out of San Francisco, dated November 10, 1946:

Martindale–Sams

Mr. and Mrs. Donald Sams of Los Angeles, California, announce the marriage of their daughter, Alma Clarice, to Bruce Henry Martindale, son of George and Patricia Martindale of 231 Sperry Road in Carson. Miss Sams is employed by the Stevens-Forrest Paper Company. Mr. Martindale is employed by the Corson Watch Manufacturing Company. A November 17 wedding is planned in Oakland.

Jackie held the yellowed scrap in her hand, turning it over as if more might be written there. Then she looked at Lanier. "This is interesting. Did your mother go up for the wedding?"

"No," Lanier said, shaking his head. "That announcement, as you can see, came out really close to the date. And she told me last night that my uncle sent it down *after* the wedding."

"So she wasn't there to see if Alma was . . ."

"No one was there, at least from my family."

She paused, turned the clipping over again, and looked at Lanier. "How old did you say that Curtis was when he died?"

"Seventeen or eighteen."

"But *which*?"

"I'm not sure. And you're right. It starts to make a difference now."

"Well, do you remember when his birthday was?"

Lanier thought for a moment. "I seem to remember it was some time in the spring."

"But you don't know the year."

"No, but I'm thinking that Angela Broadnax would know."

Jackie thumped a fist on her knee. "You're a genius."

She left Lanier with the phone in the living room, and then picked up the extension in her bedroom. Lanier dialed Angela's number, and the phone rang once, twice, three times. On the fourth ring, someone picked it up.

"Yeah," said the impatient young voice on the other end.

It took Lanier a second to remember her name. "Renee," he said finally. "Hi, is your mom there?"

"Yeah," she repeated, and then she dropped the phone and yelled out, "Mama!" In another few seconds, the phone was picked up again, and Angela Broadnax said hello.

Lanier identified himself and asked how she was. She inquired about their efforts and he told her it was looking good, they were getting close to approaching the District Attorney. Then he said, "Listen, I'm wondering if you could help me with something. When exactly was Curtis's birthday?"

"March twenty-fourth."

"You're sure."

"Yeah—same day as my oldest brother. Why?"

"We're double-checking the boys' ages, to make the case against Lawson look as bad as possible. So Curtis was born March twenty-fourth, nineteen forty . . ."

"Seven."

"Great," said Lanier, and he and Jackie did their calculations. "Thanks. I couldn't find anyone else who remembered."

"Well, he was born up in Oakland, you know. His mother moved up there to live with her sister, and that's where she met his dad."

"Right," Lanier said again. "The sister was Althea, right? Do you know where she is now?"

"Curtis's aunt? No, I don't. I'm sorry."

They made small-talk for a minute or two about the people they knew in common, and Lanier assured her once again that they were tightening the noose on Lawson. When they hung up, Jackie ran back out to the living room.

"March twenty-fourth, 1947," she said.

"And Alma was married in November of '46."

"So she was four or five months pregnant when she married your uncle."

"Yep. But we can't get too excited. I mean, she could have been pregnant by Bruce."

Jackie paused. "You're right. We need more. Is there anyone else who might know about it?"

"Well, Alma's sister, I'll bet. Althea."

"But she's got to be dead by now, right? She was older than Alma."

"She was your grandfather's age." He smiled. "And I happen to know she's alive."

Jackie had just sat down, but now she stood back up. "What? Really? Where?"

"She's in a nursing home somewhere in Oakland. I don't know which one. But my mother said that Bruce still heard from her sometimes, and she wrote him again a couple years ago, not knowing that he'd died. Her married name was Dickson, I think. My mother's going to find out for sure."

Jackie clapped her hands once, loudly. "Should we call the nursing homes up there? Try to find her?"

Lanier put the wedding announcement back in his folder. "We could. But see, there's this other thing. My friend Allen called again yesterday. He had someone look through the pension records at the LAPD and found the address for Oliver Paxton, Robert Thomas's old partner. He's living up in East Palo Alto now. And I'm thinking that even if Hirano's not fit to testify and Thomas is covering up for Lawson, Paxton might be willing to tell what he knows. And I'm sure he knows something, Jackie. I don't think he just left the force by chance."

"I thought he moved back east," said Jackie, thinking, pacing.

"I did, too. Maybe he came back out to California."

"Or maybe Thomas was trying to throw us off-track. Have you tried to call Paxton yet?"

"No. But he lives in East Palo Alto. Althea Dickson, or whatever her name is, lives in Oakland."

Jackie considered him for a moment. "What are you saying?"

Lanier leaned back, cupped his knee with his hands, and smiled up at Jackie. "Wanna go on a road trip?" he asked.

CHAPTER TWENTY-NINE

1945

IT WAS the palm tree that did it. Not the soft swell of calf, which was what he saw first, or the white dress, summer-thin, that curled around it. When Frank turned the corner that morning, headed for the store, she was leaning against the palm tree by the curb. She was young, he thought, no more than seventeen, and she was waiting for somebody. His eyes took in the brown calf, and then moved over to the other leg, which was tucked behind her, sole pressed flat against the bark. She had one smooth arm wrapped around her side, the elbow of the other arm resting on top of it. Fingers slowly stroking the back of her neck. Frank saw the combed-back hair, which was glistening, restrained, and when she turned her head toward the street for a moment, he saw how it was gathered into a small curved bun, a dark seashell on the back of her head. The curve of her jaw made a dry spot open at the back of his throat. And as he drew closer, walking in smaller steps in order to extend his view, he saw how the tree had changed for her, framed her, stooped down so she'd be protected. The rough, peeling skin of the tree made hers appear softer; the shifting sound of the leaves betrayed the tree's pleasure. This palm tree, removed from its brothers near the ocean and set down in the midst of bungalows and concrete, had never looked so beautiful, so proud. And the girl, the way she leaned there, at ease but not relaxed, small and thin but not delicate. Her body was tightened, taut, and despite the dress and the tree and the sunshine, Frank could see in her the trap ready to spring, the lit fuse, the coiled tension.

He kept walking, and just as he was about to pass, she turned away from the street and looked at him. Her eyes were brown, large and liquid, but sharp beneath the long, graceful lashes. The familiarity, the matter-of-factness with which she considered him, made him wonder if he was imagining things or if he really knew her. Some of his old friends had little sisters; he tried to match her features with those of Barry and Don, but quickly realized that they had never met. He lifted his thumb and first two fingers to tip the hat that wasn't there, nodding beneath his raised hand. And when she pulled her hand from her neck and smiled in reply, he felt something shift in him that would never shift back.

He was late that morning. His mother had a fever and he'd stayed a few extra minutes to press a cold pack to her head, but when he walked into the store, his breathlessness was not because of hurry. For the first twenty minutes, he straightened the shelves and piled the fruit in tight intricate pyramids while Old Man Larabie worked in the office. In that time, a customer came and went, and then another. The bell jingled again, a few minutes later, and because Frank was balancing a pile of oranges, he didn't look up right away. Then he heard the high, solid voice, which pulled him toward it by the collar. "I'd like half a dozen of those," she said.

Frank looked up, and his grasp on the two oranges in his hands loosened, softened; he caressed the cool fruit with his thumbs. "Weren't you waiting for somebody?" he asked. Her arms hung at her sides now, and he saw the small, square shoulders that his hands itched to cover and touch. He saw the soft convergence of collarbone and neck, like two wishbones set down to face each other, containing all the world's wishes.

"Yeah," she said. "Don't matter, though. Never get what you wait for, anyway."

He smiled, pulled a paper bag from underneath a table, and chose the plumpest, brightest fruit to place inside. As they walked toward the counter, Old Man Larabie came out, said hello to the girl, and kept moving toward one of the aisles. Frank felt watched now, and pulled himself up straighter. He rang up the oranges, took the money she held out, and let his hand linger, just a moment, beneath her touch. "Come back, now," he said, and he watched as she left, dress clinging to the curves of her hips.

Old Man Larabie, who usually caught everything, didn't wonder why his young employee looked like he'd swallowed a whole piece of fruit. "How's your mama?" he asked, tugging his pants up to contain his growing belly. "Still got a fever?"

"Doing better. It's down to a hundred now." Then, looking down at the counter, pretending to wipe something off: "That girl who bought the oranges. She ever been in here before?"

Old Man Larabie turned toward the doorway, as if the girl might still be standing there. He shook his head slowly and seemed to be thinking about something more than the young man's question. "Don't think so. She's a Sams girl. Family's had some rough times. Her daddy started drinking a couple years ago, after what happened with his boy, Reese. One day in boot camp he just went crazy—shot five members of his unit and then ended up shooting himself."

Frank shook his head. He'd heard of men losing control like that, and he almost understood. He knew what it was like to be completely overtaken by fear; he knew the urge to strike out at the earth, the enemy, your friends, yourself, in order to prove you were still a man, you still existed. He thought of the girl now, her tightness, her power. "What's her name?"

"Alma."

"Alma," Frank repeated, and he took the name into his mouth, held it on his tongue, carried it there all day.

Alma, that morning, wasn't waiting for anything; she'd been on her way to Tracy's house to show off her new white dress. But then the sun, the breeze, the tree had beckoned, seemed to say, "Wait, if you stay here with me, I'll give you something." She wasn't usually partial to palm trees—they were nothing like the thick, cool, sheltering trees down home—but this one seemed so lovely, and, in the light of the sun, she knew both she and her dress would look irresistible resting up against the trunk. When the man had turned the corner and come walking down the street, she knew the tree was fulfilling its promise. He walked toward her, against the backdrop of white and yellow houses, and the green lawns seemed to part like waters before him. His hair was in a crew cut and was shiny blue-black; his skin brown and toughened by the sun. His pants were loose, but as he walked, she saw his firm thighs, the muscles expanding and contracting against the cloth. He moved with confidence and quickness, and the slight, rolling hitch in his step suggested experience to her, not damage. His white sleeves were rolled up to reveal his strong, muscled forearms. And when he passed her and tipped his imaginary hat, she saw the hands, which were square, strong, and beautiful. There was a silver watch on his left wrist; his left hand was missing half its middle finger. She couldn't help but smile at him, this offering, this stranger, and when he walked on she watched the muscles of his back.

She was seventeen then, and just out of school. She had plans—to study more, become a teacher. This was 1945 and the war was over, and the country that allowed black soldiers to die would surely let a black girl go to college. But her family didn't think she should try to—not now, not yet—and they needed her to work, so they found a whitewoman, Mrs. McDermott, over in West L.A., a friend of Mrs. Tucker, her mother's boss. For twenty dollars a week, two meals a day, and hand-me-down clothes, Alma bore the indignation of having to be polite to a woman she hated; of washing her husband's stinking clothes; of being searched every night for stolen goods before she left for home. And although they didn't say so, her parents also encouraged her to work for the McDermotts because they wanted her close by—because of Althea running away, and because of what happened with Reese.

What happened with Reese. The Sams children moved out to live with their father's sister when Alma was eleven, Althea fourteen, Reese just turned sixteen—because they had a chance here, their parents said, to do something more than work someone else's land. The L.A. kids had laughed at how they talked, at their easy, slow-moving ways, and their aunt Sophie, denying all traces of the south she believed had made her family ignorant (the children had another aunt, back in Texas, who had killed her own husband), was not especially happy with their presence. But at the start of the war, Alma's parents had moved out, too, renting a house off of

Crenshaw. And so the family was reunited, but fragmented—like distant relatives forced by circumstance to live with each other; like lovers, once separated, trying to recapture what was already lost. In Texas, all the Sams, adults and children, had gone out to the fields together—the scathing hot sun, their aching backs made bearable by the presence of the rest of the family, by the songs they all sang while they worked. Alma had picked cotton from the time she was five, but the hard hours, the heavy sacks of harvested blossoms, seemed very far away to her now, the only proof of her family's sharecropping days the small scars on her hands from the sharp, hidden parts of the cotton plants. To be sure, no one missed the work itself—the pain, the extreme heat, the soul-shaking cold, the frozen cotton balls like ice cubes when they finished picking in December. But after they moved to L.A., her parents did miss seeing their children. Mr. Sams now worked at the toy factory all day, Mrs. Sams downtown for the WPA. Alma and her siblings were off at school, and afterward they disappeared into the social lives they'd mysteriously created for themselves in the two years away from their parents. The only time the whole family saw each other was on Sunday, at church, where the parents, so intense was their hunger for other people, went with the same excitement the children reserved for the county fair. Sundays they were a family; Sundays were good. Maybe it was the other six days of the week that they lost sight of Reese, although whether his departure was gradual or sudden Alma still didn't know.

Alma had been in California for two years, and was just beginning to feel like she belonged there, when the war started and her brother was gone. And then, just six months later, the news from Mississippi. Reese had gone into his own barracks and started firing his rifle, calmly loading and reloading while the screams and pleas rose up all around him. He had killed five people. He had spilled the blood and brains of five black boys, and seriously wounded seven others. Then he'd put the muzzle of the gun in his own mouth. And although Alma and her family hadn't told anyone, word had traveled, in stops and starts, in twists and permutations, across the entire country and back to L.A. And suddenly Alma saw the whispering, the heads bent together, the eyes low-

ered and then turned away. *"Isn't she the one whose brother . . . ?"*
"All black boys, too. At least he could have killed white . . ."
"Must run in the family. They have an aunt who took a knife . . ."
*"Better stay away from her. She and Reese were tight, and who
knows what kinds of things . . ."*

They *had* been close, which was why her brother's crime, and
death, haunted her more than it ever haunted Althea. She should
have felt it, Alma thought. She should have known. Her parents,
especially her father, put themselves through a similar torture.
They went to church the first few weeks after the news had
reached the coast, but they couldn't keep it up; Mr. Sams was
drinking constantly now, taunted by the whispers. Worse, his faith
was slipping off of him like clothing he could no longer fill. He
shut himself away in the house except to go to work, commencing
a self-imposed exile that would last the rest of his life. And for
Alma, there was also this: If Reese could do such a thing, if he was
capable of such murderous brutality, then what did that say about
her? She was the one most like him, everyone said. The intense
one, whose inner workings no one else could figure out. And look
what that had meant for her brother. So now, Alma held her fear
and shame outside of her, but they clung to her like shackles. And
instead of pressing anything—tears, talk, grief, anger—out, she
directed it in. She pushed herself to work, to succeed. Always a
good student, she became a great one, working hours each night
on schoolwork although the resentful and uninspired teachers at
her school did not see fit to give assignments. She organized a
walkout to protest the paltry number of math books (six for thirty-
three students, and most of those missing half their pages), and
was rewarded with a new set of textbooks for all her classes, and
by the administration skipping her up a grade. She took over the
care of her family's home, cleaning it, cooking for her mother and
father, constructing and fulfilling lists of tasks and groceries. If she
just succeeded, she thought, in everything—if she was unparal-
leled, unbreakable, like all the other strong-backed women in her
mother's line—then maybe she could prove she was different from
her family; maybe she could even pull them up along with her.

At seventeen, she had dated a few boys, but had never known

a man. That morning, when Frank tipped his imaginary hat and walked on to the store, she knew she had finally found one. Nevermind that she didn't know him, or that he was Japanese. Nevermind that she saw herself as always alone, despite the many people in her life. She leaned against the tree for what seemed like a good amount of time, feeling the sun on her face and on her chest. Then she walked to the store, two blocks away, where she knew the man worked. She watched his arms against the rolled white sleeves, the tan skin, the light covering of hair. And she watched the firm hands as they worked with the fruit, stacking, positioning, confirming. She longed to find out what else those hands knew; to feel them lift and open her. And she yearned to touch and kiss the blunted finger. He turned toward her then, and she saw his face head-on—the strong nose; the dark, firm lips; the high, prominent cheekbones; the black, just-now-softening eyes. "Weren't you waiting for somebody?" she heard him ask, and the low, layered voice went through her ears and settled down in the bottom of her stomach. What she said out loud was different from what she answered in her mind. Yeah, I was, she thought. I just didn't know it.

They met nighttimes, after Old Man Larabie had left for the day. They both claimed work as the reason for their late arrival home— Frank saying he had inventories, accounts to add up, Alma blaming her boss, Mrs. McDermott, damn heifer made me cook for her and wash the dishes, too. Alma would come around back to the door on the alley side, knock twice, and run her fingers over the place her knuckles hit the wood, thinking of Frank's tight skin. He always asked who it was even though it was always her, and then he'd open the door, and lock it behind her, and follow her into the office. He loved those few seconds between the door and the office, when he walked in back of her, watching, without her seeing him look. She still wore her white work dress and scuffed black shoes, sometimes a light sweater if it was cool. She was loose-jointed, liquid smooth, but there was something hard in her, efficient and precise. He loved the contradiction—the easy and tight, the quick and slow. The muscles in her calves and thighs were firm and apple-round; when they were wrapped around him, he felt enclosed by them, contained.

In the office, she'd go straight to the couch, where she wouldn't collapse with exhaustion, but instead sit down on it, hard, as if daring it to prove it could hold her. Frank would go to the desk and turn the chair around to face her, creating the space it would please them both, later, to cross. They talked first, and the talking was easy—details, minor triumphs and complaints about their days. For the first two weeks they met like this, they didn't touch at all; they were like old friends trying to catch up on each other's lives. And they realized, then, that they *did* know one another; before the war, Frank had been in her sister's class. Frank found, with Alma, that he didn't have to explain things—that when he told her his sister and father had died, she seemed to know what it had been like, marching slowly up the spine of Italy, grieving for the family now placed in the ground, praying for his sinking, jailed mother. That when he said he couldn't find a job after the war, he didn't need to tell her about the "No Japs Wanted" signs, the hoots and laughter when he said he was a veteran. That when he told her about traveling up through San Diego after he'd been discharged, he didn't have to add that the first three motels wouldn't take him, and that when he finally found one that would, someone heaved a brick through the window in the night. Alma knew these things; she felt them. And while she gradually gave Frank the straightforward, newspaper facts about her family's history—Reese's murders and suicide; her aunt's repeated stabbing of her violent, cheating husband; her father's drinking and struggling faith—she didn't have to explain to him, either.

But Frank still wondered. Wondered not about the details of these various horrors, but about what each of them, the sum of them, had done to her. He couldn't know the abandon with which she threw herself into her work, the beating of rugs, the scrubbing of floors she used to exorcise her rage. He couldn't know that as much as she hated working for Mrs. McDermott, she was relieved, almost grateful, to have something to pour herself into. Someplace where she worked so hard and so long she didn't have the energy to think. And what little was left of energy, of thought, pain, herself, she flung at Frank those nights in the back of the store.

He loosened something in her, and he both loved what that

meant and feared it. Every other woman had been surrender, acquiescence, soft pleasure wrapped in whispers and laughter. But Alma Sams was like a tidal wave. She didn't want to be overpowered, or to overpower him. She needed to hurl herself at Frank, and to know that he would be there to catch her. Never, never, as Frank smoothed his lips over the side of her breasts and took her nipples in his mouth; as he ran his fingers over the silky skin on the insides of her thighs; as he pushed as if through a wet, windy storm, he the traveler she both welcomed and resisted; was he not awed by her abandon, or her power. She took him. She contained him without giving way. Those times—wet lashes fluttering over half-closed lids—were the only moments there seemed to be cracks in her, when he could see in through the tiny spaces. The rest of the time, as they sat talking, or even afterward, as they lay naked on the couch, she possessed herself completely. He knew how tightly she kept herself wrapped, how intricate the structure of her defense. If she removed, or let someone else remove, even one small invisible brick, the whole structure might crumble, collapse. And he feared this, and also prayed for it. She was so neatly wound, she had no loose ends; and he loved this about her, admired it. But occasionally, he yearned for some stray end to come free, so he could unwrap it, unravel her, reveal the raw wounds underneath.

She, on the other hand, feared she revealed too much. She thought by showing Frank the result of her need and fury, she was giving him the narrative behind it. But he met her halfway; he let her empty herself with him, and for this she was grateful and loved him. Each of them thought that the other was stronger. Only he was right.

It would be wrong to think their need for each other had nothing to do with race. What he loved in her was not just her intensity, her beauty, but everything she'd come from. He saw in her earth-brown skin not just the girl he loved, but the faces and families of his moved-away friends whom he loved and missed so deeply. He heard their easy laughter as they played football on Sundays, as they passed each other in the hallways at school. He heard the music and saw the swirling smoke of the jazz clubs Victor had taken him to in Watts; tasted the cornbread and catfish and red beans and rice Mrs. Conway sometimes fixed them after practice. And Alma was also simply not-Japanese—not like the small folded-in young women who were so constrained and accepting of him; not the women he had failed to protect.

For Alma, Frank was gravity and fortitude—not a forced, oppressive silence, but a man who didn't air his grief; who bore his cross alone. She knew that he was pained, but also knew he would never ask for pity. His silence made hers acceptable. And he was not her brother, or aunt, or father—whatever difficulties and self-hatred their lives had conferred had passed over him, or at least taken another form. And yet he *was* her brother, also—another soldier, a man of color. His skin was brown but of a different shade—wet sand, and not the earth.

Years later, when Frank saw her—on the street, with her sons, with other women in the neighborhood—she seemed to him the same. Her face had a few shallow lines now, and her clothes were different; she looked a bit more tired. But the tightness, the tension, were still there. He wondered about her husband, if she unleashed herself with him. He wondered, as she laughed with her friends, if she had any regrets; was struck, all over again, by the pride in the angle of her neck. She would walk by on the street, say hello to him, and the heels of her shoes would tangle and twist his insides. He wondered if he still touched her, or if he ever really had. He wondered if she ever remembered.

CHAPTER THIRTY

1994

M OST OF California is wide-open spaces, huge expanses of land unsullied by buildings or people. Jackie and Lanier rediscovered this fact as they drove north through the state, windows rolled all the way down. Lanier had taken half a day off from work, and Jackie had skipped her Friday classes. It was warm—another Santa Ana—and the sky was tinged with smog. Still, as they sped along, wind brushing back their hair and music playing so loud they couldn't talk to each other, they felt alive, refreshed, set free. They'd driven through the Hollywood Hills; battled traffic in the Valley; climbed into the Angeles National Forest. And when they came through the Tejon Pass, clouds clinging to the car, and found the green and brown fields spread out endlessly before them, Jackie thought she could see the end of the world. Only then did Lanier finally speak. "Ho-ly shit," he said, and Jackie laughed, and felt that laughter break up the tension in her stomach. She realized she hadn't laughed like that in months.

Jackie had waited until Tuesday to tell Laura about her trip. She had avoided the task for days—not because she knew she'd be telling a partial truth, but because she didn't want to communicate with her at all. And Laura had not taken the news very well. It wasn't that Jackie was going someplace without her—or, at least, it wasn't *only* that. And it also wasn't that she was going with somebody else—Jackie had omitted the fact that Lanier would be joining her. But when Jackie told her over dinner, she'd gone quiet and started to cry, and her sorrow, Jackie knew, was not even about the trip, but about the fact that things were so strange between them that Jackie hadn't mentioned it before.

But Jackie did not want to think about that now. Neither she nor Lanier spoke much during the six and a half hours of their drive, and the silence was easy between them. As they approached the Bay Area, Jackie felt herself tighten as she thought about the things that awaited them.

They checked into a small, two-story motel on the border of the Mission and the Castro. Although their business was in Oakland and East Palo Alto, both of them had wanted to stay in San Francisco, which Lanier hadn't visited in years. That night, they walked up 16th Street to Market, and into the Castro, breathing in the cooler, cleaner ocean air of Northern California, and staring like wonder-struck children at the city around them. Jackie felt both at home and out of place here; both happy with Lanier and uncomfortable. They passed groups of gay men talking in high, fluttery voices, and a couple of built-up macho gays who nodded at Lanier, in challenge and invitation. Jackie watched Lanier smile, ironically, more interested than threatened. And when they passed lesbians on the sidewalk, either low-key and clad in Doc Martens and jeans, or made-up and stylized, they looked at Jackie with their eyebrows raised, or with small sly smiles of recognition. She didn't know how to react to them—whether to avoid their eyes or smile—and she realized she was acting like Laura that first summer, when they'd walked down these streets every day. Lanier looked at her questioningly, sensing her discomfort. She felt awkward and oddly ashamed of herself, and finally, more out of a need for escape than hunger, she touched him on the arm and indicated a restaurant, a Mexican place on Market.

They went inside, secured a booth, and ordered margaritas. They talked about their plans for the following day—Lanier had found Althea Dickson at St. Mary's Rest Home in Oakland, and they were going to show up there first thing the next morning, just after the residents had eaten their breakfast. He didn't ask the woman who'd spoken to him to inform Mrs. Dickson of his visit; they both figured that surprise might yield more answers. His mother had told him, though, that Alma's sister was fond of

crullers, so they needed to leave time in the morning to stop at a
donut shop.

They sat with their hands folded on top of their menus, as if
praying to each other. Finally, their waitress arrived—a tall, slinky,
long-haired Latina whose voice snagged when she got a look at
Jackie.

"And our special tonight is crab chimichangas. They come
with Mexican rice and black or refried beans. They're our most
popular special and I recommend them highly. They're really very
. . . tasty."

At this last word she glanced at Jackie, and Jackie smiled at
her and blushed. If Lanier weren't there, she would try to flirt
back—say something silly and suggestive about the drinks or the
special, or ask how tasty the things in the restaurant actually were.
But she felt watched and restrained, so awkwardly, she ordered
enchiladas. Lanier ordered a burrito and the waitress—whose
name tag read "Lucy"—dutifully jotted this down. Then she
touched her tongue to the tip of the pen and looked back down at
Jackie. "If you need anything else, or if"—and now she glanced
meaningfully at Lanier—"you're *displeased* with your selection,
please feel free to let me know."

She spun away, the ruffles of her skirt brushing against Jackie's
arm. Jackie looked at Lanier, embarrassed, and found him laughing. "Well, I guess *you're* a hit. Maybe we'll get a free meal out of
this."

"Yeah," she said. "Well, you know, it comes with the territory."

"Not necessarily. The guy who took our drink order didn't try
to pick me up."

"Are you offended?" she asked, smiling.

"No, just jealous. Your friend Lucy is all that and then some."

Jackie laughed, feeling slightly more at ease.

"You lived here for awhile, right?" Lanier asked. "Went up to
school here?"

"I went to Berkeley, but I came into the city almost every
weekend. And then I lived in San Francisco for a year between college and law school."

"Did you like it?"

"Yeah, I loved it. I mean, I was working really hard, but I still played more than I ever have since." She took a sip of her drink. She felt like she was standing on the edge of a cliff, but it was finally time to jump now, so she stepped out into the air. "This is where I met Laura."

Lanier's expression didn't change—he looked interested, not bothered or surprised. "How'd she end up in L.A.? Because you were there?"

"Only partly. The main reason was that she got a job with the city. Also, her mother lives in Beverly Hills. I was a factor too, I guess, but not the only factor." Her hands were clenched on the table now, and she realized they were sweaty. At that moment, Lucy reappeared, bearing another basket of chips although their first was half-full; they all knew this wasn't her job.

"Just thought I'd replenish you," she said. Then, looking at Jackie, "Let me know if there's anything I can do." She prolonged and softened the words "anything" and "do," offered them up like truffles. Watching the waitress's bright, direct eyes, Jackie felt her heart jump and her cheeks turn red. Lucy walked off again, and Lanier burst out laughing.

"I gotta tell you," he said. "You really don't flirt very well."

Jackie threw a chip at him. "Shut up. You're cramping my style."

Their food came shortly and they talked of other things—the animals and ranches they'd seen on their drive, their previous adventures in San Francisco. Lucy continued to flirt with Jackie, and Jackie, much to Lanier's amusement, continued to fumble her replies. She felt the same relief she always did when some person she cared about finally acknowledged her sexuality. Then, after yet another disparaging comment on her horrible flirtation skills, she said, "What? You think *you* could do any better?"

"Not with *this* crowd," said Lanier. Then, more seriously, "Actually, no. Not with any crowd."

"Oh, come on. I find that hard to believe. From what I hear, good-looking, dependable straight men are a fast-dying breed. And I see the way women look at you."

"Well." He looked thoughtful. "I don't have a hard time starting things. But I have a hard time keeping them going. I'm not that great at talking to people."

"Oh, bullshit," Jackie said. "You talk to *me*."

But it was different, Lanier thought, and Jackie knew this. Jackie didn't ask things of him. She wasn't trying to get inside. He didn't feel the same need to protect himself with her. That need had gotten so intense in the last few years that he'd stopped trying with women altogether. But Lanier didn't want to analyze his deficiencies, so they exchanged stories about crazy ex-es—the veterinarian he'd dated who'd insisted they share the bed with her three large dogs and four cats; the stoner-biker she'd dated her first year of college who'd gotten Jackie's name tattooed on her rear. Two hours later, after several margaritas, they stumbled back to their hotel, both ready for a good night's rest. They stood fifteen feet apart from each other, working the keys for their separate doors. Lanier opened his and stepped partway inside. "Sweet dreams," he said. And then he grinned. "Hope they're about the right person."

The next morning, they got up at 7:30. They bought three large crullers for Mrs. Dickson at the coffee shop next door, and donuts and coffee for themselves. As they drove through the city and crossed the Bay Bridge, they didn't have much to say. Jackie looked at all the traffic on the other side of the road, and beyond it, the green headlands and the dark blue, welcoming ocean. It was a clear, bright morning, theatrical in its beauty.

St. Mary's was a few blocks off the 580 Freeway. The building was one-story, tan, and unremarkable. They walked through the glass double-door, which was smudged with fingerprints, and nodded at the bored young security guard. Behind the front desk sat a middle-aged nun who wore a white habit and thick black glasses. Her nose was red and bulbous, as if swollen from the effort of holding up the heavy frames. Her name tag read "Sister Elizabeth." When Jackie and Lanier approached, she said, "Good morning," and her voice sounded exactly as Jackie expected: medium-pitched, thick, without shadows or potholes—the voice, Jackie thought, of someone who'd steered clear of the tribulations of life in this world.

"Good morning," Lanier said. "We're here to see Mrs. Althea Dickson."

"Is she expecting you?" asked the sister.

"Not exactly."

"Are you a family member?"

"Yes."

It took Jackie a moment to realize that this was actually true. Still, the nun examined him closely. He and Jackie had both dressed neatly—Lanier in pressed gray trousers and a bright white dress shirt, she in tan pants and a black blazer.

"I don't recognize you," said the sister. "Have you visited before?"

Lanier cleared his throat. "Actually, no. I live down in L.A. And I'm kind of a distant relative—I'm a nephew of her sister."

The nun looked at him again, and then at Jackie. Jackie realized, suddenly, that the nun was scared of Lanier. The dress shirt and pants couldn't hide the prominence of his muscles, the breadth of his athlete's shoulders. She wondered, all of a sudden, what it was like to be him, to inspire fear in people he hardly even noticed. Finally, Sister Elizabeth instructed them to sign the guest sheet, then called an attendant over to take them in.

"She's in the television room," explained the attendant as they walked down the hall. Her name tag read "Sophia." They passed several open doors, and when Jackie glanced in she saw old people, lying in bed or sitting in wheelchairs, almost all of them with their arms stretched out toward the door, crying "Help me" to whoever went by. She looked away from them in shame and thought of walking past jail cells, skinny arms held out through the bars. They soon reached a large room full of ratty couches and discolored chairs. Most of the residents in attendance sat in long-backed wheelchairs, set up in two rows to face the television. A morning talk show was on, and the volume was turned up so high that Sophia had to shout.

"Just a second," she said, "I'll tell her you're here."

She approached one of the chairs, bent down to talk into an ear. Then the wheelchair spun around. Jackie and Lanier stood quietly as the occupant wheeled herself over. Although Jackie knew the woman was her grandfather's age—seventy or seventy-one—she looked younger. Her curly hair was only slightly gray, and her skin was barely wrinkled. She had funny black glasses, the kind that Jackie associated with phone operators from the 1950s. She wore a blue and green plaid robe over a pair of pink sweat-pants. Althea Dickson did not have the withered, sunken look of the other people in the room; as she stopped in front of them, Jackie half-expected her to jump out of her chair.

"Hello," the woman said, and her voice was loud, command-ing—qualities that had nothing to do with her hearing. "I'm Althea Dickson. Who are you? I hear you supposed to know me."

Jackie smiled, especially when she saw the look of surprise and slight alarm on Lanier's face. He had expected—they'd both expected—someone elderly, deflated.

"I'm James Lanier," he managed, collecting himself and offer-ing her the paper bag. "I'm Bruce Martindale's nephew."

Althea's eyebrows shot up and then lowered into a straight, suspicious line. She took the bag from him, opened it, and peered inside. Only one eyebrow rose this time, and she looked back up at them. "Ain't really sure if I've heard of you," she said. Then, to Jackie, "And I *know* I don't know who *you* are."

Jackie gave Althea her name, and Althea nodded in acknowl-edgment before looking back at Lanier.

"I'm wondering if I could talk to you," he said politely. "About my uncle and aunt."

She tapped her foot against the footrest. "Well, I don't mean to be rude, young man, but I didn't like your uncle too much."

Lanier nodded. "That's all right. Neither did I. I liked Alma a whole lot better."

"She was my sister, you know."

"I know," Lanier said. "I'd like to know more about her."

Althea looked at him hard, and Jackie thought she was about to tell them to leave. But then she wheeled around without saying a word and headed down the hall. Lanier and Jackie glanced at each other, then followed; they had to walk fast to keep up. About halfway down the hall, without appearing to slow down, Althea took a sharp right through an open door. Lanier and Jackie hesi-tated at the doorway and then stepped in.

There were two beds in the room, both with guard rails.

Everything on the near side was heavy and dark—wooden dresser, velvet chair, pine-green duvet. The far side, near the window, was minimalist and neat, all the furnishings in black and white or light wood.

"I hate this shit," Althea said, flinging her arm as if throwing a frisbee. She had rolled up in front of the window, which faced a small courtyard, and was pulling a crumpled pack of cigarettes from under her mattress. "My son Luther bought it for me. He sold all my old furniture and our house when I went into the hospital last year."

"I'm sorry," Lanier said. "How long have you been here?"

"Three years," Althea answered. "Feels like thirty. Being around all these people make *anyone* feel old. And the staff!" She cranked the window open, lit her cigarette, puffed, and blew the smoke out through the crack. "They just as bad as the patients. Spend the day looking at the clock, you know, and thinking about their boyfriends." She paused and took a long drag of her cigarette. "They treat us like we're babies. You're not even supposed to smoke. I wouldn't be able to if my grandson Marcus didn't sneak me my cigarettes. But he just went to jail last week to start a six-month sentence, and this here's my final pack."

Jackie did not have a thing to say; she stood self-consciously beside Lanier, who had taken the only chair. On the other side of him, on the white dresser, stood several framed photographs; Althea saw him glancing at them and said, "Go ahead, take a look."

Jackie took this as an invitation for her to look as well. She and Lanier leaned over the dresser. One of pictures showed a much younger Althea in a plain white wedding dress, smiling widely next to her handsome and dazed-looking husband. Another one showed three young men, all sporting tight striped shirts and large afros; Althea informed them that they were her sons. Then there was a picture of an even younger Althea, with her arm thrown over the shoulder of a girl Jackie recognized as Alma. She looked the same as she had in the bowling-alley picture, but wider-eyed, more girl-like. Finally, there was a picture of Alma and her husband, sandwiching two young boys. Alma was much darker than

her slightly overweight husband, with the children ranging somewhere in between. Cory, who looked about five or six, was staring
off at something over the photographer's shoulder. Curtis, who
must have been fourteen or fifteen, stood proudly, hands behind
his back, looking straight into the camera and smiling. He was a
bit lighter-skinned than his brother, but still darker than Bruce—
dignified and handsome. And he was wiry and slight—like Alma,
but also, perhaps, like Frank. She tried to see signs of her grandfather in him—the set of his mouth looked familiar and there was
something around his eyes. But she couldn't tell for sure. All she
knew was that even at this age he was self-possessed and confident;
he looked more grown-up than he was. Then she thought, this is
the boy that Grandpa loved, whatever the connection. She glanced
at Lanier and saw that he was biting his lip. "That's my cousin,"
he said softly. "That's my man."

Althea had finished her cigarette now, and she cleared her
throat to get their attention. "Listen, why exactly you here?"

Lanier moved forward in his chair. "A couple of things. See,
the truth is, we're trying to build a case against the man who murdered Curtis and the other boys. But it's all gotten kind of personal,
and Curtis was like a brother to me, and, well, I just want to know
some more about him."

Althea turned her wheelchair toward the window and squinted;
Jackie couldn't tell if she was upset or just trying to see more clearly.
"There ain't a word bad enough to describe the man who did that
to them," she said, "and I hope you do catch him and punish him
good. But as for the rest of it, honey, I don't know. Don't know
what good it would do. It ain't gonna bring Curtis back."

"I know," replied Lanier. "But it would make me feel better.
He was born up here, right? How did Alma meet my uncle, anyway? And what was he like?"

Althea continued to look out the window. "Your uncle," she
began, "was a catch. Least he was back then, anyway. He was
strong and he was faithful and he had a good job. Didn't smoke or
drink at all—that started later."

Lanier nodded, encouraging her to go on.

"Alma came up to live with me at the end of the summer. She

was eighteen years old. Bruce was a man then, twenty-eight or twenty-nine, and he'd been living here in Oakland for a couple of years. Every day, on her lunch break, she'd go across the street to this diner, and Bruce would be there—he was having coffee before he started his shift at the Corson factory. They started sitting together, and pretty soon Alma was going there after work, too, to meet Bruce for his dinner break. They met and got married in just a couple of months. I was glad for her—she got real lucky."

"Why did Alma come to live with you?" asked Lanier.

Althea leaned forward, as if she spotted something moving outside. "She needed work. And a change of scenery. And the companies up here was hiring."

"Why did you come up here?" Jackie asked.

Now Althea leaned back again and laughed. "Our daddy always took the car to a gas station over on Imperial Highway. One day, he brought home this skinny man said his car engine blew up. He was a sailor just back from the war and he was on his way home to Oakland. Anyway, he asked did I want to come with him, so I did. Stayed with him for forty-four years, till he passed back in '88."

Jackie smiled at this story, but Lanier didn't seem to hear it. "Mrs. Dickson," he started gently, "was work the only reason that your sister left L.A.?"

She turned to look at him now, and her eyebrows were raised. "What you trying to ask, young man?"

He bent forward, hands spread against his knees. "I found a wedding announcement that said that Bruce and Alma got married on November 17, 1946. And Curtis was born in March of '47."

"So she was pregnant when she married him. So what?"

He looked away for a moment, and then back. "You said that Alma came up to live with you at the end of the summer. But if Curtis was born the next March, then she must have gotten pregnant in June or July."

Althea looked away and pulled another cigarette out of the pack. She lit it and kept her eyes on the burning tip.

"Do you have any idea," asked Lanier, "who the father was?"

She took a long, slow drag before she answered. "It don't

matter. Bruce raised him. And I don't think Curtis ever knew."

Lanier looked at Jackie, who was still standing by the bed. "Mrs. Dickson," he said gently, "it *does* matter. It matters to me, and it matters to Jackie here. Her grandfather was Frank Sakai."

At the mention of this name, Althea swung her head around.

"Listen," Lanier continued, "I'm sorry. I know this is a shock to you. But the more we look into this, the more we hear that Alma and Frank knew each other, and that they were . . . close." He paused, but Althea didn't say anything. "We're just not sure how *long* they knew each other, or if—"

"I know all about that," the old woman snapped. She puffed on her cigarette, not bothering, now, to blow the smoke out the window. Jackie and Lanier remained silent. When Althea spoke again, her voice sounded tired. "I knew Frank, you know. He was in my class at Dorsey. But I don't think he knew Alma then—she was still in junior high. He sure noticed her later, though—after the war." She paused and waved away the gathering smoke. "He was working at the store already, and I guess she would stop in there on her way home from work. I wasn't around for most of this 'cos I came up north with Raymond—but it didn't take long for our parents to figure out what was happening. They forbid her to see him, but that didn't work. I don't know how long they were together. But sometime in the summer of '46, my mother realized Alma was pregnant and she sent her up here to live with Raymond and me."

"Why didn't she stay in L.A.?" Jackie asked.

The old woman gave her a look that made her feel naïve. "A lot of reasons that I can think of."

Lanier nodded at Jackie. "And then she married Bruce, and Frank married your grandmother."

"But they knew each other after," Jackie said. "And Curtis started working in the store."

Althea nodded. "What happened between the two of them, I don't exactly know. Alma never talked to me about it. But I do know she didn't say anything to Bruce or Curtis. Curtis never knew Bruce wasn't his daddy, and Bruce never found out who the real daddy was. Resented it, though. And resented Curtis, too.

Thought he saw the father hiding behind every tree." She crushed out her cigarette. "I saw Frank again at Alma's funeral. He seemed real sad."

Jackie nodded—remembering, suddenly, Frank's unexplained trip to San Francisco, the postcard he had sent her. "I had no idea about any of this," she said. "I don't think anyone in my family did."

"That surprise you?"

Jackie realized, with a start, that the old woman didn't like her grandfather. What was she thinking? Why was she upset? Did she think that Frank took advantage of Alma? "Mrs. Dickson, I think my grandfather really loved your sister. I mean, you said yourself that he came up here for the funeral."

Althea swung around and looked at her. "Love ain't something you *feel*, young lady. Love is something you *do*. And what'd Frank Sakai ever do for my sister?"

"A lot," Jackie said.

"He did," Lanier concurred.

Althea raised her eyebrows. "Hmph."

Jackie and Lanier were silent as they drove back to San Francisco. Jackie had expected to feel exhilarated after talking to Althea; instead, she just felt sad. And so when they reached the hotel, she said she wanted to take a nap and retreated into her room. She had so many questions, so many things to mull over. Did Curtis ever know that Frank was his father? Did Jackie's grandmother have any idea? Had Frank and Alma continued their affair after she'd moved back to L.A.? And this she kept coming back to, over and over: What had it been like for Frank to watch another man raise his son? These were not the kind of issues she wanted to talk about with Lanier. So she said goodbye to him, showered, and then, still wrapped in her towel, lay flat on the bed and stared up at the ceiling.

Lanier, for his part, didn't want to be alone. He started walking—through the Mission, through the Castro, all the way up to Haight Street and over to Golden Gate Park. None of the people he saw left a mark on him, though; all he could think about was

Curtis. Curtis, his cousin, who was also not his cousin. Curtis, who was, however, Jackie Ishida's uncle. Curtis, his first and best example of what a man was supposed to be; his debt; his reason for doing all he did. Curtis, whose real father—unlike his own— was there right in front of him, but also just outside of his reach.

CHAPTER THIRTY-ONE

FRANK, 1985

H E HAD no right to grieve. She wasn't his wife, hadn't even been his lover since before all his children were born. But when he heard of her passing, it was like a piece of shrapnel pierced his heart. Then there was an emptying. He felt nothing, vacated, the insides of him absent. And the world around him lost all texture and meaning, so that the thunk of the phone shocked him when he dropped it on the counter; the people in the street, when he stumbled outside, opened their mouths and spoke words he couldn't hear.

It was Victor who had called and told him. Victor had been the one Alma wrote to when she finally left her husband, and she still sent him a Christmas card every year, which was how Frank had heard she'd moved back to Oakland. And Victor had found out about her death from her sister Althea, who'd called from Oakland and was arranging the funeral. Victor did not feel up to another funeral, and he hadn't left L.A. in twenty years, but he suspected enough about Alma and his friend to know that Frank might want to make the trip. Ovarian cancer, Althea had said. She hadn't even known until near the end that her sister was sick.

Victor's call had come at eleven a.m., while Mary was out at the store. When she got back an hour later, she called out that she was home. No answer. She didn't worry, because Frank often took walks on Saturday mornings or went to visit with a neighbor, although he usually told her first or left a note. After putting away the groceries, she began to prepare lunch. They always had Japanese food on Saturday, and today's fare was simple—broiled salmon, steamed rice, *tsukemono*. She had just turned the rice down to a simmer when she heard her husband come into the house and then enter the kitchen. She greeted him and he said hello. He seemed in a dark mood, but Mary didn't worry—he would tell her what was wrong when he was ready. As he sat at the table, she turned her back to him, cutting open the sealed package of *takuan*. She told him of the new saleslady at the Japanese market, a serious young girl who reminded her of their Rose. Slowly, carefully, she squeezed out a few inches of the pickled yellow *takuan*. She laid it out on the cutting board, positioned her knife a centimeter from the end, and pressed down.

"I have to go out of town," said Frank, suddenly, and his voice sounded strangely heavy.

Mary paused, then repositioned her knife and cut another piece. "Oh?"

"A funeral," Frank said. "Up in Oakland."

Her shoulders tightened and lifted, but he couldn't tell if it was from nervousness, anger, or working the knife. She cut another piece. "Did she die?"

Frank started, but then discovered he wasn't really surprised. It would be disrespectful, to both women, to give a long explanation. Things had been so much easier with Mary since Alma moved away; their marriage regained the calm, affectionate equilibrium it had had in the first few years. He knew how disappointing their life together had been, how he had lived elsewhere from her the years he was running the store. When Curtis was in the neighborhood, and Alma too, Frank had felt too guilty about what he wasn't giving his wife to do anything but avoid her—after their first few years in the Mesa, she'd become as invisible to him as she had ever been in Little Tokyo. But after the store, the move to Gardena, he came back to her again, trying to fulfill the promise he'd made to her all those years ago, when he'd taken her out of her parents' restaurant. The two of them would sit out on the porch drinking iced tea together, talking, or reading in easy silence. And he hated to disturb that calmness now, but he had to, there wasn't a choice. "Yes," he said. "I'll be back in a couple of days."

Now, at the church, wearing his one gray suit, Frank wondered why he had come. He'd flown in the night before, the first plane he'd taken in forty years, and he still felt as he had in the air—the sense of weightlessness, the total disconnection. He sat alone in a pew near the back of the church, recognizing no one but Althea. The casket, a simple cream-colored design, was closed, which Frank was thankful for. He didn't want to see Alma less than totally alive. The other mourners, well-dressed people of different ages and colors, were friends and admirers and coworkers from Alma's life outside of him. *They* all had more right to grieve, he thought, than he did. But he loved her, he'd loved her almost all of his life, and the terrible thing about failing someone is that you keep on failing them, no matter how you try to make up for it. They should have been together—he, Alma, and Curtis. And it hurt when she left the first time, came up here to Oakland without telling him. And it hurt every time he saw her through the years, when she came by to pick up Curtis from the store. And it hurt when she moved up here again, after she left Bruce, because he knew it was for good this time. But despite how he felt, he stayed, he took it, choosing not to run as he had all those years ago by rushing to enlist after his father and sister died. Because the world was always a full and sweet place while he knew that Alma was in it, and her absence now was bigger than all the people in his life put together. He ached for her the way his finger ached for its tip, the way his foot ached for its toes, feeling them there, knowing they would never come back. The way he'd felt, in his heart, only one other time, when in the space of a year he lost his mother and his son.

His son. How happy he'd been when Alma brought him back to L.A. He'd heard, through the grapevine, why she left, but he had no idea where she had gone. And the pain of seeing her with another man now, or with her friends at the Holiday Bowl, was bearable only because of Curtis. The boy had wandered into the store on his own—although Frank had run into him with his mother a few times on the street—and Frank had sent him home with a coloring book and a brand-new box of crayons. The letter Curtis sent back let him know that Alma was thankful, but cautious; he kept it in his office until the day he shut down. She kept her distance, going out of her way to acknowledge his family; to comment on the beauty of his daughters. But she got easier, gradually, seeing how the boy and the man took to each other, and asking Frank, finally—although she didn't have to; he'd have done it regardless—to hire him to work in the store. And as Curtis got older, was finishing high school; as Frank started picturing him sitting in the office, the owner, Frank wanted Alma to tell their son the truth. It was the second disagreement they'd ever had. And then he was dead, and it was too late, and Frank couldn't stand to be in the store. And the money he got for selling it he didn't know what to do with. He tried to give it to Alma, who refused it; she only accepted half the cost of the funeral. But it belonged to them, to Curtis and Alma, and if *they* couldn't take it or didn't want to have it, he couldn't give it to anyone else, or deposit it, so he simply put it away. In the back of the closet where he kept all his pain. Boxed-up and hidden from sight.

After the words of the service he did not hear, the mourners rose, touched each other, spoke in hushed whispers, and slowly began to leave. Frank drove over to San Francisco, where he went to a bar in Pacific Heights and drank until it closed. He was absent of thought again, trying to fill the emptiness with whiskey and beer. It had been years since he'd drunk like this, probably since the war, and he was surprised by how well his stubborn body resisted the poison he fed it. But finally the alcohol engulfed him and the bar, the whole world, tipped and spun. He paid for his last whiskey and wandered outside. The cool air immediately took four drinks off his night, and his vision was clear enough to read the street signs. He walked. He walked several miles, stopping twice to vomit, until he found himself at the Golden Gate Bridge. It was late enough now that there was only a scattering of cars and pedestrians. He walked out onto the bridge, his jacket flapping in the strong ocean wind. His hair flew into his face but he didn't bother to brush it away; he just kept going, mostly by feel, the railing checking his stumbling body. Halfway out, he stopped and faced the bay. The painted red metal was cold beneath his hands and he leaned into it, the hard curve against his stomach. He heard the ocean and peered down at it; the water looked dark and welcoming. With the wind still whipping his jacket and hair, he screamed and screamed and screamed. The wind ripped the sounds away from him, but he felt the violence in his throat. Sobbing, he threw one leg over the railing and tried to hoist himself up. But then, through his hair and tear-blurred eyes, he caught sight of the city. The lights were spread out before him like diamonds in velvet. In one of those buildings lay the body of the woman he loved better than anything in this world or the next one. But in other lighted rooms, in another city, were his wife, his daughters, his grandchild. If he got up on that railing and offered himself to the air, they would be without a husband, a father, a grandfather. Awkwardly, half regretfully, he brought his leg back down. One family was enough to betray.

CHAPTER THIRTY-TWO

1965, 1994

1965

The air outside was heavy and Louisiana-thick. All week, the whole city was confused. People who hadn't seen the South in thirty years woke up expecting to hear the sound of tractors and cotton gins; of cows mooing and roosters proudly announcing the day. But instead they heard sirens and car engines and far-off factory whistles, and when they opened their eyes, they were in L.A. The heat of California was usually dry, unoppressive. Not like this. This kind set you sweating and wore you out, made you feel like you'd worked a full day by nine in the morning. This kind made you feel like you were swimming. People didn't want to move—it was too hot to work, to eat, to fuck. And when skin *did* come together, you could be sure it was nothing good—a mother losing patience with her crying little boy, a husband enraged by what his wife served for dinner, a group of teenagers itching for something to smash. Everyone was laid low by the heat, but struggling against it. There was a watchful suspense in the air. And the Southerners knew the only thing that could break the grip of the heat was an old-fashioned, earth-shaking storm.

This particular storm had been a long time coming. Anyone who kept an eye on the horizon, a nose lifted to the wind, had known it was on its way. They'd known their whole lives, maybe, and their parents had known for *their* whole lives, too. All it took, finally, was the proper combination of elements, the crashing together of gas and cloud. A young black driver pulled over by a motorcycle cop, some words, a misunderstanding. A gathering crowd, including a pregnant woman who witnesses later said was slapped by a policeman. More people, drawn by the noise, the crowd, the steadily rising voices. No one knew who threw the first rock.

All through the night, the storm was building, gathering force and dimension. A few bursts of fire split the sky like heat lightning. The storm, inflamed by history, swept down in curtains, sheets, and shrouds, all twisting together, forming rivers and collecting in pools. Those who were not part of the storm were locked away safely inside. By morning, all was clear again, although a black sooty cloud still lingered over Watts—darker than the usual imagined one, which hung there all the time. But nightfall brought the storm again, larger and more powerful, the odd and all-consuming partnership of water and fire. Hundreds, thousands of people now, their anger and energy stoking the fires that stoked the ever-increasing heat. More stores and factories hit by lightning, brightening with flame. Someone picked up the phrase that Magnificent Montague was always saying on the KGFJ morning show—*burn, baby, burn*. And the words traveled from mouth to mouth, like fire passed on through the touched tips of torches. Soon, that phrase was one of the sounds of the storm, along with the whoops, the smashing glass, the greedy feasts of fires, the shots that ripped through the rest of the noise like thunder. A deluge—torrential and blinding. Those who got stuck in the storm—outsiders and even some long-time residents who should have known better—did not make it home unscathed. They got dragged from cars and beaten, but not a single outsider died. That fate was reserved for the people who lived there—engulfed in the storm they helped along or tried to contain, or caught by the armed outsiders who tried to quell the storm by force. By late Thursday night, Watts was glutted; by Friday it started to flood. And all the powerful, churning water that had gathered there spilled over the banks, streaming into other parts of the city.

The flood reached Crenshaw on Saturday. Just a few yards away, on the boulevard, the rivulets were sweeping past them; Curtis saw groups of boys and men running up the street. They whooped and yelled—out of exhilaration, out of a mad destructive frenzy, out of the pure undiluted relief of smashing back at the land that had beaten them down for four savage unspeakable centuries. Curtis stood in front of the store, along with David, David's little brother Tony, and Tony's best friend, Gerald; Derek, who'd been there earlier, had left. With them too was Akira, who was home for the summer. The door behind them was closed and bolted; Mr. Sakai had locked it up before sending everyone home. But there they stood, Sakai himself already long gone, shut at home with his family like almost everyone else, except for those who stepped out to join the flood or those who were finally drowned in it. Curtis and the other boys watched, mostly silent, occasionally muttering a sound in concern or disbelief. Most of the men who ran by were empty-handed, but some bore bats or bricks; a couple of them were waving guns, as casually as napkins. And the return foot traffic, going the opposite way—people running by with televisions, shoeboxes, diapers, and bread. Curtis saw no cars—after the first couple of days of this conflagration, people knew better than to try and drive. The body of the city itself was at a virtual standstill—but within it, the cells rampaged freely, cancerous with life. Curtis heard the smashing glass, smelled the smoke blown north from Watts. He heard, too, the occasional crack of a gunshot, and far away, the sirens. For the first time, he was glad the store wasn't on Crenshaw—they lost the incidental traffic they might have gotten on the boulevard, but this different traffic now passed them by. Still, he intended to stand there until the flood had spent itself, washed through. He told David that maybe the younger boys should go on home, but that entailed crossing Crenshaw, so they stayed. Occasionally he looked over at Kenji Hirano, who was standing on his steps, preaching, voice deep and firm and certain. He was about to tell Kenji that it wouldn't do any good, but then the gardener went into his house. They kept watching the scene on Crenshaw and they were all facing right, so they didn't see the squad car that approached from the left until it had pulled up beside them.

"Gonna go join the party?" asked the voice that was instantly familiar to Curtis. He looked and saw the cop who'd beaten him, his harsh eyebrows, his metallic yellow hair. Curtis still bore a scar on his cheek where the cop had opened his face two years before; unconsciously, he reached up to touch it.

The cop continued, arm slung casually out the window. "Or you going to just knock out this store right here? Looks like no one's looted it yet. You boys have got first dibs."

Akira stepped forward and said, with a gall that Curtis found both admirable and reckless, "Why don't you keep driving, asshole? They need you up on Crenshaw."

The cop's partner, who'd been silent so far, let out a quiet laugh. A larger man than his partner, his edges more blurred, he usually stood back and watched Lawson's antics. He enjoyed the citizens' comebacks as much as his partner's acts themselves; saw them all as part of the same larger comedy. But Lawson's face colored, and now he shot an angry look at his partner. "Oh, you think it's funny now, do you?"

Curtis watched the men fearfully, hoping that Lawson's venom toward his partner would distract him from the boys. But now he turned toward them, got out of the car. "I appreciate your advice," he said, looking at Akira, "but I think I'm needed *here*. To get some punks off the street so they don't hurt anyone."

Curtis felt, in his chest, a spasm of fear. The boys moved closer together. The cop passed all of them once, like an officer inspecting his troops. Then he said, "Now get on into the store."

Curtis didn't know what the cop had in mind—probably another beating—but he knew instinctively that they must stay outside. The other boys seemed to know this, too. On the street, behind Lawson, the Irish cop drove by, and they all appealed silently for him to stop. He didn't, and Curtis's heart sank. "We ain't got no key," David lied.

The cop turned and walked past them again. "Maybe *you* don't," he said, not looking at David. Then he took his gun out of its holster, cocked it, and aimed it at Curtis's head. "But *you* do." The silence in Curtis's chest was so long and complete that he knew his heart had stopped. He felt the cool mouth of the gun pressed lightly against his temple; it was almost a relief against the melting heat. And then he felt his heart resume, thunderous and loud, beating so violently he didn't know how his chest could contain it. "No, no I don't," he stammered.

"Yes, you do," said Lawson, leisurely, in command of himself again. He stood at arm's length from Curtis, in a relaxed, easy posture, as if he were caressing the boy's head with a feather. "I *know* you do. You work for the Jap and he trusts you with everything. In fact, I've seen you close the place up."

Curtis was afraid to look away from the cop, afraid to look at his friends, but he felt their eyes on him, their paralysis and shock.

"Open it up," the cop commanded, and Curtis reached into his pocket and pulled out the jangling keys. Fumbling now, feeling the snout of the gun hover near him although it no longer touched, he moved unsteadily toward the door. He thought of telling the others to make a run for it, but he knew it was useless. The best thing to do was go along with the cop and get inside. And there, in his territory, amidst the aisles and objects he knew so well, maybe the boys could summon up some kind of defense. He unlocked the door, pushed it open, and stepped inside. The cop stood under the awning now, like some kind of demented doorman, and waving the gun, he ushered the other boys in. He ordered them to stay in view, and then called, without turning, for his partner to join him. Both cops moved inside quickly, the partner sighing as if bored with the game. "Lock the door," instructed Lawson, and his partner obeyed. Lawson swept his gun back and forth, looking pleased with himself. The boys huddled together like sheep.

"I don't see why you boys have to act like this," said Lawson. "Burning things. Stealing things. You think it's going to make people like you better?"

Curtis shivered and didn't say the obvious—that the boys in the store had done no such thing; that they were, in fact, protecting the store.

"Shit, over on Central, we had cops backing up the firemen trying to put out a fire, because a bunch of stupid niggers—oh, excuse me, '*brothers*'—were shooting at them. And the firemen were trying to help them, trying to put out a fire in their neighborhood. In their *own neighborhood. Imagine.*"

Lawson was enjoying himself. While his colleagues' reactions to the riots had ranged from the disgust of his commanding officer to the complacency of his partner, Lawson's own feeling about the unrest was a kind of glee. The blacks were finally doing it, acting like the senseless animals he had always known they were. He could say anything to them, do anything, and there was no one around to stop him. Now he lowered his gun and approached the boys, looking David up and down. "What exactly were you doing outside, anyway? Figuring out which place you were going to break into first?"

David's eyes were open wide, his lips quavering. "Naw, man!" he insisted. "We was trying to keep *this* place safe."

"Shut up," the cop said, and at the same time, he brought his knee up hard into David's groin. David doubled over, grabbing himself, making high gasping sounds. "Come on, what were you planning to do?" asked Lawson, moving down the line. "What were you boys going to steal? Maybe you started *out* protecting this place, but you would've joined in eventually. You can't help it, *man*," he mocked. "It's in your blood."

"Just like beating the shit out of people is in *your* blood?" This was Akira, and Lawson turned toward him.

"You better be careful. None of your Yellow Brothers are around to protect you now. What the hell's wrong with you, boy?"

"What's wrong with *you*?" Akira shot back, stepping toward him. "Why don't you just shoot us, man? That's what you want, isn't it? That's all you seem to know how to do."

Lawson swung out with his gun and struck Akira on the side of the head. Akira jerked back at the impact and then put his hands to his face; between his fingers, blood trickled out. Curtis gulped and tried to stop shaking, but he was nervous and bumped into the cereal boxes, which fell onto the floor. He had an arm around Gerald, David's brother's friend, and the boy was stiff with fear. Lawson came and stood in front of them. His eyes slid down Curtis's face, settling on the scar on his cheek, and Curtis wondered if he remembered putting it there. Lawson looked him in the eye now and lifted his hand, fist clenched, callused fingers blunt and solid. Curtis held his breath and put his arms up as he waited for the punch.

* * *

1994

Lanier walked for several hours, and by the time he got back to the motel, he'd made a decision. He banged on Jackie's door. It was 5:15.

"Hi," she said when she opened the door. She was in sweats and a T-shirt, and her hair was wet.

"Hi. Listen, I think we should go talk to Paxton."

"You don't want to wait till tomorrow?"

"No," he said. "Do you?"

She brushed her hair back off her face with a long sweep of her arm—a tired, unself-conscious motion that made Lanier realize how self-aware she usually was. "Actually, no. Let's go."

Oliver Paxton lived in East Palo Alto, about an hour south of San Francisco. Once they left the freeway, they had no trouble finding the house. Jackie was surprised—although she'd heard that this city was rough and run-down, Paxton's block was full of neat one-story houses with well-trimmed lawns. Lanier parked at the curb and the two of them looked up at the house. "This is our case," he said. "Right here."

As they walked up the driveway, mounted the stairs, and rung the lit-up doorbell, Jackie half-hoped that Paxton wouldn't be home. It was as if by leaving the end of the story blank, by never hearing how Curtis and the others were murdered, the boy she'd come to know in the last few months—her uncle—would still be alive, would never have died at all. But just a few seconds after the chime died down, someone approached and then opened the door.

Lanier could not believe the man in front of him. Oliver Paxton looked just as he had in the picture in Thomas's office— tall, fair-skinned, solid. He'd put on a few pounds since his police days, and his hair was mostly gray, but otherwise, the two images were almost identical. There were laugh lines all around Paxton's eyes and mouth. "What can I do for you?" he asked.

Lanier cleared his throat. "Officer Paxton?"

The man raised his eyebrows. "No one's called me 'officer' in almost thirty years. What can I do for you, son?"

Lanier held out his hand. "Mr. Paxton—I'm sorry—my name is James Lanier. This is Jackie Ishida. We just drove up from L.A. yesterday, and we were wondering if you could talk to us about something that happened while you worked for the LAPD."

Paxton shook his hand, and then shook hands with Jackie, finally looking back at Lanier. "That was a long time ago. I don't remember much. I was a teacher from '67 until I retired last year."

"Yes, I know," said Lanier. "You see, we're trying to find out about something that happened during the '65 uprising, when four boys were locked into a freezer."

"Are you on the job? Internal Affairs?"

"No, sir. We're family. Jackie's grandfather, Frank Sakai, was the man who owned the store and found the bodies. And one of the boys who was killed was my cousin Curtis." He felt more confident now, and pushed ahead. "We have a couple of witnesses who saw Nick Lawson take the boys into the store. But none of the cops we've talked to seem to want to give him up. I spoke with Robert Thomas and he didn't have much to say. Anyway, I saw a picture of you in his office."

Just then, they heard a voice in the background. "Who is it, Ollie?" A middle-aged woman in a neat cardigan appeared at Paxton's side. She smiled at them, but, reading her husband, seemed cautious.

Paxton, Jackie thought, was looking disturbed. His lips were pressed together and he furrowed his brow. To his wife he said, "These people are here to ask about the boys in the freezer." And her face fell, and she put a hand on his arm protectively. To Jackie and Lanier he said, "You better come inside."

He moved out of the way, and Lanier glanced at Jackie before stepping through the door. *We've got him*, his eyes seemed to say. Inside, Paxton directed them to a couch. Jackie noticed small, random things—a *Sports Illustrated* on a table, a plaque that said "District Teacher of the Year," a recent portrait of Paxton, his wife, and two grown women who Jackie assumed were their daughters. Paxton sat in an armchair, almost knee-to-knee with Lanier. His wife pulled a chair up beside him. "Tell me what you're trying to do here," he said.

Lanier leaned forward. And watching this man with his wife, seeing them here in this peaceful house, he was almost sorry to have to disturb them. He couldn't quite imagine Paxton working with Thomas—he already rather liked this man. "We're trying to build a case against Lawson," he explained. "We're trying to line up witnesses so we can present the whole thing to the D.A.'s office." He paused. "We were hoping that you could help us out, Mr. Paxton. Someone told us you drove by the store that day. Did you happen to see anything?"

Paxton looked down and was silent for so long that Lanier and Jackie started to fidget. Mrs. Paxton took her husband's hand and they looked at each other. "I saw something, all right," he said finally. "But I don't think it's what you want to hear."

Lanier and Jackie looked at him. "What do you mean?" Lanier asked.

"Nick Lawson was a racist and a violent man, no doubt about it. But he didn't kill those boys in the store."

Lanier stood up and then sat down again. "But people *saw* him. We have *two witnesses* who saw him go in."

"Oh, he went in, all right. But he came out again. And he got shot that very day, if I remember correctly." He paused. "No, it wasn't Lawson who did it."

"Well then, who?" Lanier demanded, almost shouting at him.

"I'm going to tell you, son. Just listen." Paxton put his head in his hands for a moment, and when he took them away, he looked not at Lanier and Jackie, but at the table. And the whole time he was talking, for the next twenty minutes, his wife kept her hand on his shoulder.

* * *

1965

Curtis held his breath and put his arms up as he waited for the punch. But then, so loud and sudden that both boys and cops jumped, someone banged hard on the back door. Curtis exhaled as Lawson whirled toward it.

"Who is it?" he called out.

"Nick? You OK?" the muffled voice inquired.

Lawson seemed to recognize it. He nodded toward the door, and his partner ambled down the aisle and into the back, unlocked the door and opened it. Two cops, both Negroes, stepped inside, one not much older than the boys.

"We were driving up the alley," the older one said, "and we saw your car parked out front. We just wanted to make sure you were OK."

"We're fine," Lawson replied.

Curtis started shaking again. What flicker of relief he'd felt had now vanished—the Negro cops, or at least the older one, were hardly any better than Lawson. Since their first encounter at the junior high school, Curtis had feared this cop, especially since he'd started watching him from the window of his squad car, parked out in front of the store. But now he thought maybe he hadn't feared the cop nearly enough. On this day, in this madness, there was no telling what he'd do. The cop said to Lawson, "What kind of problem you got here?"

"Oh, these boys just need a talking to."

Thomas saw one boy doubled over and another holding his bleeding face. He laughed. "Looks like you been talking pretty good."

Lawson smiled a mean smile. "Yeah, well I know how it is with your people, *man*. Only one kind of talking gets through."

"We are *not* his people," Curtis said without thinking.

"Hell," said Akira, "he ain't even a man."

At that moment, they heard the crackle of a walkie-talkie. All four cops looked down at their belts. Westphal, Lawson's partner, took his walkie-talkie out, deciphered the distant fuzzy voice, and looked at Lawson. "They need us over on Crenshaw."

"All right," Lawson said. Then he turned to the boys. "Sorry to cut this date short. I guess I'll have to take a rain check." And he and his partner went out the back door and were gone.

The boys were left with the two black cops, and Thomas fixed them with a look of seething hatred. He walked toward them now, his partner a little behind, continued past them and over to the door. Thomas re-shut it and tested the lock. His back was turned.

And at the precise moment that Curtis was noting the huge sweat marks around the policeman's armpits, Akira tapped him and nodded toward the back of the store. Curtis shook his head no—the younger boys would never make it—and he watched his friend take off. Akira was lightning quick and silent, and by the time the cops turned, he was almost at the door already. Thomas whipped his gun out, but Akira was gone. Paxton moved to follow him, but Thomas grabbed his arm and held him back. "Let him go," he said.

He faced the boys, as Lawson had done—officer-like, as though they'd just been handed over to his command. He tried to swallow his humiliation at being insulted by Lawson. He tried to swallow his humiliation at being mocked by these punks. Everyone, everywhere, had it in for him. And he was going to take the respect that was his due. "Now what were you boys doing that got Nick so mad?"

"Nothing!" insisted Tony.

Thomas looked at him and laughed. "Nothing? Nothing? You must have done *something*. Unless you were the only niggers on the street—the *only* ones—who weren't getting themselves in trouble."

"He's telling the truth," Curtis said.

Thomas considered him now and cocked his head. "Oh, really? Just like *you* were telling the truth, boy, when you said you didn't break into Audubon?"

Curtis looked down at his feet, remembering the stuffy office where Thomas and his old partner had grilled him; the satisfaction on the policeman's face when he admitted to the break-in; the icy stare and hard-set jaw when Alma drove him away from the school.

"What I don't understand," the cop continued, "is why you have to do this. Some little punk told me yesterday that this was a rebellion, but what all are you rebelling against? People can do whatever they want now—anyone, even Negroes. I mean, look at Ollie and me."

Yeah, Curtis thought. Just look at you.

"And all you hoodlums on the street, you're destroying your own neighborhood. I don't see *white* people out there on

Crenshaw or Central. It's you." He glared at them. He was not one of them, never had been, no matter what they or Lawson believed. He thought of his father, how much smarter and more refined he was than the ignorant blacks they'd had to live among. And now these punks in front of him, who were just as useless as the ones he'd grown up with. "It's niggers like you who give the rest of us a real bad name. White people don't treat you the way you like? Well, it's because you do *this* kind of shit."

He waved his arms expansively, and Curtis suddenly felt very calm. "We were *protecting* the store," he said, looking Thomas in the eye. "You *know* that."

It was more than Thomas could bear. This fool talking to him as if he, Curtis, were an equal. When it was fools like him that made his job so hard, made men like Lawson not see him as a peer. This riot the worst thing he'd ever experienced, and beneath his anger at the punks who were tearing up the city was a deep and gnawing shame. Shame that he was the color of the arsonists and looters. Shame that other people's worst beliefs had been confirmed. "Protecting *this*?" he said weakly. "Why would you want to protect this?" And he raised his arms, both taking in the store and dismissing it, and Curtis saw the sweat marks again. His own T-shirt was soaked clean through, and he felt perspiration trickle down his legs. It was hot enough on the street, but even worse inside, the closed doors and windows making the old store feel like some medium circle of hell. He wiped his brow with the back of his arm, a gesture which Thomas caught.

"You hot, boy?"

Curtis shrugged.

"Yeah, it's hot. Well, I'm sorry you're so uncomfortable. But I got just the thing to cool you off." He pulled his gun out quickly, and Curtis squeezed his eyes shut, waiting for the impact of the bullet. But when he opened them, the cop was gesturing toward the back. "Go on," he said. "Go back there."

The boys obeyed, wondering what he was up to, and the partner followed in silence. At the back of the store they halted, and Thomas moved past them. He went to the freezer door, and as his fingers touched the handle, Curtis felt a twist of nausea.

The cop opened the door and nodded. "Get in."

Curtis and David looked at each other, tightening their hold on the boys. None of them moved. Even Paxton looked at Thomas like he was crazy, but the older man would not be made a fool of. Thomas said again, louder, "Get in!"

They still didn't move, so Thomas raised his gun and cocked it. "Don't fuck with me now," he said calmly. "I don't have the patience today. Get in."

They remained where they were, until the cop fired a warning shot that made them yell and duck. The bullet smashed through the window, and they heard the tinkle of falling glass. "Jesus, Bob," the young partner said, but Thomas ignored him. He stuck the barrel of the gun between Tony's eyes, and at that, the older boys finally obeyed and moved into the freezer. As soon as they'd all crossed the threshold, the door shut with a sucking sound.

It was pitch black, and cold. Curtis swung his hand around blindly until he found the string that was connected to the light bulb. He yanked it down and all of them blinked in the sudden light. "Let's wait till they leave," Curtis said. "Then we'll get out."

Around them hung slabs of frozen meat, like huge bizarre stalactites. On the floor were bags and blocks of ice. In one corner, stacked cartons of ice cream. At first the cold felt good against their overheated skin, but then the sheen of sweat turned chilly and the soaked shirts began to feel like veils of ice. They all started to shiver. They waited ten, twelve, fifteen minutes. Then Curtis placed his hands against the door and pushed. Nothing happened. He thought he hadn't tried hard enough, so he put his shoulder to the door and pushed again, harder. Still nothing. He looked at David, trying not to be alarmed, and the other boy came up next to him. The two of them pushed the door together. Nothing.

"What's wrong?" Tony asked.

"I don't know," Curtis said. "Maybe the suction or something. But this should open. There's nothing holding it shut."

David looked around and found a crow bar that someone had left in the freezer. He tried to pry the door open, to no avail. Curtis watched this, not believing that the door would not open. The younger boys hugged themselves and shivered harder. "I'm cold," they complained, and Curtis felt his eyes water. He and David tried to open the door—with hands, shoulders, backs, feet—rested, and tried again. They stemmed their own rising panic by comforting Tony and Gerald.

"Mr. Sakai will come in and find us," Curtis assured them. "I'm sure he won't stay away very long."

Gerald was the first to sit, against a wall that, for some reason, wasn't quite as cold as the others. Soon, Tony sat beside him. The older boys decided to wait, conserve their energy, and try to keep warm, so they flanked the younger boys, David next to his brother and Curtis next to Gerald. Curtis put his arms around Gerald, feeling Tony's shoulders against the back of his hands. David did the same with Tony. At first they felt a bit warmer, but after a few minutes, there seemed to be no heat rising off the younger boys' skin, and they were almost as cold to the touch as the slabs of meat. Curtis wondered about his mother, if she'd come looking for him. He prayed, they all prayed, and Tony began to cry. Periodically Curtis or David would try the door, but none of them expected it to open anymore. They had no idea of how much time had passed. But eventually, Curtis stopped worrying and began to relax. Mr. Sakai would be there soon. The younger boys were quiet now, and Curtis felt, to his surprise, a gradual sensation of warmth, starting with his feet and his hands, and spreading slowly through the rest of his body. He didn't feel cold at all anymore. It was going to be all right. He thought of Angela, and Cory, and his little cousin Jimmy—how happy he'd be to see them; how he'd describe and embellish this adventure. He was sleepy, his eyelids heavy, and he finally let them close. Feeling safe now, he floated off to sleep.

* * *

1994

When Paxton had finished, the room was silent. Jackie couldn't bring herself to look at Lanier. And Lanier, for his part, could not move or speak. Then Paxton started talking again. "It was only my second year out of the Academy, and I was scared to death of Bob. He was so angry all the time, he took everything so personally, and no one saw it except for me and the people he beat. There were some complaints against him, but, well, that only made our bosses like him better." He picked a glass up and set it down again. "I didn't stop him. I thought he was just scaring them, pulling a stupid stunt. And when I found out they were dead, I couldn't do anything. Bob never mentioned it again—it was like it never happened. I should have reported it, I know, but I just couldn't. I was scared of him, and I didn't want to rat on him, and I was just a damned coward. The only thing I could do was leave the job, and that's exactly what I did."

"And escaped to the north," said Jackie.

"And escaped to the north."

Lanier, throughout this, had not said a word, and when Jackie glanced over at him, he looked like he was going to be sick. Now, he stood abruptly, and said, "Thank you, Officer Paxton." Then he headed toward the door without looking back.

Jackie thanked Paxton, who didn't seem to notice they were leaving, and followed Lanier out to the car. For the entire drive back up to San Francisco, neither of them said anything. Jackie stared at the lights and felt as if her heart had been removed. Lanier didn't know whether to cry or scream or drive his car into the bay. All those years he thought he knew who'd been responsible for killing his cousin. And while he'd realized that something was wrong about Thomas, he couldn't fathom that this man—that any black man—would commit such an act against children. He felt his knowledge of the world had been wrong and naïve; he felt impotent, enraged, and betrayed. The murders were even worse, somehow, because Thomas had committed them. It was as if Curtis had died all over again. He parked the car in the motel lot and they both stared straight ahead. Then, finally, his voice:

"I can't believe this shit. I can't . . ."

And he felt the world heave up from under him and toss him like a toy, and he put his head in his arms to try and stop the motion. The sobs came then—jagged, uncontrollable. Twenty-nine years worth of grief. Jackie sat beside him, not sure of what to do. But then she reached across the seat and touched Lanier's neck. He had his hands over his face, and she watched the huge shoulders heave and shake. She reached across with both hands now, unbuckling her seatbelt, then his, and pulled him gently toward her. She brought his head to her chest and stroked it, touching the shockingly warm skin of his cheek, his thick, curled hair. She felt his breath against her skin and the heavy strength of him; he smelled of aftershave and something deeply male. He cried for what seemed like forever and they clung to each other, spinning, holding on as if for their lives. Finally, his sobs died down and he pressed his cheek against her. She felt his soft lips on her collarbone, on her shoulders, on her neck, and then his face was right in front of hers, his great head between her hands. They kissed, softly at first and then harder, hands grasping and caressing, trying desperately to leave themselves behind. She felt the hard, shifting muscles of his shoulders and back. She touched the rough scar on his face, and he felt her body rise against him. But then they opened their eyes and looked at each other.

"I'm sorry," Lanier said, voice raw with emotion. He pulled away, back into his seat. "I'm sorry."

"Don't be sorry."

Something was wrong here, they both knew it, but it wasn't simply that Lanier was a man; that Jackie desired women. She knew that she'd never be in this situation, feel so open and connected, with any man but Lanier, but it was also the fact that it *was* Lanier that kept it from going further. And he knew he *didn't* want this as much as he did. Not because of the limits and idiosyncrasies of desire, but because, they both realized, with a clarity that shocked them, they were, at least in some sense, family.

"Listen," he said. "I lost control of myself. I'm just upset, and I—"

"Stop," Jackie cut him off. "I was here, too."

They sat there for a moment, silently noting the steamed-up windows, and then they got out of the car and walked to their rooms. At their separate doorways, awkwardly, they said goodnight. Jackie sat down on her bed and stared at the wall, too tired to miss the dinner she now remembered she hadn't eaten, too spent even to turn on the television. She felt the injustice of not desiring the person she connected with, and loved. Then there was a knock on the door. When she opened it, Lanier was standing there, looking as miserable as she.

"I won't touch you," he said.

"I know."

He stepped inside, she shut the door behind him, and they lay down on the bed. She pulled the covers up and put her arms around him, and they drifted off to sleep.

CHAPTER THIRTY-THREE

1965

WHAT HAUNTED Jimmy the most later was not his cousin's death itself, but what happened a few hours before it. It was early on Saturday morning, the fourth day of the uprising, and the action was still a few miles away—although they could see dark smoke in the sky to the southeast and faintly hear the relentless sirens. Jimmy was over at the Martindales' house, playing with Curtis and Cory. The springer spaniel from next door was outside with them and the boys took turns throwing a baseball, for the pleasure of watching the young dog fly, her ears riding the air like wings. But Curtis's demeanor was serious, without its usual ease or delight. He knew that while the fires were mostly in Watts, people had started to loot all over; he knew their neighborhood might be swept along with the tide. For the younger boys, though, the air of disorder, the smashing down of rules, was more thrilling than genuinely frightening. Curtis stayed very alert, lifting his nose every few minutes to read what he could from the winds. He tried to take the ball from the dog's mouth, but she shook her head no and growled playfully. He finally managed to get it back from her and then launched it down the street, and Jimmy was amazed, as always, at the power in his cousin's thin body. The younger boys' throws were shorter, but the dog didn't care; she kept barking at them and jumping up, oblivious to the watchful atmosphere.

It was a little before ten when Curtis handed the baseball over to his brother. "I'm going to the store now," he said. "I'll catch up with you all tonight."

Jimmy, who was sorry to see him go, ran to keep up with him as he headed down the street. Behind them, Cory continued to play with the dog. "Tonight?" Jimmy said. "That's a long way away. We'll just come down to the store after lunch."

Curtis kept walking, not looking at him. "I don't want to see you in there today. Go on home now. And stay off the street."

Jimmy moved faster, three strides to each one of his cousin's. He felt panic rise and spread in his chest. "You don't want to see us? Why you don't want to see us?"

"I do," Curtis replied. "Just at your house, or my house. I don't know what's going to happen today, so you all should just go home and sit tight."

Jimmy didn't hear the sense in this, only the rejection, and now he burst into hot, bitter tears. "I'll do whatever I *want* to. You big scared pussy."

Curtis turned to him, and although his voice was stern, his face looked more tired than angry. "Don't you talk to me like that, Jimmy. 'Else I'm not gonna come see you at all."

"I can talk like I *want* to. *You* ain't my daddy. And I don't wanna see you, anyway." He stopped and crossed his arms.

"All right, then. Suit yourself." Curtis resumed walking, ignoring him, and Jimmy couldn't stand the sight of his older cousin's narrow back moving away, or the voice of his younger cousin, which was calling from behind, telling him not to be such a baby.

"You big pussy!" Jimmy yelled again. "I hate you!"

Cory wanted to keep on playing after Curtis disappeared, but Jimmy wasn't in the mood anymore; he sniffled a couple of times and walked back home. There, to his surprise, he found his aunt Florence, who'd come over with his other cousin, Daphne. They were sitting in the living room, in front of the TV, his sister running back and forth in excitement.

"Mommy can't get home! Mommy can't get home!" she announced. And Florence then told him the rest—her employers would not let her leave their house until they knew that the riot had ended.

They stayed in the living room all day, watching the images of burning and shooting on TV, faintly hearing the commotion on the boulevard. Florence fed all the children snacks every couple of hours, cooked catfish and rice for dinner. Jimmy's mother called a few times, apologetic, worried; she told Jimmy and Alice she'd get home just as soon as she could. And Jimmy—bored with the television, uninterested in his toys—kept wondering what his cousins were up to. He was still furious at Curtis, and glad he'd cursed him out; he wouldn't speak to him, he decided, for a week. But he had been too hasty in leaving Cory behind—if he was with Cory, he wouldn't feel so imprisoned now. They might even sneak over to Crenshaw to watch the action.

Jimmy stayed up late—Florence didn't put them to bed—and he eventually fell asleep on the couch. So he was barely awake when his mother came in at six the next morning and smothered him and his sister in kisses. And he was still half-asleep three hours later when he looked out the window and saw Mr. Sakai mounting the steps. And when Mr. Sakai told him what he'd come there to say, Jimmy wouldn't believe it at first, thought he was in a bad dream, but the man's drawn face and tear-stained cheeks convinced him it was true. And Jimmy struck out, crying *No!,* punching and kicking at the news, his fists and feet landing on the man's body—until Frank, while fending Jimmy off, also somehow gathered him in and held him, until the boy's anger and regret and denial and grief were finally exhausted.

CHAPTER THIRTY-FOUR

1994

JACKIE AND Lanier were both suspicious by nature, and neither of them wanted to believe what Paxton had told them. He could have been lying, just as he claimed his colleagues had done—he could have been protecting Lawson, or even himself. They came to this, slowly, on their drive back down to L.A., and over the next couple of days at home. On Wednesday night, they met again at Jackie's apartment, after she remembered that they'd never gotten in touch with Akira Matsumoto. But *she* wasn't about to make the call to some Tokyo newspaper office, and so she'd had no choice but to bring in Rebecca, who'd been dying to get involved anyway. Lanier wanted to be there when Rebecca called, of course, and Jackie was glad she didn't have to be alone with him, so she invited them both over for dinner. She hadn't told Rebecca the rest of what had happened on her trip—the steamed car windows, the night in the hotel—and she wondered if her friend could sense the awkwardness between her and Lanier, the new and strange formality. Jackie made a big pot of pasta and fresh, messy sauce, scattering oregano and basil all over the kitchen. They ate at the table, Rebecca covering the pauses in conversation with funny stories about her victory with Jackie during the moot court trials, and with updates on her work with Legal Aid. And this time, she didn't seem to be playing for Lanier's attention at all; her audience was obviously Jackie.

"Hey, where's Laura?" she asked, as she mopped up her extra sauce with a piece of bread. "You should call her. We could have a little party."

"At home, I suppose," Jackie said. "I'm not really sure." She frowned. Rebecca knew damned well that Laura wasn't privy to what was happening. And this exclusion was applying to more subjects than just Frank and Lanier. Jackie hadn't been in any mood to call Laura when she'd returned on Sunday, and on Monday, when she finally did go over to Sierra Bonita, their interchange had been so strained and tense that they both gave up and Jackie walked home. She hadn't spoken to Laura since. Something serious was afoot and she knew this, but couldn't bring herself to move one way or another. At any rate, now, she couldn't look at Lanier. And try as he might to talk of work, to engage with Rebecca, to make suggestions about the call, he didn't feel comfortable, either. They were both a bit ashamed—they'd opened up too much, let the other too close, and now they were trying desperately to draw the curtains shut, to pull back into themselves.

"Did Jackie tell you about the waitress she met?" Lanier asked Rebecca.

"What?" Rebecca said. "No, she did not." And she was smiling, but there was an edge to it, which Jackie was too rattled to notice.

"Oh, it was nothing," Jackie said. "Just a girl who was desperate for someone to flirt with." She didn't know why Lanier was doing this—as accusation, or deflection?—and she tried to catch his eye, but he looked away.

Jackie gathered up the dishes and began to wash them off, and Rebecca came up behind her and put a hand on her shoulder. "Hey, are you OK?"

"Yeah, I'm fine." But Jackie felt shaky, uneven—devastated by what they had heard about Thomas, confused about the strangeness between her and Lanier, twisted and uncertain about what to do in her crumbling relationship with Laura.

Rebecca seemed to sense that something was wrong, and so she took care of everything. She made Jackie and Lanier sit down while she brewed a pot of coffee, and then kept talking so they didn't have to face each other. Finally, at nine p.m.—one p.m. in Tokyo—she slapped her knees and looked at them. "Let's do it," she said. She could hardly contain herself. For the last two days she'd been driving Jackie crazy with stories of her childhood in Tokyo; of the year she spent there between college and law school. "Where's the number?"

Jackie handed her the sheet of paper she'd been carrying since the bookstore, and Rebecca picked up the receiver. Lanier and Jackie watched silently as she dialed a long string of numbers, and they all waited half a minute. Then Rebecca perked up and took a sharp, quick breath. She spoke in fast, flawless Japanese, which escaped Jackie completely. There was a pause, Rebecca spoke again, and then bowed with the phone in her hand—a move that Jackie had seen her great-grandmother make, and which would have amused her at any other time. Another pause, and then Rebecca spoke in English. "Is this Akira Matsumoto who grew up in L.A.? Hi. You don't know me, but there's someone here who wants to talk to you."

She handed the phone to Jackie, who received it with shaking hands. Lanier scrambled into the bedroom to pick up the extension. Jackie introduced herself, quickly informing Matsumoto that she was Frank Sakai's granddaughter.

"Frank Sakai," said the man on the other end. "Now that's a name I haven't heard in a long time." His voice was deep and cigarette-ragged. Jackie could hear other voices in the background, and she envisioned a crowded and smoke-filled room lined with rows of metal desks. She couldn't believe how close Matsumoto sounded, as if he was working in an office down the street.

"I've heard that you've been living in Japan for years," she said. "When exactly did you move there?"

"The fall of '65. I didn't mean to stay so long, but then I got a job and fell in love. You know, the typical story."

Jackie noted the date he left, and then jumped right in, telling Matsumoto why she was calling. She and Lanier had decided beforehand not to reveal all they'd heard, figuring they could get more out of him this way. So now Jackie told him about Lanier, and related their conversations with Hirano and Conway. "And you're the one other person we've heard of who might have been a witness. So I'm calling to see what you know."

There was a long silence, and if it hadn't been for the voices

in the background, she might have thought they'd been discon-
nected.

"Listen," Matsumoto said finally. "I'm glad you're doing this,
but you're going the wrong direction. I don't know who killed
David and Curtis, but it sure as hell wasn't Nick Lawson."

"How do you know that?" Jackie demanded. "Two people
saw him take the boys inside."

"Well, I was there also—did your witnesses say that? He led
me into the store, too, and he was roughing us up, and then
another set of cops came in—the black ones, the partners—and
Lawson and his partner disappeared."

"You were in the store?"

"That's what I said."

"No, I *didn't* know that. So how did you get out of there?"

"I ran for it. The cops turned their backs and I just took off
for the door. It wasn't me they had a problem with, anyway. That
older cop had some kind of grudge against Curtis—against black
kids in general, I think."

"So the boys were alive when Lawson left, and you left them
with the other two cops?"

"Hey, I didn't want to. I had no idea what was going to happen; I just thought they would get beat up. And I tried to get the
others to run for it with me, but Curtis wouldn't move."

"So Nick Lawson didn't kill them."

"It must have been the others."

"And yet it's Lawson who got shot in revenge."

Matsumoto laughed, a harsh, flat sound. "He didn't get shot
for what happened in the store. He got shot for years of beating
the shit out of people."

"How do you know?"

"I should know. I did it."

"*What?*" Jackie exclaimed. "*You* shot Nick Lawson?"

"I went looking for the bastard when I got out of the store. My
house was a block away, and I went and got my father's gun and
found Lawson up on Crenshaw. I snuck up behind him and gave it
to him, but I only hit his leg, and to this day I can't decide if I'm
happy or unhappy that I didn't kill the racist motherfucker."

Jackie didn't know what to say. After a moment she asked, "Did anyone see?"

"Oh, I'm sure they did. His partner didn't—he was talking to some kids around the corner—but I'm sure that *somebody* did. I was out in the open, not exactly in disguise. Why do you think I came running to Japan?"

"You went to avoid getting caught?"

"Damn straight. Not only that, but my brother was killed during the riots, by a cop in Culver City. I feel real bad for Curtis's cousin; I know exactly what he went through. That weekend, I lost my brother, David, and Curtis, and a couple of friends from Dorsey. And to top it all off I almost ended up killing a cop. L.A.'s trouble, you know. It's gotten worse since then. There was really no reason to stay."

Rebecca, who was gathering bits and pieces of the story through Jackie's responses, was walking back and forth, punching the air, completely beside herself. Lanier, sitting silent on the edge of Jackie's bed, shook his head in disbelief. Jackie waved at Rebecca and tried to make her stop, and then cradled the phone in both hands.

"Would you testify?" she asked. "Would you testify that when you left the store the boys were with the two other cops?"

"What, and maybe risk standing trial for shooting Lawson?"

"We don't have to mention that. It's irrelevant. We're not going after Lawson."

"He's going to come up, though. Even if *you* don't use him as a witness, the other two probably will. And Lawson might stick up for them and say they all left the store together."

"But everything I've heard about Lawson seems to suggest that he wouldn't stand up for black cops."

"Maybe, I don't know." Then Matsumoto sighed. "I need some time to think. Truth is, if one of those cops *did* do this, then I'd like to see the bastard punished. But I need to know that if Lawson comes up, I can work something out to protect myself."

"We can try to talk to the D.A. about immunity," Jackie said. "Please. Kenji Hirano's not the most reliable witness, and we need all the corroboration we can get."

Matsumoto was silent for another few moments. Then finally he said, "OK. What the hell."

It was over, Jackie thought, or at least their part of it was through. Matsumoto's story, his shooting of Lawson, the appearance of the partners—what the other men had seen was accurate; they just hadn't seen it all. Paxton had told the truth—at least about Lawson's innocence—and both she and Lanier believed the rest of it now. Lanier felt, once again, the cloudy sense of apprehension that surrounded his memories of Thomas; he knew it was Thomas, not Paxton, that his cousin had feared. He could picture the younger Thomas—huge, with billy club in hand; Oliver Paxton he couldn't envision at all.

Neither Jackie nor Lanier slept well the night Rebecca called Japan, and first thing the next morning, Jackie put in a call to the D.A.'s office. She told them what she was calling about and arranged a meeting for the following Monday. And so they had to sit tight until then.

Except Lanier couldn't. The answers they'd found had engendered more questions, which kept him twisting in his sheets for two nights. Robert Thomas. How *could* he? A black cop, too. And why didn't Paxton try to stop him?

By Friday afternoon, Lanier was jumpy and exhausted—too tired to work, too tense to fall sleep. And so he left work at five and drove up to Fairfax and knocked loudly on Jackie's door.

"What's up?" Jackie said when she answered, mouth still full of the burrito she'd been eating.

"I'm going to go talk to Thomas," he announced. "You wanna come with me?"

"We shouldn't," Jackie said calmly, noting his red eyes, the pulsing veins in his forehead and neck. "I mean, we've got an appointment at the D.A.'s office next week. Trying to talk to him now might scare him off. It might even be illegal."

"I don't give a fuck. I want to speak to him. Now."

Jackie knew she couldn't talk him out of it. But maybe, if she went along, she could prevent him from doing anything stupid.

Fairfax, at that time, was clogged with commuters; it took

them fifteen minutes to travel the mile and a half to Hollywood Boulevard. This too was full of cars, but they drove without comment until they reached the Hollywood Station. By sheer chance, they found a parking space across from the lot. They waited there until a little after seven, when Robert Thomas emerged in street clothes and walked to his car. Jackie reached for the door, but Lanier put his hand on her arm. They both felt the new weight of this gesture, but didn't speak of it.

"Let's follow him home," he said. "I'd rather get him in private."

Thomas drove a green Explorer, which was easy to keep sight of in the traffic. They followed him to Carthay Circle, where the Explorer turned into the driveway of a tidy one-story Spanish house. Lanier parked at the curb across the street. By this time, Thomas knew he'd been tailed; he slammed his door shut and stared down the driveway as Lanier and Jackie got out of the Taurus. Lanier crossed the street quickly, while Jackie lingered behind. She saw Thomas's eyes widen as he recognized Lanier.

"Captain Thomas," said Lanier, and his voice was sheer ice; the cop's hello slid smoothly over it, unheard.

Lanier came to a stop, and the two men stood sizing each other up. Thomas was big, well-built, and Lanier wouldn't necessarily take him in a fight. Jackie saw the bitter lines around his mouth, the narrowed, suspicious eyes, the tired but defiant set of his shoulders. This man gave her a totally different feeling from Paxton, who'd seemed very much like the schoolteacher he was. Paxton she'd trust with the welfare of a baby; this man she'd cross the street to get away from.

"It's Lanier, right?" asked Thomas. "What are you doing here?" He looked from Lanier to Jackie and back again.

"I think you know," replied Lanier, and when Thomas just stared, he added, "I talked to Oliver Paxton last weekend."

"Oh, really?"

"You told me he moved back east. You didn't say East Palo Alto."

Thomas's expression didn't change, but he raised an eyebrow. "I must have made a mistake. How *is* Ollie? I haven't seen him in, what, probably thirty years."

"Well, that was lucky for *you*. He had some interesting things to say about you."

Thomas looked at him, not speaking, not moving. Behind him, someone stirred at the window.

"He was with you in '65, Bob. At Frank Sakai's store. And this here is Frank's granddaughter, Jackie."

Lanier was staring at him, hard and hateful, and Jackie watched Thomas's face. Over the last few days she'd wondered what he would do when he was confronted with the fact that his partner had finally spoken. She'd turned over in her mind the possibilities—would he deny it angrily? Get threatening and mean? Try somehow, self-righteously, to justify himself? But now, on the driveway, Thomas did none of these things. His shoulders dropped and loosened, and, amazingly, he started to laugh. "You've got some nerve, Lanier," he said. "Coming to my house."

Lanier fought to keep still. "I'm glad you think it's funny," he shot back. "We've got witnesses, and *they* don't think it's funny."

"You *couldn't*," Thomas said. "There was nothing to see. Their word's no better than mine, Lanier. Now please get off my property."

"You're going to stand there and tell me you had nothing to do with it?"

"I'm not telling you anything. There's nothing to tell. Now please leave before I have to *make* you leave." He turned and started walking toward the house.

"You're *caught*, Bob," Lanier called after him, voice drifting out of control. "You're a *murderer*, Bob. How does it feel to have blood on your hands?"

Thomas turned around, slowly, and stepped back down the driveway. He looked as angry as Lanier now, and Jackie was scared—the age difference between the men had totally vanished. "Listen, you know-it-all fuck," Thomas said. "You have no idea what it's like to have people's lives in your hands every day. You have no idea what it's like to find an old lady whose guts are splattered all over her kitchen, or a man who's been stabbed to death because he wouldn't give up six bucks, or a little girl with a knife sticking out of her cunt. I know what it's like, and even so, I don't take it lightly when my job requires me to hurt someone. There's a lot of animal punks out there who I'd like to see drawn and quartered. But to take them down personally is no small thing. No cop likes to hurt people, no decent one anyway. What happened to your friends, if a cop *did* do it, I'm sure it didn't happen on purpose." He stopped here and smiled again, an expression that chilled Jackie to the bone. "Not that it breaks my heart. At least it got them off the streets. Probably saved everyone a lot of trouble in the long run."

Lanier moved before Jackie could stop him. He hit Thomas in the face with a hard right hook, and Thomas dropped to the ground with a thud. "You fucking *bastard*," spat Lanier. "You murdering racist bastard."

The front door opened now, and a middle-aged woman in a business suit came out and stood on the doorstep.

"James," Jackie said, stepping closer, afraid to get in his way. Lanier floated up to the older man, and away again, trying to regain his control. "James, come on," Jackie urged. "It's not going to help us." She grabbed his arm, which was rock-hard, veins bulging with blood. "Come on, let's go. Let's get out of here."

Lanier let himself be dragged backwards down the driveway, but he kept his eyes on Thomas. "We're going to get you, Thomas. No matter what you say. Your ass is going to jail."

Thomas lay on the ground, hand on his jaw, blood trickling out of his mouth. "You've got no case, Lanier. I'm a thirty-five-year veteran. Whatever you've got will never stand up in court."

Lanier drove blindly on the way back to Jackie's. His earlier sadness and ambivalence had been supplanted by fury; he cursed and hit the dashboard several times. They both feared that what Thomas said was true—it *was*, essentially, his word against Paxton's—and now they didn't know what to do with themselves. And Lanier felt what he'd been feeling more and more these last few days—that he was somehow letting Curtis down again, which he'd done over and over up until the last moment he ever saw him. At the apartment, Jackie invited him in, but Lanier declined the offer. And so they separated, each left to fend for themselves with their anger, their dissatisfaction.

CHAPTER THIRTY-FIVE

JULY, 1946

O N CERTAIN evenings, the young man stayed in the store after the older man had left for the night. He told the older man that he had some work to do; he had to check accounts or the inventory. It wasn't hard to convince him there was reason to stay. The place was busy, shelves emptying as fast as they could stock them, new money in the neighborhood, from home-owners and companies, finding its way in through their doors. The young man was trustworthy—a devoted son, a veteran—and he knew the older man intended for him to take over the store one day.

A little after nine, there'd be a light rapping on the back door. He would always walk to the door slowly, delaying his pleasure. When he opened it, she would be standing in the shadows, smil-ing, and he would offer his hand and then wordlessly pull her inside. After he shut the door, they'd embrace, still silent. Then, she'd tell him what excuse she'd given her parents that night: she was at the movies with Constance, or working, or bowling with her girlfriends from school. He'd tease her—*Would you like some popcorn, miss? I hear the feature is very good.* And they'd look at each other, eyes ravenous for what was denied to them in daylight. He, to her, smelled of fresh earth and sun—and cardboard, and soap from the store. She smelled to him of wide-open plains, clean laundry, and a touch of perfume.

He was twenty-two then, and she was eighteen. They both still lived with their parents, and he took care of his mother, who'd been knocked flat by the loss of her husband and daughter. Her parents, so strict and religious, would never understand what she saw in this man; they'd borne down on her harder since her sister had fled up north the year before. But once, twice a week, they escaped them all and met in the closed, quiet store.

They walked, hand in hand, to the little office behind the counter where the older man kept all his records. There was a couch against the wall—the older man napped here regularly, and sometimes, during the rougher patches of his marriage, would stay here overnight. But now he was gone and the store was closed. The young woman sat down on the couch, and the young man in a chair, and they talked, caught up on their days. The young man smiled—he hadn't noticed her when she lived here before; she'd been the pigtailed younger sister of a classmate. Now, she was the axis on which his entire existence spun. He couldn't wait anymore and moved next to her, and they kissed each other long and deep. He lifted his hand to brush her cheek with his thumb, then smoothed her hair back with his fingers. She curved her hand around his neck and pulled him closer. He loved the feel of her body—the small breasts pushed up against him, her soft-but-hard shoulders, her hands that touched him everywhere at once. She unbuttoned his shirt and placed her hands on his chest, touched him through his pants. He moved under her blouse and then down to her skirt, unhooked, unzipped, unbuttoned. They worked between, through, and beneath each other's clothes, never quite removing them all. He curled his body over hers, and she touched his black hair, ran her fingers down his now-moist back. He placed her hand between his legs and then said, "This is yours."

She pulled him into her and said, "This is yours."

They ran into each other on the street sometimes, when they were with their friends or parents, and it thrilled them both to pretend they hardly knew one another, and were only saying hello to be polite. On those occasions, he would have to look away from her, lest his smile or heightened color betray his love. They told no one—her girlfriends, she knew, would never approve, and he had no friends there in the Mesa anymore. He wondered if, given the chance, he'd tell his old friend Victor, but Victor was living in Watts now, and they hadn't really talked in several years. He didn't know if Victor would understand, anyway—he wasn't sure that *he* even did. What he did know was that each night was like a generous gift; each sunset and sunrise so gorgeous and fresh it seemed the world was reinventing itself just for him. As he walked down the street he felt lighter, stronger, as if nothing could ever worry or defeat him. And she felt, for the first time, like she was no longer alone; like she'd finally found a home in the world. Instead of her daily routines growing tedious, interfering, she went about her tasks almost cheerfully. She polished silverware so hard and efficiently it was almost too bright to look at. He took a greater pride, all of a sudden, at setting up precise rows of soup cans and cereal boxes. Sometimes, to get him through the day, he went back to his locker in the office to look at the picture she'd given him of herself and a group of her friends at a bowling tournament the summer before. Then he went back out into the store and worked even harder. It was a wonderful and heady thing, now, to simply be alive; they both took joy in every moment. And the better and faster they completed their work, the sooner they could be with each other.

There were times they each felt bad about their secrecy. Her parents would come into the store to buy vegetables or milk, and he'd be overly solicitous—not out of guilt, exactly, but instead a kind of awkwardness. He was so close to them, so intimate, and they didn't even know it. And she felt strange when her parents discussed her sister's husband, of whom they didn't approve, and who they felt had taken advantage of their hospitality. His mother started pressing him to find a suitable wife—she had candidates and it was time, she said, and it was hard for him to find reasons to put her off. She couldn't understand why, suddenly, his spirits were so good. He cooked for her with no complaint, and mowed the lawn, whistling, and she was worried; she'd never seen him so light-hearted. Once, he saw the girl's sister, his former classmate, when she was down for the holidays, and that was the only time he really thought about their difference in age—she was younger, in eighth grade when he'd been taken away to the camps. But her youth—her serious, burdened, but still undeniable youth—was part of what drew him to her. For four years, since the start of the war, he'd seen nothing but carnage, blood, and sorrow. And now he knew, and discovered in himself, something fresh and untouched, still capable of wonder.

They talked about taking a trip together to the mountains or up to the country, some place where the long and lazy days could luxuriously unfold and not be broken up into endless stretches where they didn't see each other, and short stolen moments when they did. But he didn't really want this—every place outside of the city, whether country, marsh, desert, or mountain, was, in his mind, the landscape of war—and neither of them could take time off anyway, let alone explain their absence to their families. So they contented themselves with their time in the store, windows open to the cool, quiet night. The anticipation they both felt on those days they'd arranged to meet—him bustling around the store, she walking quickly down the sidewalk at dusk—was more intoxicating and real than anything either of them ever felt before or after.

They met like this for nine, ten months, going on a year. And then one night in midsummer, lying, spent, on the couch, the young woman told the young man that a friend of hers had gotten engaged. She leaned against him lovingly, kissed him on the neck, and said she envied her friend—she wondered if *they'd* ever get married. The young man didn't utter a word, but she felt his whole body stiffen, and she pulled away and looked at him, confused. Wouldn't you marry me? she asked, and though she thought she meant in theory, she realized she wanted to know. Yes, he said. Yes, of course I would.

"But then why did it take so long to answer?" she asked, buttoning her shirt. "You got so nervous just then. I felt you."

"No, I didn't," he said, sitting up. "Of course I'd marry you. I *want* to marry you."

"You bastard."

"What do you mean?"

"You hesitated. You had to think about it. I can't *believe* you. I'm not good enough to marry?"

"That's ridiculous," he said. "You know I love you."

"Do you?" She glared at him. "Is it?"

They argued—or rather, she yelled at him and he tried to

explain himself. Eventually she stormed out of the office. He didn't see her for one week, then two, and pride and confusion kept him from tracking her down. But those weeks were worse than anything, worse than fearing for his life in Europe, and her absence weighed on him so heavily he could hardly draw breath. He did not know how to fix this, how to take back or make disappear the two seconds before he'd said yes. Because she was right. If it was true that he wanted to bring their love into the daylight, to be with her forever, it was also true that, at least for a moment, the thought of it had scared him. He needed to make her understand that she was his life, as vital as water or air. And so finally, hat in hand, he walked over to the young woman's house for the first time since he'd known her. And the sour-faced man who answered the door informed him she was gone.

CHAPTER THIRTY-SIX

1994

O N MONDAY morning, Jackie drove downtown again, this time with Lanier at her side. They were both wearing suits, and Lanier kept teasing Jackie; he'd never seen her so dressed up.

"So what happens after this?" she asked as they drove past Crenshaw. She looked right, off the freeway, down the boulevard she saw as a timeline now, a measuring-stick of her history.

"Just what you said. The D.A.'s office takes the information and decides whether or not to press charges, and then, hopefully, we all go to court."

"I know *that*," Jackie said. "I mean . . ." What *did* she mean? She meant, what was going to happen with them? Without even giving it a second thought, she'd assumed that she and Lanier would still see each other a couple of times a week, and talk on the phone every day. But now it occurred to her that their work was done and she had no reason to see him again until the trial— provided there was one. "I mean, what are we going to do with ourselves now? We don't have any more people to chase around."

Lanier smiled. He understood what she was really saying, and he felt the same way. Jackie had been his only constant for the last three months—the person to talk to, the thing he could always do. And, as awkward as things still felt between them now, he hadn't realized how used to her he'd gotten. "Well, we could find some other mystery to solve. Or you could come down and volunteer at Marcus Garvey."

Jackie laughed. "But I'm not a young father. What good would I do?"

"You don't have to volunteer in *my* programs. There's a lot of other stuff going on—tutoring, job training, that kind of thing."

Her first reaction was to say no, she was too busy, but after all the time she'd spent on extracurriculars that winter and spring, she knew that wasn't the case. Her second reaction was that she wouldn't be any good—what did *she* know about tutoring, or even teens, for that matter? But then she realized that these reactions were silly. It was a wonderful idea—a way to see Lanier regularly, and to honor her grandfather. And it was a way for her, finally, to do something useful; to get out of herself and give to somebody.

They met Lois on the steps of the Hall of Administration and Jackie made the introductions.

"This is my aunt Lois," she said. "It's her who started all this. And Lois, this is my friend James Lanier."

They shook hands and looked closely at each other. "I'm trying to figure out if I remember you," Lanier said, laughing.

"I don't know how much I remember, either," Lois replied. "But I feel like I know you already."

It was a beautiful morning, the sun bright in their faces, and Jackie could see that meeting Lanier and the prospect of resolving the boys' murders had made her aunt more bouyant than she'd been in several months. And something about meeting Frank's daughter sent Lanier back in time, and he turned away so the women couldn't see his moistened eyes. Lois felt this, too, the collapsing of the years, and she thought of her old neighborhood, children riding on bikes, and above all she thought of her father. Frank, who'd taught her what it meant to call a place home. Frank, who was so much a part of the neighborhood that he was never the same after the family moved away. But the memories made her feel connected to something again, and it was more a reclamation than a loss. This man, Lanier, was part of her father, too. He'd been a child with her, back in the Mesa.

Inside the D.A.'s office, they checked in with the receptionist and took seats in uncomfortable chairs. Lois and Lanier spoke of the old neighborhood, the people they knew in common. Jackie asked her aunt about the new house that she and Ted had just purchased, their plans for the move, the final packing of her grandfather's things. Lois asked Jackie about her conversation with Matsumoto, and, watching her niece and Lanier answer together, finish each other's sentences, she saw a closeness between them she wondered about, an intimacy she'd never seen Jackie share with anyone else.

After they'd been waiting for twenty-five minutes, a voice called out from the doorway. "Mr. Lanier? Ms. Ishida?"

They all looked up and saw a short, slim woman in her middle or early thirties. "Yes," they all answered, standing. Lanier straightened his tie.

"I'm Pauline Richardson," the woman said, extending a slender hand to Lanier, and then to Jackie and Lois. "I'll be sitting in with Deputy District Attorney Silverman today. He asked me to bring you back to his office."

She turned and walked back through the door. At the end of the hallway, Pauline stepped into an office, and Jackie saw the words "Alan Silverman, Deputy District Attorney" on the door. Inside, sitting down, was a tall, thin man whose head was rimmed with graying hair.

"Hello, Alan Silverman," he said, reaching across the desk to take their hands. "So you're James Lanier." Then he turned to Jackie. "And you must be Jackie Ishida. Professor Greenberg had some very nice things to say about you. You're starting at Turner, Blake & Weinberg in the fall?"

"Yes," she answered, slightly embarrassed. "Thank you for agreeing to see us."

"Well, it sounds like you have an interesting story, so fire away. Ms. Richardson will be sitting in, if it's all right with you."

"That's fine," Lanier replied.

"This all started about three months ago," Jackie began.

Silverman leaned back in his chair. "When exactly?"

"February 5th," said Lois. "The day of my father's funeral." She told them about the old will and the box of money, and Jackie gave a summary of what she and Lanier had uncovered. When she reached the part about Robert Thomas, Silverman looked up from the yellow legal pad where he'd been furiously scribbling notes. "Are you sure it was him?"

"Yes," Lanier responded. "His partner gave him up. And one more person saw Lawson leave and Thomas go in when the boys were still alive."

Pauline Richardson was scribbling also, looking down at her pad. "Did the second witness actually see this Thomas kill them?"

"No," Jackie said. "Only the partner did."

"And you believe the partner?" Silverman asked.

"Yes, we do." Then she and Lanier, together, told them why. They laid out the story in greater detail, including Thomas's refusal to cooperate with Lanier; his misleading information about Paxton; his reputation in the neighborhood; his behavior when they finally confronted him. They gave Matsumoto's account as well, including his later encounter with Lawson, withholding his name until they knew the D.A. would consider immunity. They gave them the histories of Curtis and Frank, omitting everything about Frank's relationship with Alma. It was irrelevant, really, to the fact of the murder. But more importantly, Jackie realized, she wanted to protect Frank and Alma and their undercover love; she wanted it to remain theirs forever.

Thirty minutes later, their voices trailed off and the attorneys put down their pads. Silverman looked very serious now; his brow had crunched into deep furrows and his mouth looked small and tight. "I knew that there were a lot of unreported incidents in '65. But this one . . ." He didn't go on. There was silence for a minute or two; then Silverman looked up at them. "I've got to tell you. I don't know how much of a case we have here. There's really only one witness, and it's Paxton's word against Thomas's."

"Couldn't we get Lawson to testify?" Pauline asked.

Silverman shook his head. "We could try. But it's not likely he'll admit to being there in the first place, let alone seeing Thomas come in."

"So what do we do?" Lanier asked. His shoulders had tightened, his breath was shallow and fast. If Thomas slipped through their fingers now, he didn't know what he would do. Even as he was trying to right things for Curtis, he couldn't stop letting him down.

Silverman knocked twice on the surface of his desk. "We'll tell the police." He put his hand up when Lanier and Jackie tried to protest. "Probably Internal Affairs. They'll send detectives out to interview all the witnesses you mentioned—just give us their names again, along with addresses and phone numbers. If they're still telling the same story, we should be able to take this to court." He paused. "But more than that, I can't really promise you."

Jackie, Lanier, and Lois were all silent. Jackie opened her bag and pulled out her datebook, then copied down the names and numbers of the people they'd talked to.

Silverman took the sheet from her and laid it in front of him. "This city, what goes on here, all the violence and racial hatred. I can't imagine how it could get any worse." He ran his hands over the paper, staring at the words. "You did a hell of a job, you two."

"Yeah, well, maybe not good enough," said Lanier.

Pauline Richardson walked them out to the lobby again, chattering, assuaging. "It'll be all right," she said. "If anyone can bring this Thomas down, it's Silverman. He'll make sure we find other witnesses, and he'll force Thomas to make a mistake. Don't worry. I'll keep you posted on developments myself."

They didn't speak as they walked back toward the parking lot. When they reached Lois's car, they all stood and looked at each other.

"Well, what do you think?" Jackie asked.

"I guess we'll have to see," her aunt replied. "But you did what you could do. I'm proud of you, Jackie. Thank you."

"No problem," Jackie said, and she didn't say what she was thinking—that it was she, Jackie, who had really been rewarded.

"You know, I've been thinking," Lois began, shading her eyes as she looked at Lanier. "I've been trying to figure out what to do with my father's money. It never seemed right that I should keep it, and I can live without it anyway, so I'm thinking that I could give it to your organization."

Lanier just looked at her. "Aw, Lois, you don't have to do that."

"Well, you didn't have to do all of *this*."

"That's very generous of you. But I mean, are you sure?"

"It's what my father would have done, I think. It's in keeping with him and Curtis. Why not give the money to you and keep it in the family?"

"You're right. But shit. Thirty-eight grand. We could do a lot with that money."

"Good."

"Hey, thank you," said Lanier, placing a hand on her arm.

"No," Lois answered, "thank *him*."

That Friday, Albert Stevens, the one gay man in Jackie's law school class, was having an "Air Out Your Closet" party to celebrate the end of the semester. Jackie had spent the afternoon shopping for business suits with Rebecca at the Westside Pavilion, and now they were back at Rebecca's place, changing for the party. Both of them were looking forward to going to Albert's; there would be students from several other departments. They'd already had an eventful day—trying on and discarding several dozen different outfits, making fun of each other, and driving all the salespeople crazy. And they were both in great moods—Jackie feeling unburdened, if not totally satisfied, after the trip to the D.A.'s office; Rebecca because a district judge had delayed the deportation of the garment workers, pending further hearings.

"What are you going to do with yourself now?" Rebecca asked that evening, as she and Jackie laid out their dresses on the bed. "You're going to be bored after *that* big adventure, and all you have to do now is study for finals and the bar."

"I don't know," Jackie shrugged. "Try to figure out what to do about Laura."

"Did you ever tell her what was happening?"

Jackie shook her head. "No, not really." She hadn't told Laura much of anything the last few weeks, and she knew it was just a matter of time before one of them brought their worn-out relationship to an end. When she really stopped to think about it, she did miss Laura, but that feeling was outweighed by the relief she felt when she didn't have to see her.

"Well, don't despair," Rebecca said. "I can think of a bunch of people who are waiting if you suddenly become available. A couple of them will probably be there tonight."

"Oh, bullshit. Like anyone cares. Hey, where did you get that?" She was pointing at Rebecca's dress, a small shimmery black thing that complemented even the bed.

"At Nordstrom's. And I look *good* in it, I don't mind telling you."

"I'm sure you do, Miss Ego. Come on, it's time to get dressed."

Jackie expected her friend to offer the bedroom or send her into the living room. But Rebecca, facing the mirror, removed her shirt right there, and Jackie realized they were going to change together. Rebecca stood there in her bra now, a delicate blend of black lace. Then she reached around with both hands and the front of the bra came forward as she unfastened the clasps in the back. The straps slid down her arms and Jackie tried not to look, but she caught a glimpse of the firm, perfect breasts, their dark and lovely nipples. Rebecca nodded at her, as if issuing a dare. Jackie felt extremely self-conscious—but also intrigued. She pulled off her own shirt, unclasped and removed her own bra. No sound except their breathing as they stepped out of their pants, folded them, and placed them on the bed. Jackie wasn't sure what to do with her eyes. She pretended to concentrate on putting on her dress and stole glances at her friend as she slipped into hers, seeing black hair spread against smooth olive skin, long toned arms, and delicate collarbone. Rebecca looked so much more fragile without her clothes, and Jackie realized she wanted to touch her. She felt loss for the breasts as they disappeared beneath the fabric; wanted again to see the flat stomach, the bits of curled hair that were not entirely contained by the white bikini panties. And she felt Rebecca doing the same thing to her—trying not to look, but unable to help herself. Once Jackie's dress was on, she examined herself in the mirror. Her short blue dress worked well with the curves of her body, and she looked good, though not as glamorous as Rebecca. They both leaned over Rebecca's vanity, inches away from the mirror, putting on make-up and doing their hair. They added stockings, necklaces, watches, and pumps. And then, completely ready, they paraded in front of the mirror, looking at themselves and at each other. They hadn't spoken since Rebecca removed her shirt, but now she turned to Jackie, who realized how fast her heart was beating, how quick and shallow her breaths had become. They'd never stood so close—only inches apart—and Jackie felt the goose-bumps, the sparks jumping off her skin, even before Rebecca leaned in and kissed her. She shivered—how long since she'd shivered!—and when they both pulled back she looked at her friend, her beautiful friend, the moist lips, the cut cheeks, the green, cat-like eyes.

"I can't promise anything," Jackie said.

"I know. You're a self-involved asshole."

"But for some reason you like me anyway."

"Yep. Always have. You've got a lot of potential. And you've improved so much these last few months."

"It was Lanier, you know. And Curtis. And my grandfather, too. But mostly it was Lanier."

"I know. And I thank him for it. Remind me to send him a card."

"And I don't know what's up with Laura, either. I mean, I know it's over, but I'm . . . tired. She really went through me. And there's still some things we have to figure out."

"There's no hurry. Neither one of us is going anywhere."

"Everything's a mess—my relationship, my family, I don't know how I feel about my job. You don't mind all this in-between stuff?"

Rebecca smiled. "Honey, look at me. I *am* in-between stuff."

And very gently, patiently, Rebecca kissed her again, and Jackie felt something loosen in her, something ancient and glacial start to creak and break free. *She* was the one, she thought, who'd had a lover all this time, and Rebecca the one who'd been alone. But it was Rebecca who seemed to know, now, where they were both going, and Jackie felt the relief, as Rebecca's hand moved down her neck and over her shoulder and onto her breast, of being with someone who was capable of meeting her halfway. Jackie touched Rebecca's face, her smooth, long back, and pulled her tighter, closer. And she knew, for the first time—and finally, with this person—that in surrendering herself, she would also, some-how, be given herself in return—stronger, newer, and complete.

CHAPTER THIRTY-SEVEN

1965

T HE YOUNG man was now an older man, and had hired young men himself. This morning, the fourth young man he'd hired, but the one he loved most, had come in early because of the burning in Watts to get his work done, and then to help lock the place up. The older man watched him as he bent over the desk, wrestling figures that weren't adding up to the number he wanted. The boy grunted to himself and scratched his head. He was a handsome boy, and smart and responsible, and the man wished he could take credit for this. He couldn't, though, and he knew it—this boy was his mother's product, and his own.

"We should get a couple more deliveries of bread each month," the boy said. "We always get real close to running out."

"That's a good idea. Anything else?"

"Yeah. I noticed the eggs been getting smaller lately. Maybe we should get them from another distributor."

"Good. We can do that."

"And the candy bars." Here, the boy grinned sheepishly. "I always take one to Angela, you know, and she's getting tired of what we got. I think we should try to order a couple more kinds."

The man smiled. "Anything for Angela."

The man left the office then, and went out into the store. They were both trying to act like everything was normal, despite the storm that was brewing outside. In a while, before the looting got worse, he'd send the boy home; he'd only come in himself to make sure everything was locked. The man walked up and down the three small aisles, straightening boxes of cereal, counting packages of flour. He loved this place—it was, more than any other place, his home. But he'd known for some time that he should leave. His daughters were sixteen and fourteen now, and working until eight o'clock six days a week he'd somehow missed most of their childhood. It wasn't too late, though—with different work, with better hours, he still had a chance to get to know them before they left his house forever. He'd lined up another job, a nine-to-five, with a local distributor, who figured his years of experience in the grocery business would help them keep up with changing markets and trends.

The boy was eighteen now, and had just graduated from high school. He'd moved into his own apartment and was about to be married; he'd worked at the store all summer, and even though he was preparing to start classes at the junior college, he'd stay on full-time in the fall. The boy didn't know the man was planning to leave, nor was he aware of what the man had in mind for him. The man knew his proposition was going to make the boy happy; just anticipating his reaction made him smile.

Although the man's wife didn't like the idea, it made perfect sense that the boy take over the store. He'd worked there nearly four years, all through high school, and he understood all aspects of the job, both personal and business. He went at everything—the orders, the books, the physical arrangements—as if it were the most fascinating project in the world, and he'd said many times that he wanted to run his own store someday. The way the man figured it, he would tell the boy what he'd planned, then spend a couple of months on formal training. Then, gradually, he'd make himself less and less present, until the boy was completely on his own. The man would still own the store, but the boy would manage it, on salary; after a few years, the man would turn it over to him. He had been thinking over this plan, pounding out the details in his head, almost all of his waking hours.

And then, the rest of it, which he'd tell him soon after. For two years, on and off, the man had been arguing with the boy's mother over telling the boy the truth about his parentage. The boy had a right to know, he felt, and things would make sense that way—the business was being passed on from father to son. But the mother had argued that it wouldn't be fair—to the boy or to her husband, who still didn't know—and she'd refused flat out the man's every appeal. But the man couldn't hold it any longer. While he respected the woman's wishes, he couldn't help himself anymore, and now that the boy was finally out of his mother's house, the man felt that the time was right. The man didn't know how he'd tell him, and he didn't know where or when, or what he'd say. But he almost shook with joy at the simple, solid prospect of finally being able to claim his son. He tried not to think about what would happen if the boy reacted badly—he'd been silent too long to worry about the consequences now. All the stories and lessons and history he'd passed on to the boy. All the things that belonged not only to him, but also to his child.

A few minutes later, as the two of them were checking all the windows, the man said, "Listen, son. When this is all over, there's a couple of things I need to tell you."

The boy looked at him quizzically—the man seemed so intent and serious—and just then, several people entered the store. It was the other boys—the two who still worked there and the older one who used to, and a couple of younger boys, the little brothers. One of the older boys, the Japanese one, waved his arms excitedly.

"Some stores are getting looted on Western," he said. "You better hurry up and shut down."

The man nodded. "Go home. Get home as fast as you can. And stay there with your families until everything's quiet."

They didn't want to go, but he shooed them out, all of them, even the one he loved. Then he rushed around, checking all the windows again. He went out the front door, locked and bolted it behind him, and quickly walked the four blocks to his house.

The boys had taken off in the opposite direction, but now one of them, the one who'd been in the store that morning, stopped short in his tracks. "We can't just leave it," he said. "If no one's there to defend it, it's gonna get torn apart."

"Well, that's a chance we gotta take," one of the other boys replied. "I mean, damn, you know? Better it than us."

"Don't be such a fuckin pussy," said the Japanese boy. "He's right. We should go back and stay there in case some fool tries to burn it down."

"No one's gonna do that. People love the store. They need it."

"That don't matter when folks are upset."

"Well, I don't care what *you* all do," the first boy said. "I'm going back. I'll see you assholes later."

He took off down the sidewalk. The Japanese boy followed. The remaining boys all looked at each other, and then the oldest one said, "Aw, shit." He walked down the sidewalk after the first boy, and the two younger ones ran to keep up. The other boy watched them go, and then went home.

The first boy, hearing all the footsteps behind him, smiled and kept on walking. They were going back to defend the store he loved. He hoped the man would be proud of him, even though he was disobeying orders; he was trying to take care of the only place where either of them felt at peace. And as he kept walking, and then jogging, down the sidewalk toward the store, he thought about the man, the strange intensity in his voice just before the other boys came in, and wondered what he'd been planning to tell him.

Also from **AKASHIC BOOKS**

KAMIKAZE LUST by Lauren Sanders
2000 Lambda Literary Award Winner
287 pages, a trade paperback original, $14.95, ISBN: 1-888451-08-4
"*Kamikaze Lust* puts a snappy spin on a traditional theme—young woman in search of herself—and stands it on its head. In a crackling, rapid-fire voice studded with deadpan one-liners and evocative descriptions, Rachel Silver takes us to such far-flung places as a pompous charity benefit, the set of an 'art porn' movie, her best friend's body, Las Vegas casinos, and the psyche of her own porn-star alter ego, Silver Ray, all knit together by the unspoken question: Who am I, anyway? And as Rachel tells it, asking the question is more fun than knowing for sure could ever be."
— Kate Christensen, author of *In the Drink*

THE WEEPING BUDDHA by Heather Dune Macadam
360 pages, a trade paperback original; $16.95, ISBN: 1-888451-39-4
"Heather Dune Macadam should be included in that rare category of literary mystery masters such as Lawrence Block, Craig Holden, and Giles Blunt, whose lyrical prose and beautifully developed characters have a great deal to say about the troubled world we live in and its legacy of violence."
— Kaylie Jones, author of *A Soldier's Daughter Never Cries*

SOME OF THE PARTS by T Cooper
A Barnes & Noble Discover Great New Writers selection (fall 2002)
A Quality Paperback Book Club selection (February 2003)
264 pages, a trade paperback original, $14.95, ISBN: 1-888451-36-X
"Sweet and sad and funny, with more mirrors of recognition than a carnival funhouse, *Some of the Parts* is a wholly original love story for our wholly original age."
— Justin Cronin, author of *Mary and O'Neil*, 2002 PEN/Hemingway Award–Winner